The Quick Boat Men

THE QUICK BOAT MEN

John Harris

HUTCHINSON
LONDON

© John Harris 1992

The right of John Harris to be identified as Author of this work has been asserted by John Harris in accordance with the Copyright, Designs and Patents Act, 1988

This edition first published in 1992 by
Hutchinson

Random Century Group Ltd
20 Vauxhall Bridge Road, London SWIV 2SA

Random Century Australia (Pty) Ltd
20 Alfred Street, Milsons Point, Sydney, NSW 2061, Australia

Random Century New Zealand Ltd
PO Box 40–086, Glenfield, Auckland 10, New Zealand

Random Century South Africa (Pty) Ltd
PO Box 337, Bergvlei, 2012, South Africa

A CIP catalogue record for this book is available from the British library

ISBN 0–09–177338–5

Set in 11\12 pt. Plantin, by Pure Tech Corporation, India

Printed and bound in Great Britain by
Mackays of Chatham PLC

Author's note

From the day torpedoes were invented the one problem that occupied naval minds was how to deliver them. Submarines were one obvious solution but they were still unreliable and minds turned to fast surface craft.

The firm of Thorneycroft – to this day involved in the development of high-speed craft – were among the first to produce light, quick steam launches but, as navies wished to put more and more armament on them as protection, they grew so big that thoughts turned towards the idea of small high-speed boats. It was an idea that appealed particularly to small countries with small navies.

The coastal motor boats of World War I were the brainchild of three officers of the Harwich destroyer force who felt there would be a use for small petrol-driven shallow-draught high-speed boats able to cross minefields to attack German bases. By the end of the war sixty-six of them had been built and among the many awards for gallantry won by the crews of the CMBs and motor launches were three VCs. Their development to the high-speed craft of World War II resulted from the work of private companies and the achievements of men who wanted to break records.

'The four horsemen were beginning their mad, desolating course . . . over the heads of terrified humanity . . . Humanity, crazed with fear . . . was fleeing in all directions on hearing the thundering advance of Plague, War, Hunger and Death . . .
And the white horse, the red, the black and the pale were crushing all with their relentless iron tread.'

Vicente Blasco Ibanez
(*The Four Horsemen of the Apocalypse*)

The Quick Boat Men

I

1905–1909

1

'This,' Edward Dante Bourdillon pointed out, 'is a torpedo.'

The announcement was received with indifference by the older of the two girls sitting in the boat with him, with grave interest by the younger.

He pointed at the slim white shape in the water just ahead of them. 'That's a yacht. Ketch-rigged.' He patted the polished teak of the long, low launch lashed alongside him. 'This is *Triton*, a quick boat. The description was first used in the last century for the fast steam launches of John Thorneycroft of Chiswick. Uncle Egg borrowed it for his petrol and paraffin-driven boats. They're capable of almost twenty knots.'

'Can we get on?' The older of the two girls could not hide her boredom. 'We haven't got all day.'

'Right, Georgina.' Edward recovered from the rebuff with an attempt at brisk forthrightness. 'This –' he patted the boat they were sitting in '– is a dinghy, muscle-powered –'

'Oh, Teddy, do get on.'

Edward frowned. He had been developing his talk carefully and he was young enough to enjoy having a captive audience.

'Right,' he said again. 'Back to where we were: this is a torpedo.' He indicated the apparatus he had mounted on the bow of the launch alongside them. 'It's what's known, in fact, as a spar torpedo. It takes its name from the fact that it's mounted on a spar.' He paused to let the information sink in. 'The spar, of course, is itself mounted on a boat. The boat is aimed at the target and, as the torpedo on the end of the spar strikes the target, it detonates the explosive and the target is destroyed.'

'So, I imagine,' Georgina Reeves pointed out from the centre of the dinghy, 'is the boat the torpedo's mounted on.'

'Ah.' Edward considered the question with all the solemnity of a seventeen-year-old male endeavouring to explain a technical problem to a female he was trying to impress. 'But it *does* work. They used a spar torpedo successfully as long ago as 1877. A copper canister on a pole mounted on a boat. Against an obsolete French naval vessel called the *Bayonnaise*.'

'*Mayonnaise* is a funny name for a battleship.' The speaker this time was Georgina's thirteen-year-old sister, Augusta, who sat in the stern of the dinghy holding the oars, something her eighteen-year-old sibling wouldn't have dreamed of doing. Augusta was all plaits, teeth, legs and enormous eyes. Edward regarded her severely. She wasn't supposed to be with them.

'Not *Mayonnaise*,' he said. '*Bayonnaise*.'

'Sorry.' Augusta lowered her eyes humbly.

'It means someone from Bayonne. As it ends with an 'e' I presume it means a *female* from Bayonne, which would seem normal as all ships are considered to be female.'

Augusta looked up, regarding him with adoration. Her sister's attitude was more cynical. A year older than Edward, she considered herself – and was – more adult than he was. She was tall and slender and already shapely and beautiful, her face surrounded by a cloud of blonde hair tied back with a huge black bow. It took Edward's breath away just having her there.

He was sitting in the dinghy, the August sun hot on his back, with Augusta firmly relegated to the stern behind him. He had hoped to sneak away alone with Georgina but she had joined them, happily ignorant of their wish to disappear quietly. It had been Edward's intention to put on a show and nobody, he felt, could put on a show with a thirteen-year-old interrupting all the time.

The launch that lay alongside the dinghy was facing the yacht, *Fairy*. Pristine and polished to within an inch of its life, it belonged to Edward's uncle, Egbert Bourdillon, who owned and ran the boatyard that lay along the shore behind them.

4

'Go on about the *Mayonnaise*,' Georgina said casually.

Edward frowned, ignoring the deliberate mistake. 'I suppose you've heard of the Battle of Tsu-Shima.'

The two girls looked blank.

'It was in all the newspapers,' Edward said. 'Out in the East. China Seas. In Tsu-Shima Strait. The Russians lost thirty-four warships against the Japanese loss of three torpedo boats.'

They still looked blank.

'*It was only four months ago*,' he explained irritably. '*27 May 1905*. It started a revolution in Russia.'

'The Russians are always throwing bombs.' Georgina gave a little shudder. Revolution in Edward VII's England was unthinkable.

She was the daughter of the vicar whom Edward regarded as a sanctimonious old hypocrite, very like the school chaplain. The chaplain did a lot of hard work on his knees and liked to get the pupils to learn by heart not one of the sterner passages from the Old Testament or the Ten Commandments but the Song of Solomon which, it was firmly believed, he admired less for its inspirational beauty than for its erotic content.

As it happened, Georgina didn't try very hard to conform to her father's mould and had enough strength of character to stand up for herself. And she was useful to have around because she was virtually the only girl in the village of Porthelt of the right age and class – and class, in 1905, was important. Unfortunately, she wasn't a good listener because in a group of two she always considered herself the more interesting.

At that moment, she was hitching at the belt at her waist and, smoothing her skirt over her knees, was showing rather more leg than was considered permissible. She didn't care much for convention, however, and Edward was enjoying the view.

But he was beginning to feel she wasn't taking him seriously. Now she was straightening the tie she wore under the sailor collar of her white blouse and wasn't even looking at him.

'After all –' he spoke loudly to attract her attention '– it was only an experiment to see what would happen. The attack was made by a Thorneycroft boat with a French naval squadron and the *Bayonnaise* was unmanned and towed by a tug. There was a story about it in the *Graphic*. I cut it out and stuck it in a scrap book. It said the whole French squadron watched, expecting the torpedo to destroy the Thorneycroft as well as the *Bayonnaise* and –'

'Who was driving the Thorneycroft?' Augusta interrupted.

It was a normal enough question for Porthelt, even for a thirteen-year-old girl, because the village was dominated by the Bourdillon boatyard. The local houses were hidden by its workshops and boatsheds which in turn were blurred by the forest of masts belonging to the yachts lying in front in the little bay made by the curve of the land.

'A French officer, I suppose,' Edward said.

'Did he volunteer?' Georgina asked.

'You could hardly expect them to order a man to do a job like that.'

'*I* wouldn't volunteer.'

Edward looked at her angrily, still not sure whether she was genuinely interested in what he was trying to show her or whether she was deliberately making fun of him.

'Well, *he* did,' he said sharply.

'How do you know?'

Edward glared at Georgina. 'Are you really interested or are you just being clever?'

An expression of mock dismay crossed her face. 'Oh, Teddy,' she said, 'I'm terribly interested. But it all sounds so silly. This man trying to blow himself up with a ship called the *Mayonnaise*. Please go on.'

Edward's manner had grown a little stiff. 'When the torpedo struck, there was a deafening –' he lingered on the word for the drama it conveyed '– a deafening report and the *Bayonnaise* sank almost at once. As for the Thorneycroft, the shock caused it to bounce back a matter of fifteen metres – that's a bit more than fifteen yards – then it went round and round in circles for a while as if dazed, until finally it resumed its course with the rest of the squadron.'

'So it was all right?'

6

'It was all right.'

'I bet it gave the crew a headache,' Georgina observed gaily. Edward frowned, convinced by this time that his demonstration wasn't being treated with the respect it deserved. He was a well-built boy, beak-nosed and lean-faced, dark hair curling tightly round his ears. Augusta thought the world of him. Georgina felt he had too high an opinion of himself and needed taking down a peg or two from time to time.

He tried to ignore her smiles and indicated the long boom he had secured to the launch. He had required help from Augusta to get it into position, but the spar had finally been lashed stoutly down the length of the bow and protruded a matter of about eight feet beyond the stem.

'I've directed it downwards so it'll strike *Fairy* just on the waterline,' he explained. 'A proper spar torpedo, of course, is rigged underwater and parallel with the surface, but, since I can't do that, I've aimed it just above the waterline so that the pressure of water against it won't slow the launch or turn it off course.'

'Won't it sink *Fairy*?' Augusta asked.

'Not on your life.' Edward laughed. 'The launch will be going very slowly. With the engine at low revs, it'll just hold her nose on to *Fairy* so we can pick her up.'

'It'll never work.' The words this time came from the deck of the yacht itself where another youngster, older than Edward, sat dangling his feet over the side, watching with a grin on his face. Edward tried not to notice him.

'Your cousin Maurice's talking to you,' Georgina pointed out.

'My cousin Maurice can go and jump in the creek,' Edward said.

'He's waving.'

'Georgy –' Edward's expression was one of pure fury '– let him wave. He can only sneer. He doesn't do anything at all himself, except sneak into Uncle Egg's study and drink his sherry wine and go around with that lout, Barney Scholes-Dever from the Manor House. He ought to be learning something about the boatyard. He's expected to take it over one day.'

'When he does, will you get a look-in?'

It was a good question. Edward's father, Hubert Bourdillon, had been a very different type to his scholarly brother, Egbert, and, having got himself into trouble over a girl in Portsmouth, had run away to sea. More adventurous than Egbert, he enjoyed himself for three years around the world before returning quietly to take his share of responsibility for the growing boatyard founded by their father. It had surprised everybody when he had brought with him an Italian wife, one Maddalena Uschetti, the daughter of another boatyard owner in Livorno, known always to British people from its association with Nelson as Leghorn. Save for the fact that she wasn't English, a state considered by the Bourdillons to be more or less essential for a happy life, Maddalena was regarded as an eminently suitable partner. But the boatyard in Livorno was much bigger than the one at Porthelt and the Italian family's indignation at Hubert Bourdillon's cheek in marrying their daughter without permission resulted in her being cast out. There might have been a reconciliation – indeed, proceedings were under way – but for the fact that, sharing her husband's love of the sea, Maddalena Bourdillon had been drowned with him when their yacht was run down in a sudden Channel fog by a coaster loaded with scrap iron bound for Cardiff. And Hubert's brother, Egg, had taken in the orphaned Edward Dante, who had been brought up at Creek House, the Bourdillons' untidy shambles of a home behind the boatyard.

'Well,' Georgina persisted, '*will* you get a look-in?'

'I'm supposed to,' Edward said. 'After all, my father and Uncle Egg were brothers and when my parents died he promised I would. He's always said I'll have a share.'

For all his quiet eccentricity, Egbert Bourdillon was essentially a fair man and a far more stable character than Edward's father. But Maurice didn't like Edward, resented his intrusion, was not as clever as Edward and had a mean streak in his character which suggested that when Egg was gone, he would do things his way, and his way was unlikely to include Edward.

'That's why I'm trying this out,' Edward explained. 'After all, Bourdillons isn't just a yachtsman's boatyard.

We build experimental stuff. The navy's bought from us. There aren't many bigger.'

It wasn't entirely true because there were plenty of bigger yards. Apart from one or two experimental craft, Bourdillons normally built orthodox boats, but were required from time to time to build on licence to hard-pressed, larger and wealthier yards.

'There's Thorneycrofts, of course,' Edward admitted. 'And people like that. They're the first string. But we're only just below. Now –' he gestured '– about this torpedo.'

'It won't work, Georgy,' Maurice called.

'Oh, yes, it will,' Edward snapped back.

'It'll just push the spar back. The lashings will give.'

'No, they won't. I've anchored the other end against the wheelhouse.'

Edward turned back to his demonstration, frowning and red in the face.

'It all sprang from the *Merrimac–Monitor* fight in the American Civil War,' he said. 'The Confederates made great use of torpedoes but in those days they were merely towed canisters of explosive and it was soon decided that small fast launches were a more suitable means of delivering an attack.'

'You do know an awful lot about it, Teddy,' Augusta said.

Edward smiled. 'The Russians were among the first to use them, on another launch built by Thorneycrofts. They hit a Turkish monitor, but they were driven off without sinking it and the commander of the launch and his observer were badly wounded. Thorneycrofts have been building quick launches ever since. Uncle Egg wants to get into that line. He has some good ideas too. He's working on one he expects to go at over thirty knots.'

'That's faster than a motor car.' Georgina was impressed at last.

'Well, yes. And he's thinking of spar torpedoes. They're normally carried above water and lowered to below the surface for the attack. All it needs is a determined captain.'

'Take no notice of him, Georgy,' Maurice shouted from the deck of *Fairy*. 'Pa's not thinking of them at all. They

9

have locomotive torpedoes these days. They have built-in motors and run on gas or something. Eddy's talking through the top of his head. Just showing off. There've been "fish" torpedoes for years. They used to carry them in davits and drop them into the water, and they had a winch to hoist them back aboard after a dummy run. These days they fire them from a tube on the bow.'

'Ignore him, Georgy,' Edward said, furious that Maurice knew as much as he did.

Georgina laughed. 'I can't,' she said. 'His voice is louder than yours.'

'You should come with *me*,' Maurice shouted to her. 'In *Fairy*. I'm taking her out into the Solent this afternoon. It'll be much better than arsing about with a kid like Eddy who likes to fiddle about with gadgets he doesn't understand.'

Augusta rose in Edward's defence. 'You shouldn't use words like "arse",' she said.

Edward looked up fretfully. 'Are we going on with this experiment or not?' he asked.

Georgina responded briskly. 'I thought we were going to row downriver. I didn't think we were going to war.'

'One of these days,' Edward said, 'we *shall* be going to war. Everybody knows the Germans are getting too big for their boots and that the Kaiser's building a fleet as big as ours.'

'Rot,' Maurice said. 'Everybody knows the Kaiser's mad and that the Germans can't build ships like we can. They wouldn't have a chance and they know it. That's why there won't be a war.'

Edward wasn't so sure. The countries of Europe were like duellists – D'Artagnan or Cyrano – quick to quarrel.

'We don't want to go to war,' Maurice went on, 'because, with the Empire, we have everything we need and the Germans just daren't. And anyway, what lunatic would attack a dreadnought with a spar torpedo?'

'I didn't suggest we'd attack a dreadnought with a spar torpedo,' Edward yelled. 'You'd have to use a mobile torpedo for that. I was just demonstrating how a spar torpedo works.'

'Why?'

'Oh, shut up.'

'Shut up yourself.'

Georgina turned her back on Maurice, who sat watching them, with all the arrogance of a nineteen-year-old who owned a motorcycle and was allowed to drive his father's car and sail his yacht.

His voice came again. 'Eddy had never heard of a spar torpedo until a day or two ago,' he yelled. 'I saw him reading it up. He ought to know they're out of date and that it's pointless experimenting with them.'

Goaded beyond endurance, Edward retaliated. 'You're an ass, Maurice.'

'Ass or not,' Maurice said, 'when Pa goes, I'll be running the yard and I'll make certain you're out on your ear. There'll be no room at Bourdillons for half-wits.'

'Uncle Egg promised me a place.'

'And I suppose you'll get one. But as soon as *I*'m running the show, you're out.' Maurice beamed and swung his legs. 'Put that in your pipe and smoke it.'

'Take no notice of him, Teddy,' Augusta said primly, '*I'm* listening.'

'Actually,' Georgina announced, 'this isn't what I really expected to do this afternoon. Still, I'll listen.' She stared at the overhanging trees and the flat calm water and the white yachts reflected in its surface.

'Considering the weather, though,' she added under her breath, 'I can't think why.'

'Well, all right,' Edward said unwillingly. All the pleasure had gone out of the afternoon. 'You have to allow for wind and tide and a few things like that, of course, but a skipper with experience could work that out in his head. All he has to do is place his boat alongside the enemy. That's what Nelson always said. And that –' he indicated *Fairy* with the grinning Maurice sitting on its deck '– is the enemy.'

He heaved on an oar and, as the dinghy with the accompanying launch swung, he drew a deep breath. 'We're now pointing directly at *Fairy*,' he said. 'What I'll do now is release the lashings, lean over from the dinghy, set the gear lever to "Ahead", and just pull the throttle back far

11

enough for her to move slowly through the water. Actually,' he pointed out pedantically, 'throttles should be designed to be pushed forward to increase speed, not pulled back.'

'Why?'

'You're pushing speed forward into the boat. The other way, you're pulling her back. Like reins on a horse. I've suggested it several times but Uncle Egg doesn't listen. Now we'll sit back and watch. Perhaps,' he added hopefully, 'Maurice will fall in the water at the shock.'

'Not if she's going dead slow,' Georgina pointed out.

'No,' Edward admitted. 'Not if she's going dead slow. Ready?'

'Yes.'

'Here goes. Gear into "Ahead".' Edward leaned over and as he pushed the lever forward, the launch began to move slowly forward from alongside the dinghy.

'A little more throttle, I think,' he went on. 'So she'll do the job properly.'

'Go on,' Maurice shouted. 'Open her full out. Then perhaps you'll sink Pa's boat and he'll realise what a dummy you are and not allow you in the firm.'

'I wish you'd go and boil your head.' In his anger, Edward pulled the throttle lever too far back and, as the launch gathered speed and began to move away from him, his clutching fingers only served to open the throttle even wider.

The rumble of the exhaust increased and the launch shot forward, watched by the horrified group in the dinghy.

'You bloody fool,' Maurice yelled, scrambling to his feet as he saw the launch heading towards him at high speed.

'You shouldn't say "bloody" –' Augusta stopped, her mouth open. 'Oh, my,' she breathed.

The point of the spar struck *Fairy* on the waterline with a resounding crash and the yacht's mast oscillated wildly as the boat heeled. Edward's idea of anchoring the stern end of the spar proved entirely successful; it didn't tear loose, it just moved backwards enough to stave in the front of the launch's wheelhouse and lift the roof.

'Christ!' he said.

12

Maurice, who was standing on the deck waving his arms as if he could repel the speeding launch, overbalanced and fell with a flat splash into the water. The launch, as Edward had predicted, the spar having struck something solid inside the yacht, bounced backwards, withdrawing the spar to leave a gaping hole, and was now setting off down the river on its own.

Ignoring the spluttering Maurice, Edward watched, helpless, as it swung in a wide arc back on its tracks. There were terrified screams as the launch threatened to do the same to the dinghy as it had done to the yacht, but it missed by a hair's-breadth and went on to run up the shingle bank. There was a bang and a screech from the engine as the propeller shear-pin went, then it stopped dead, blue smoke rising slowly into the air.

The *Fairy* had listed sharply, and the hole in her side began to take in water. Sitting horrified in the dinghy, Edward watched as his uncle's pride and joy sank lower and lower until she finally gave up the ghost, heeled over and lay on her side. The horrified spectators heard her lockers burst open and all the pots and pans Aunt Edith kept aboard for instant waterborne parties, cascade on to the cabin sole. As she sagged beneath the water, her mast at an angle of 45 degrees, Edward stared about him in desperation.

Maurice was still swimming, but at the crash windows had opened in nearby offices and workshops and people were running out. Someone was climbing into a dinghy and he was relieved to hear the clatter of oars. Pushing Augusta out of the way, Edward seized the oars of the dinghy and started to pull.

'Where are we going?' Georgina asked placidly.

'Downriver,' he said.

'You're in trouble, old Teddy,' she said, beaming at him.

'That's why I'm going downriver.'

'What about Maurice? Won't he drown?'

'Unfortunately not.'

'I think that's your uncle in one of the dinghies. He looks peeved.'

'I don't blame him.'

13

'What are you going to do?'

'Row down past Porthelt. You'll have to row back.'

'When I go out in a boat,' Georgina said coldly, 'somebody else takes care of that department.'

'I'll do it,' Augusta said stoutly. 'I can row. Where will you be, Teddy?'

'God knows. I think it might be a good idea to join the French Foreign Legion. People always do that when they're in trouble, don't they?'

'Africa's a long way,' Georgina pointed out cheerfully.

'Perhaps I'd better just go to sea for a while. It might be a good idea if I never came back.'

'Oh, Teddy,' Augusta sighed.

As he tugged at the oars, Edward sighed with her. 'There's one thing,' he added. 'It proves my point about the throttle. If I'd been pushing instead of pulling it wouldn't have happened.'

2

Despite his despair at Uncle Egg's anticipated reaction, Edward's real reason for such a hurried departure was to put as much distance as he could between himself and Cousin Maurice. Since the death of his parents, he had had to put up with Maurice's bullying without complaint. He'd promised himself that one day Maurice would pay for it but now, he felt, was not the time. Maurice was a great deal bigger than he was. Having felt the weight of his fists on more than one occasion, Edward had no desire to make their acquaintance again. The day would come, however, when he would be as big as Maurice.

Edward wasn't eager to disappear immediately into the wild blue yonder. He loved the river and the boatyard. Bourdillons built small tugs and lighters, driven by reliable steam, paraffin and heavy oil engines. They tackled steel hulls, lightly-plated boats for tropical waters where the destructive ship worm attacked wood; they made wooden barges for Europe, petrol-driven cedar craft, and launches, whalers, dinghies and tenders for the Admiralty. They had slips, a foundry where propellers and other castings were poured, a smithy with furnaces and a steam hammer to forge crankshafts and connecting rods, a boiler shop for plate work, a machine shop with lathes, planers and shapers driven by old-fashioned overhead leather belting, a fitting shop where engines were fixed and small craft could be brought in to have machinery installed. Practically every craftsman in wood and metal in the area worked at Bourdillons and Edward desperately wanted to be part of it.

For a day or two, in constant fear of being seen, he hung about the river. A note in the post to Georgina brought not Georgina but Augusta on her bicycle.

'Georgy says she's busy,' she announced. 'She sent me.'
'What's happening?'

15

'Your uncle's livid,' she announced, extracting plenty of drama from the occasion. 'But your Aunt Edith told Mother he'll get over it. Mind you, she's not all that happy herself. She spent a lot of money on new curtains for the cabin and restocked the galley with crockery and the bunks with new mattresses and sheets. It's all got to be replaced. But she said you ought not to worry, just to give it a bit of time. Did you join the Foreign Legion?'

'They haven't got a recruiting office round here.'

'So what are you going to do?'

'Perhaps Sam Nankidno could let me know how things are at the yard.'

'I can tell you that straightaway. Everything's stopped for the salvage of *Fairy*. Your uncle's got his shotgun in the office, and Maurice has gone into training.

'What for?'

'What do you think?'

'Oh, Christ!'

'Father says you shouldn't use words like "Christ" and "Jesus" as oaths. He says they're blasphemous.'

'Your father's never been in a situation like the one I'm in. I don't suppose you could lend me some money, could you? I've spent all I had with me and I'm starving.'

'I've got a bit in a money box. About two or three pounds. I don't know exactly. You could have that.'

'Good old Gussie. Could you send it down with Sam Nankidno? Tell him I'll be outside the Three Eels at seven tomorrow.'

'You're not going drinking, are you?'

'Of course not,' Edward said.

But he did.

Sam Nankidno was only a year older than he was and they had often indulged in wrestling matches behind the boathouse when Sam was supposed to be working. Sam was an apprentice, a dark-visaged youth whose family came from Cornwall, with the build of a fox terrier and a strange ability to tease recalcitrant engines to life. He had first appeared as a skinny thirteen-year-old, and it was Uncle Egg who had discovered in him an instinctive ability

16

with mechanical things. He came from generations of seafarers and knew all there was to know about the ways of sailors. He and Edward had taken to each other at once.

Since he brought £2 6s 10d, the entire contents of Augusta's money box, and had gone to a lot of trouble, it seemed only fair to offer Sam a drink.

'I had a date,' Sam said, 'with Alice Appleby. I had to cancel it to come here. She probably won't go out with me again.'

'You need a drink,' Edward suggested.

'Gussie said the money was for food and lodgings.'

'I don't think even she would object to *one*. A small one.'

'You're not old enough to go in pubs.'

'I'm big enough. And when you're big enough you're old enough.'

Sam grinned. 'Come on then,' he said. 'Keep your money in your pocket. I'll pay. After all, it would cost more to take Alice out. She drinks port and lemon. And it's payday tomorrow.'

Eyed suspiciously by the barmaid, Edward stared into his half-pint of mild, which was the cheapest thing available.

'Think it's safe to go back?' he asked.

Sam grinned again. 'Not yet,' he said.

'What shall I do, Sam?'

'Shouldn't you be going back to school soon?'

Edward shook his head. He was sick of Greek and Latin and French verbs and wasn't particularly enamoured of Shakespeare. Above all, he detested the chaplain, whom he suspected of an unnatural interest in the smaller boys.

'How about getting a job then? Temporary, sort of. When it's blown over I can let you know.'

'I thought of joining the Foreign Legion.'

'I wouldn't.'

'Why not?'

'The conditions are supposed to be terrible.'

'Perhaps I could go to sea?'

'Same difference. But weekly boats go from Portsmouth.'

'What are weekly boats?'

17

'Coasters. Ply round the coast. Short trips. Portsmouth to Bristol. Perhaps to London. London to Tyneside. That sort of thing. You could sign off after a week and see what the situation is. If it's still a bit warm round here, you could sign on for another week.'

'It's an idea.'

'Better have another beer. It'll give you backbone.' Sam grinned. 'If it was me, I'd go home, take the hammering and call it quits.'

'Uncle Egg's got a shotgun.'

'He'll never use it.'

'What about Maurice?'

'You could wipe the floor with him.'

'I'm not a fighter, Sam.'

'Then it's time you was. Especially if you're going to sea. Everybody needs a good fight under his belt before he settles down, and everybody's a fighter when he has to be. All you need to know is how to set about it.'

'How *do* you set about it?'

'For a start, you don't think of fighting fair like they teach you at school. None of this stiff upper lip and straight left stuff. Maurice is flabby. He smokes too much and I've seen him in the pub swilling beer with that Barney Scholes-Dever from the Manor.'

'So what do I do?'

'Don't give him a chance. Not even to square up. As soon as he says "Go" – or even before – rush him. Use your feet to get his shins and the top of your head to get his nose. That'll daze him. After that, keep him back-pedalling. If he cops you one, don't for God's sake stop to draw breath. Forget it and keep going.'

Sam appeared again the next evening, bringing with him a kitbag. 'If you're going to sea,' he said, 'you'll need something warmer than what you've got on. There's a jersey in here, some rubber boots and a pair of new dungarees. There's also an old oilskin and a sou'wester and some warm socks.'

'Whose are they?'

'Mine, o' course. I heard, by the way, that there's a weekly going from Portsmouth on Saturday night. Ask at

18

the pub across the road from the docks. That's where the skipper drinks. He'll listen because it's never easy to make up numbers on weekly boats.'

'Thanks, Sam. I'll never forget you.'

'Don't talk daft. There's another thing: Gussie said she'd be near the Three Eels at eight o'clock. She wants to say goodbye.'

'Tell her to tell Georgina to come.'

'She prefers to come on her own. I think she's stuck on you.'

'She's only a kid.'

'She won't always be a kid,' he said. 'And I wouldn't mind being her old man's curate when she grows up a bit.'

'Why not Georgina?'

'She's got her eye on Barney Scholes-Dever. He's got more money than you. Meantime, I have to see Alice. She has to be home by half-past ten. She's got that kind of Ma.'

Augusta was on her bicycle, looking nervous.

'I can't stay long,' she said.

'Why wouldn't Georgina come?'

'She said she was busy. Mother thinks I'm visiting Dulcie Quinton about going back to school. If I'm seen with you I'll be in trouble. I've raised another pound. Aunt Grace gave me two pounds for going back to school. You can have one of them.'

The sacrifice took Edward's breath away.

'Sam said you were going to sign on a ship. Will you be all right?'

'Why not?'

'All those rough men. Father worked with the Missions to Seamen for a time and he's always telling the most dreadful stories about them.' She glanced about her. The sun had lost its brilliance and the white glare had changed to a bronze glow. 'I think I ought to be going. Teddy. But I wanted to say goodbye.'

'I'm only going for a week.'

'All the same –' Blushing furiously, she leaned over the handlebars of her cycle and kissed him.

'What's that for?'

19

'Just in case,' she said.

'Just in case what?'

'Just in case it's more than a week.'

He walked round the village, lonely and at a loss to know what to do with himself. It was still daylight when Sam appeared. He had the look of a cat that had been at the cream.

'I thought you were going out with Alice,' Edward said.

'She had to go home,' said Sam. 'We were going to the church social but her Grandma had a turn and she was only allowed a couple of hours.'

'Where did you go?'

'Down Acre Lane.'

'There's nothing down Acre Lane.'

Sam grinned. 'There's fields,' he said. 'Some of 'em with tall corn.'

'You never –?'

Sam grinned from ear to ear. 'Mind your own bloody business.' Changing the subject, he said, 'Where are you spending the night?'

'Don't know.'

'Where did you sleep last night?'

'Brown's barn. There was plenty of straw. It was warm enough.'

As they talked, the door of the Three Eels opened and Maurice emerged, in white flannels, boater and blazer.

'We've got company,' Sam said.

'Oy!' Maurice looked as though he had had a bellyful of beer. 'Brat!' With him was Barnaby Scholes-Dever from the Manor House, Colonel Scholes-Dever's son, a good-looking blond young man carrying a cane. He had recently been sent down from Cambridge.

'You talking to me?' Edward's voice was shaking and he fought to hold it steady.

Maurice advanced on him, smoking a cigar, his face damp with sweat.

'One in the guts ought to sort him out,' Sam murmured. 'I'll be off.'

'Why?' At the very least, Edward had been expecting moral support.

'I still work for the boatyard,' Sam said hurriedly.

20

'You little bastard,' Maurice said. He seemed to tower over Edward. 'You nearly drowned me.'

Edward swallowed. 'Pity I didn't,' he said.

'You're asking for a hiding. I've given you hidings before. You're due for another.'

'Sort him out, Maurice, old boy,' Scholes-Dever said. 'And make it quick. It's time we were off. The girls'll be waiting.'

Maurice suddenly lashed out. It wasn't a hard blow but it sent a whole core of vengeful fury surging up inside Edward. As his cousin paused to remove his blazer, Edward's right fist struck him on the side of the head and sent him reeling.

While Maurice was still stumbling about with his arms trapped in the sleeves of his blazer, Edward rushed him head-first, fists swinging. Maurice was knocked flat on his back.

'You rotten little cheat,' he snarled.

As Maurice struggled to his feet, one arm still in the sleeve of his blazer, Edward rushed at him again. Maurice tried an uppercut. The buttons on the cuff of the free sleeve struck Edward across the eyes, almost blinding him, but the material took away the force of the blow. He sent Maurice hopping with a kick on the shins and, before he could recover, swung hard with left and right. Maurice was on his back again, startled, dazed and wondering what had hit him.

Edward was about to step back, when he remembered what Sam had said about not letting up. Diving on top of his cousin, he grabbed a handful of carefully-oiled hair, yanked up Maurice's head and slammed it back on the pavement. Maurice's eyes rolled.

As Edward climbed to his feet, Scholes-Dever lunged at him with his cane.

Swinging round, Edward snatched away the stick and, swiping out with it, heard Scholes-Dever yelp with pain. Breaking the cane across his knee and tossing it aside, he managed to punch Maurice again as he struggled to his knees.

'All right! All right!' It was the voice of the landlord of the Three Eels. 'Stop this bloody lark! I'm not having

21

fighting on my premises. Bugger off, the lot of you! I've sent the potboy for the police.'

Maurice staggered upright, his face suddenly green, as the landlord interposed himself between them. Remembering bouts he'd seen at fairs where old pugilists, well versed in the tricks of the trade, had taken on all comers for a sovereign, Edward recalled how they had used the referee as a shield. Now, as the landlord struggled to separate them, Edward dodged under his outspread arms and landed a right hook to Maurice's stomach.

Maurice went down again, sat up, lifting himself on one elbow, and vomited the beer he had drunk into the gutter and down the front of his blazer.

'You bastard,' he panted. 'You didn't give me a chance.'

'I'll never give you a chance again, Maurice,' he said. 'Remember that.' He turned to find himself facing Scholes-Dever who backed off.

'And you keep out of my way, too,' he said, 'or I'll do the same to you.'

'Never you mind doing anything to anybody,' the landlord yelled. 'Just you wait until PC Spicer arrives. He'll sort you out. Fighting on my forecourt. Committing a public nuisance. Drunk and disorderly.'

God, Edward thought, there was going to be hell to pay when Uncle Egg found out. He could see Constable Spicer, portly and sporting a large moustache, puffing round the corner on his bicycle from the police house.

'Time I was off,' he said to the landlord. 'Thanks for the warning.'

Rubbing his ear where Maurice had hit him, Edward walked away with as much dignity as he could manage.

'Oy! You there!'

The sound of Constable Spicer's voice set his feet moving faster. Once round the corner into Acre Lane, he started running.

'Hold it, kid.' Sam Nankidno caught Edward's arm and pulled him behind the hedge.

'Well done,' he said. 'But, make no mistake, you've made a nasty enemy there.'

Edward suddenly felt rather shaky after the elation of his victory.

'What are you going to do now?' Sam asked.

'Walk to Portsmouth, I think.'

'You'll need a good meal and a bed first. Come on home with me. My Ma'll see you right. I'll tell Gussie in the morning what you intend.'

'You'd better not tell her about tonight.'

'No need. She saw the lot.'

'What?'

'She'd just reached the corner when the fun started.'

'Oh, Christ!'

Sam shook his head. 'I shouldn't worry, if I was you. I heard her say, "Go on, Teddy. Hit him." '

3

Sam's weekly boat turned out to be a tatty old barge that looked as though she was normally used to carry rubbish. The skipper wore a bowler hat and the rest of the crew seemed to consist solely of a boy and a dog. Edward had a feeling he could do better.

It had started to rain and the lights reflected from the wet pavements, but Edward could smell the sea, the real sea, not the river where the boatyard lay, and he experienced a violent surge of emotion, as the bonds that held him to home dropped away. He gazed at the tall cigarette-shaped funnels and, beyond them, the masts and spars of sailing vessels.

'You thinkin' o' goin' to sea, son?'

The voice seemed to come from under his left arm and he swung round to find himself facing a small man in a cap with a face like a ferret.

For two days he had been debating with himself. Was he doing the right thing? Ought he to go home and throw himself on Egg's mercy? Ought he even just go back to school and let them sort it out?

'Yes,' he said decisively. 'I am.'

'In that case,' the little man said, 'you'll need a ship, won't you?'

'Do you know of one?'

'Not half. *Dolly Colgate*. Tramp. Due for Cape Town and the East. Mixed cargo. Birmingham tools. Manchester cloth. Scrap iron.'

As the little man moved closer under the light of the gaslamp, Edward noticed that his teeth fitted badly and jiggled in his mouth as he spoke so that he still seemed to be talking after the sound had stopped.

'Do they need a hand?' he asked.

'Looking for a deck boy and an ordinary seaman. You'd do for the deck boy.'

'Who're you? The mate?'

'Not bloody likely. Name's Jimmy Oxshott. I just give a 'and now and again to 'elp 'em make up numbers. What some people call a tout.'

'Oh.'

'Don't let that worry you. *You* don't 'ave to pay. The *Dolly Colgate* sorts that out. Now then, what about your gear?'

'I haven't got much.'

'In that case, you'll need some. You'll also need a few tips on what to do. Everybody needs a few tips first time out.'

'How do you know it's the first time?' he asked.

Oxshott sniggered. 'Sticks out like the warts on a wart-hog, son,' he said. 'So just watch yourself. Don't let 'em bully you. They're bastards for that. And avoid fights. If you get into one, remember the old maxim. *Twice blest is he who knows his cause is just, thrice blest is he who gets 'is blow in fust.*' It was much the same advice as Sam Nankidno had offered. 'And keep away from women.' He sniffed. 'Tell the feller on the dock gate I sent you. It'll be all right.'

The little ferret vanished as abruptly as he'd appeared. For a while Edward debated what to do, then he headed for the dock gate. A whiskery man in a little cabin looked up. He was drinking tea from a mug with a vast black crack down its side that looked as if it were a breeding ground for germs.

'I've been told to report to the *Dolly Colgate*,' Edward said.

'God 'elp you. Who sent you?'

'Chap called Oxshott.'

'That old bugger. All right. If he's sent you, you can go. She's down here to starboard. You'll see her. There's a sign up on the bridge.'

The docks were silent except for a steam winch in the distance clattering as stores were hoisted on board. The rain had slowed to a fine drizzle that raised damp haloes round the gaslamps.

25

Edward found the *Dolly Colgate* without trouble, a towering black hull and a tall funnel like a Woodbine, linked to the quay by ropes and a solitary gangway. An old man was sitting on a large upturned crate at the end of the gangway reading *Peg's Paper* by the light of a hurricane lamp.

'This the *Dolly Colgate*?' Edward asked.

The man didn't bother to look up. 'That's what it says up there.'

'I've been told to report aboard.'

'Who're you?'

'Edward Dante Bourdillon. I'm the deck boy.'

'First time?'

It seemed there was no point in denying it. 'Yes,' Edward said.

'Christ help you. Up the gangway, then forrard. As far as you can go without falling off the end. You'll see two alleyways. Take the one on your right. T'other's the black gang's. They'd murder you. You'll see two cabins. Don't go in them. One's the bosun's. The one beside it's the carpenter's and he's a swine. The little cabin next door's for the deck boy and the ordinary seamen. Right at the end's the forecastle. Don't go in there. They don't like people pinchin' their bunks and they're a right load of buggers. Other side of the alleyway's the messdeck and the daymen's cabin. Don't go in there, either. They're old hands and they don't like new boys.'

Edward slowly climbed the gangway. Clearly, there were more hazards to going to sea than he'd imagined. He picked his way among coils of heavy rope hawsers, winches, ring bolts and hatch covers. Finding the forecastle, he stared about him.

It looked like a prison. Painted a uniform grey, it consisted of a group of bunks made of iron piping and iron slats on which were sacking mattresses. These, he discovered later, were filled with straw and known as donkeys' breakfasts. With each was a pillow of the same material. The minute cabin next door contained three bunks and three lockers.

Tossing his few possessions on to one of the bunks, he sat down on a wooden bench which was the only other furniture, and contemplated his future. If the surroundings were anything to go by, it looked pretty bleak. He was tempted to bolt. But he couldn't face the old man at the end of the gangway. 'Don't fancy it? Bit too rough for you? No Mummy to tuck you up at night.' He could imagine the comments already.

There was a sudden commotion on the quayside. It sounded as if someone were being murdered. Gradually the shouting died down to what sounded like pleas for help and Edward decided someone had been attacked and rolled for his money. His conscience told him he ought to help, or at least investigate, and he climbed back on deck.

'Stupid old sod,' the watchman said, to no-one in particular.

'Who?'

'Him.'

The old man jerked a thumb and by the pale glow from a cluster of lights above the deck, Edward saw a sprawling figure, swathed in a twisted overcoat, lying face down in a puddle on the cobbled surface of the quayside.

'Is he dead?' he asked.

'Nah,' the watchman said. 'Drunk.'

They knelt down beside the prostrate man and turned him over. The stink of booze was enough to rock Edward back on his heels.

'Pooh!' the watchman said. 'Ripe as an old kipper.'

'Swimming,' the drunken man mumbled. 'Swimming for me life.'

They helped him to a sitting position, which wasn't easy. His arms and legs seemed boneless.

'Touch o' sciatica,' he said. 'Gets me knees.'

'Sciatica be buggered,' the watchman commented. 'You're pissed. It's the donkeyman,' he explained to Edward. 'He always gets hisself paralytic.'

The donkeyman choked suddenly and fished in his mouth to hook out a set of false teeth which he stuffed into his pocket. 'That's better.' he said. 'I can hear what you're sayin' now.'

He was screwing up his eyes to peer at Edward but he could obviously see no more than a blurred image. As

27

they lifted him to his feet, somehow their legs became entangled and they all fell down.

'Excuse me crossing your bows,' the donkeyman apologised solemnly above the bitter curses of the watchman as they sorted themselves out. 'Steam always gives way to sail. Me balance's gone. Sunk without trace.'

The watchman tried to drag him upright by his coat sleeves.

'Leave it out,' the donkeyman said peremptorily. 'I can manage.' Squinting at the watchman, he muttered, 'Bugger me, if it isn't 'Arry Armitage.'

The watchman spat.

'There'll be plenty more like him tonight,' the watchman said, as they lowered the donkeyman on to his bunk.

Edward was just making up his mind to try and get some sleep himself when another row started. This time it was the bosun and the carpenter. They were both Swedes and it was hard to tell whether they were helping each other or having a fight.

About ten drunks later, Edward climbed into his bunk. Straw, that protruded through the sacking pillow, pricked his cheek. But Edward didn't care. He was exhausted. As he pulled the coarse blanket over him, he heard a roistering voice somewhere on deck.

'There was Brown, upside-down,
Moppin' up the whisky off the floor –'
The song was interrupted by a crash, and then silence. But suddenly the song started again.

' "Booze, booze," the fireman cried
As they came knockin' at the door –'
There was a thump and a curse.

'Oh, the wheel flew off the hearse
An' the coffin fell out in the road –'
The singer now was outside the door.

'An' the widder got outa the carriage
An' she said "Goddam the –" '
The song came to a full stop as the door smashed open. Framed in the entrance was an enormous man.

''Tis a quare ole song, that one bhoyo,' he shouted.

His face was worn by the wind and the weather and his eyes were glazed in a luminous opal stare. His hair was black and stood stiffly upright as though he'd had an electric shock.

'Francis Xavier McWilliams,' he announced. 'They also call me Xavier William McFrancis and William Francis McXavier. Sure, it don't matter. I have the dhrink taken.' Like a falling oak, he slowly toppled to the floor. Edward left him where he lay, and was not even bothered by the snores.

The following morning, dressed in dungarees and nervous as a lion tamer going solo for the first time, Edward breakfasted off burgoo – a rather tasteless porridge – eggs, fried to the consistency of stones, and bread.

Three bright-eyed youngsters, who clearly had been sober the night before, produced the meal in huge dixies.

'Tuck in,' one of them said. 'There's plenty. The rest of 'em won't be out for a while yet.'

They were all able seamen and very young – one was only sixteen. Knowing it required four years at sea to become an able seaman, the startled Edward realised the boy must have first gone to sea at the age of twelve. What, then, had he to worry about?

'Enjoy it while you can,' the youngest said. 'It won't be this good tomorrow. It'll be fried liver out of tins with all the pipes in and it'll taste like boot soles cooked in paraffin. I know the cook. I've sailed with him before. This is just to kid everybody she's not a starvation ship.'

When the call came to go on deck to cast off moorings, in his anxiety Edward was ahead by a long way. The next to appear were the three youngsters. The mate produced the ship's articles for Edward to sign on, whilst the rest turned up, grey-faced, in ones or twos. As they hefted the heavy mooring ropes, they moved like zombies.

The rain had stopped and the skies were clear. A cold wind whipped the top of the bow wave to a feathery spray. As the *Dolly Colgate* felt the open sea, she dug her nose into the waves, and the spray blew back into glittering rainbow-coloured fans. She creaked and groaned like a living thing. Around the masthead wheeled the gulls, bril-

29

liantly white in the morning sunlight against the dark clouds.

The bosun arrived with a chipping hammer and Edward was sent to hack at the paint on the poop. Within an hour he had enormous blisters on his hands.

'Keep going,' the bosun said. 'They'll get hard in time.'

The blisters burst and began to bleed, and the day became one of sheer agony. The evening was a dark shadow ahead of him. He had seen nothing of Francis Xavier McWilliams except at mealtimes when he sat opposite Edward, nursing a splitting headache.

On his bunk after supper, Edward took out the only book he had brought with him – a pocket copy of *Omar Khayyam* Gussie had sent via Sam.

'This your first thrip, bhoy?'

Looking up, he saw McWilliams' bright red face and black hair upside-down within an inch or two of his own. Blue eyes rimmed with red glittered at him.

'Yes, it is.'

'Youse get lotsa trouble first thrip. What's that you read?'

'It's called *The Rubaiyat of Omar Khayyam*,' Edward said nervously.

'The rubber what?'

'Not rubber anything. *Rubaiyat*. It's a poem. Persian.'

'Yerrah, bhoy, ye have the Persian?'

'It's been translated into English. By a chap called Fitzgerald.'

'Oirishman?'

'I expect so.'

''Tis great poets the Oirish are. What's that rubber t'ing like?'

Edward started to read it aloud.

'Awake! For Morning in the bowl of Night
Has flung the Stone that puts the Stars to Flight . . .'

McWilliams swung down from his bunk and sat next to Edward. 'I know a poem,' he confided, as Edward closed the book.

Shutting his eyes he began to quote:

'The last rose o' summer
Left bloomin' alone,

All her lovely companions
Is faded an' gone.'

'Tom Moore,' Edward said.

'Is it now?'

'A great poet.'

'Oirish.'

'That's right. Go on.'

'I don't know no more. Say a bit o' that rubber fella again.'

Edward obliged.

'The darlin' craytur. Ye know any more poems, bhoy?'

'I know Cassius' speech from *Julius Caesar*.'

'Where's Julius Caesar?'

'It's not a place. It's a man. It's a play.'

They went through chunks of *Macbeth, Romeo and Juliet*, even *The Song of Solomon*. Edward had had them all hammered into his head at school.

'Sure, I like that *Song o' Solomon*,' McWilliams said. 'The fella who wrote that musta been a sailor. That's how sailors t'ink when 'tis hot and they're lyin' in their bunks in the middle o' the night.' He tapped his chest. 'I know the *Hail Mary*. Hail Mary, full of grace –' He stopped as if he weren't sure of it after all. 'Holy Mary, Mother of God,' he tried, 'pray for our sins, now and at the hour of our death.'

'*Santa Maria*,' Edward said. '*Madre di Dio, prega per noi peccatori, adesso e nell' ora della nostra morte.*'

'What the devil's that?'

'Same thing. In Italian.'

'Holy Mary, Mother of God, ye have the Italian as well?'

'I learned it from my mother. She was Italian. She's dead. So's my father. I'm an orphan.'

McWilliams eyed him. 'Ye're terrible big for an orphan, bhoy. Tell me, how do yez say "I love you" in Italian?'

'*Ti amo. Ti adoro. No potrei vivere senza di te.* Something like that. Why?'

'I got a girl in Naples.' He fished in his locker, and took out a small box, from which he removed a wallet. From the wallet he took a sheet of paper carefully wrapped in tissue paper.

31

''Tis a love letter, so 'tis. You t'ink you can read it for me. I ain't never read it before.' The letter was opened as carefully as an ancient script and spread out on the bench.

'It came just as we was leavin'. What's it say?'

' "Carissimo Xavier –",' Edward began to read.

'Always called me Xavier,' McWilliams explained. 'Afther St Francis Xavier. 'Tis a saint he was. Saints is important in Italy, y'see. Next time I'm in Naples oi'll show her what this saint is made of.'

'I shouldn't if I were you,' Edward said. 'She writes that her husband's found out and he's going to shoot you.'

McWilliams' jaw dropped, then he grinned. 'Sure, there's other fish in the sea. You speak any other languages?'

'A bit of French and German.'

'We'll make a grand partnership,' McWilliams said. 'Wherever the ship puts in, you talk to the girls and I take 'em to bed. And anybody who messes wit' yez, I tear 'em to pieces.'

4

For eighteen months the *Dolly Colgate* ploughed around the Middle and Far East before docking in Cape Town. After a wild night on the town, McWilliams ended up carrying Edward back to the docks draped over his shoulder like a sack of corn, only to discover that the three teenage boys in the crew had gone missing.

There had been no sign of a disagreement at any point during the trip, but it had emerged that they thought South Africa was a land of opportunity.

'You can still make a fortune in the diamond fields,' one of them had said, and they had obviously decided to try.

'The bastards have gone up-country,' the bosun said sourly. 'We'll never find 'em. And neither will anybody else.'

The captain raged up and down the bridge and cursed the mate, who took it out on the bosun who lashed into Edward, because he was the most junior member of the crew.

The ship was delayed for three days until new crew were found. They were all old shellbacks soaked in beer and rum and when two of them failed to turn up as the ship was about to leave Port Elizabeth, Edward decided he had had enough.

When they put in to Durban, he and McWilliams walked off, went to a pawn shop where Edward got rid of his watch and McWilliams a gold chain and cross which had belonged to his mother, and took a train to Johannesburg. That was where the diamond fields were. Stepping on to the platform, they did a jig together, cavorting wildly to the amusement of other passengers.

''Tis a quare old place,' McWilliams said, gazing about him at the mine headings. 'But 'twill make us a fortune, bhoy.'

Unfortunately, Johannesburg was going through a slump and there were riots. The unemployed – whites as well as blacks – were demanding jobs. And the antagonism that had existed between Boer and Briton during the recent war in South Africa only exacerbated the ill feeling. More than once, finding themselves on the edge of an angry crowd, Edward and McWilliams had to bolt down a side street to avoid being flattened by a blow from a police truncheon.

Within a month they were back on the coast, broke, hungry and searching for a ship. Moreover the police were looking for Paddy McWilliams over a little business of a fight in a back-street shebeen.

'Sure, thim cops would disbelieve the blessed saints thimselves,' he panted as they hurried for the docks. As they ran, they got caught up with a group of cadets from a Portuguese training ship, *Vasco da Gama*, who had been enjoying a night ashore. When they reached the ship, they slipped on board with them. The cadets enjoyed the joke and looked after them, but, when the ship reached Cape Town, Edward and Paddy were tossed ashore by the indignant officers. The Cape Town police took a lenient view, and suggested it would be a good idea to find another berth – within twenty-four hours.

The only ship available was a four-masted barque, the *Culloden*, which appeared to be going north towards England. Though they didn't fancy spending their time at sea climbing rigging, there wasn't much choice.

By this time, the blisters on Edward's hands had toughened into callouses and the foul language that had shocked him at first came as easily to him as it did to everyone else.

But once more, Edward and Paddy found they had jumped out of the frying pan into the fire. The quarters in the *Culloden* were more cramped than in the *Dolly Colgate*, and the food was filthy. The crew were a mixed bag. There was a black West Indian, a Frenchman, a German mate, and a vociferous Russian cook called Pushkov who had fled Russia in 1905. He claimed to be from the mutinous Russian cruiser, *Potemkin*, whose crew had murdered their officers, and become the centre of an attempt at revolution in Odessa.

Pushkov couldn't cook to save his life, but he was intelligent and, speaking a little English, managed to communicate with Edward, who was the only man on board he would acknowledge as his intellectual equal. In a mixture of English, French, German and Russian, they exchanged reminiscences of what life had been like before they had gone to sea. They were both homesick and Pushkov often melted into tears.

'You different,' he said. '*Anglichanin* very stiff. No tears. *Zhelavu schastiya*. Very upper lip.'

Climbing the rigging made Edward's stomach churn and he decided it would be wise to return to steam as soon as possible. The first time up the mast left him with a thumping heart. The lower part of the climb wasn't difficult but at the top was a roughly semi-circular platform of gratings. To get on, he had to climb outwards on the rope ratlines with his back almost parallel with the deck. As he paused, Edward was hailed by a shout from the mate on the deck below.

'Go on. If you fall, you'll only fall in the water. It's only fifty feet. Mebbe you could turn it into a dive.'

Gradually he grew used to the climb and, though he always hated it, he learned to do it with some efficiency. But in bad weather the forecastle was a heaving, groaning hellhole, a steaming dive where the condensation dripped off the bulkheads and the men lay watching the oilskins and dirty clothing swinging backwards and forwards in monotonous arcs to the pitch of the ship. In cold weather the *Culloden* was an ice box so that their clothes were never dry and Edward shivered beneath his two inadequate blankets and swore he'd never go to sea again.

But, almost against their will, he and McWilliams learned the functions of the multifarious ropes, the difference between a brace, a halliard and a downhaul, between a royal and topsail, between a staysail and a spanker, a crossjack and a topgallant. They experienced gales that put the fear of God into Edward as the Cape Horn waves came over the deck big as houses, grey, forbidding and ugly. The hawsepipes were blocked with wood stoppers, lifelines were up and wire safety nets rigged to prevent anyone being washed overboard, while the cargo in the hold was held in place with railway sleepers lashed with chains and secured with wedges driven home with sledge hammers. More timbers were laid across the hatch covers and lashed to ring bolts as the ship drove headlong before the wind, rolling her lee rail to scoop up avalanches of green water.

Unfortunately the ship wasn't going to England as they'd thought, but to Australia initially and, following the winds, they were never far north of 60 degrees south, travelling via Geelong and east – about Cape Horn across the southern oceans. Nowhere en route did they encounter glamorous places or beautiful girls, and in the end they found themselves back in Cape Town where they had started.

The desire to go home was becoming an obsession. Both men walked off the *Culloden* and signed on a tramp steamer, *Magdalen Gladbrook*, which was due to head north for Swansea within twenty-four hours. Like all tramps, she was finding her cargoes wherever she could, and dropping them where she had to. They unloaded tobacco in Freetown and, picking up coconut fibre, headed for Dakar where they loaded castor beans. At Dakar, they received orders to proceed to Alexandria to pick up a cargo of Egyptian cotton for Rio de Janeiro.

'Bloody hell,' said Edward. But at least he was glad of the calm of the Mediterranean as they chugged past the Balearics, the southern tip of Sardinia, Sicily, Malta and Crete.

In Alexandria, they lay alongside a small barquentine, the *George V. Cotterill*, due for England as soon as she had discharged her cargo. Stores and gear were being replenished in Egypt because they were cheaper there and her owners were mean. The master, a man called Budd, received Edward and Paddy with joy because two of his men had just gone into hospital after an accident. Both men clearly knew their way round a sailing ship. Budd asked no questions and welcomed them aboard.

'The Medway, boys,' he said. 'You'll be home with your loved ones before you know where you are.'

Budd was an old man who had been passed over for promotion to a bigger ship, and had a habit of going to his cabin during increasingly frequent periods of depression to lose himself in a bottle of whisky.

The first mate was a bully who had the sourer members of the crew threatening to push him overboard one dark night when no-one was looking. But none of them ever tried, because he was a giant of a man and they were all terrified of him. His weakness was the opposite sex and he vanished ashore every night looking for the drinking dens where the women were as wild as the men.

The weather was hot for late autumn, and there was no sign of seasonal rain. With every day that passed the heat increased until the very air seemed to have burned away. There were rumours of disease in the poorer quarters of the city.

Several nights after they had signed on, McWilliams dragged Edward with several more of the crew in tow along to a place where he claimed girls did the most extraordinary things for the amusement of sailors. As they approached the dive, down a dark and narrow street, an Egyptian staggered against them. He was well-dressed and was carrying an armful of books. As he stumbled past, he dropped his books, then his knees slowly gave way, and he collapsed full length on the pavement, his face in his own vomit.

'Ah, the curse of dhrink,' McWilliams said sympathetically.

They were about to go to his assistance when a man pushed them away.

'You British?' he said. 'Then keep away. It's cholera.'

Paddy and Edward decided to give the show a miss, and went back to the ship, where there were fierce arguments on deck and in the forecastle.

'Plague's brought by rats,' someone said.

'It ain't plague,' someone else retorted. 'I saw that in China. That feller was just sick. Somethin' he ate.'

A British doctor from the Embassy appeared to examine them. They were lined up on deck and checked one by one, but there was nothing he could find wrong, though he made their hair stand on end with his stories about the effects of cholera.

'Any sign of diarrhoea?' he asked Edward.

'No.'

'Thank God for that. That's how it starts. Perspiration, a feeling of faintness, unsteady limbs, a fluttering in the stomach, then a prodigious emptying of the bowels followed by abdominal cramps, a desperate thirst, vomiting, retching and the massive evacuation of a colourless liquid from the rectum.' He turned to Budd. 'Miraculously, you have no signs of it aboard your ship, Captain. It's playing the very devil in the shanty areas.'

Budd's face fell and he headed for his cabin and the whisky bottle.

'He looks as if the cook's spat in the stew and t'rown the ladle at the ship's cat,' McWilliams said.

They still had most of a mixed cargo to unload but, because of the epidemic, labour was hard to find. The dockworkers had disappeared to their own quarter of the city. Because he could speak a little French, it was Edward who was sent by Captain Budd to the agent's office to chivvy him into finding help.

It was while he was away from the ship that McWilliams vanished. There were rumours that he'd been waylaid and left for dead, but Edward knew his disappearance sprang from something far less dramatic. Unlettered and superstitious, he could face danger and bad weather, anything the mate could throw at him, but he couldn't face the prospect of an epidemic.

5

The *George V. Cotterill* remained alongside despite the noisy demands from the forecastle that she should leave. Business in the city was still being carried on, newsboys cried the names of papers and urchins scrambled for discarded cigarette ends. But the cafés were empty and cabs stood idle in ranks. A few shops had shut and people hurried past, not even stopping to talk.

With the increasing number of deaths, rumours spread, many of them wildly exaggerated. Gradually the city became isolated. The streets no longer grated under the wheels of waggons bringing in food. Bonfires were lit in the streets in the belief that the smoke would ward off the pestilence. But still the deaths continued and even the quacks, hawking their medicines in the streets, fell dead and were buried with the money still in their pockets because no one would touch it.

The heat was intense, but there was a storm building up in the west. Edward could sense it. Edward prayed the ship would leave because he was terrified. While he had been in the agent's office one of the clerks had collapsed. He had seen him for two or three days, looking as if he were disappearing pound by pound, his eyes slowly receding into his head. As the clerk fell off his stool, he almost knocked Edward over. Turning on his heel, Edward had fled.

Now there were reports of other outbreaks in the eastern end of the Mediterranean – in Istanbul, Smyrna, Beirut and Alexandria, all destinations for the *George V. Cotterill*. In the end a deputation was sent to Captain Budd demanding the crew should be free to leave. Budd's eyebrows vibrated and his face grew red.

'Are you lot telling me what to do?' he roared.

'Yes.'

'A ship has to give notice of her arrival and departure,' Budd yelled. 'Nationality, tonnage, cargo, where she's been, where she's going, when she leaves and how long she plans to stay. I'm the master of this ship and I don't ask the piss-arsed members of the crew what I should do.'

He blustered mightily, but was as frightened as they were. Nobody bothered with the drinking dens and bars any more. The ship was ugly and uncomfortable but they had taken on their water at Gibraltar and, by rationing it, they seemed to be safe so long as they didn't go ashore. Only the mate seemed to crave the pleasures of the land.

Captain Budd remained all a-twitter and continued to send Edward to chivvy the agent to hurry the unloading. He was itching to leave, but he couldn't ignore the owners' instructions. And his cargo was still only half-unloaded.

That night, the mate, who had gone ashore as usual, failed to return to the ship. Edward was sent to find out what had happened. He managed to track him down to a drinking den where he had last been seen, but the place was closed and there was a board nailed across the doorway with a skull and crossbones insignia scrawled on it. Underneath it was scrawled, '*Fermé. Choléra.*'

'Oh, Christ,' Captain Budd said when Edward delivered his report.

The cholera cases were being taken to an isolation hospital which had been set up outside the city, but the place was in total confusion. There had been no time to take down the names of individual victims but Edward was offered the chance to check the wards to see if he could identify the missing man. He took one look and backed away. They were crowded with twisting, wretched figures. Their faces were hollow, their eyes deep-sunk, their skins yellow, their clawing hands appealing for help. There were men and women crammed together, of all colours and races, but mostly Egyptians from the poorer quarters of the city. There was no sign of the mate.

The nurse, a hollow-eyed Scottish woman, who looked ready to drop with exhaustion, answered Edward's questions. She seemed to remember a European who had been brought in.

'He was a sailor, I think,' she said.

'Where is he now?'

'I think he died.'

'Damn. So what happened to him?'

'They're taken out and buried immediately.'

'Have you any proof?'

'They'll have kept his belongings. Most people here come from the poorer quarter and don't have anything at all so it shouldn't be hard to identify them. They'll be burned.'

The mate's wallet, watch and chain lay in a neat heap on a large table. There were other neat piles, obviously the possessions of Europeans who had died and been hurriedly buried. Edward was careful to touch nothing. When he went outside again, he found the man who'd driven the carriage had vanished.

'He's inside,' he was told when he enquired. 'He collapsed.'

When he reported the facts to Captain Budd, the captain licked his lips nervously. 'I don't like this,' he said. 'He ought to have been brought aboard. Sick or distressed British seamen are supposed to be conveyed to their home port.'

'The crew would have walked off immediately,' Edward pointed out bluntly, 'and the ship would have been quarantined.'

'He was in here last night,' said Budd. 'He had a drink with me.'

'Perhaps you've got it now, Captain,' Edward said cheerfully.

Budd gave him a startled look and vanished to his cabin. His steward reported sounds of heavy gargling, and, during the afternoon, orders were issued to single up the mooring ropes ready for departure.

About noon the next day, when they were all congratulating themselves on their escape, a cloud as big as a pocket handkerchief arose out of a clear horizon. The second mate, a thin little man who suffered from the captain's bullying, decided it meant rain and sent Edward for sou'wester and oilskins. By the time Edward returned, the cloud had spread across the entire sky. Lightning flashed through and there were growlings of thunder.

41

As the vanguard of the clouds passed over the ship, rain began to fall, growing heavier until the sea seemed to protest at its weight. From the weather-side of the ship came the threatening roar of a huge wind sweeping across the sea, awe-inspiring and terrible in its power.

The second mate immediately ordered the royals taken in. But as he did so, Captain Budd appeared on deck and insisted they stay where they were. As the squall struck, with the howl of a banshee, the *George V. Cotterill* leaned over, water leaping up through the scupper holes in solid jets. Another squall followed and the ship lurched further until the rail dipped beneath the waves, and the captain finally ordered the royals to be lowered.

But because of the angle of the yards, it was impossible to bring them down, and another gust drove the lee rail out of sight, sloshing water along the deck.

'Jesus God!' Washed out of his galley, the cook was clinging to a life line. 'She's on her beam ends!'

In a panic, the captain gave the order to let go the royal halliards, and started to scream a succession of wild orders.

'She'll go like the *Eurydice*.' The second mate was muttered in his fury by the wheel.

'What's the *Eurydice*?' Edward asked nervously.

'Naval training frigate. Nine hundred tons. Caught by a sudden blow off the Isle of Wight in 'Seventy-eight. One minute it was bright sunshine and calm seas, and she was under plain sail. Next minute she was upside down. Three hundred and fifty men lost.'

The *George V. Cotterill* heeled over. She had been caught with every scrap of sail on her and as she leaned it was difficult to keep a footing on the deck.

The second mate was struggling to help the helmsman put the wheel over so the ship would pay off, and there were moments when Edward was sure he was as good as dead. Then the gaff topsail blew away. There was a crack that lifted every head, the outer edge of the mainsail which was trailing in the sea lifted clear, and gradually the ship came upright.

The rain drove horizontally into the canvas. Sails and gear were clattering and banging in the wind as the crew began to haul away the mainsail. The hands went aloft, Edward with his heart in his mouth as usual. By the time they returned to the deck, darkness was sliding across the sea, and it was blowing a full gale. Edward's muscles seemed to be caught by iron bands, his eyelids drooped with weariness and he was half-dead for want of sleep.

But the wind began to abate and, with the mainsail back in place, the *George V. Cotterill* stood to west and north in a backing wind.

The following evening, a group of faint lights was seen.

'Tip of Sicily,' said the second mate.

There was no sign of Captain Budd, and the steward said he was in a drunken stupor. The second mate was haggard with fatigue. As they edged closer inshore, Budd appeared and hovered near the wheel. The word went round that he was aiming to pass round the tip of Sicily and put into Naples, and everyone began to look forward to a disease-free port where they could enjoy themselves.

'We'll be there for Christmas,' the second mate said.

The wink of a lighthouse appeared through the darkness.

'Cape Spartivento,' the fifteen-year-old apprentice suggested.

Budd decided to go on thrusting before the wind which was still blowing strongly. The plan was to make for Reggio di Calabria, to ride out the storm in the entrance to the Straits of Messina.

'That's a terrible place,' the second mate observed. 'The wind and current come through there like the hounds of hell.' He was extremely nervous. He felt they were too close to land and suspected they were heading for trouble.

'We should stand off till daylight,' he said.

'We're getting pretty close,' the apprentice squeaked.

Almost as he spoke, through the mist of spray, they caught the flash of a green light and saw the bulk of a steamer crossing their path.

'Christ!' Budd yelled. 'Hard over!'

Instinctively, the helmsman, helped by the captain, heaved on the wheel and the *George V. Cotterill* swung to port. The steamer loomed to starboard, lights blazing.

'For God's sake,' the mate yelled. 'We'll be ashore.'

'We're all right,' Budd yelled back. 'There's the light-house.'

'That's not a light,' Edward screamed. 'It's a fire ashore.'

Everybody was on deck, both watches waiting tensely for the next order, knowing that some of the canvas should come off the ship, and convinced something horrifying was about to happen. The steamer had vanished into the murk.

'That *is* a fire,' Edward insisted. 'You can see the sparks.'

The mate had sent a hand forward with a leadline and he was singing out the depths. 'By the deep – ' he yelled. Then he stopped. 'Bloody hell!' he screeched, 'we're aground.'

Even as the captain turned to bawl fresh orders, Edward was thrown forward as the ship struck. The howling surf swung her up and she drove forward then dropped heavily. The topmasts bent and came down. Sails flapped and hammered, the chains clattering against the yards. Then the yards themselves came down as the lifts and ties carried away, and the mizzen topmast fell in a blanketing cloud of canvas. The ship stopped dead, the helmsman groaning on the deck by the wheel with broken ribs.

Budd seemed petrified, and it was the second mate who took control.

'Rockets,' he ordered. 'Carpenter, see how much water we're making.'

The rockets flew up with a shower of sparks as the hull continued to bump and crash on the rocks. Now they were closer, they could see land just ahead of them, even lights, beyond the foaming sea. A backing gust of wind drove the ship back into deeper water. On deck it was pandemonium, with flying chains and wires twisting and whipping like living things.

'We're taking water fast,' the carpenter announced.

As he turned away a heavy spar, swinging down from aloft, swept him into the scuppers.

'Get him below,' the mate shouted. 'I'll attend to him later. The rest of you stand by the boats.'

With the apprentice, Edward struggled down to the officers' saloon. It was canted at an odd angle and the crockery that had been on the table had all slid to the deck, while the curtains with which the steward had attempted to decorate the place hung at an angle from the porthole. As they placed the injured man on the leather bench, he promptly rolled off and they had to snatch up clothing from the hooks on the bulkhead and wedge him in.

When they reached the deck again, the lurching seemed to have stopped.

'I think she's floating,' the apprentice piped. 'She seems steadier.'

'She's floating,' the mate agreed. 'But she's full of water.'

But the deck was tilted crazily, and the boats the mate had ordered out could not be swung because the topmast had fallen across them, shattering one and pinning the other to the skids. Finding a new, vile oath for every wire and spar that got in their way, the men worked furiously to clear them. The surf roared among them as they struggled. All the *George V. Cotterill*'s upper masts had gone, leaving only the thick stumps of the lower masts, the yards-a-cockbill at crazy angles. The masts and spars which had fallen into the sea swung back and forth like battering rams to grind against the hull.

Every man in the ship was on the poop now, struggling to release the shackles that held the hammering spars, fighting off the hampering folds of canvas that flapped and beat at them in the wind. It was impossible to release the shackles.

'You two.' The mate pointed at Edward and the apprentice. 'Go forrard. Find lamps, chisels and hammers.'

Fighting his way through the spider's web of ropes and wires, Edward could see the sea sweeping unhindered across the deck. The black shape of the forecastle head appeared in front of them, dark against the sky. Beyond it lay the land, near enough, it seemed, to leap to safety. Fallen gear impeded their path and, as they struggled, the ship shook like a rat held by a terrier.

The apprentice was swearing in a cracked and terrified voice inside the locker, trying to find what he was seeking in the pitch blackness. Waiting outside, Edward was in a nightmare of fear, expecting the ship to vanish beneath his feet at any moment.

'For Christ's sake!' He yelled, 'come out of there.'

There was a crash from inside the locker and a squeal of fury, and the apprentice burst out, holding his head. Blood was pouring through his fingers and he seemed dazed. The ship lurched and he fell backwards into the darkness. Edward plunged after him, pawing like a blind man until he found him. As he dragged the apprentice clear, a spar smashed down on the locker, reducing it to splinters.

Supporting the boy with one arm, Edward struggled aft, forgetting the lamps and tools they had been sent for.

As he negotiated the tangle of spars, wires and chains amidships, he was startled to see the white shapes of the boats ahead of him slowly sinking from sight. Deck planks splintered, iron plates bent and tore like paper. Rivets popped, and Edward saw the great fore and aft sail come roaring down with a shriek of blocks and the twanging of wires to cover the huddle of men struggling on the poop. Then the stumps of the main and mizzen masts canted slowly to one side, and fell backwards, and he realised the ship had broken her back. The poop was disappearing before his eyes.

Dumping the unconscious apprentice, Edward ran aft to find that between him and the rest of the ship a vast chasm of wild water had opened. It dawned on him that the stern half of the *George V. Cotterill* had fallen away, taking with it every other member of the crew. All of them, the second mate, the captain, the cook, had been fighting to clear the rigging on the poop when the huge sail had come down, swamping them with its folds, and now they had all been swept into the darkness, every one of them, together with the unconscious carpenter stretched out on the bench in the saloon.

Already he could hear shouts and splashing somewhere below him. Grabbing one of the halliards, he tossed it down into the darkness. For a while he could feel it moving in the swirl of water, then he felt a tug that almost jerked him into the sea. Realising a man was on the end of it, he tried to haul it in but it was too heavy and his hands were frozen. Desperately he looked round for help but the apprentice was still in a huddled heap on the deck among the wreckage.

A hoarse voice croaked up from the darkness. 'Take a turn round something, you bloody fool. I'll climb.'

Edward swung the bight of the rope round a bitt and held on. A minute or two later, the bosun's head appeared, his hair in his eyes, blood pouring down his face so that he looked like some sort of spectral being rising out of the sea.

'Well done, lad,' he said. 'Let's send it down again.'

But even as they stood staring down into the maelstrom, the shouting died away beneath the crashing of the sea.

6

The wind dropped as suddenly as it had risen. Daylight revealed the three survivors aboard the wallowing forepart of the ship still clinging, bewildered, dazed and exhausted, to the wreckage. The bows were swinging in the waves but the after half of the ship had disappeared, leaving only a tangle of splintered planks, hatch covers and twisted deck houses, all held together by a network of rigging. A corpse was floating face-down in the shallows but it was impossible to tell who it was. The rest of the crew were somewhere beneath the great carapace of torn canvas that shrouded the tangle.

Soon after daylight, with the sea abating all the time, a steam tug appeared alongside. On its side it said *Compagnia di Orlando, S.A.*, and the registration on its stern showed it came from Messina in Sicily. The sun had come out unexpectedly, and in the distance it was possible to see houses and fields.

On the stern deck of the tug was a stout, bearded man in a formal suit, hat and coat. A rope was thrown and the survivors scrambled down the heaving deck.

'*Subito. Spicciatevi. Fate presto.*'

The harsh voice of the man at the wheel nagged at Edward but, having survived the night, he had no intention of falling in the sea through too much haste.

'*Chi va piano,*' he snapped back, '*va sano e va lontano.*'

As he reached the deck of the tug, the man with the hat helped him to his feet.

'You speak good Italian,' he said.

'My mother was Italian. She came from Livorno. You may know her family name. It was Uschetti.'

There was no response. The tug went astern, swung about and eventually arrived at what looked like a ferry harbour. Dumped ashore, the survivors were left standing, dazed and bewildered, in the lee of a corrugated iron shed on which a loose sheet swung and rattled in the dying wind. After about five minutes, a trap appeared. Behind it was a horse-drawn cab and a motor car, clanking and steaming. Blankets, food and bottles of wine and brandy were brought and pressed on the wretched survivors. Within an hour, exhausted and still hungry, Edward was half drunk.

Eventually, he and the others were pushed into the trap, which cantered off inland, bouncing and bumping over a rough unmetalled road to what appeared to be a hospital. There they were undressed and pushed into bed. For the first time in months, Edward was sensuously aware of clean sheets and a soft pillow. He fell asleep in minutes.

When he awoke Edward found himself staring into the face of a nun. She was young and pale and unbelievably beautiful.

'*Dove?*' he said. '*Dov' e qui?* Where am I?'

'Messina,' she said. '*Ospidale della Santa Maria Ringraziamento.*'

'*Quanto sopravvivente?* How many survivors?'

She held up three fingers.

Feeling himself gingerly, Edward realised that apart from a mass of cuts and bruises he was unharmed and no one objected to his getting out of bed to see the other survivors. The apprentice's head was covered with bandages.

'You saved my life,' he said.

Edward smiled.

The bosun had a wound three inches long over his right eye and a ferocious headache. 'That stupid old bugger, Budd,' he snarled. 'Sicily's surrounded by beaches and the old fart chose about the only bit of rock in the whole place to put us on.' He was already making plans to look up a woman in Reggio di Calabria he'd met on an earlier trip.

'Widow,' he said. 'Nice and plump. All I got to do is take the ferry . . . That bloody Budd nearly did for us, lad.'

'Do you think there will be an enquiry?'

The bosun grimaced. 'Shouldn't think so. She was an old ship and nobody's bothered about sailing ships these days. It's 1908, son, nearly 1909. All they think about these days is reciprocating engines and steam-driven tubs. Just thank your lucky stars you're alive and go and enjoy yourself at the expense of the government for a bit.'

It had only just begun to dawn on Edward what had happened. Hitherto his only achievements had consisted of playing cricket for the school, winning one or two minor prizes and beating the living daylights out of Cousin Maurice. Since then he had been in half a dozen fights, had jumped ship, travelled to Johannesburg, fled from the police, just avoided a cholera epidemic which had killed hundreds, survived a shipwreck and, he supposed, been responsible for saving the lives of two people.

He was looking forward to going home and telling people like Sam and Georgina about it. Even Aunt Edith and – he paused – probably his Uncle Egg. Somehow, he felt that, while Maurice wouldn't be very impressed, his uncle might now be able to forgive him for what he'd done.

A young man from the British Consul's office turned up. He had no chin, wet lips and a high collar that sawed at his ears. He wore a white linen suit, yellow patent leather button boots and a boater. He spoke excruciating Italian and was there, he said, to assist the nuns and a man from the police to take down the names of any relatives and dependants of the survivors.

'I can't help, I'm afraid,' Edward said. 'I know nothing but their names – you'll have to ask them yourself.'

'*E Lei?*' The policeman pointed at him and licked his pencil ready to write.

'No father,' explained Edward. 'An uncle.'

'The name, Signore?'

'Marmaduke Egbert Bourdillon.'

'Marmo Duca Eghbertabo Dillon.' The Italian's spelling was interesting. '*Un nobiluòmo?*'

'He thinks your uncle's a nobleman. He isn't, I suppose?'

'No. Just an ordinary chap.'

They managed to get the address down, then the doctor arrived to say that, as Edward was uninjured and not suffering from shock, he would be allowed to leave the hospital.

'Where do I go?'

'Just hang on a jiffy,' said the man from the Consulate. 'I'll go and make a few telephone calls. It won't be much, of course. Just a room or a bed in a dormitory. That sort of thing.'

It was at least an hour before he returned. 'Found you a place,' he said. 'Rather good, actually. Offered to take you in for Christmas and the New Year. Can't think why. But there we are. Never look a gift horse, eh what?'

'Never.'

'The di Orlandos are an extremely wealthy family. Two young children.' The young man leaned forward and Edward noticed how the high collar bit into the soft neck. 'I say, old chap,' he said, 'you won't let us down, will you?'

'What the hell do you mean?'

'Everybody knows what sailors are. They're an important family, as I say. It seems you speak Italian. Is that true. *Parlo Italiano?*'

'A damn sight better than you do,' said Edward.

The di Orlando family ran a large old-fashioned export-import and chandlers' business and were the owners among other things of the tug that had taken the survivors off what was left of the *George V. Cotterill*. A motor car laboured from the hospital up a winding white road to a village called Friddi beyond which was the di Orlandos' home. This was reached through a pair of huge cast-iron gates set in a high wall. The south end of the house incorporated the ancient walls of a former palazzo, which still retained the original marble pillars and floors. A wide entrance was adorned with statues, and the windows were wide open to a soft breeze that set the leaves of wisteria and roses trembling. The land was enclosed by Roman pines and a long line of cypresses that marched up the hillside like a regiment of soldiers.

Di Orlando was there with his wife to meet Edward as he stepped from the car. It was the same man who had spoken to him on the tug. 'Welcome,' he said in English. 'I speak a little of your language but I feel more comfortable with my own.'

Edward smiled, as they all shook hands. 'I speak them both, sir.'

51

He was given a pleasant bedroom overlooking the slope of the hill and provided with a nightshirt and clothes to wear. 'My son's,' Di Orlando explained.

The di Orlando children were hardly the youngsters Edward had expected. Salvatore, the son, was a strapping eighteen-year-old, articled to a solicitor in Messina. His passion was girls, and, when he wasn't in the office, he was to be found hanging round the village pump in Friddi eyeing the local talent. He wasn't the slightest bit impressed that his family was entertaining the survivor of a shipwreck. He began to remind Edward of his cousin, Maurice.

His sister, Rafaela, was a lance-straight scornful beauty, tall for an Italian with a stateliness beyond her years. She was a little older than Edward, slender and exquisitely formed, and her thick raven hair was plaited and bound over the top of her head in Sicilian style. Beneath it great, dark eyes smouldered.

'Your mother,' di Orlando said after a delicious supper of roast chicken. 'Her name was Uschetti and she came from Livorno. Would she be related to the Uschetti family who build boats?'

'She was their daughter.'

Di Orlando frowned. 'She was a headstrong woman, as I recall. Runaway marriages are not how things are done in Italy. It was a great disappointment to the family.'

'It wasn't for my mother,' Edward said. 'She and my father were very happy.'

'Is your family important?'

'Not particularly. But it's an old family and well known.' Edward was beginning to resent the line of questioning.

'I am surprised you are not an officer,' said di Orlando. 'In Italy the sons of good families are always officers.'

Edward explained how he had sunk the *Fairy* and run away to sea. 'I thought it safer to stay away for a while.'

'I hope the sparks will have stopped flying.'

The family seemed in no hurry to send him on his way, and did everything in their power to make him feel at home. Signora di Orlando even took him with her daughter in the carriage on a picnic near Taormina, where he dutifully admired the remains of the Roman theatre.

They drove along the lower slopes of the hills. They were fringed with a scrappy covering of cactus – chiefly prickly pear and sisal, whose tapering leaves ended in a long black spike as hard as ebony and as sharp as a needle. The carts that rattled round the island, painted with the pictures of saints in gaudy colours, stirred up a white dust that left all the foliage by the roadside looking grey and dead. The land was dry as a desert with occasional patches of cultivation, where the earth had been ploughed and dug by wooden implements whose design dated back to Christ. Edward had heard snatches of bird song but had barely laid eyes on a bird. But now and again he spotted a herd of cattle or a few goats and sheep.

'Our land,' Signora di Orlando explained, as they passed through a grove of olive trees, 'stretches as far as you can see. Most of the island is owned by people who live in Rome and Naples. People prefer to work for us.'

Rafaela, the daughter, lifted her head proudly. 'Because we take care of them,' she said. 'And unlike some on the island, they eat meat regularly. We provide schools and a doctor for their illnesses. We are successful because we've never been absentee landlords. We've never been troubled by the Fasci.'

'The Fasci?'

'A secret society the peasants formed to protect them from oppression. In Italy the North gets everything and Sicily nothing. The di Orlandos have always stood up for the South and the people trust us.'

The di Orlando business consisted of warehouses near the ferry jetty, and a gloomy but impressive office in the city near the Church of Santa Maria Alemanna, where Edward was introduced to the staff. The manager, Dummo, was a short, pompous man with pince-nez, and his deputy a long thin man called Jenschi. They reminded Edward of a circus act.

'And this is Evrone, the chief clerk,' Dummo said casually. 'And his deputy, Zoparella.'

The clerks bowed. Since Edward was di Orlando's guest no one knew how to address him. Everybody in Italy had a title – Ingeniere, Professore, Dottore. In the end, since he had been a sailor, they settled for Capitano.

But little time was wasted on the clerks, and, as they sipped cold wine in di Orlando's office, they were joined by a couple of business associates. Clearly di Orlando considered Edward someone of importance.

But Salvatore continued to ignore his existence. Rafaela was friendly but aloof. One evening, taking a stroll after supper, Edward met her on one of the garden paths. Someone was strumming a mandolin on the slopes below the terrace and Edward suggested they should dance to the music.

'Certainly not,' she said, backing away. 'That would not be correct.'

Sicilian life seemed to be centred round traditional feast and saints' days. Then, the marketplace filled with weightlifters, sword-swallowers, quack-medicine sellers, conjurors and jugglers. As Christmas approached, Edward lent a helping hand in the house with the decorations. And, for only the second time since he arrived at the di Orlandos', he found himself alone with Rafaela. Their hands touched for a moment, as she shifted the position of a porcelain Madonna Edward had just placed above the fireplace in the dining room.

For a moment, they both stood there in silence, Rafaela gazing fixedly at the floor. Then she raised her deep, dark eyes to his. 'You must know,' she said, 'that I am to be married.'

It appeared the groom-to-be was the son of Salvatore's boss, Bruno di Porto, a man of thirty-nine. He did the legal work in Messina for his father's business which was similar to the Di Orlandos'.

'Do you *want* to marry him?' said Edward after a while.

'No,' she said, and her eyes flashed.

'Then why must you?'

'Because that is how marriages are made in Sicily. The businesses will merge and become powerful. The dowry is agreed. That seals the marriage and helps the husband set up home.'

'But this Bruno di Porto – he's nineteen years older than you are.'

She shrugged. 'He is also a chaser of loose women. But he is a sound businessman, I believe.'

'It's ridiculous,' said Edward. 'Why do you have to marry an old man you don't love? My mother didn't.' But then the rest of the family arrived, and the conversation was over.

Christmas came and there was an exchange of small presents. Edward was embarrassed to receive a suit from the di Orlandos and a gold watch from Rafaela. There was nothing from Salvatore. Friends appeared for dinner and listened open-mouthed to Edward's story of the shipwreck. He improved it with every telling.

On Christmas Day they went to mass in an ornately decorated church in Messina, driven there in the di Orlandos' carriage. Salvatore insisted that he preferred the church in Friddi and, being Salvatore, he got away with it.

Silent in the lofty church, his nostrils stung by incense, and his ears tingling from the glorious choir and the high chant of the priests, Edward was tautly aware of the presence alongside him of Rafaela. She looked overwhelmingly beautiful, and he found himself wondering what it would be like to hold her and kiss her and how she would respond.

When it was time to take the bread and wine, Edward was about to follow the family when she laid a hand on his.

'You are a Catholic?'

'No.'

'Then you are not allowed to take the sacrament.'

But she gave him a little smile and her fingers remained on his hand, a little longer than they needed to.

It was the first time she had shown any warmth towards him. As they sat on the verandah in the evening, under the watchful eye of Signora di Orlando, he sat quietly, enjoying the slender column of her neck, the patrician nose, the fine eyes, the luxuriant and glistening hair. Salvatore, as usual, had vanished and was doubtless already involved in some amorous escapade with one of the village girls. Later, Rafaela played the phonograph, but she seemed impatient with Gigli and Galli-Curci, and they played a decorous game of chess instead. Occasionally, their hands met, often enough for Edward to suspect it was deliberate, and several times he caught her looking at him. When their eyes met, Rafaela's dropped at once.

No-one was hurrying to send him back to England and the di Orlandos seemed to be treating his stay with them as an extended holiday. With di Orlando and his son occupied with their own affairs during the day, Edward and Rafaela had often gone into Friddi, occasionally doing a little shopping.

'We must watch out for vipers,' she warned, as they took a short-cut home through the fields.

When he took her hand to help her over a wall, she didn't try to reclaim it when they reached the other side. But when they slipped descending a grassy bank and rolled together in a giggling heap to the bottom, she sat up, her face close to his and her laughter died abruptly. She pushed him away, her face suffused with blushes as she brushed the grass from her skirt.

One day during the week after Christmas Edward asked, 'Could I take you into town this evening?'

'Not alone.' There was a long silence. 'But Zia Monica would be allowed to act as chaperone.' Rafaela seemed to read Edward's thoughts. 'She is not difficult to lose,' she smiled. 'For a short time only, of course. For half an hour or so, we can slip away.'

'Have you done this before?' Edward looked at her quizzically.

She blushed. 'Only with my girl friends,' she said. 'Never with a man. First, of course, you will have to ask my father. I will tell him I wish to buy New Year presents. Then you must ask him if you may accompany me. He will think hard about it but he will say yes, but that Zia Monica must come along.'

It seemed as grave an undertaking as asking for Rafaela's hand in marriage, and di Orlando considered it with the greatest seriousness. Eventually, he agreed.

'I will inform Zia Monica,' he said. 'Rafaela wishes to buy presents and she will be glad of your help with the parcels. I will arrange for you to use the carriage.'

Zia Monica was a desiccated woman in black. As Rafaela had said, she was not intrusive and sat opposite them in the carriage, staring straight ahead while they talked. She carried a prayer book and wore a shawl round her shoulders and a black bonnet on her head.

As they wandered round the shops, the young bloods leaning on the walls and corners pretended to faint as Rafaela passed. When she took no notice they whistled and sighed and pretended to shoot themselves.

Later, Edward and Rafaela sat talking in a street café over coffee. Zia Monica still didn't interfere and studied her prayer book. It was the oddest courtship. Eventually, strolling back through the town, they managed to give her the slip while she was looking in a shop window. There was a side street with a gate and a shady garden with trees, and lights showing dimly through the branches. Edward found himself pulled into the darkness. Immediately, two soft arms went round his neck and he felt Rafaela's mouth on his. It was a tremulous kiss, so much so that he wondered if Sicilian concepts of honour had made it her first attempt. But as he kissed her back she clung more tightly and the kiss became fiercer.

'It is terrible,' she said. 'We have only a few minutes and next year I have to marry Bruno di Porto.'

'For God's sake Rafaela, you don't have to. Marry me.'

'Don't be silly,' she replied. 'You have no money and I don't wish to live like a pauper. Nor do I wish to have my family constantly bemoaning my treachery as the Uschettis do about your mother.' She was suddenly a different person, vibrant, forthright and full of initiative. He was tremendously aware of her near him, of her perfume, her beauty and sexuality.

'Married to this Bruno fellow,' he said, 'you'll be stifled.'

'Yes,' she said calmly. 'Bruno is old and I shall always be alone with dozens of children. I don't want that kind of life.'

'What will you do?'

'Some women take lovers.' She gave a sudden grin. 'The Borgias used poison. Sicilians prefer bombs. Perhaps I'll try something like that.'

'Perhaps that's why my mother ran away with my father.'

'I expect so. I want to be treated as a woman, not a clause in a marriage settlement.'

'Have you ever . . . kissed Bruno di Porto?'

She gave an exaggerated shudder. 'Never,' she said, then smiled. 'If we were older, I would say come along to my room tonight when everybody's asleep.'

'You can't mean that.'

'No, I don't. Oh Edward. I want to do so much. I want adventure. I want to run a business. I want to make money. If I could run my father's business, I would modernise it, revolutionise it. There is so much opportunity. Everything's so backward here.'

This was not quite the adventure that Edward had in mind, but he could see she was quite serious.

'Do you know anything about it?'

'Of course. I used to go to my father's office as a little girl and sit at a desk he provided for me. I still do. He thinks I am just playing. I was when I was a child, but I learned about things. I watched him work with the accountants. Tax evasion is a national sport in Sicily, you know . . . He thought my interest was just the whim of a silly girl because girls don't go into business, but by that time it was more than just a game to me.'

'What about Salvatore, when he takes over?'

'He will ruin everything. I would do things much better than he ever will.'

'Wouldn't he let you help?'

'I've told you. Girls don't do that sort of thing. In any case, Bruno di Porto wouldn't allow it. Have you an arranged marriage waiting for you?'

'*I'll* decide whom I'm going to marry.'

She was silent for a moment. 'Salvatore will waste his money, his chances, everything. If I had my way, I would immediately open a depot on the other side of the strait in Reggio di Calabria and have imports for the mainland landed there, not here to be transported by ferry across the water. I'd have an office in Rome and use Civitavecchia and look into the possibilities of Brindisi, Venice and Genoa. Orlandos could be as big and important as anyone

58

in Italy. And quickly, too. Italy has been a united country only for fifty years and it is growing all the time. Opportunity is everywhere.'

Talking business seemed a strange way to conduct a lovers' meeting but they clung to each other a few minutes longer. The heat was intense and for a while Edward thought it was the heat of lust. Then he noticed dogs were barking all over the city, asses were braying, and a cock crew frantically despite the hour. The night had become close and very oppressive.

They found Zia Monica in a panic, looking for them, but Rafaela apologised humbly enough to calm the old aunt's fears. As she turned to lead the way back to the carriage, she threw Edward a glance that almost made his knees give way.

'Storm coming,' di Orlando said, when they got home.

It was impossible to sleep. Edward lay on the bed, wondering if Rafaela were expecting him to make a foray down the corridor to her room. Sweat trickled down his forehead, and his throat was dry. He wanted her desperately. But did she really want him? He took a deep breath and closed his eyes.

7

It was just becoming light when Edward awoke. He had no idea what time it was, only that Salvatore had returned from his carousing in the village. He had heard him shout goodbye to his friends and the slam of the door. Then the house was silent again.

Edward's thoughts returned to Rafaela. He knew her room lay at the end of a corridor on the upper floor of the house, and that, since the floors were made of marble against the summer heat, there would be no creaking boards to negotiate. Her mother and father slept at the opposite end of the house, while Salvatore had a room on the lower floor because he came in late so often. There seemed to be no possible snags, but Edward continued to resist the temptation.

In the distance there was a rumbling. At first Edward thought it must be thunder, but every dog in Friddi immediately started barking and the rumble grew louder until it became a roar. The bed lurched violently and he was flung to the floor. For a moment, there was dead silence as he lay, clutching the sheet, then there was another screeching rumble and a crash as the whole house started to shake. The windows fell in, showering him with glass and he heard screams from outside and someone yelling in a hoarse voice.

'*Terremoto!*'

It was a word with which he was unfamiliar but it wasn't hard to translate. Part of the wall crumbled and the ceiling caved in.

Covered in plaster, but miraculously unhurt, Edward decided the safest thing was to get outside. But the floor was heaving like a rough sea and he was flung down and half-stunned as a beam from the ceiling struck him a glancing blow. The noise and the shuddering seemed to

60

go on for hours but in fact the tremor could have lasted only a matter of seconds. The room was hazy with dust, but he could make out a huge split across the centre of the floor, one side of which was cocked up at an angle of 30 degrees. A colossal chunk of stonework had smashed his bed to smithereens.

Scrambling among the debris, he managed to find his clothes and dragged them on. Part of the corridor had collapsed, but Edward jumped the gap. Suddenly there was another shuddering rumble and the floor shook. Rafaela's door burst open of its own accord as he arrived. She was sitting on the floor among the tangled bedding, half-naked.

'Edward,' she screamed. '*Madonna Santissima*, are you all right?'

'For God's sake,' he yelled, 'put something on. They'll be coming any minute to see if you're all right. They'll think I've been here with you all night.'

But Edward could not help feeling a twinge of regret, as her breasts were covered by a silk nightgown.

His arm round her waist, they slipped from the room just as the ceiling crashed down. The balustrade had fallen away and lay in a heap in the hall, covered with plaster that had fallen from the ceiling. Keeping to the wall, they stumbled down the lopsided staircase. The statues that had stood in the hall were all on their sides, broken, and the pictures hung askew on the walls. Dust was everywhere.

Once outside, Rafaela flung herself at the first person she saw. 'Edward rescued me,' she cried, shaking the flakes of plaster from her hair. 'But for the grace of God and His Blessed Mother I should be dead.'

Dishevelled and terrified as Zia Monica was, she glared at Edward. Then Signora di Orlando appeared. Her eyes were wild and her face and her nightclothes were covered with blood.

'*Mio marito*,' she was wailing. '*Mio figlio!*'

The side of the house where the older di Orlandos and Salvatore slept had collapsed, crushing the kitchen area and the servants' quarters. A miasma of dust drifted over the fallen blocks of masonry and the rubble that surrounded them. There was no sign or sound of life. The outhouses had gone, trees were uprooted, the wall surrounding the garden had collapsed, bringing down the great cast-iron gates, and a rift in the earth ran straight across the lawn.

Finding a gap between two great blocks of masonry, Edward crept between them. He recognised a tapestry that normally hung in the salon, but alongside it was a bed and dust-covered clothes. Then he saw di Orlando lying on his back among the rubble. There was blood across his face and down the front of his nightshirt. Heaving away the wreckage, Edward began to drag the body to the gap where he had come in. It was hard work, but then Rafaela was beside him, taking hold of her father's arm.

'Is he dead?' she cried, tears falling in rivulets down her dust-covered cheeks.

The earth seemed to groan beneath them. Several blocks of stone fell and a great slab of marble that was leaning crazily slammed down flat. For a moment, they clung to each other in terror, but the rumbling subsided, and the cascade of plaster dust changed to a trickle, and finally stopped.

'He's still breathing,' said Edward, when they succeeded in dragging di Orlando outside. His wife gave an agonised scream, and started tearing at her hair, beating her forehead and wailing prayers, transformed abruptly from a modern, civilised woman of wealth, poise and position to a Sicilian peasant.

'*Siccome Voi, o Gran Dio, siete giusto e santo in tutto le opera Vostre –*'

'I'd better try to find Salvatore,' Edward said.

Pushing through the gap again, he began to explore the wreckage. There was no movement, no sign of life. He found a foot but it was a woman's. He managed to shift the debris that covered her. It was Elsa, one of the maids. Her neck was broken. Then he found a hand which he identified as Salvatore's from his signet ring. But, try as he could, Edward was unable to pull the body out. A great oak beam had crushed Salvatore's back. There was nothing he could do.

The carriage horses had escaped from the stables and disappeared. Only one, the oldest, stood calmly cropping grass, blood drying on its neck from a slight cut below one ear.

'I'll go for help,' Edward said, having found reins and a saddle. Rafaela waved him goodbye, then went back to her father.

The scene in the local village was one of total devastation. Houses had been flattened as though by a giant's foot. Edward headed for the town. But the town, if anything, was worse.

The air was full of wails and shrieks. A shattered gas main blazed. The doors of the prison had been thrown open by the tremors and some of Italy's most notorious criminals were at large among the ruins. Soldiers were beginning to arrive, however, and some effort was being made to round them up, and to rescue trapped people. A few doctors had also appeared and were trying to help survivors dragged from the ruins.

Without warning, the earth trembled, and Edward's horse reared up. Dozens of half-naked people rushed into the streets, screaming with terror. It was a vision of hell. Over their cries, Edward could hear the splintering roar of buildings collapsing and for safety he dismounted in the centre of a square, holding his horse's head and stroking its muzzle. A house behind him subsided gently into a heap of rubble, as though it had suddenly melted.

Spitting the dust from his mouth, Edward realised his quest was hopeless. Then the rain started, turning dust into mud, coming down in long shining stair rods that bounced from the flooded streets. In places it was impossible to tell where the streets had been. The churchyard of San Fiorenzo was strewn with coffins, split wide open. Rotting corpses lay sprawled in front of the church. A terrified congregation had been crushed while they prayed. A few men tore with bleeding hands at the stones in search of relatives. Women sat in the ruins, frozen-faced, shivering in the ice-cold wind that blew from the mountains to the north, while a priest moved among them, dispensing what little comfort he could. There was no help to be had.

As Edward headed out of town, fishing boats were taking people to ships which were standing out to sea.

The foreshore was littered with broken bodies and the carcasses of dead animals.

When he reached the Casa Orlando, Edward was met by Rafaela, dry-eyed and blank-faced. 'My father is dead,' she said. 'And so is Salvatore. The doctor came from Friddi and said he couldn't possibly be alive. One of the maids is also trapped but I have sent for spades to dig her out. There is nothing left. I've sent my mother to Agrigento to stay with her sister.'

They worked until dark, rescuing what was possible, then as it grew dusk, Zia Monica and the maids were sent to their families in the village and Edward and Rafaela dragged a mattress into the stable, which seemed the only place left standing, and lay down together, fully dressed, under the same blanket. There was no question of a chaperone and she clung to him in the darkness.

The next morning, the bodies of di Orlando and his son were buried in the garden. It was impossible to wait until the overworked undertakers could be found to take them away.

The rescue work continued during the day. In Friddi most of the dead and injured had been brought out. There was little left of the Casa Orlando but Edward and Rafaela managed to rescue a few pictures and artifacts as well as a pair of shotguns belonging to Salvatore. They stored them in the stable out of the rain which continued to fall, icy-cold and drenching. The family lawyer, a man called Montesi, his clothes muddy, his hat dented, and his glasses bent, appeared. On hearing that Salvatore was dead, he informed Rafaela that if her mother died she was the sole inheritor of her father's wealth. She didn't seem very interested.

'Signor Montesi,' she said with an authority that had only increased since the disaster, 'we can deal with that later. What we're doing now is more important than money.' Dismissing the lawyer, she returned to directing the work of sorting through the rubble. When they reached the wine cellar, it was a pleasant surprise to find so many bottles unbroken. They had to push the corks in with their fingers, and, as the rain stopped and the sun came out, both Edward and Rafaela were mildly tipsy, and some of their helpers fell asleep where they had been working.

The following day, Edward went into town again on the old limping horse to arrange for help from men who had answered the call from the other side of Sicily. What had happened to the two other survivors of the *George V. Cotterill* he didn't know and couldn't find out because the hospital had collapsed. The sewers had been shattered and the rats had been driven out and were everywhere, huge, pink creatures as terrified as the human beings. There was a dread of cholera.

Only one chemist was open, an old-fashioned *farmaccia* with a row in the window of old faenza urns carrying Latin inscriptions. On a shelf, Edward observed glass jars containing a snake in alcohol and an embalmed rat that had been born with two heads. The old man behind the counter was dishing out doses mostly from bottles marked *Morte alla colera* and *Filtro d'amore*.

The whole city stank of carbolic and lime and, watched by nuns with saintly faces, long convoys of carts piled with corpses were making their way to a cemetery which had been dug outside the city, where soldiers and half-drunken *becca morti* were burying the dead in immense pits.

Edward found himself roped in with a party who were digging for a group of women trapped in a cellar. As they drew nearer, they could hear a woman moaning and a high-pitched squeaking. When they finally broke through and shone their carbide lamps in, the whole cellar was alive with rats. They were huge with long red tails and had been feeding on the corpses. There was only one woman left alive and she was out of her mind.

Sailors from four large Russian warships that had been passing the island from the Black Sea towards Gibraltar, put men ashore and they were working like madmen to release people who were still buried alive. The submarine telegraph to the mainland had been broken and it was difficult to summon help. The only news came via the fishermen, which indicated that Reggio di Calabria across the strait had also suffered considerable damage.

65

Houses on the coast had been washed away by the tidal waves that had built up as the seas receded then returned. But British, French and German ships were constantly arriving and Americans were organising assistance from Taormina. Many of the city officials were dead and there was no money, food, clothing, blankets or tents, and the cold winds had grown stronger. The soldiers were shooting the prisoners from the gaol when they found them looting, but bandits from the centre of the island were on the move, too, rounding up stray cattle and driving them into the hills. There was no question of stopping them.

The casualties in Messina alone numbered thousands and the danger of a cholera epidemic increased. But yachts loaded with provisions were arriving from the north and from France. Newspapermen were also gathering like flies.

The di Orlando warehouses were largely undamaged, because they had been protected from the tidal waves from the south by the Forte San Salvatore on its spit of land. The offices were also still standing, and several clerks wanted to know if they were still employed. Their spokesman was the chief clerk, Evrone, a small man with a curlicue moustache and glasses. He had learned that the banks were proposing to start business again, guaranteed by their parent offices in Rome, Milan and Turin. Money was available for help if only someone would grasp the need for it.

Returning to Friddi, Edward told Rafaela what he had found out and begged her to go to her father's office and encourage his staff to carry on.

'Now is your chance,' he urged.

Remembering what he'd heard about the escaped prisoners looting anything they could find, that evening Edward led the old horse into the stable. Dragging a broken bed in after it, he erected it alongside the stall, a brick under one damaged leg. Repairing the door to keep out the wind, he also built a rough fireplace from pieces of broken masonry and lit a fire. The larder had survived more or less intact, so they were not immediately short of food, and by the light of a hurricane lamp he and Rafaela ate a stew he had cooked, listening to the old horse munching hay.

Rafaela sat staring into the flames. 'I need someone, *caro* Edward,' she whispered. 'My mother will be of no help. I have no one.'

Suddenly, the horse whinnied. 'Shh,' said Edward. Putting the lamp out, he and Rafaela waited, listening in the darkness. Edward reached for Salvatore's shotgun and thrust two cartridges into the breech.

'What are you going to do?' whispered Rafaela.

'I don't know yet.'

They kept absolutely still. Through the broken door, they saw two dark figures moving against the night sky.

Rafaela picked up the other gun.

For a long time nothing happened, and Edward felt he would choke with tension. Then, with a crash, the door flew open. Framed in the opening were two men. Each held a gun and as they saw Rafaela they started grinning. They hadn't spotted Edward in the shadows, and one of them stepped forward and made a grab for her. Edward was at a loss. He couldn't fire without hitting her. Then, the other man stepped inside, and Edward swung the gun on him and pulled the trigger. The roar filled the stable and set the horse neighing and kicking in terror. The intruder was hurled back off his feet, his face and chest a horrifying mash of blood and pulped flesh. As he fell, the first man turned and, as he did so, Rafaela hit him in the side of the head with her gun. One barrel went off and Edward felt the blast and the searing heat of the shot. Dust poured down from the roof of the stable. With a groan, the man fell but scrambled quickly to his feet and, dropping the gun he had been carrying, stumbled out into the night, clutching his head.

'You all right?' Edward panted.

'Yes. Oh, *Santa Maria, Madre di Dio*, I almost killed you. Are you hurt?'

'I don't think so.'

At the end of the stable the old horse had settled down again, and was munching away at the hay. Rafaela put down her gun. 'I didn't realise it was loaded,' she said.

'We'd better get rid of the body,' Edward replied.

While she held the lamp, he struggled in the lashing rain to scrape a shallow hole at the end of the garden, then they dragged the dead man by the heels across the grass and rolled him in. The hole was barely deep enough but the task took long enough for them both to be soaked to the skin.

Throwing the last of the muddy soil over the body, they trudged through the beating rain back to the stable. Inside, half-frozen, Edward unbuttoned his shirt and threw it down.

'Take off your wet clothes,' he said. 'And get into bed, or you'll die of pneumonia.'

She stared at him doubtfully for a moment, then she dragged the remains of the flimsy slip she was wearing over her head and flung herself down alongside him. Dragging the blanket over them, he put his arms round her and held her close. She was shuddering with the cold, but gradually their body warmth returned. And in sheer exhaustion they fell fast asleep.

When Edward woke it was almost daylight, and Rafaela was still curled up in his arms. As he opened his eyes she was gazing at him and he kissed her gently. She returned his kiss, cautiously at first, then with passion. Her arms tightened round him and before they knew what they were doing, their hands were exploring, caressing, drawing comfort from each other's bodies. There were no whispered words, only a wild exhilaration that swept away all the horrors they had seen.

8

Dressed once more in their damp and wrinkled clothes, Edward and Rafaela felt awkward and avoided eye contact.

'We must see Father Anselmo,' Rafaela said.

'Remember, I'm not a Catholic.'

'It doesn't matter. Father Anselmo will know what to do. He will make it all right.'

The old priest didn't ask questions. He did no more than tell them to kneel, and muttered a few prayers in Latin over them.

Two policemen arrived on horseback during the morning. Behind them came a cart pulled by a mule and driven by one of the villagers. They dug up the corpse and without much ceremony threw it into the cart. As it drew away, Father Anselmo raised his fingers in blessing.

'I shouldn't bother, Father,' one of the policemen said. 'He was inside for murder and rape. He wouldn't have made old bones. Nor will his mate. Not with half his head shot away.'

Rafaela gasped and went pale.

'There was no choice,' said Edward. 'No choice.'

In the days that followed, Rafaela became increasingly withdrawn. There was nothing Edward could say or do, so he occupied himself with practicalities.

Messina was still full of people clothed only in whatever they could find. A few had followed the example of the escaped prisoners and looted whatever clothing shops they could find. No one stopped them.

With the aqueduct broken, there was no water except from a few tainted wells, no bread, meat, pasta or vegetables, and no fish because most of the fishing boats had been swamped by the waves that had swept across the beach, carrying away hundreds of people who had rushed there to escape falling buildings. Many bodies had been washed back onto the beach and lay decomposing in the sun.

The stink was appalling and everybody wore handkerchieves over their noses and mouths. There was cholera in the poorer quarter of the town, and the rats were said to be spreading typhus. Thousands of homeless cats and dogs slunk about the ruins, gnawing at human flesh, and more than a few disappeared into the cooking pots of starving people.

The wine shops had been emptied and the drunken orgy that had followed the first invasion of looters had ceased. But tremors continued and people had taken to heading for the orange groves at night to sleep under the trees. Business was at a standstill because everyone was concerned simply with survival. But Orlandos was one of the few businesses beginning to function again.

Evrone was delighted to see Edward. 'There is much to do here, Capitano,' he said, twisting his curlicue moustache nervously. 'Food and building materials are going to arrive soon in great quantities, but there will be no one to handle them. Orlandos should be doing the work. We have the facilities and the experience. Di Portos have vanished, and the whole family perished.'

'Including Bruno di Porto,' thought Edward unworthily.

'The Caniglias and Della Setas are gone. We are the only importers left here and the Banco Meridione have told us they are prepared to advance money. Signor Capitano, somebody should be here to give the orders.'

'I can't do it,' Rafaela said later.

'Yes you can.'

'It's not a job for a woman.'

'It's a job for anyone who can do it.'

Next morning, dressed in odds and ends of her own, her mother's and Zia Monica's, she twiddled her thumbs while Edward harnessed the old horse to the carriage, which had been polished till it shone by Zia Monica's brother, an old man who until the earthquake had worked as a gardener for a convent.

The Banco Meridione had been only partly damaged and they were putting on a brave show. Rafaela was shown with some ceremony into a small office where the manager had been temporarily transferred.

'Signorina di Orlando,' he said. 'What sadness. Please accept my condolences on the death of your father. What can I do for you? What do you wish?'

Rafaela swallowed. 'Money,' she said.

To her surprise, the bank was only too eager to supply her and, drawing out a substantial sum, she headed for the Orlando office to pay the wages of the clerks.

Urged on by Edward, she made a short speech. 'My father counted on you. I need you,' she ended. 'Just be patient. And we will make this company great again.'

That night Rafaela insisted on retreating to the far end of the stable, where she erected a barrier of blankets, boards and sheets of cardboard to form two rooms. A mattress was dragged in and placed on boxes. Rafaela even found some sheets. They could still hear the mice scurrying about and the shuffle of the horse, they could hear each other, but they had a privacy of sorts.

Edward lay awake for hours, staring at the cold moon slicing through the warped planks of the door. There was the muted rumble of a new tremor and Rafaela whimpered on her side of the barrier. Then she called out his name and he went to her. She was warm with sleep but her limbs were stiff with terror.

'Oh Edward,' she said, 'please don't leave me.'

He kissed her gently, and her arms went round his neck, drawing his head down to her breast.

Food started to arrive with the government officials from the mainland. The man from the Ministry of the Interior in Rome who appeared in the Orlando offices was a small stout bureaucrat with a spade beard and pince-nez spectacles.

'You?' he said, frowning at Rafaela. 'We need a man of experience.'

71

'What's wrong with a *woman* of experience?' Rafaela rounded on him, lips curling, contempt in every curve of her body. 'I have sat by my father and watched what he has done. When he was busy I have even done it for him. I can do all that one of your stupid men can do and more.'

The man from Rome disappeared in a hurry, a pained expression on his face. Edward grinned at Rafaela. She glared back at him, but as the door slammed, she hugged him quickly then she swung round and shouted into the outer office.

'Evrone! Can you come in a minute, please.'

Evrone appeared, plump and dainty, fiddling with his moustache.

'Where's Dummo?' Rafaela demanded. 'He's the manager. He should be here.'

Evrone shrugged. 'Signorina, he's dead.'

'What about Jenschi?'

'Also dead, Signorina.'

For a moment there was silence then Rafaela said, 'How much do you know about the business, Evrone?'

'Everything there is to know, Signorina. I have been with your father for twenty years.'

'Then why are you only the chief clerk?'

Evrone shrugged again. 'Because my education came from the nuns and the parish priest, Signorina. I was an orphan. I was not considered to have enough education. Signor Dummo had been educated at a private school.

'Signor Dummo,' Rafaela said, 'was an old snob who had his eye on me. How would you like to be manager?'

Evrone's jaw dropped.

'Could you do the job?'

Evrone stared at her wildly, then his back stiffened. 'Si, Signorina. Of course.'

'Very well. You've been appointed. Who would you recommend as your assistant?'

'Carlo Zoparella.' The name came at once. 'He is young but very bright and very forceful.'

'He's your deputy from this moment. But teach him your job as well, and see he finds a good chief clerk.'

Evrone shuffled his feet. 'May I make a suggestion, Signorina?'

'You're the direttore now, Evrone, looking after my interests. You have every right to make a suggestion. Speak up.'

'You need a man, Signorina. In the office of the head of the firm.'

Rafaela's face darkened. 'I shall sit in that office.'

'Not immediately, Signorina.' Evrone was insistent. 'At first you need a man. Preferably some member of your family. For a figurehead. So the people from Rome will not turn round and walk out of the office as they have just done. Let us get things moving, and then consider what else to do.'

Rafaela frowned. 'There isn't anyone.'

'There must be someone,' said Edward, 'surely. What about Zia Monica's brother? All he has to do is look important.'

'*E bene,*' said Zia Monica, when she heard Rafaela's proposal. 'It's good.' They found her brother trying to sort out the damage to their house and snatched him away. Putting him in one of di Orlando's rescued suits, they brushed him down and drove him down the hill and stuck him in di Orlando's office.

The old man was in a daze. He couldn't believe his luck. He was to be paid for doing nothing. All he had to do was sit.

Avvocato Montesi, the lawyer, raised objections to their plans at once. 'A woman can't carry on a business like this. Especially one of your age.'

Rafaela stared coldly at him. 'I was old enough to be married, Avvocato,' she said. 'You know that, because you arranged the contract. If I am old enough to be responsible for a household and for bringing up children, I am old enough to handle a business that will keep me alive. Not only me, but you, too Avvocato. Your firm handles all our legal work.'

Montesi looked baffled.

'I am willing to offer you a directorship,' Rafaela continued. 'But only under certain conditions. You will draw the usual salary and bonuses but you will deal only with the legal aspects. I am running Orlandos from now on. I have already appointed a manager.'

'Who?'

'Alfonso Evrone.'

'Signorina, he is a man without education.'

'He is a man with twenty years' experience of this business. If you don't accept my appointment, I shall have no alternative but to terminate our association with your office and find someone who *will* agree.'

Montesi's lips tightened across his teeth. 'Signorina,' he said. 'I have no option but to agree.'

'I don't want you to agree because you have no option, I want you to agree because you believe in what we're doing. We're going to modernise this business. You'll not get much in the way of bonuses until we've built things up again, but after that I promise you there'll be plenty.'

Montesi managed a bleak smile. 'Then I will give it a try, Signorina. I will give Evrone all the help I can.'

'*Signor* Evrone now. He's the manager of the firm, not just a clerk.'

Montesi coughed behind his hand. 'Signor Evrone,' he said.

9

The relief supplies were beginning to trickle into Messina now and Orlandos were handling everything. Meat, milk, grain, flour came first, and then the materials of reconstruction.

The men from Rome were shown into Zia Monica's brother and the old man sat like a sphinx saying nothing. When addressed, he gestured silently at Evrone or Zoparella who answered for him. Eventually, he even began to develop his own characteristics and guess what the answer should be.

The American official from Taormina who was organising the relief was by no means unwilling to work with a woman. He was very young and obviously much attracted to Rafaela.

'In New York, Signorina Direttrice,' he said, 'we would have done our business over a lunch. But there are no restaurants.'

'Perhaps Orlandos should open one.'

'Good idea,' he replied, smiling.

In another room, Edward was considering lists. When the crunch came, Rafaela found she didn't know as much as she thought she did and Edward knew nothing at all, but they were young and adventurous and, with Evrone and Zoparella to guide them, they were beginning to see daylight.

'We exported grain, wood, beans, grapes, wine, fruit, sulphur, rock salt,' Evrone said. 'The producers on the island used us as a depot and also as a co-operative. We imported flour, treated wood, cement, machinery, cloth and household equipment that isn't available on the mainland. Again we acted as a depot for those firms who needed the things.'

'Apart from what's being given free,' Edward said, 'you'll have to double – no, quadruple, if not more – the cement you're importing. There's going to be a lot of rebuilding.'

Evrone nodded. 'We must buy glazed drain pipes, plaster, glass, planks, nails, screws. Those are the first essentials. They're needed immediately.'

'You ought also to think about crockery and glassware. There can't be a whole plate or glass on the island.'

Rafaela sighed. 'I feel guilty about charging for these things when people need them,' she said.

'They're arriving free at the moment,' Edward pointed out. 'And no-one's going to buy until they can afford to. Give things free if you wish. The first essential is to get the place going again.'

Zoparella interrupted. He was a young, spaniel-eyed man who looked about seventeen and he was wearing one of Salvatore's jackets, because he had lost his own and needed to look properly dressed for his job.

'Someone should go to Reggio di Calabria, Signorina,' he suggested. 'Twenty thousand people have been killed there. I crossed by fishing boat during the night to see my sister who, thank God, is safe, and returned this morning. All the small towns – Scilla, Canitello, Villa San Giovanni, Gallico, Archi, San Gregorio – they say that they are nothing but a vast cemetery. There are thirty thousand dead in the ruins, they say, and several thousand more injured. In Pellaro there are only two hundred left alive. Someone should be there to help. We have no-one on that side of the strait and a lot of materials are coming down from the north. It needs organising.'

'Can you deal with it, Carlo?' Rafaela asked.

'I'm sure I can, Signorina.'

'Then you go. We'll find someone else here to replace you. Set up an office. You can draw on our account. I'll want to see all paperwork, of course.'

Zopparella gave her a sly look.

She stared back at him, then they both grinned. 'I think we understand each other, Carlo,' she said. 'The time may come when there'll be more than just a small office over there. And you could be running it.'

That afternoon, Edward was surprised to find a letter from his uncle waiting for him at the Orlandos' office. It was full of warmth and promised him a tremendous welcome home. When he told Rafaela, she was silent. Then she said, 'You will never come back.'

'Of course I will.'

'When?'

He reached for her hand, but she turned away.

Edward gradually became aware, as he went about, of long slow stares from the people of Friddi, and they were not friendly.

'There have been murmurings in the village,' Rafaela said. 'According to Zia Monica. And I have had letters from cousins. They think you're planning to steal their birthright.'

The following day, Edward was jostled in the street, and when he protested he was immediately surrounded by a crowd of hostile youths.

During the afternoon, three men in dark suits came to see Rafaela at Orlandos. When Edward went to join her, he was politely ushered outside and the door shut in his face. He was about to insist when Evrone laid a hand on his arm.

'Not now, Signore,' he said quietly.

When the men left, Rafaela called Edward into her office.

'What the hell is going on,' he asked furiously.

'These are friends,' she replied.

'And what am I?'

'These are people I know, people my father knew. They came to warn me. I have lived here all my life and I can play my enemies at their own game. These men will raise a small army to stand behind me because there are enough people in the island who are grateful to my family.'

She frowned. 'But when my enemies can't get at me, they will find another victim. You are an outsider. I can't argue against that.'

She laid a hand on his arm. 'Perhaps it would be wiser if you *did* go home for a while. Until we can arrange things on the mainland. I intend to open in Rome and other places, and it would be safe there. But it needs time. For the moment it may be better if I am seen to be alone. Then the cousins can't complain. There are other reasons, too.'

'What other reasons?'

'Reasons I can't tell you at the moment because I'm not sure of them. Do you love me?'

'What do you think?'

She stamped her foot. 'You English are cold-blooded,' she snapped. 'An Italian would declare his love at once.'

'And not mean it. Did Bruno di Porto tell you he loved you?'

'Yes.'

'But he didn't love you, did he?'

'I love you, *carissimo* Edward. I'll always love you. All my life.'

II

1909–1911

10

It was strange to see the green fields of England again
after the arid landscape of Southern Italy. Even in the rain
Sicily was bare and devoid of colour except where gardens
had been planted or the sea glimmered through the olives
in an ever-changing pattern of blue, purple and grey.
England looked too lush to be real. But though the fields
were green, the skies were grey as gunmetal and full of
harshly crying crows. The sea that lapped its shores was
the colour of lead.

As Edward stepped from the Southampton train at
Porthelt, Egg was waiting on the station, tall, dome-
headed, bearded, more like a professor than a boat-
builder. He was bubbling over with excitement.

'Good God, boy, how you've grown.'

'It wasn't the food, Uncle Egg.' Edward paused. 'Uncle
Egg – about *Fairy*.'

'Forget it, boy.'

'I'm so sorry. It was supposed to be an experiment. I
was probably showing off to Georgina.'

'It's over and done with,' Egg insisted. 'Forgotten. But,
perhaps you could tell me, Edward, what exactly *were* you
trying to do?'

'I was trying to torpedo her.'

'With a pole?'

'It was a very strong pole. I'd been reading about a spar
torpedo and I was trying to show Georgina how they
worked. In the old days they aimed the boat –'

'– and blew themselves up.'

'Well, sometimes. But sometimes it worked. I was
trying to show her how. But the throttle moved. Uncle
Egg, you really have got it wrong. The throttle should go
forward to advance it and come back for retarding it.
That's the automatic thing. It's like reining in a horse.

Forward to give it its head. Back to slow it down and stop it.'

'You could be right, boy.'

'And it did torpedo her.'

'You can say that again. It cost me a small fortune to raise her and pump her out. Your Aunt Edith was furious. She got over it, though. Especially when she heard about the shipwreck. It lifted a load off her mind when she found you were safe and well. She'd been thinking you'd got into bad company.'

Edward grinned. 'I did at times, Uncle Egg.'

'Well, that's all over now.' Egg laughed. 'You're home and part of the family again and we want to know what you got up to, what you've done.'

'Why didn't you write more often?'

'Because I never received any letters from you or Aunt Edith. Or Georgina come to that.'

'We wrote,' Egg said. 'We all wrote. Well, perhaps Maurice didn't. But the first news we had of you was from that man, Orlando.'

'I'm sorry to say he's dead. In the earthquake.'

They climbed into Egg's sit-up-and-beg De Dion Bouton.

'This all your luggage?'

'I've got used to travelling light.'

'Didn't the family who took you in help at all? Distressed British seaman and all that sort of thing? Jerseys and so on from the slop chest.'

'Uncle Egg, after 28th December nobody had *anything*. Not even the wealthiest.'

'Sorry. Didn't realise. Talk to you later about that. Now tell me, what are your plans?'

'I don't really know.'

'I could use a good seaman.'

'Here? In the boatyard?'

'While you've been away I've developed some new ideas. There's a demand for quick motor boats. Whitehead's self-delivering torpedo's revolutionised thinking in the world's navies. They all want torpedo-carrying craft and they want the fastest that can be devised. Builders in every country in the world are designing for paraffin/petrol engines and the refinement of round-bilge forms, and boats are reaching thirty-five knots. Hydroplanes are probably exceeding that with less power and lower fuel consumption, and hard-chine planing hulls called skimmers are coming into fashion.'

Egg developed his idea with enthusiasm, gesturing wildly, often with both hands off the steering wheel. 'People think torpedoes are becoming such a menace – especially after the Japanese wiped out the Russian fleet at Tsu Shima – they're building ships to destroy the torpedo boats. They call them torpedo boat destroyers – or just destroyers. So the torpedo-carrying craft have to be faster still so they can't be hit. I've designed one or two types that hit the nail on the head.'

'What kind of engines? Petrol, paraffin or steam?'

'Not steam. Not for speed.'

'So where would I come in?'

'Ever thought of becoming a salesman?'

'What of?'

'Boats. My boats.'

'What about Maurice?'

'You know Maurice. He isn't the type. He's an office man. We'll talk terms later.'

Vibrating heavily, the car drew up at Creek House. Through a grey mist, Edward could see varnished masts and spars and the familiar white shapes in the steady drizzle. Beyond them, the trees at the other side of the creek were ghostly shapes with long, reaching arms.

'Mother! Maurice!' Slamming the door open, Egg began to shout. 'We're back. It's Teddy.'

Aunt Edith came hurrying down the stairs. Maurice appeared from the study. He was smoking a cigar. 'Ah ha,' he said, exhaling a puff of smoke. 'The prodigal returns.'

'Hello, Maurice.' Time had done nothing to soften their mutual animosity.

'Teddy!' Aunt Edith enfolded Edward in her arms. 'You look half starved,' she said, wiping tears from her eyes. 'We'll have to feed you up, I can see!'

With the smell of roast beef coming from the kitchen, Edward flicked idly through *The Times*. England seemed like a foreign country, he was so out of touch. Then there was a ring at the doorbell and the Vicar and his wife and daughters were announced.

'Teddy,' Augusta shrieked as she ran towards him.

'Gus.' He held her at arm's length, aware that she had grown taller and rounder and that the parts of her that had touched him felt soft and pleasing. 'You look lovely.'

Georgina presented her cheek for a chaste peck and the Vicar's wife kissed him. 'Like father, like son,' she said. 'Rushing off to sea and forgetting your responsibilities.' The Vicar offered a limp hand and expressed the hope that in Edward's dire straits in the shipwreck and at Messina he hadn't forgotten God.

'Didn't have much time to think about Him,' Edward confessed. 'I was rather busy.'

Egg dispensed thimble-sized glasses of sherry – which, after what he'd drunk in his time at sea, Edward considered a very tame beverage. He noticed that Augusta was allowed it now, as an indication that she was grown up. Maurice dashed his down in one gulp and wandered out of the room. When he returned, he was holding a larger glass, and the liquid in it smelled of whisky.

Lunch started noisily, with everyone asking questions but by the end of the meal, Edward was doing the talking and everybody else was listening.

'How absolutely awful,' Augusta said. 'Being in a shipwreck.'

'He's not the only one,' Maurice pointed out. 'I've been in a shipwreck, too. You remember? You helped.'

After lunch, Egg called Edward into his study to discuss his plans. It sounded exciting but Porthelt was small and not very accessible, and Edward couldn't imagine a high-powered buying committee from the Royal navy, or any other navy, wasting their time looking for it.

'We should take the boats to them,' he suggested.

'What have you in mind?'

'There are regattas during the summer, all along the coast. Portsmouth, Poole, Plymouth, Cowes. There are always motor yacht sections. Why not show the boats there? Enter them for races. If they're as good as you say they are, they'll wipe the floor with the opposition and you won't need to sell them. They'll sell themselves.'

'I think you might be on to something,' he said. 'You'd have to know how to handle the boats. You'd have to be quite expert and that would mean spending some time getting used to them. It would end with a directorship, of course. You and Maurice would be running the place eventually, Maurice handling this end, you handling sales.'

It all sounded splendid in theory, except for Maurice.

'That's settled then,' said Uncle Egg. 'How about coming to the boatyard on Monday? That'll give you time to settle down. Get yourself some decent clothes, though. Can't have you frightening the coastguard.'

That evening Edward walked down to the water's edge. It was cold but, wearing a heavy jacket loaned by Egg and one of Aunt Edith's scarves, he stood at the end of the jetty and stared over the misty river, suddenly aware of how suffocated he had felt surrounded by family and friends.

There was no wind and the water was still. A few seagulls screeched overhead, and across the creek there was a splash as a rat dived in. As he gratefully drew in deep breaths of salty air the boards of the jetty creaked and he turned to see Georgina materialise out of the mist with the Vicar's spaniel.

'Georgy.'

'Thought I might find you here,' she said. 'I was taking the dog for a walk.'

Edward couldn't think of anything to say.

'How does it feel to be home?' Georgina prompted.

Edward shrugged. 'Odd.'

'Being at sea didn't sound like much fun to me.'

'It had its moments.'

'All those rough men.' She shuddered.

'Some of them were good chaps.' He thought of Paddy McWilliams and the first trip on the *Dolly Colgate*. 'They pinched my money to get drunk, but if I was in trouble – with the police, for instance – they'd see me all right.'

'*Were* you in trouble with the police?'

'Once or twice.'

Silence fell between them once more. The spaniel cocked his leg against a wooden spar, then yanked at his lead.

'I think he wants to go back.'

'I'll see you home,' said Edward.

They walked to the Vicarage, not speaking, and stopped in the porch just as it began to grow dark.

'Thank you, Edward.' Georgina turned to face him.

There'd been times at parties when she'd been soft as silk, waiting for his kiss outside the door in one of the games they'd played, and at other times with needle-pointed elbows and knees and bursts of breathless laughter.

She was standing close to him, her face lifted, her eyes on his. He thought of Rafaela in Messina, his promises and what had happened between them, when she leaned forward and kissed him on the lips.

'There, Edward,' she whispered. 'A home-coming present.'

He drew a deep breath but as he reached for her she slipped away.

'I must be going now.' She smiled. 'I expect your Uncle's got a lot to talk about now you're joining the firm.'

She turned away abruptly and stood for a second in the open doorway, framed in the glow from the gaslight inside. Edward walked slowly to the gate. 'Goodnight, Georgina,' he said.

11

On the following Monday morning Egg took Edward to the boatyard and led the way to the drawing office.

'As you know,' he said, 'this firm's been involved with quick boats since my father started it. We build river boats for South America and our launches have been used in the university boat race for the officials. We produced sixteen-knot boats as long ago as 1890 and they brought us loads of orders. Now, as we know, it's torpedo boats. The need these days is for something fast and sturdy which is a good sea-keeper. The engine's the thing. We've made experiments, but, of course, so has everybody else: Hydraulic jet propulsion. Propellers of all shapes and sizes. In the end it always comes back to the power plant.'

He paused and adjusted his spectacles. 'We've had our disasters too. *Snake*, which was built for the navy, was lost and the court martial claimed it was structural weakness. It wasn't, of course. No court martial is qualified to pontificate on causes but they always do if only to show it isn't naval slackness that's to blame.'

He gestured at the drawing board. 'This is the Bourdillon Mark III. Hand started. There was a bit of a problem over it having to be set low but I've overcome that by using an extra shaft and a chain. It's fast.'

Edward studied the drawings. 'Is that what I'm supposed to be selling?'

'Not yet. For you I'm thinking of forty-five-foot launches powered with two Bourdillon IIIs, each developing seventy horse power. Their weight's only about one and a half tons and we think we can reach seventeen knots with them – ideal for naval purposes.'

'As torpedo boats?'

'The navy's used fifty-six-foot picket boats with a dropping gear carrying two eighteen-inch torpedoes and they're

87

found to be stable if the boat doesn't exceed ten knots. I think mine could go faster.'

Edward frowned. 'Seventeen knots isn't very fast for a torpedo boat,' he said.

'That's because the navy insists on paraffin. They lose about fifteen per cent of their power output from the same engine capacity. But the navy doesn't like petrol. They consider it dangerous.'

'So is being hit by gunfire. There'd be less chance of that if the boat were faster.'

Egg's idea intrigued Edward. It seemed to have great potential. Selling boats would make him virtually his own master, and he would be able to travel where he pleased so long as he justified it with sales. Above all – and the thought kept returning to him – it meant that eventually he could talk on equal terms with Rafaela.

'When were you thinking I should start?' he asked.

'In two or three months' time,' Egg said. 'You'll need to be well acquainted with the boat. We have two available at the moment. It'll mean using them constantly and reading everything you can about them.'

'I'll need a mechanic with me.'

'All the time?' Egg looked startled.

'If these boats are what I think they are, I'll need someone to answer finer points about the engines. And he'll need to keep them in tip-top condition because it won't look very good if they break down while they're being demonstrated.'

'Did you have someone in mind?'

There was only one contender. Edward spoke to Sam Nankidno the next morning as he crouched over the shaft of one of Egg's steam launches.

'How goes it with Alice Appleby?' he asked.

Sam looked up. 'She's took up with that young feller who runs the dairy counter in the grocer's.' He sounded bitter. 'A bloke who slaps water into butter all day.'

'So you'll be free now?'

Sam grinned. 'There are plenty of other fish in the sea.'

'I meant, free to do what you please.'

'What are you getting at, Eddy?'

'Ever thought of travelling, Sam?'

Sam looked up. 'Me? Can't afford it.'

'Would you like to?'

'Who wouldn't?'

'What about these new boats the yard's turning out?'

'The forty-five-footers? They're good.'

'And the engines? Have you worked on them?'

'The older men get those jobs.'

'Fancy having a go at them?'

'Not half. Look, what's all this about?'

There was a little grumbling at the engine shop as the news about Sam went round. But the grumblers were all older family men who had no wish to leave home, and adjustments were made in shifts to allow Sam in.

As soon as the boats were ready, one was put in the water and the trials began. They spent a few minutes admiring it, then Egg gestured. 'Start up,' he said.

The engine came to life with an explosion and a puff of blue smoke then settled down to a steady rumble that spoke of power. The trials went well and the boat's speed was calculated at 15 knots. With Sam's tinkering, they pushed it up to 17 knots but could go no further.

'If we ran on petrol,' Edward asked, 'how fast would she be?'

Egg rubbed his nose. 'Twenty-five. About there.'

'Suppose we converted them wholly to petrol. Would it take long?'

Sam explained. For petrol and paraffin there were two separate fuel tanks and two separate leads to the carburettor. The engine started on petrol then switched to the vaporising oil. When they stopped they switched back to petrol so that the carburettor was left with petrol in it.

'Otherwise you have to drain the whole system,' Sam said.

'Good,' Edward said. 'All we need now are the throttles changing. Forward for fast. Back for slow. Let's do it.'

The boat moved down the creek, its engines rumbling heavily. There was a lop on the sea but with Egg, Edward and Sam aboard the boat showed she had good sea-keeping qualities and they soon reached a speed of $22\frac{1}{2}$ knots.

Egg's eyes shone with delight.

Edward and Sam now had virtually full control of the trials of *Dido* and *Aeneas* as Egg had christened the two boats. As the summer holiday period arrived, they found themselves moving about the south coast, either towing a Bourdillon on a huge trailer hauled by a clanking steam engine, or putting it on board a coastal vessel at Southampton and dumping it in the water at their destination. Most of the comments at the various regattas were complimentary, but the yachting fraternity did not really approve of anything that didn't carry canvas. Nevertheless, the boats won everything they entered and started to sell.

12

Edward argued for a design that would make the craft lighter.

'My skimmers,' said Uncle Egg, 'will be the lightweight boat of the future. Fast as hell. These are heavy boats. Designed for the navies of the world. War boats.'

'No one's at war, Uncle Egg,' said Edward.

'They will be before long, the way the Kaiser's behaving. The French have a boat that does twenty knots, with a forward central-firing torpedo. Everybody wants them now.'

'But Uncle Egg, if you want to sell these things as torpedo boats, aren't we wasting time doing what we are doing? We should be selling them to the navy.'

Egg liked the idea. But getting the navy interested was more of a job than they had anticipated. When Edward finally managed to obtain an interview, he was dismissed with a condescending lecture.

'The navy doesn't deal in small boats,' he was told. 'We have the biggest fleet in the world and it's made up of huge steel ships. If we were interested in going fishing, then we might consider your proposal, but we are too busy.'

Edward returned to Porthelt in a fury. 'If those pea-brained, self-satisfied arses don't want them,' he said, 'what about selling them abroad? There must be someone – France, Holland, Denmark, even America, who'd be interested. And what about Italy?' Edward deliberately left the Italians until last in case his eagerness made Egg suspect he might have other motives.

Egg smiled. 'I think Italy might be a very good place to start. There's a chap in Naples called Gaspare Boboli. Army man. Your father knew him. He'd be a perfect contact.'

With the two boats almost ready, Edward sent off a telegraphed message to Rafaela. '*Coming soon,*' he wrote.

Within a day he received a reply. '*Make it very soon. I send you kisses. Rafaela.*'

A torpedo and launching gear arrived the following week.

'Where did you get it all from?' asked Edward admiringly.

'Chap called Zaharoff,' his uncle replied. 'He'd sell you a battleship if you had the cash.'

'It looks wicked,' Sam said, staring at the shining cigar-shaped tube.

'They are wicked,' Egg agreed. 'But not that one. The warhead's full of cork and water.'

The launching gear consisted of two sliding chocks which held the torpedo, and two fixed chocks which secured it in position on the side of the vessel. The two fixed chocks were connected by a bar which carried the firing mechanism, and an electrical release system. On firing, the chocks carrying the torpedo slid out and dropped over the side of the boat so that the torpedo fell into the water.

'What sets it off?'

Egg's hand moved along the firing bar. 'This. It carries a special gyro-starting tripper which sets off the gyro by means of a special starting lever fitted to the weapon. As the torpedo enters the water the air lever which starts the motor is thrown by a tremendously complicated device known as a piece of wire, made fast at one end to the boat; the other end's looped over the air lever.'

'Does it really work?'

'Let's give it a try,' said Egg.

The weight of the torpedo reduced the speed by three knots but this didn't matter because it still remained faster than most launches. The big problem was that steering was difficult and they found that no matter how hard they worked to keep the helm up the boat always had a tendency to turn to starboard. Trying the weight on the port side made no difference because then the boat turned to port.

'We need a compensating weight on the other side,' Sam said. 'Could we carry two torpedoes?'

'Too expensive,' said Egg.

There was no time to do more. Egg had booked them aboard the SS *Fabricius,* due in Naples by the end of the month.

13

Built round a beautiful bay, Naples demanded and received affection. Superstitious, religious, and vital, it bubbled with warmth, colour, noise and music. People lived with the constant jangling of church bells, the vibrant throb of mandolins from cafés and the prayers of priests, with the smell of horse dung and incense.

Red, white and green Italian flags flapped everywhere and everybody was wearing rosettes. The brash new Italy had decided to chivvy tired old Turkey into giving up her North African possessions. Though Turkey's dominion was supposed to run through the Middle East along the North African coast and into the Balkans, it was in fact Britain who controlled Egypt. France controlled Algeria and Tunis, and Spain had Morocco. To take her place in the community of colonial nations, Italy wanted Libya, and the streets were packed with young conscripts wearing large sun helmets and baggy trousers.

Sam and Edward spent the first night at a small family hotel. The next day, they went round to see a family named della Strada, relations of Zoparella, who lived near the Vomero and to whom they had received an introduction via Orlandos. Edward dropped back into Italian life with ease, but Sam found it harder to adjust. It was the first time he had been away from home, he didn't speak the language, and wasn't sure that he liked the food. But he was too busy to worry for long. They found a workshop near the slip, in a small-boat basin called the East Aghieri Quay. It was arranged for the boat to be brought there, complete with crates of spare parts. The workshop was shared with a carpenter-boatbuilder called Bartolini. He was also related to the della Stradas and until Sam got the hang of things and could find his way about, the youngest della Strada, Alessandro, was hired to look after

94

him. The boy was obsessed with America and keen to improve his English.

'In America,' he said, 'everybody has a motor car. Also they eat meat every day of the week – with ice cream to follow. I have cousins in Florida.'

There had been no letters from Rafaela, just a card from Switzerland. All it had said was '*I am so happy. Kisses. Rafaela.*' Edward looked forward to seeing her eventually in Messina, but for the time being he was preoccupied with work.

They set up a fitter's bench and found rope, blocks, tackles and spares; tools, paint, varnish, files, batteries; even an oxy-acetylene welding outfit. Sam was in his element.

It didn't take long to discover that Major Boboli – now, it seemed, Brigadier General Boboli – was not in Italy. Letters addressed to him in Taranto were returned with an accompanying letter to explain that he was in Somaliland and could not be reached.

'Well,' Sam said, 'that seems to be that. Where do we look now?'

'God knows, Sam,' Edward replied. 'I thought this was going to be a doddle. Now Boboli's disappeared into the wild blue yonder I don't know what the hell we do. Have a good time on expenses and go home . . .'

But the following morning a letter arrived from Rafaela. She was coming to Naples, and was very interested in seeing Edward's boat.

Dido was lowered in her cradle onto the quay, and moved round to the East Aghieri Quay. Work started immediately. Within a week they were ready to slip her.

'There's nothing wrong with her,' Sam said. 'A few adjustments, that's all. Things we'll find out when we run her at speed.'

The boat was sent down the slip and floated off its cradle. Edward found a launch to tow them to clear water. Around the bay lay the blue mountains, with Vesuvius towering in the distance and Capri and Ischia shadowy shapes out to sea. As they cast off the tow, the hired launch stood by in case of problems, Alessandro watching enviously from the deck.

They made several runs, one with Mama della Strada's son shouting with excitement, as they raced across the water. Towing the boat back to the boatyard, they switched the paraffin tank and petrol tank lines. When they towed her out again, the difference was magical. The boat seemed to fly over the waves.

'Sam,' Edward yelled. 'We can't muck about with paraffin anymore. Not when you can get this speed from petrol.'

'What about the navy?'

'Stuff the navy. It's run by a lot of old fogeys who think they're Nelson. Times have changed.'

Everything was ready when Rafaela's telegram arrived. Edward met her at the station. She was accompanied by a smart young woman with short, fair hair. Rafaela gave Edward a hesitant kiss.

'This is Adela Cremoni,' she said. 'She goes everywhere with me. She is Italian-Swiss and very, very efficient.'

Feeling awkward, but putting a brave face on it, Edward took them by carozza to the East Aghieri Quay. Rafaela slipped her arm through his, while Adela Cremoni sat opposite, clutching a bag and a briefcase, bolt upright, her hat over her nose against the sunshine.

'How did you find me?' Edward asked.

'Orlandos know everything,' Rafaela smiled. 'Tell me what you've been up to. Tell me about your boats.'

'We reached thirty knots yesterday,' he said, with a huge grin. 'But I want to hear about you.'

'I've been quite busy, as you can imagine. After you left it was like living in purdah. But now I do as I wish. I've been all over Italy, and to Greece and Albania, setting up business deals. People seem to have got used to having a woman in charge. I'm thinking of going into shipping. And motor cars, and typewriters. Clothing and shoes, too. We have to expand.'

'Sounds like it,' said Edward. 'Tell me, do you live alone these days?'

She hesitated. 'Not quite,' she said.

The carriage came to a halt and Sam rushed forward to help Rafaela down. His admiration was obvious. Rafaela was dressed in pale yellow with a wide hat and a sunshade of the same colour. The months since Edward had seen her had changed her. She had grown even more beautiful.

'Lucky bastard,' whispered Sam. 'You must tell me your secret.'

'You have to get shipwrecked,' muttered Edward.

'Now, show me this boat of yours,' said Rafaela. 'I want to try her.'

'You will get oil on your dress,' said Edward.

'I can buy another.'

Sam produced an oilskin, but Signorina Cremoni dived into the bag she was carrying and brought out a spotless lightweight white mackintosh and cap.

Rafaela beamed at Edward. 'You see,' she said.

With Sam driving the launch, they towed the Bourdillon into the bay, Alessandro handling the ropes, Signorina Cremoni sitting sulkily in the cabin.

'She thought we were going on a ferry,' Rafaela laughed. 'I hope she's not sick.'

'Does she live with you?'

'Just her and Zia Monica and the maids and gardeners. And Beppo, of course.'

'Who's this Beppo?'

'There's no need to be jealous. He drives me about in the carriage. But he says I am in too much of a hurry. I should buy a motor car. He's probably right.'

Stopping the engines, they anchored the launch and transferred to the Bourdillon. Signorina Cremoni looked alarmed. 'Am I to be left alone?' she bleated.

Rafaela laughed. 'Don't worry. The little boy will look after you,' she said.

The roar of the engine starting made Rafaela jump, but as the boat made its first run she shrieked with delight. As they shut down and the boat wallowed, the stern lifting under its own wash, Rafaela said, 'Now it's my turn.'

'Throttle by your right hand,' Edward said. 'Forward to increase speed. Try it. Slowly.'

She advanced the throttle, her eyes gleaming.

97

'How much more?'

'Push it all the way.'

The Bourdillon surged forward. Spray lashed their faces, and Rafaela's hair came loose. 'She's wonderful,' Rafaela cried, breathlessly. 'You'll sell hundreds.'

That evening, they dined at Rafaela's hotel and she listened carefully while he outlined his plans for the boat.

'Why didn't you come back?' she asked abruptly.

'I was busy.'

'Too busy to come back?'

'Rafaela, ours isn't a great firm like Orlandos. I don't have a lot of money behind me. My uncle gave me the chance, and I'm determined to make it work.'

'You forgot me.'

'Of course I didn't.'

'I needed you.'

Edward was saved by the telephone. It was a man he'd met from Lake Maggiore. 'I'd like to buy one of your Bourdillons. But I've had the devil's own job tracking you down.' He insisted on talking about prices, guarantees and delivery dates and Edward was conscious that his replies could be heard all over the dining room. When he returned to the table, Rafaela was fuming, her eyes bright with anger.

'There were things I wanted to tell you,' she said.

'I'm sorry about the telephone call. But it is the first nibble.'

'Oh, Edward. This is impossible. I think you should leave now.'

'Can I see you tomorrow?'

'Tomorrow I shall be in Venice. I have business there.'

'Rafaela . . .' Edward reached out to take her hand, but she pulled away.

'Goodnight, Edward.'

He wanted to overturn the table and take her in his arms. But instead, he stood up, pushed back his chair and walked out of the dining room without looking back.

Edward took the Bourdillon to Genoa, Civitavecchia, Brindisi and Rimini. There was plenty of interest, but no offers. The man on Lake Maggiore withdrew at the last moment. Feeling very low, Edward returned to Naples.

There was no one in the office. Edward sat down at his empty desk, and felt overwhelmingly tired. Then, suddenly, the door burst open, and in rushed Sam.

'Spaghetti alla vongole,' he said in his atrocious accent. 'Out of this world. I never thought I'd think it, but this stuff beats English food any day.' He fished in a drawer and produced a letter. 'We've had a nibble,' he said, casually.

It was from a lawyer's office and asked for a demonstration.

'For God's sake!' Edward leapt for the telephone.

The lawyer, who introduced himself as Avvocato Ferignani, confirmed he had a client.

'May I ask his name?' Edward was half-hoping he might be a naval man.

'Signor Marco Matschek. Can you show him the boat tomorrow? He is in Naples only for a limited period.'

Thank God he had returned when he had, Edward thought.

'Tomorrow will be fine,' he agreed. 'Who's he buying for? Do you know? Himself?'

'I am not aware that anyone else is involved.'

Slamming the telephone down, Edward said, 'We'd better give her a trial run this afternoon.'

'You can if you want,' Sam replied. 'But there's no need. She's running as smoothly as a sewing machine.'

They did a trial run, nevertheless. As Sam had said, there was nothing they could fault.

At first light the next day, they were both standing by the boat. They didn't have long to wait. Signor Matschek arrived minutes after them. He was tall with a long blue-jowled face. He was dressed in a black raincoat, wore a grey felt hat and carried a black leather briefcase.

They offered him coffee, even brandy. 'No thank you.' His voice was clipped and nasal. 'I've come to see a boat, not for a drink.' He examined the Bourdillon thoroughly, asking questions which were to the point and knowledgeable. They discussed prices, fuel consumption, technical

99

and financial details, and he insisted on studying the engines, then listened, his head on one side, as they started up.

'Bourdillon Mark II, petrol,' Edward said nervously.

'I see no point in building a fast boat and running it on slow fuel,' said Matschek. 'Shall we see her in action?'

He took off his hat and handed it to Alessandro who solemnly carried it to the office. Then he took a cap from his briefcase. It had earflaps that tied under his chin. He buttoned his raincoat to the throat. 'Shall we go?' he said.

They were towed into the bay by the launch with Sam at the wheel and Alessandro watching the stern.

'Do you always have to tow her out to start her?' Matschek asked.

'It's just a precaution. There's a lot of flotsam near the quay.'

'Perhaps you should hire a decent basin.'

Perhaps they should. If they could only sell the bloody boat, Edward thought savagely, they bloody would.

The launch stopped and dropped anchor, and Sam joined them on board and cast off the towrope. The engines exploded to life with a satisfying thump and a roar. Opening the throttle, Edward raced the boat along what he judged to be a kilometre then slowed down.

'That was fast?' Matschek said. 'What about longer distances?'

'Where would you like to go?' Edward asked sarcastically. 'Posillipo?'

Matschek's expression didn't change. 'Perhaps Capri,' he suggested.

Edward swung the boat round and roared south. The boat behaved perfectly.

'Perhaps,' Matschek suggested, 'we should stop for a drink. I am interested to see how well she restarts.'

'The Emperor Tiberius,' Matschek pointed out, as they sipped their wine on the quayside, 'liked to throw his enemies off there.' He gestured at the high cliffs.

They watched the donkeys labouring up the slope to Anacapri, tottering on tiny feet with Thomas Cook's tourists on their backs.

When they returned to the boat they found it being studied by a large crowd. Matschek solemnly put his cap back on, tied the flaps and buttoned his raincoat. There was a titter from one or two of the onlookers, then a cheer as the Bourdillon restarted, first pop.

Roaring back towards the mainland, they shut down alongside the launch. They towed the boat back and made fast. Matschek stepped ashore, still frozen-faced.

'Well?' Edward asked.

Matschek removed his cap and replaced it with the grey felt hat which Alessandro brought from the office, carrying it carefully before him as though it were a platter with John the Baptist's head.

'Your boat,' said Matschek, 'is strong and powerful. But you are trying to sell it as a pleasure boat to playboys who will be terrified.'

'But are *you* interested?' Edward asked.

'I will let you know. *Buon giorno.*'

Turning on his heel, Matschek marched straight-backed through the boatyard gates where he waved to a cab and vanished among the teeming streets of the city.

14

'Perhaps he was right,' Edward said, staring through the window at the untidy East Aghieri Quay. There was an old tug which hadn't moved for years, green slime hanging on her mooring ropes, a sagging lifeboat from a sunken ship which was half full of water, launches with peeling paint, pinnaces with drab unpolished brass funnels. 'Perhaps we *should* find somewhere better.'

'It wouldn't make a better boat,' said Sam.

A week passed and they heard nothing. Edward was composing a letter to Uncle Egg, explaining their failure, when a young man wearing an ear-biting high collar appeared in the doorway. He removed his hat to show a parting top dead centre as if it had been cut with a knife.

'Bassani, Andolfo,' he said. 'At your service, Signori. From Avvocato Ferignani. Will you please call on him as soon as possible?'

Ferignani had Edward shown to his office immediately he arrived. He produced papers and what looked suspiciously like a bank draft.

'You have sold your boat, Signor Bordillone,' he beamed. 'Signor Matscheck was most impressed.'

After the initial euphoria had worn off, Sam and Edward were sad to see the Bourdillon go. They cradled the boat and saw her lifted by slings to the deck of a coaster heading for Brindisi and then up the Adriatic to Venice. Ferignani had made enquiries but couldn't find out who wanted it.

For the first time Edward began to grow suspicious. The British newspapers were full of the growing jealousy of the German Kaiser for the British fleet. 'If the Germans have got the Bourdillon, there's nothing to stop them copying it.'

It was a chastening thought.

'There's nothing to stop the Austrians taking her from Venice,' Edward went on. 'There's nothing even to stop a German ship picking her up and taking her round to Hamburg or Kiel.'

'So now we've got a torpedo and launching gear and no boat,' Sam said. 'Let's go and celebrate.'

Sam dressed for the occasion in a suit pressed by Mamma della Strada with a stiff collar so tall it made his eyes bulge. They invited the whole della Strada family to join them at a restaurant near the Castel Sant' Angelo, but Mamma della Strada had enough sense to refuse and simply allowed her two daughters, Rosina and Teresa, to go.

'They chaperone each other,' she said with mock severity.

After supper, they all went dancing. The dances were old-fashioned and the music was provided by accordions, guitars, mandolins and violins. For a while, Edward was swept away with the noise, the crush and the nearness of the girl in his arms. They danced till they dropped, then wandered home, careful not to keep the sisters out too late.

'If you ask me,' said Sam later, 'you should be taking yourself back to England, and having a word with your uncle. We're going to need a couple more boats out here at least – and not fitted for paraffin either. Don't worry about me. I'll be all right.' Sam grinned. 'But I can't make up my mind. Should it be Rosina or Teresa?'

It was as though he had never been away. Uncle Egg was bubbling with enthusiasm and talk of bonuses, and the Vicar and his family were coming round that evening. Augusta was away at school, but with them came a tall young man with cold eyes and a lock of dark hair that drooped romantically over one eye.

'My curate,' the Vicar said. 'Alexander Owen-Smith.'

'He's a nephew of Lord Howhill,' the Vicar's wife whispered. 'He's also related to nobility in Germany. His full name's Von Rauche Owen-Smith.'

Edward took an instinctive dislike to him. He never took his eyes off Gerogina, and when she played the piano and sang he stood by her to turn the pages.

'Give us a song, Alexander,' the Vicar's wife suggested.

Owen-Smith feigned modesty but he sang. He started off with Beethoven's lullaby – '*Guten Abend, gut Nacht, mit Röslein bedacht –*' and for an encore sang a ditty which Edward had learned from the German bosun of the *Culloden* with very vulgar variations. He had a light tenor voice and Edward, who couldn't tell a tune from a warthog, seethed with jealousy.

But a moment later Georgina was at his side, all smiles. Was Aunt Edith still encouraging the Vicar's wife to think that Georgina and he were made for each other?

Georgina was peaches and cream, all an English girl should be, but suddenly seemed a pale shadow alongside Rafaela.

'When are you coming home?' she asked.

'I'm not,' he said. 'I'm setting up an office in Naples.'

'All those foreigners. I couldn't bear it!'

'They're not savages.'

'But actually *living* there.'

'It's where my work is. It might be a long time before I come home for good.'

He saw her face tighten. That's torn it, he thought. But then the curate oiled in, and Edward was ignored by both of them for the rest of the evening.

Edward spent three weeks supervising the fitting out of *Aeneas* and a third boat they christened *Achates*.

'Something to show you, my boy,' said Egg one morning, taking Edward into the workshop. He pulled away a huge sheet to reveal the mock-up of a slender 50-foot-long boat with a stepped flat-bottomed hull.

'What do you think?' Egg said. 'Hydroplane design. They've been forced on us by the interest in motor–boat racing in Monaco. Petrol engines made it possible. Just imagine what they could do in wartime.'

'Can I take one to Italy?' said Edward eagerly.

'Not yet. She's too light forrard. I haven't got it right

and the water's lifting the bow too high. But you'll have it soon, I promise.'

Itching to be off, Edward made some last-minute arrangements with the office, and stopped for a brief chat with Sam's old girl friend, Alice Appleby, who was still tapping away at her old typewriter. Maurice, charming as ever, didn't bother to say goodbye.

'It's all down here,' he said irritably, shaking a piece of paper in Edward's face. 'Your bloody boats will be on their way within a month.'

Crossing the Channel in a freezing gale. Edward found himself looking forward to the warmer climes of the Mediterranean. Sam was there to meet him. He had acquired a small van with a box body for moving spares.

'Didn't take long to learn to drive it,' he said. 'I only ran over a few pedestrians.' He chuckled. 'And we've had a couple more enquiries. One from that feller on Lake Maggiore again, and one from the navy. The Maggiore one sounds like it might come off this time. The navy one's only a query. Ferignani's in touch. He's a good bloke that. I took him fishing the other day in the towing launch. He's on our side all right. I've also found another workshop in West Aghieri Quay. It's the place the yachtsmen use. There's a workshop with everything we need including a private basin, a yard with a good gate and a solid lock. There's plenty of room for two boats. We are *getting* two boats?'

Edward grinned. 'More if we want them.'

'Did you talk to him about Matschek?'

'He promised to look into it. But I don't suppose he will. He's too busy. But he agreed we ought to know to whom we're selling in future. Which reminds me, what about the final documentation from Matschek? Has it arrived?'

'All signed, sealed and delivered, and stamped to within an inch of its life. And you wait, he's going to love the new place. He'll be sure to tell all his friends.'

Sam was right. The West Aghieri Quay had style, and it couldn't do any harm to be neighbours with the smart yachts and motor boats of Neapolitan businessmen. It was a very pleasant change after the tumbledown shacks of the East Quay. They hired a cart hauled by two mules, and slung the crates containing Egg's torpedo and the launching gear aboard. Sam's truck was stuffed with everything else.

They had barely unloaded when news came that the boats had arrived, and they headed straight for the Bacino Principe. Both boats had been painted yellow because they had decided the varnished hull didn't encourage second glances from the Italians who liked bright colours.

After they had towed the boats to their new base, the della Strada family turned out to help again, all the way down to Alessandro who at thirteen was now squarely on the payroll for the simple reason that he refused to leave their side.

The paperwork involved was heavy but Rosina, who seemed to have her eye on Sam, offered to help. She worked as a secretary at the railway station and was a dab hand at office work.

They chucked out the old plywood desk that Sam had knocked up, and invested in a solid mahogany job with a leather top. It made Edward feel he wasn't just pretending to be a businessman.

There was a letter from the man at Lake Maggiore, headed with the name of one of the great Milan engineering firms. There was also a letter from the Admiralty in Rome. Edward started answering letters, offering demonstrations and dates, and it was late evening before Rosina said that her back ached, her head ached, and her fingers were tired of typing.

Sam took his leave very shortly afterwards, and Edward got down to studying the final documentation for the boat they had sold. The papers included the bill of sale, registration papers, importation documents, references to patents, documents about fuel, and plans showing the bulkheads and stringers and the type of propellers. The change of ownership documents were at the bottom and consisted of several parchment-like sheets covered with signatures. Matschek's name was prominent among them and there were others Edward had never heard of, but not one that indicated any German connection. But at the bottom, tucked away in a corner where they could hardly be seen, were some initials which leapt out at Edward as if they were a jack-in-a-box.

They were scrawled with a broad pen-nib in black ink. Normally he wouldn't have looked twice, but he had seen these too often to miss them. They were Avvocato Montesi's, and Avvocato Montesi acted only for Orlandos.

15

The train was crowded and Edward was crammed into a compartment with a large family and two priests. The evening was stiflingly warm and the mother of the family produced bread, sausage and wine and offered it round.

The newspaper he bought carried a warlike leader that challenged Turkey to do their worst. 'ITALY MUST ACT,' the headlines screamed. 'THE NATION DEMANDS NORTH AFRICA.'

The train was full of young conscripts heading for a depot in the south, all wearing scarves bearing the date of their call-up. One of them started singing. He had a high clear tenor such as only Italians seemed to possess and before long others had joined in.

Edward barely noticed. He was seething with anger. All his genuine hopes that the navies of the world would be eager for his boats had come to nothing. He hadn't even considered the idea of Rafaela as a buyer.

He was sure the sale hadn't gone through to make Orlandos more efficient or to satisfy some whim of Rafaela's. The secrecy precluded all that. He couldn't even imagine her ever using it to cross the strait to the mainland. She had bought it to help him. It was charity.

As dawn broke, the train reached the coast and Edward saw some of the unrepaired damage from the earthquake – houses with collapsed roofs, mule carts still carrying away rubble, forests of roof timbers, and dozens of workmen slapping mortar and bricks down as though their lives depended on it.

Heading for the ferry at Reggio di Calabria he bumped into Carlo Zoparella. His face lit up with pleasure at the sight of Edward.

'Capitano. You're going to Messina? You'd better hurry. The ferry leaves in a few minutes.'

'How is the Signora, Carlo?'

'Magnificent, Capitano. I would not have believed it possible for anyone to grasp the details of a business so quickly. She exhausts us all.'

The ferry was packed with people, most of them Sicilians returning home. The deck was stacked with sacks of grain. There were several sheep and a number of goats, bleating as if their hearts were broken, and exuding a stink that made its way even into the crowded saloon.

As the ferry slipped round the Peninsula of San Rainieri and the Forte San Salvatore into the harbour station, Edward realised he was feeling rather nervous.

The gate posts of Casa Orlando had been set straight again and the gates, freshly painted, hung in place. The new house was rising like a phoenix from the ruins of the old. The ornate nineteenth-century decorations had vanished and the surviving statues had been consigned to the garden.

Stepping down from his carozza, Edward saw Rafaela in the doorway. She ran towards him and grasped his hands.

'You've come, Edward. How wonderful. I thought you might not. We've waited so long. There's so much to talk about.'

She kissed him warmly on both cheeks, but drew back as she became aware that he had not responded with equal fervour. And looking into his face, her eyes suddenly filled with tears.

'Come inside,' she said briskly, taking his arm. 'You must be tired from the journey.'

Zia Monica met them in the entrance hall. To Edward's surprise she was smiling. Good God, he thought, Rafaela wasn't the only one who had been liberated by the earthquake.

Signorina Cremoni walked briskly down the stairs, with an armful of papers.

'Not today,' Rafaela said. 'Today I shall stay at home.'

'But –'

'No.' The word was sharp and commanding. 'Not today. Appointments can wait. Everyone can wait. I have business to attend to here.'

They chatted inconsequentially for a few minutes then Zia Monica appeared with a tray of coffee and rolls.

'I take it you haven't breakfasted,' Rafaela said.

'I'm not hungry.'

She stared at him for a while, suddenly wary. 'Why are you here?' she asked sharply.

'Why did you buy the Bourdillon?' he demanded.

She stared at him, at a loss for something to say, a hand clutching at her heart. 'Because I wanted it.'

'Have you ever used it?'

'No. It's too wet for a woman. It's a man's boat. Why are you asking me these questions?'

'You bought it out of charity. Because you had money and thought I needed help.'

She was growing angry and her eyes blazed. 'Well, you did. You were good at telling me what to do but you weren't doing very well for yourself. I was watching.'

'You did it to help me.'

'Yes.'

'To encourage others to buy.'

'It did, didn't it? Commandante Matschek's name is good enough to make people interested. I did it through him to save your pride. Pride is important to a Sicilian.'

'It's important to me, too. I would rather sell on my own.'

Her voice rose. 'You could well have gone on trying for another year.'

Signorina Cremoni kept moving in and out of the room as once or twice did Zia Monica, and they were obliged to keep switching their conversation to other subjects.

'It was Montesi's initials on the contract that told me what had happened,' Edward said.

'I told him not to sign anything,' she snapped. 'But I suppose he had to put his name somewhere on the document.' Her eyes blazed. 'It was wrong of you to come here. It was wrong of me to come to Naples. But I wanted to see you. To see how you were. My eyes ached to see you. But I realise now it's not possible. You have your life

110

to lead and I have mine. I had things to tell you. They were beautiful things.'

'Then tell me.' He was growing tired of this litany of how much she had to say to him.

'How can I?' she snapped. 'When we face each other with angry words and bitter tongues.' Just then, with her fierce eyes, she was pure Sicilian. 'That isn't the mood for what I have to say.'

'For God's sake, Rafaela, spit it out.'

'No.' Her eyes glittered back at him, sharp with Sicilian hauteur. 'Not *now*. There are other, harsher things to think about now. There is a war coming. And the country isn't ready for it. The politicians as usual were in too much of a hurry. They have had to hire horses, carts, motor vehicles from us. They have even asked us to find them ships. They came to see me. Fortunately Evrone and Zoparella were here. They still refuse to deal with a woman. We showed them all the documents they wanted. They couldn't argue. But I am frightened. So much money is involved.'

He stepped forward but she drew a deep breath. 'It won't concern you, though,' she said. 'You are English, secure in your Empire, safe in the knowledge that you're powerful. I am part of a small country struggling to be noticed in the world. We're different. I see it very clearly, now. From different worlds. It isn't as if we were lovers.'

'What were we then?' Edward snapped.

'Two frightened people. Afraid, cold and wet and in need of comfort.'

Edward stared at her, not knowing what to say.

'You may stay the night if you wish,' Rafaela said coldly. 'It's too late to catch the night ferry. Zia Monica will see to anything you need. I have to go to Rome. I don't know when I shall be back.'

Edward turned on his heel. 'Goodnight, Rafaela,' he said.

Outside, he gazed up at the night sky, and cursed himself for being such a blundering fool.

16

'Where the hell have you been?' Sam's indignant bleat greeted Edward as he reappeared at the Aghieri West Quay. 'There's a war on. Didn't you know?'

Edward knew only too well. The train had been held up to allow troop trains heading for Brindisi to pass – lines of carriages jammed with yelling young men, horse boxes full of excited cavalry mounts, and flat cars loaded with guns and equipment.

The station and the Piazza Garibaldi had been crammed with troops, thousands caught in the pools of light from the gas lamps that protruded from the smoke-blackened walls, saying goodbye to their families in the shadows of engines that snorted showers of smut. They were squeezing concertinas, plucking at mandolins, embracing their women, exchanging bread, wine and sausage, voices echoing under the glass and iron of the vaulted roof.

'They've sent an army to occupy Tripoli,' Sam said. 'Oughtn't we to go home?'

'Why? It doesn't affect us. Italy's not been invaded. Tourists are still arriving. I saw a carriageload at the station.'

That evening, they ate at a small trattoria near the quay. Everybody in the place seemed to be shouting, not only at their companions but across the restaurant to other diners.

'We must get rid of corruption,' a man on the next table was shouting across them. 'The army's short of guns and the navy's short of boats.'

Edward's ears pricked and he leaned forward. 'Sam,' he said, 'this sounds like an opportunity for us.'

The following day, he wired Egg to be prepared to push up production and managed to get an interview with a naval commander in the Ammiragliato in the building of the Ministro della Marina.

'It's true we have invaded Libya,' he conceded. 'After four hundred years of Turkish misrule, it's time someone else had a go.'

'Where did you land troops?'

The commander smiled. 'You don't seriously expect me to tell you?'

Edward smiled back. 'I have a reason for asking. Do you have all the boats you require? Because I can supply them if they're needed.'

'What sort of boats?'

'Pinnaces, barges, motor torpedo boats.'

'Where would they come from?'

'From England. They could be here within weeks.' Edward crossed his fingers behind his back.

A long discussion followed on cost, fuel and delivery. For a moment it looked as though a contract might be in the offing. But in the end the commander decided his authority wasn't sufficient for him to risk it, and backed off.

From the newspapers Edward learned the Italians had landed near Tripoli and had proceeded to blockade the city. And, from a small paragraph at the bottom of the page, it appeared that another blockade was taking place at Arina, near Benghazi, and that the man in command was Commandante di Brigata Arnaldo Boboli.

The following week, when the 6000-ton French coaster, *Liberté*, came alongside at a small port called Sanauen, 20 miles west of Arina, Edward and Sam and two of Egg's 45-footers, *Aeneas* and *Achates*, were aboard, together with their cases of spares.

Edward didn't waste any time in tracking down the Commandante. A shabby hotel of whitewashed mud bricks near the waterfront called the El Abid had been taken over for the military staff and Boboli was established there. From the hall of the hotel Edward spotted the Italians on the verandah. A table was covered with charts and maps and a loud argument was going on.

He waited impatiently while his business card was presented. There was no response. Then, abruptly the

113

charts were rolled up, and the officers on the verandah dispersed. Edward himself was about to leave, when a young captain, all smiles and moustache, appeared.

'Signor Bourdillon?'

Edward rose and the Italian clicked his heels.

'You wished to see the general?'

'To pay my respects.'

'Come with me, please.'

Boboli was a short stout man with a black beard in which the white streaks appeared to have been introduced artificially, they were so exact.

'Signor Bourdillon,' he said. 'How nice to meet you. I remember your father well. Your mother was a cousin of mine.'

This was news to Edward, but he didn't let on.

A bottle of wine was produced by the young officer and they sat on the verandah and chatted inconsequentially about the Bourdillons.

The formalities over, Boboli asked why Edward had come to see him.

'I believe you are short of munitions, Commandante?'

'We have the men and we have the guns.' Boboli stroked his beard. 'Unfortunately, Rome misjudged the situation. They expected the local tribesmen to greet us as liberators. No-one observed that they are Muslims and prefer to side with the Turks. The tribesmen are massing at Ain Zara to the south, and Benghazi and Derna are too far away.'

Boboli frowned. 'We need the harbour at Arina. It isn't a deep-water harbour but it would do. There are lighters that can be brought up. Unfortunately, the Turks are in position and we dare not attempt a landing. If we could only take Arina, Benghazi would fall like a ripe plum.'

Suddenly he smiled, revealing acres of excellent white teeth. 'When the Balkan countries finally decide to throw off the Turkish yoke, it will be wonderful,' he went on. 'The Turks will find all their supplies are on the wrong side of the Mediterranean again. They'll have to take everything back again. For the time being, however, I am obliged to kick my heels here while the Turks sneak ammunition and men past every night.'

'You need small fast shallow-draught armed boats to intercept them, Excellency.'

'Two or three would do the trick. They could lie in wait under the shadow of the cliffs.'

'I know where there are two such boats.'

Boboli raised an eyebrow. 'Tell me more,' he said.

'They are Bourdillon boats, Excellency. They can do thirty knots.'

'That's fast, my young friend.' Boboli smiled again. 'But these boats. They are steam launches?'

'No, Excellency. They have petrol marine engines.'

'Are they armed?'

'They are strong enough to take a gun.'

'What I want is a torpedo. There is a Turkish gunboat, the *Tahaf*, lying in the harbour at Arina. Her guns cover the entrance. She escorted a small coaster, the *Huda*, carrying ammunition. The *Huda* lies beyond her. They ran her aground to make unloading easier. There isn't much in the way of harbour installations. They're building a jetty and rigging a derrick. Bring me your boats when they can fire a torpedo and I might be interested.'

17

The following day, wearing a galabiyah and a towel round his head so that he looked like one of the Libyan boatmen who plied up and down the coast, Edward took an Arab dhow past Arina harbour.

The gunboat, *Tahaf*, guarded the entrance, her guns trained to sea. She looked a little like a large flat-iron, with low decks, a low freeboard and a high bridge and upperworks. The red Turkish crescent flag flapped at her stern. The entrance to the harbour was narrow, with high cliffs on either side and, surrounded by small yellow buildings and palm trees, it looked like a seedy oasis. The *Huda* lay on the beach, beam-on to the sea beyond the *Tahaf*, leaning inwards, her tall stack canted over, her masts charcoal marks against the sky.

Edward was in a thoughtful mood when he returned to the little quay at Sanauen where Sam was bent over *Dido*'s engine.

'Sam, we need to convert these bloody things to men o' war.'

'Charming,' Sam said. 'And how do you propose to do that? The water pump on this bastard has gone on the blink.'

'What about the other one?'

'Not much better.'

'Have we the torpedo launching gear with us?'

'You know bloody well we haven't.'

'If we could use that torpedo –'

'It's a dummy.'

'No, it isn't. Only the warhead. Suppose we change it for one stuffed with explosive.'

'Then what?'

'Sink something.'

'Jesus.' Sam stared at Edward in awe. 'What?'

'One of these caiques that bring in the Turks' supplies. It'd show what the boats could do.'

'That's an act of war. Where are you going to get the explosive from?'

'You've heard of this chap, Zaharoff, haven't you? He sells anything from grenades to battleships.'

'I think you're barmy,' said Sam, grinning.

Edward grinned back. 'Am I? Sam, if we could hit something we could sell a couple of dozen of these things. And think what that means as commission. You could go home and marry Alice Appleby.'

Sam laughed. 'Bugger Alice Appleby. A bird in the hand's worth two in the bush. Rosina della Strada'll do me.'

It took a fortnight and a little bribery to get the torpedo across the Mediterranean. They found a French ship in Sanauen heading for Brindisi and managed to sweeten the captain enough to give Edward a passage. He returned aboard an Italian naval tug.

'Where the hell did you get the warhead?'

'I had it taken to pieces and filled with explosive.'

'Who did it?'

'Fabbrica Farinese. Pappa della Strada told me about them. They do work for the Italian navy. At this moment they're trying to produce torpedo boats. I used a little of Uncle Egg's expenses to persuade one of the directors I was an Italian naval officer and that we've got a high-speed launch to fit the torpedo. I said it was *multo urgento*.'

'You cunning sod. One of these days you'll get your head stuck in the railings and won't be able to get it out. Who's paying?'

'The Italian Navy. At least, I hope so. If they refuse or we fail, Christ knows.'

'Jesus,' muttered Sam. 'I have to hand it to you, kid.'

'Does *Dido*'s engine work?'

'Like a bird.'

They worked on the boat all that night and the next day, hauling on tackles to swing the torpedo to its position against the clamps on the deck.

117

'It looks bloody ugly,' Sam observed, eyeing the equipment. 'Has it ever been tried?'

'Apparently.'

'Are we going to test it?'

'We don't have time. If it works, we're in the money. If it doesn't, we could be in the clink.'

Frowning, Sam studied the tilt of the deck. 'Will she steer?' he asked. 'She's got a hell of a lot of weight on one side. She'll probably go round in circles.'

She did.

Towed out by a hired launch driven by an Arab in a fez, they tried her out the following day. The sun was blisteringly hot and they could see the dun line of the desert behind the shore. The boat moved in a definite arc.

'She'll be hell to aim,' Sam decided. 'And what if they see us?'

'We do the job after dark.'

'God help us. What are we going to do about this bloody circling?'

'Sandbags.' Edward gestured at the great sweep of desert baking under the African sun. 'There's plenty of sand.'

It worked. The sandbags didn't provide perfect balance but they didn't have to use as much helm to keep the boat heading on a straight course.

'Just one little thing,' Sam said. 'What if somebody starts firing at us?'

'Let's see if Boboli will give us a machine gun.'

But Boboli had disappeared. They found him eventually outside Sanauen, where a whole battalion of men were clearing stones and smoothing ridges of sand.

'My airfield,' Boboli said proudly. 'We are bringing our air fleet up from Tripoli.'

'Your what?'

'We have two Bleriots, two Farmans, two Etrich Taubes and three Nieuports.'

Edward had never heard of aeroplanes being used for war. He'd never seen one, in fact, though he'd heard of people floating around above the ground.

'What do they do?' he asked.

'Reconnaissance work. That is how we know the tribesmen are gathering at Ain Zara. They are the cavalry of the clouds.' Boboli gestured at a young officer alongside. 'This is Captain Piazzi. He made the first operational flight in the world from the field we established near Tripoli. We are going to destroy Arina with bombs.'

Edward's jaw dropped. 'I thought you wanted to torpedo something.'

Boboli shrugged. 'It won't be necessary now. The air fleet will reduce the opposition to dust.'

Edward was in a gloomy mood that evening. He had spent a great deal of money that wasn't his. The bomb was an occupational hazard among European rulers but nobody had ever dropped any from an aeroplane before.

News came that Boboli's aeroplanes had arrived and Edward hired a carriage to take himself and Sam to see them. The horse looked on its last legs, the stuffing was sticking through the leather of the seats and the fringed awning was faded and torn.

'Looks like a bloody funeral,' said Sam.

'Ours,' Edward replied.

Boboli's air fleet, the engines covered with tarpaulins, was lined up, being scrutinised by groups of Italian soldiers. The atmosphere was sulphuric. Boboli was furious because only part of the air force had arrived, and more than one of the planes was out of action. A sandstorm had overturned two, breaking spars, while three more were having engine trouble because sand had blown on to the exposed tappets of the engines.

'Christ,' exclaimed Sam. 'I used to fly them things on a piece of string when I was a kid.'

Three days later, two of the Farmans struggled off the ground, engines buzzing like faulty sewing machines.

Boboli looked pleased as they gained altitude.

'Sottotenente Gavotti is going to drop bombs. The size of melons and weighing no less than two kilos each.'

As the aeroplanes vanished from sight, he began to prowl up and down, gnawing at the end of his swagger stick.

An hour later one of the machines appeared out of the clouds. They could hear the engine missing occasionally and saw puffs of blue smoke as it circled the airfield.

It landed finally, bounced and came to a stop. Everybody started running. A moment later a major on a horse tore up to report. 'Sottotenente Falcioni had to drop his bombs in the desert, Excellency,' he said. 'Gavotti dropped all of his on the target. Four altogether. Three exploded.'

Boboli was almost dancing with rage. 'And the damage?'

'Two or three camels, Excellency.'

Boboli turned away, furiously slapping at his boot with his stick.

'Perhaps I can do what the aeroplanes couldn't do, Excellency,' Edward said quietly.

Boboli's head turned. 'How?'

'We have acquired a torpedo.'

Back at the harbour of Sanauen, Boboli studied the strange apparatus fitted to the boat and the missile resting on the chocks on its side.

'Will it work?' he asked.

'Of course it will, Excellency.'

They managed to persuade Boboli to give them an old lightweight Hotchkiss which the army didn't like because of its tendency to jam. It was fitted to the bow and a Sergeant Custalozzi and five men armed with rifles were provided to handle it. Two soldiers would have been sufficient for Edward but Boboli insisted.

The men were dewy-eyed conscripts but the sergeant had fought in Abyssinia and Somaliland, and had the medals to prove it. His grandfather had been one of Garibaldi's followers and Custalozzi was itching to prove himself a chip off the old block.

As they prepared to go aboard, Boboli said, 'You can't go to war as a civilian, Signor Bourdillon. You could be shot as a spy. You must be sworn in as officers of the reserve. From now on you are Tenente Bordillone and Ingenière Nanchino. We will find the uniforms. Just in case. The Turks are not noted for their civilised treatment of prisoners of war.'

120

A trial run, fully loaded, was scheduled for the afternoon. The guns plus the military overload reduced the boat's speed considerably.

'Sink me a ship,' Boboli said, 'and I will make sure your boat is bought.'

Edward glanced at the sky. The sun was shining and the sea was still. 'Would tonight suit you?' he said.

Followed by a small tug loaded with drums of petrol, the *Dido* left the quayside as dusk arrived, engines rumbling hollowly as they made for the open sea. There was a whiff of wind and Edward prayed the weather would not change. They had twenty miles to go and a heavy lop might sink them with the boat so dangerously unbalanced.

She handled badly and the soldiers were far from happy. As the spray broke over the bows, Sergeant Custalozzi moaned it would ruin his gun. One of the soldiers was seasick, and lolled unhappily in the stern.

After two hours they were in view of the lights of Arina. By this time everyone was cold, damp and far from confident of the operation's success. Edward stopped the engines. Above the swish and lap of the sea, Edward was surprised to hear voices.

'Turkish caiques bringing in supplies, Signor Tenente,' Custalozzi hissed. 'They come every night. We must be very quiet.'

Sam gave the thumbs up.

'Chocks going to work?' Edward asked.

'Christ, I hope so.'

'Firing bar fixed?'

'Yes.'

'Air lever forward?'

'Yes.'

'Wire loop attached.'

'Yes. For God's sake, let's get on with it.'

The engines restarted with a thump and the *Dido* moved closer. Points of light gleamed ashore and there was a line of yellow portholes where the Turkish gunboat lay. Without being able to see them, Edward was aware of the caiques drifting past them in the dark.

121

A slight wind made it extremely difficult to keep her on course. Waves slopped over the bows, and there were muffled cries of alarm from the soldiers.

'For Christ's sake,' Sam muttered, 'if we don't get rid of the bloody thing soon, we'll be swamped.'

'Just a bit closer,' Edward muttered. 'Tell 'em to bale.'

Clouds obscured the moon and cast a dark shadow over the sea. The *Dido* was manoeuvring in the entrance to the harbour now with the *Tahaf* beam-on to them. Her deck lights picked out a number of men on her stern.

'Get rid of the sod,' Sam growled.

Edward held his hand a little longer. 'Stand by.'

'For Christ's sake –'

'Go.'

Sam heaved on the lever that released the chocks. Nothing happened.

'Give it a shove.'

Cursing under his breath, Sam threw his weight against the chocks. Reluctantly they moved, the connecting rods sliding and clicking as the torpedo settled with a final solid clunk into firing position over the side of the boat. Then, as Sam heaved, the clamps opened abruptly like claws. The torpedo fell and Sam almost followed it overboard as it ploughed into the sea. The control wire sprang taught with a twang then dropped loose. As the torpedo's motor started and it moved away the boat swung to port.

'Jesus,' said Sam, staring into the darkness. 'It worked.'

At that moment the moon came out like a searchlight. They were surrounded by caiques. But not one changed direction and it was obvious the low freeboard of the Bourdillon made them almost invisible in the swell.

They could see the torpedo track moving away from them at a tangent, nose-up and making a small bow wave.

'The bloody thing's not running straight,' Sam groaned.

'It'll hit her, though,' Edward replied. 'It'll hit her.'

The soldiers quickly forgot their seasickness and their concern for the gun. Then the torpedo vanished.

'It's gone underneath.'

The language was frightful.

'Well, that's that,' muttered Edward. 'We'd better go home.'

'We've lost the bloody thing,' said Sam, 'but at least we're alive.'

Edward brought the boat's head round towards the west, disconsolate at having failed.

'We'll never get another chance like that,' he said.

As he spoke there was a tremendous explosion ashore, followed by another that seemed to split the heavens open. A great red flare of flame blossomed out like a vast tulip.

18

For a while everyone was silent, awed by what they had done.

The moon vanished again, behind a huge bank of cloud. The sea was like ink and they could see nothing of the caiques. One minute they had been there; now they were invisible.

The boat was still tending to yaw to port under the counterweight they had added to balance the torpedo.

'Get rid of those bloody sandbags,' Edward snapped.

Leaping forward, Sam wrenched out his knife and the sandbags began to plop into the water. As they disappeared and the boat began to answer the helm better, they became aware of a heavy shadow bearing down on them and Edward heaved the boat's head round. It was the last of the Turkish caiques and the deck was jammed with men, eyes glued to the huge flare of flame ashore. Fragments of the *Huda* were still dropping into the sea and they could hear the Turks' cries of dismay coming over the water. Nobody on board the caique seemed aware of the low sleek shape of the Bourdillon in the water astern.

Edward was surprised by the rattle of the gun on the foredeck. Eager to strike a blow for his country, Custalozzi had snatched the cover off the Hotchkiss and was firing at the caique. The startled Turks dived for cover behind the wheelhouse. As the Bourdillon moved along the beam of the vessel, Custalozzi let rip with another burst.

So far he didn't seem to have hit anybody but the opportunity was too good to resist. Edward drove the Bourdillon at speed across the bows of the caique so that Custalozzi could treat the Turks to a third fusillade. As they swung to starboard to run down the other side of the caique a white flag was run up the masthead, faintly pink in the glow of the flames ashore.

124

'The buggers are surrendering,' Edward yelled.

'You've started a bloody war,' cried Sam, 'you mad sod! What are we going to do now?'

'Accept the surrender.'

'Sergeant,' Edward said to Custalozzi, 'can you get aboard that vessel and batten everybody down below deck? Take four men. Leave one man to handle the gun. We'll dodge about a bit, firing here and there so they'll think there are more of us. When you've got them all below and the hatch secured, shout and one of us will take over.'

Custalozzi and four of his men clambered aboard the caique, guns at the ready. While Edward circled round, the remaining Italian fired short bursts over the caique.

Edward was wondering nervously if he'd bitten off more than he could handle when a shout came from Custalozzi, and Edward took the Bourdillon alongside.

'You jammy sod. A Turkish general. Sufra Adem Bloody Bey, no less. *And* his staff.'

Sam stared at Edward, not sure whether to laugh or cry.

They had struggled back to Sanauen against a rising wind. And a downpour of rain left the Bourdillon almost swamped. When they reached the harbour a cavalcade of officers, splendid in sashes and braid, with Boboli at their head, came thundering down to the quay.

Custalozzi sprang to attention, quivering with pride, his arm raised in a shuddering salute. Men with carbines were quickly dispatched to the caique and a string of Turks, complete with fezzes and medals, soon emerged on deck. They were a bedraggled lot. Locked below, most had been seasick.

The senior officer, a major general, bowed and offered his sword to Boboli who, with a magnificent gesture, indicated that Edward should take it. Startled, Edward accepted the sword, then proffered it to Boboli who shook his head and smiled.

'*E la vostra*,' he said. 'You captured him. It is yours. *Bravo. Bravissimo, Tenente Bordillone*. Italy is grateful. It was a brilliant idea to attack the ammunition ship first. Without her, the *Tahaf* is nothing.'

125

Three-pounder guns were quickly mounted on the bows of the two Bourdillons and they raced up and down outside the entrance to Arina harbour, firing on the *Tahaf*, while she replied ponderously with her heavier guns, her shots always wide of the mark. After a week the rate of firing slackened then stopped. With her ammunition gone and none in reserve, the *Tahaf* was useless. A white flag went up and the Italian soldiers moved in from the desert.

Inevitably Boboli took the credit, but he was as good as his word. The day following the ceremony of the surrender at Arina, as the red, white and green flag of Italy was hoisted over the Customs House, a man from the navy arrived to arrange to take over the boats.

Benghazi fell within a few days, followed by Derna. By the end of the year Italy was in formal possession of the coastal area towns and was organising an expeditionary force for a movement to the interior.

The newspapers had the story by this time with Edward referred to as Tenente Eduardo Dante-Bourdilloni and Sam as Ingenièro Samuele Nachino. Still wearing the uniforms Boboli had supplied, the two heroes appeared in a parade in Rome among several thousand soldiers and sailors. They were presented with enamelled medals with red, green and white ribbons and were kissed on both cheeks by the King, a minute figure wearing a shako half as tall as he was. When they finally returned to Naples, the della Stradas were almost hysterical with pride and delight. A huge celebration was organised at the best restaurant in the city, and Sam and Edward were clapped by the staff and customers.

Sufra Bey's sword was admired by all, and old della Strada who, like Custalozzi, had fought in Abyssinia, made a few passes, which encouraged further roars of approval.

One of the della Stradas' neighbours turned up with a bundle of letters addressed to Edward.

Edward felt almost embarrassed by the effusive congratulations. Montesi, Zoparella, Evrone, Avvocato Ferignani, had all written, even to Edward's surprise, the frozen-faced Matschek. There was also one from Egg, with an important postscript. '*Enquiry today from Italian Navy concerning 20 more boats*.' The final letter was postmarked Messina.

'Lucky Edward,' Rafaela wrote in her strong spiky hand. 'Your boats have been sold to the navy.' He wondered how she knew before he did. 'You now have everything you wish. If only I had.'

III

1911–1914

19

Since the Armenian massacres, no one was sorry to see the Turks humbled. But there was little praise for Italy's aggression.

It was soon obvious also that in Libya she had bitten off more than she could chew. The benefits were meagre and the Italian Army felt betrayed by its politicians, who were being heavily castigated by a young journalist called Mussolini in a new newspaper called *Avanti*.

With the hostilities now confined to skirmishes with native tribesmen, it was time for Edward to go home again. But Sam remained behind. He had acquired a small flat at the top of the funicular though he continued to eat occasional meals with the della Stradas.

'No Alice Appleby?' Edward enquired.

'Not a chance.'

'One of the della Stradas?'

'That's why I moved out.' Sam gave a shamefaced grin. 'The temptation was getting too great!'

Egg was over the moon at the Bourdillons' success and his nephew's new-found celebrity. Maurice was rather less enthusiastic.

'Anyone can lick the Turks,' he said.

The Portsmouth newspapermen came with their cameras and demanded pictures of Edward in heroic poses with Sufra Bey's sword. On the Sunday after his return Aunt Edith insisted on his accompanying her to church.

Expecting to see Georgina there, Edward raised no objections. But she wasn't there and he was obliged to sit through the service with only Augusta to look at. She was nineteen now and had grown into a good-looking girl, daintier than her sister, but with the same blonde hair and

131

blue eyes. The Vicar's prayers concluded with thanks for the return of the wanderer, and afterwards, outside the church, Edward found his hand being shaken by people he had never met before, even by Colonel Scholes-Dever from the Manor House.

'Jolly well done,' he said. 'High time those damned Turks were taken down a peg or two.'

As the crowd parted, Augusta approached and kissed him on the cheek.

'Augusta. How lovely to see you. What are you up to these days?'

'I thought I'd try nursing. I've been helping at the hospital at Winchester. Mother doesn't approve, of course. She says well-brought-up young ladies don't work for a living.'

That evening the Vicar and his wife and family were invited for sherry. Edward had the suspicion it was a put-up job and he wasn't the only one.

'Your beloved's arrived,' Maurice announced with an evil leer. 'But you'd better watch out for the curate. He's a randy little sod. I've heard he's got a woman in Porthelt already.'

Georgina looked stunning. 'Home is the hero,' she said, with a smile.

'I'm no hero, Georgy. It was sheer luck. Like being a survivor from the *George V. Cotterill*.'

'You blew up that ship, didn't you?'

'I was aiming at a different one.'

'You're just being modest. And I hear from my cousin at the Foreign Office that they are anxious to talk to you.'

Two days later a letter arrived summoning Edward to London. He went expecting to have lunch with the Foreign Secretary but it turned out to be a dreary deputy to the man who held the Italian desk. They met in a small office down a back corridor. It was stuffed full of books and the desk was piled high with files and papers. The official behind it was a cold, bloodless type in an ear-clutching stiff collar and pince-nez spectacles. He offered nothing in the way of refreshment, not even a glass of water. He pumped Edward for information – what were the Italians up to? What did he know about this man, Graziani, who was behaving with such cruelty against the tribesmen? Did he think there was any chance that Libya under Italy might become a threat to Malta and British possessions further east? There was a suggestion that the French were involved – was it true? Did the Italians show any sort of ability or were they, as everybody believed, incompetent and lazy?

Many of the questions were insulting and Edward's answers were appropriately brusque. The official stood up abruptly, indicating the interview was over, and Edward was shown out.

'You can tell your cousin,' he informed Georgina when he got back to Porthelt, 'that I think the Foreign Office might do a lot better in affairs abroad if they learned a few manners.'

It was obvious that Aunt Edith and the Vicar's wife were in collusion. And as far as convention and propriety allowed, they threw Edward and Georgina together and left them alone. Away from the malicious gaze of Maurice, the two escaped to the garden and drifted to the summer house. It had been built near the water, among the trees and close to the boatshed. Here they kept the cane lounging beds for the summer, the umbrellas, the deckchairs, the mattresses, the oars and sails for the dinghies. It was a large building with room to have meals in and even two beds for guests when the house was too full during the holidays.

As they stopped for a moment in the doorway, their arms brushed against each other. Then Georgina's fingers touched his and she gave a little gasp. Edward turned to take her in his arms, but there was a sudden call from Aunt Edith in the garden.

Alexander Owen-Smith, the curate, had arrived. He was sitting on an upright chair, wilting over a glass of sherry which he clutched in slender white fingers.

Georgina, Edward noticed, crossed to the curate and touched his arm in a sort of greeting before seating herself next to her mother.

133

'There was a piece about you in the *Illustrated London News*,' Owen-Smith said. 'I saw it at the home of a friend, and obtained permission to cut it out. They were very impressed that I knew you. I put a note in with it because I wasn't sure you would be here.'

Aunt Edith passed over a sealed envelope which rested against the clock on the mantelpiece. Inside was a short paragraph cut from the magazine. It was a rehash of all the other stories which had been printed about him. The note, short and sycophantic, was signed *Alexander Clifton Owen-Smith* with a whole battery of flourishes and twirls.

'Thanks,' Edward mumbled without much enthusiasm. 'How kind.'

Georgina turned up a few days later as Edward was packing his bags to return to Italy. Egg was at the boat-yard with Maurice, and Aunt Edith was in Porthelt, shopping, and had taken the maid with her to carry things. The house was empty and he had a sudden suspicion that Georgina had made sure it was.

She arrived with a book and a card of pressed flowers for Aunt Edith but he knew they were only an excuse.

'Aunt Edith's out, Georgina,' he said from the landing. 'So is everybody else. There's only me. Come up.'

'Upstairs? I couldn't.'

'Don't be silly, Georgy. I'm only packing.'

She feigned surprise at the labels on his luggage. 'You're not going back already?'

'A man has to earn a living.'

'The trouble with you, Edward, is that you have itchy feet. You can't stay still.'

She was wearing a pale blue dress with a deep sailor collar, complete with three stripes. In admiration for its navy it seemed the whole country was trying to look like jack tars.

She picked up a pair of socks and folded them.

'I don't think I should like Italy. I hear it's very hot and very smelly.'

'Who tells you this?'

'Alexander.'

'Alexander?'

'Father's curate. He says Italy's absolutely filthy. He went to Lugano with Mr Thomas Cook.'

'Lugano's in Switzerland.'

'*Italian* Switzerland. Very like Italy. And he's been to Milan.' She pulled a face. 'I don't know how you can bear to live there.'

Reaching out, Edward pulled her to him and kissed her full on the mouth.

'Edward.'

He kissed her again. Her hand went up as her straw hat was knocked sideways but then her arms were round his neck and her mouth opened to his.

'Edward,' she said as he released her. 'We shouldn't.'

His answer was to caress her breast. She brushed his hand away. He put it back. She pushed it away again. He persisted and this time she resisted no longer. But she was trembling all over.

For a while they wrestled with each other on the edge of the bed, Georgina trying to keep him at a distance.

'Not here,' she whispered. 'Someone will find us.'

'The summer house.'

She didn't argue and, holding his hand, ran with him down the garden. Slamming the door behind them, Edward flung a pile of mattresses to the floor. They stood together for a moment, not touching. Georgina's eyes glowed with a mixture of excitement and fear. Then Edward took her in his arms and they sank to the mattresses, kissing with a passion that seemed almost like despair.

'Edward.'

Edward's fingers fumbled at the buttons of her dress. She gave a murmur of protest as his fingers found her breast but the way her body arched against him told Edward something else. Her hat had fallen off and her hair had come loose and drifted in a blonde cloud about her face.

'Edward,' she panted. 'Do you love me?'

He was too busy fiddling with a difficult button to answer.

'We shouldn't be doing this,' she whispered, her hands now at work on his shirt.

Her dress had ridden up to reveal her long legs encased in white stockings. Her bodice was open to the waist so that her breasts, white and pink-tipped, were soft under his hand.

'Oh, Teddy,' she said. 'Yes. Yes.'

20

Egg was too absorbed in his boats to notice what was going on under his nose, but Aunt Edith was in no doubt. Even though she didn't say anything, certain sharp glances informed Edward that she did not approve, and he made sure to keep out of her way as much as possible.

Georgina did not come back to the house, and sent no message. Driving with Egg to Porthelt, Edward saw her riding through the village on her bicycle, accompanied by the curate. As he stared at them, Egg rambled on about the Foreign Office interview.

'I expect,' he snorted, 'that those toffee-nosed, pea-brained stuffed shirts have ruined more business deals than I've had hot dinners.'

Edward was only half listening, but he did perk up when his uncle started talking about the new boat he was designing.

'Hydroplane,' he said. 'Hard chine. Stepped hull. I expect it to do thirty-five knots even with a load. The navy already have a boat with four Napier engines that reaches thirty knots. But it's over a hundred feet long, which is too big. They'll soon be so big, they'll need smaller boats to escort them. Mine's only forty feet and could carry torpedoes. The trouble is how the hell to launch them.'

'Not over the side, Uncle Egg,' Edward said. 'You'd have to have two, which would reduce the speed. And they'd both have to be fired together. Believe me, I've tried it.'

'It doesn't really matter,' Egg replied. 'Nobody wants to torpedo anybody at the moment, anyway.'

'When will the hydroplane be ready, Uncle Egg?'

'Not yet. There's no rush. Besides, I've another idea – forty-five-foot pinnaces. The Navy'll jump at them. And we have to live off run-of-the-mill boats, my boy, not bright ideas. The time will come for the hydroplanes. But what Bourdillons need now is cash.'

'Try painting 'em a bright colour, Uncle Egg. It worked in Italy.'

'Our lines are something special.'

'You can't see a winning boat's lines at half a mile. But you *can* see the colour. Try yellow. People will call 'em the Yellow Perils but at least they'll be noticed.'

Edward wasn't sorry to take his leave of England. Georgina had stayed away. Her surrender had been complete but she had not sought him out again.

Egg had been wrong about the 45-footers. The original twenty boats were cut to ten. But two of them had been ordered direct from England to be delivered to Venice.

'Who for?' Edward asked.

'Orlandos,' Sam said.

'I don't want to sell to them, Sam. It's charity.'

'It's business,' Sam replied. 'You're not telling me that Rafaela di Orlando would buy anything but the best.'

Edward couldn't argue and telegraphed Egg to send the boats as soon as possible with all instructions, plans and spares. In the meantime, Sam had taken on a fitter-mechanic on a temporary basis so that he could help new owners with any problems.

He was away in Venice when, unexpectedly, Edward was informed by the manager of the hotel he used for lunching possible clients that someone was looking for him.

'He didn't give a name –' the manager looked serious '– but I suspect, Signor Capitano, that he's Turkish.'

'Turkish?'

'The war is over. Turks may now travel in Italy.'

For a day or two Edward went about his business and forgot all about the enquiry when a man called Emil Bodschen wrote requesting a meeting.

They agreed to have lunch at the restaurant at Santa Lucia. Bodschen was a stout, pink-faced man with a thick neck that bulged over his collar. He wore white duck trousers, a striped blazer and a panama hat and seemed to spend most of his time mopping the perspiration from his face.

'You are not an easy man to find, Herr Bourdillon,' he puffed.

Edward smiled. 'I've been away,' he said, and then without more ado, 'I presume you're seeking boats, Herr Bodschen. What did you have in mind exactly?'

Bodschen coughed behind a pudgy hand. 'The sort that sank the *Huda* and forced the *Tahaf* to surrender.'

Edward was silent for a moment.

'I am, of course,' Bodschen continued, 'acting for someone, someone in high places. It would be a substantial contract.'

'Would you care to tell me who you represent?'

'Kabat Pasha.'

'Egyptian?'

'Turk.'

Bodschen presented his card with another for the absent Kabat Pasha. Beneath Kabat Pasha's name were the words, *Société Ottoman, Compagnie Intéressée des Constructions Maritimes (et Arsenaux)*.

Edward pursed his lips.

'The Société Ottoman,' Bodschen explained, 'buys for the Turkish Government. They are interested in your boats.'

'But you are not Turkish.'

'No. Swiss. I come from Romanshorn on Lake Constance.'

Edward nodded.

'Turkey doesn't wish for another fiasco like Libya. And Germany has arranged loans.'

'How many boats do you want, Herr Bodschen?'

'What was your Italian order?'

'Ten.'

'Then I think we would be interested in fifteen. Big nations, Herr Bourdillon, go in for dreadnoughts. Small nations go in for torpedo boats.'

'Would you like a demonstration?'

'We had one.' Bodschen smiled. 'At Arina.'

The sale was arranged and telegrams were sent off to England. It suddenly seemed to Edward that he might be

missing opportunities to make money not only for Bourdillons but also for himself and Sam. He resolved to keep
his eyes open for the main chance when it appeared.

A few days later, he and Sam stopped on the Via Car-
raciola, to watch a boat moving at speed out in the bay.
They knew what it was immediately – a new boat designed
and built by Motoscafo Armato SVAN with Ischotta-
Franschini engines, and considerably faster than the
45-foot Bourdillons. Sam and Edward weren't the only
spectators. A group of expensively dressed men had
alighted from two chauffeur-driven cars, and were watching the display with more than casual interest.

'That's an incredible boat,' one of them said.

'It ought to be,' Edward said loudly. 'It's a Bourdillon.'

The man turned to look at him, but didn't speak.

A few days later they were invited to lunch by a man
who gave his name as Pausanios. So now the Greeks were
interested in doing a deal.

'I don't like it,' Sam said.

'Bourdillons will,' Edward pointed out. 'For God's
sake, Sam, we're not gun-runners. We're selling Uncle
Egg's quick boats. What people do with them is none of
our business.

Boboli hadn't forgotten them either. For his part in the
affair at Arina he had received the Order of the Crown of
Italy and had been pushed up to full general. But he was
aware that he had taken credit that was not rightfully his,
and wished to make amends to Edward.

'I think,' he said, 'that you should get in touch with
King Ferdinand of the Bulgarians.'

Sam and Edward exchanged amused glances.

'He is fascinated by expensive mechanical toys. Loves
motor cars – especially if they are driven by blond, blue-
eyed chauffeurs. He has a collection from half a dozen
countries, electric and petrol-driven. He also has a passion for trains. I believe he also has an aeroplane or two.
I think he might well like one of your boats, especially if
you assure him it's really fast.'

Edward wasted no time in contacting the Bulgarian ambassador in Rome, who agreed immediately to set things in motion.

Back in England, Maurice of all people had come up with a bright idea. Moving pictures had started to entertain thousands and a little flat-footed man with a black moustache, a bowler hat and a cane kept them laughing. America had found a new industry and two-reelers – even longer films these days – drew people together in village halls and cinemas.

Arranging for a camera to be mounted on the deck of a lighter, hatched over and well filled with ballast to keep it stable, Maurice filmed the full range of Egg's boats in bright sunshine as they roared past the cranking cameraman. The wash caused a problem but by shooting only the boats' passing and drawing away before the wash hit the lighter, they were able to produce pictures which, however grainy, spotty and grey, showed clearly what the boats looked like and how fast they went. It was even arranged for a tug, with a known speed, to be passing as one of the 45-footers tore past in a welter of spray.

Edward went to meet his uncle in Switzerland, which he was visiting with Aunt Edith on one of Thomas Cook's tours, and managed to arrange for boats to be available whenever he wanted them.

While in Lucerne, by sheer chance, Edward ran into the man from Lake Maggiore and finally clinched the sale of the 45-footer they had been arguing about for months. It was arranged that the boat would be delivered to Monza by rail. After that it would be up to the new owner to get it to the lake. Since the man owned a huge engineering works in Milan, Edward didn't think this would produce any problems.

The contracts with Italy, Turkey and Greece delighted Egg. 'We've taken on extra men,' he said, 'and opened new premises. We bought out the corn chandlers next door and acquired two barns from the farm beyond.'

They celebrated that night with a five-course dinner at Egg's hotel. Aunt Edith, pink-cheeked from a trip to Mount Pilatus, was keen to relay the news from England to her nephew.

'Georgina always asks after you,' she said, 'You should write to her, Edward. You didn't even say goodbye.'

Later that night, after his uncle and aunt had gone to bed, Edward stopped in the bar for a nightcap and got talking to a South African who had made a fortune in diamonds. Having once been a sailor, it appeared he had been unable to endure life 500 miles from the sea in Kimberley and had invested his money in a whaling fleet which was operating from a place called Saldanha.

'I know it,' Edward said.

'You're the only bugger I ever met who did,' the South African said. 'If it only had drinking water it would be a better port than Cape Town. How'd you come to be there?'

'Sailing ship, *Culloden*. I was deckhand aboard her. I swopped her for the *George V. Cotterill*, which was wrecked off Messina in 1908.'

'The year of the earthquake. I remember. Seventy-five thousand dead in Messina alone!'

The South African ordered fresh drinks and started to talk enthusiastically of his whalers. 'Based at Langebaan. It's at the end of a long lagoon. Goes for miles. They say it's no good but that's a load of kak. I've often thought of building a house there. At the moment there's nothing but a few fishermen's cottages. Black fellers. It would be handy for the whaling station. But it's too goddam far.'

'Why not use a boat?' Edward suggested. 'A fast boat.'

'Where would I get a boat that fast?'

Edward smiled. 'I could sell you one. Is money any object?'

'None at all. Where is this boat?'

'Naples. Does your European tour cover Naples?'

'It does now. What is she?'

'A Bourdillon. Forty-five feet. Capable of twenty-five to thirty knots. Slim hull. Good sea boat. Can carry eight. You'd need a cabin, but that could be built on for you.'

'Dammit, I own a bloody whaling station. It's full of bloody boat-builders. Look, you must meet the family.'

'The name's Bourdillon. Edward Dante Bourdillon.'

They shook hands.

141

'Leroux,' the South African said. 'Frederic Leroux. Call me Fricky. Bit of French in me. Bit of Dutch. Bit of God knows what. My wife's up a mountain somewhere with the rest of the family. I suppose they'll come down eventually. Have dinner with us tomorrow night.'

'Uncle Egg,' Edward said. 'I need banking facilities here in Switzerland.'

'Good God, boy, why?'

'It's ridiculous telegraphing home every time I need money.'

Egg still looked dubious.

'Uncle Egg, I've done some things in my life you didn't approve of. Sinking *Fairy* was one. Perhaps going to sea was another.' Perhaps Georgina would have been a third, he thought. 'But,' he went on, 'I've never cheated you.'

'More than I can say for Maurice.' Egg frowned. 'What's in your mind?'

'I need money for expenses. For Sam. To pay for the premises we hired. To pay for the carpenter-boatbuilder and the fitter-mechanic. I can't wait for monthly cheques. I need an account here on the Continent I can draw on and pay into, linked to Bourdillons' account in England. We're into big business suddenly and Switzerland's a good central place with excellent banking facilities. We're selling to Turkey and Greece now but I don't want to carry a cheque or a bank draft around with me until I return to Naples or to England. I want you to arrange facilities with a reputable bank so I can use them wherever I happen to be. Whether it's Naples or Paris or Berlin or Dubrovnik or Vienna.'

'Are you seriously expecting to be selling boats in those places?'

'The world's wide open, Uncle Egg. I think I've just sold one in South Africa.'

Egg was thoughtful. 'Ought we to be building bigger craft?' he asked. 'Torpedo-boat destroyers, for instance.'

'You haven't room, Uncle Egg.'

'Well, why don't we buy *more* room?'

'In the river?'

'It's got to be a sea frontage,' he said. 'At Southampton or Portsmouth. Somewhere like that. Keep the place we've got for building small craft. Pinnaces. Tenders. Launches. We can afford it, my boy. I'll go into it with Maurice.'

'He's not exactly my favourite cousin, as you know, but why not let Maurice run things, Uncle Egg, so you can concentrate on design? You can't really do both.'

Egg patted his hand. 'I'll think very seriously about it, I promise.'

The next day they went together to see the Swiss Banking Corporation of Basle. Egg produced documents to prove his identity and the bank spent the rest of the day checking them. That evening a message was waiting for them at the hotel. 'Facilities available for Bourdillons.'

Edward grinned at his uncle. 'Now I can go to dinner with Fricky Leroux with an easy conscience,' he said.

When he returned to the hotel after seeing Egg and Aunt Edith off at the station, Edward found a tall cold-eyed man waiting in the lounge for him.

'Venturi,' he said. 'Vittorio Venturi. I am from Ticino, Italian Switzerland. I have heard of you, Signor Bordilloni.'

'Good,' said Edward. 'How may I be of help?'

'I am interested in your boats.'

Edward was puzzled. He had been selling chiefly to navies and Switzerland was landlocked.

'Switzerland is not just a land of mountains,' Venturi read his mind. 'She has lakes. Four of them have common frontiers with other countries. We need to see they are well patrolled. We don't expect our neighbours to attack us. However, we do need to patrol the border down the centre of the lakes. For smugglers. We are thinking of several boats. I assume for more than one the price would be reduced. And that if there were any hold-up, you would forfeit some of the price as a compensation for the delay.'

Edward was reminded why the Swiss were considered such good businessmen.

'How do you see my idea, Signor Bordilloni?'

Edward smiled. 'I see it very clearly, Signor Venturi. And the name, by the way, is Bourdillon.'

Leroux's wife was a slim good-looking woman with thick blonde hair. The 'family' comprised one member, a daughter, Kristiana.

'We call her Krissie,' Leroux said. 'My son Trompie's not here. He's holding the fort till we get home.'

Krissie Leroux was slender and blonde like her mother, and possessed a wide smile and violet eyes. She showed some interest in the plans that were spread between the coffee cups after dinner, but began to get fidgety as her father fussed over details.

'When can you deliver?' Leroux asked, eventually.

'Directly. To your own slip at Saldanha Bay. We can also arrange for someone to be there with her if you wish.'

'Ag, man, we don't need experts. I've got a dozen of my own. Send us a manual and the plans and we can handle it.'

When they discussed prices, Leroux suddenly said, 'You're a bit young, man, aren't you, to be handling goods at those figures. You can't be much older than my daughter, here.'

'My age is no barrier to experience,' Edward replied, vaguely irritated.

It was at this point that Krissie joined in. 'Hey, Pa,' she said. 'Sometimes you are slow. This is *the* Edward Bourdillon.'

'Which Edward Bourdillon?'

'The small boat expert. The Edward Bourdillon who sank that Turkish ammunition ship.'

'With a Bourdillon 45,' Edward added. 'Same boat I'm offering you, Mr Leroux.'

It didn't take much longer to shake hands on a deal.

As midnight approached, Leroux rose, scooping up the papers to study later. His wife had long since grown bored and vanished.

'Krissie?'

'I'll stay here a bit, Pa.'

Leroux kissed her and headed for the stairs.

'I've had more than enough of boats for today,' Krissie said. 'I went on an endless dreary steamer trip down the lake. I think I'd like a bit of terra firma for a change. Do you fancy some fresh air?'

They walked for a while in silence, then Krissie slipped her arm through his and steered him to a patch of deep shadow under the trees. When he kissed her, she kissed him back enthusiastically.

'Hey, man,' she said. 'It's too damn cold here. I've never understood why people go barmy over Switzerland. When it isn't snowing it's raining. I have some booze in the hotel. Let's go back there.'

There was no nonsense about Krissie Leroux. Back in the room she offered him a drink he didn't have time to swallow, and started taking her clothes off.

'Why don't you come to Cape Town?' she asked as she nestled close to him afterwards. 'Sell a boat or two down there. And spend some time with me.'

Edward kissed her forehead, and ran his hands through her luxuriant hair. 'I've been to Cape Town,' he said.

'Where did you stay? The Mount Nelson?'

'Not exactly. The Missions to Seamen.'

'If you came back with us, Pa would find you a job, I know he would.'

'Not if he knew about this, he wouldn't.'

When the Leroux family left for England, Edward headed for Naples, reflecting that there was another side to selling boats that could be very exciting, and sometimes exhausting.

Sam was still lying low while Rosina and her sister made up their minds which of them was more interested in him. But the Bulgarian ambassador in Rome had some positive news.

'His Majesty,' he informed Edward, 'has a seaside villa near Varna. He feels a boat could be very useful when he's there.'

'What would he use it for?' Edward asked. 'Fishing?'

The ambassador wrinkled his nose. 'King Ferdinand does not fish.'

'What does he do?'

'He amuses himself. His Majesty finds it a most amusing idea to drive himself from his palace in Sofia to the station, then drive himself by train to the coast, and finally drive or steer, or whatever people do, to Varna. He regrets the delay in letting you know but matters are extremely delicate at the moment.'

Edward looked sideways at the ambassador. Something was definitely in the wind. The nations of Europe were on edge. France was worried about Germany. The Germans were envious of Britain and nervous of Russia. Russia was seething with discontent. Italy was itching to prove herself. And newspapers had been calling the Balkans the powder keg.

The ambassador smiled. 'There will be no war I can assure you. The King would not be contemplating buying anything so expensive as a fleet of boats if there were a danger of war.'

'A *fleet* of boats?' Edward's heart leapt.

'Why not? He has a fleet of motor cars.'

Returning to England, Edward found the boats couldn't be ready for Bulgaria before the end of the month, so he concentrated on seeing the boat Leroux had bought prepared for its journey from Southampton to Cape Town. Shipping boats had become almost second nature by this time.

There was plenty to do and he cabled Sam that he was staying in England until he could see the King of Bulgaria's boats off, and would then take the train to Naples to be there when they arrived. The only ship he had been able to find which was going anywhere near the Black Sea was a small French freighter called the *Maréchal MacMahon* carrying mules and other assorted cargo. It was due in at Southampton in a month's time from South America and would be loading its extra cargo before leaving for Naples, Taranto, Athens, Smyrna in Turkey, Istanbul and Batum before doubling back and touching Bulgaria at Varna.

'Why can't she go to Varna immediately after Istanbul and then go to Batum, which is at the other side of the Black Sea?' Edward asked.

'Because,' the clerk pointed out, 'what we've loaded for Varna is underneath what we've loaded for Batum so that the Batum cargo – the mules – must be unloaded first.'

'Why the hell don't you load the other way round?'

The clerk sniffed. 'We take cargoes as they come. If a cargo arrives, we take it, before it goes to someone else. We then have to follow the routes they dictate. There's no choice. Not if you want to stay in business. Your boats will have to go as deck cargo, which means that at Batum they'll have to be unloaded. They will then be reloaded for the ship to proceed to Varna.'

'Then so be it,' said Edward, shaking his head.

The next day he borrowed Egg's car to go and see Georgina. The ghastly curate was just leaving and he smiled thinly at Edward. Georgina looked rather flustered and Edward wondered what on earth they had been up to. The Vicar was attending a meeting at Porthelt and his wife was visiting sick relatives in Plymouth. There was only the maid in and she was in the kitchen with what Georgina called 'her follower'.

'Come upstairs,' she said skittishly, and was unbuttoning her blouse as soon as the door shut behind them.

'Georgina,' Edward said as they combed their hair and smoothed themselves out. 'All this sneaking about is ridiculous. I can't relax. You're terrified the maid will walk in. Come away with me.'

'Come away? Where to?'

'A hotel, for God's sake. Other people do.'

'Where could we go?'

'Have you any friends who'd swear you'd spent the night with them?'

'Mother's coming back tomorrow morning. I can arrange to go to my ancient aunt's the day afterwards. I can't stay there because the house is too small so I can arrange to spend the night at the George in Exeter. You could meet me there.'

Two days later, announcing he was off to Exeter to see Sam's sister, Edward took the train west. He spotted Georgina at the other end of the platform, half-hidden by steam. She was dressed in her favourite blue. He pretended not to notice her but changed compartments as the train stopped at Bournemouth.

For safety, they ate at a different hotel, having first surveyed the scene to make sure there was no-one there who could possibly know them. Georgina drank more wine than Edward believed she could and was a little light-headed as they rode in a cab to the George. Dropping her at the door, Edward rode the cab a few hundred yards down the road, where he dismissed it and walked back to the hotel.

Georgina flew into his arms, when he walked into her room. 'This isn't something I make a habit of,' she said, as they paused for breath. 'I think we're being very wicked.'

He kissed her hard on the lips. There was a new-found experience in the way her mouth and tongue moved against his, in the ease with which she divested herself of her clothing, the eagerness with which she wrenched at his shirt, even the way she moved against him.

'Can't we telegraph your parents that you have to stay another day?' Edward nipped her gently on the ear.

'It won't be necessary,' she said. 'They already think I'm going to visit Stonehenge on the way back. It's something Father's always saying I should do. So now I'll do it. We can stay at a little hotel in Salisbury I know of.'

He looked at her curiously.

'A friend of mine stayed there,' she said. 'A friend from school.'

The Pheasant in Salisbury was smaller and more rudimentary than the George, but it seemed clean and the clerk's expression didn't flicker when Edward asked for a double room.

A group of farmers fresh from the market and full of drink suddenly spilled into Reception, and the two lovers beat a hasty retreat. Slamming the door behind them, they kissed hungrily, before falling heavily across the bed. The giggles lasted only for a minute before they became silent.

They ate quietly in the hotel dining room, while the farmers guffawed, glugged and drank themselves even sillier. Afterwards, arm-in-arm, Edward and Georgina walked together through the centre of town as darkness fell. Edward felt proud and possessive because heads turned to look at her. He even wondered if he should suggest they get married. But her chatter was light and bubbling, and Edward opted for caution. Marriage was a big step – one that Sam, who was more experienced, was obviously hesitant to take. Edward felt too young to die.

They had a glass of Armagnac in the bar, sitting close together in a corner in the shadows before retiring to their room. A couple of farmers were left, glazed and sleepy. To his surprise, Georgina suggested another drink. Edward was surprised, and assumed that perhaps Georgina had acquired the taste for brandy from the occasional nip from the medicine cupboard, when the boredom at the Vicarage was too much to bear.

As he slid the bolt home in their room, Georgina fell into his arms. The drink seemed to have smoothed away any lingering inhibitions. Georgina made love with lascivious abandon. And later Edward found himself saying, 'Georgy. Why don't we get married?'

'Good God, why?' she murmured sleepily.

He didn't persist.

Paying the bill next morning, Edward asked for a cab to be called.

'Oh, by the way sir,' said the clerk. 'You forgot to sign the register. Perhaps you'd be kind enough to do it now.'

Edward momentarily was flummoxed. Mr and Mrs John Smith was the best he could come up with. He decided to be an accountant and to live in Yeovil. And while the clerk's attention was distracted by an inquiry from a very pale and bloodshot farmer, Edward flipped idly through the register, wondering how many other Smiths had spent the night there.

There was at least one. His home was claimed to be Ely and his profession was given as publisher. Slamming the book shut, Edward picked up his bag and headed for the door. The cab had arrived and, tipping the boy, he climbed in after Georgina and they drove to the station together.

Edward hadn't the slightest doubt who John Smith, publisher, of Ely, was. The signature and the writing were full of ostentatious curlicues. It was equally clear who Mrs Smith had been.

22

The Bulgarian Embassy was in a large house in a side street in Kensington. Like the Embassy in Rome, it was full of pictures of Bulgarian peasants in fezzes and what Edward had learned were called 'crap-catcher' trousers.

The ambassador kept him waiting but was informative enough when he was finally shown in. 'The problem is Macedonia,' he said. 'Its borders touch Albania, Greece, Bulgaria and Montenegro, which creates a volatile mix of people. Yet it belongs to Turkey.' He cleared his throat. 'Greece, Serbia and Montenegro have allied themselves with our country and are already driving the Turks out of Thrace. The war will be over soon and there is no reason whatsoever why the King should not buy your boats. I would recommend that you proceed as planned.'

It seemed risky but, after a conference with Egg and Maurice, it was decided to go ahead as the ambassador advised.

'If Ferdinand turns them down,' Maurice added, 'you can always sell them to some millionaire in Monte Carlo.'

'Are we selling them as war equipment?' Edward asked. 'Because, if we are, the Turks are going to have something to say about that. To get them to Bulgaria we have to go through the Dardanelles and the Bosporus, all Turkish territory. They could seize them.'

'Why not go by rail through Austria.'

'Austria's opposed to Serbia establishing herself on the Adriatic,' Edward pointed out. 'She'll think the boats are for use against her.'

'Russia?'

'Russia's opposed to Bulgaria controlling the Sea of Marmara.'

'My, aren't we the little expert,' Maurice sneered.

151

Edward ignored him. 'We'll go via Batum as planned,' he said. 'It'll be all right.'

There were still over three weeks to go and Edward saw Leroux's boat off to Cape Town on the deck of a freighter. He still seethed about Georgina. The thought that she had been in the same hotel, probably in the same room, even the same bed, with Owen-Smith infuriated him. But he was besotted, and wanted desperately to see her again.

Nobody answered his knock, and the door was unlocked. Edward walked into the hall.

'Let me go!' It was Augusta's voice.

He saw her jammed in the corner at the foot of the stairs and struggling with a man. Edward yanked him away, and hurled him against the wall. It was Owen-Smith.

Edward didn't hesitate. He grabbed hold of the curate, dragged him down the hallway and flung him out into the drive.

'If I find you round here again,' he yelled, 'I'll break your neck.'

Pale and wild-eyed, Owen-Smith picked himself up. 'My hat –'

Augusta handed it to Edward who walked over to the curate, slapped him twice round the face with the hat, then dropped it to the ground. As Owen-Smith bent to pick it up, Edward gave him the benefit of a boot up the backside.

'I'm not sure if you can forbid him the house,' said Augusta, having got her breath back in the living room. 'After all, he is father's curate!'

They both laughed.

'I expect you've come to see Georgina.'

Suddenly, Edward wasn't so sure he had. He wasn't even sure he could face that knowing half-smile she put on that made him feel like a schoolboy again.

'It's just as well. She's gone to London. She'll be home later.'

'As a matter of fact,' Edward blurted out, 'I came to see you. We haven't talked for ages. I wondered how you were.'

152

'I'm fine. I have a job if I want it. In London. But I have a feeling it'll be harder than I expected. The rules about nurses seem very inhibiting. One half-day a week. In at night by ten o'clock. No followers. I like that word "followers". It sounds so innocent, but they clearly think followers *aren't* innocent at all. How do they expect girls to go in for nursing when they place so many restrictions on them? Would you like some tea, Teddy? I offered Mr Owen-Smith a sherry. I think it must have gone to his head a little.'

'You're pretty, Gussie.'

'Thank you, Teddy. And thank you for saving me.'

'From a fate worse than death?'

'Well, he *was* getting a bit hot under the collar.'

It was as though Edward was seeing her for the first time. He admired her spirit, and couldn't understand why he hadn't noticed before how beautiful she was.

'Will you marry me, Gussie?' he found himself saying.

She stared at him with her huge eyes. 'Me, Teddy?'

'Why not? We've known each other all our lives.'

'I always thought it was Georgina you were after.'

'It was.' He paused. 'Once. But I don't think she's interested in me.'

'So you thought you'd try someone else . . .'

'I didn't mean it like that,' he said, feeling hot with embarrassment. 'I thought I was in love with your sister. But I was wrong. I've been a fool.'

There was an awkward pause. 'So what do you think, Gussie. Will *you* marry me?'

'Oh Teddy! I've adored you all my life. You must have known.'

'Yes, I suppose I did.'

She took his hands. 'Oh, Teddy! Dearest Teddy. Don't you think we ought to kiss each other?'

'Do you mean you will?'

'Yes, Teddy. Yes, I will.'

He kissed her on the lips and found it curiously satisfying.

'We'll need at least three weeks for the banns to be called.'

'We could do it by special licence.'

'Don't be so cruel. This will be Mother's day and she'll want to make something of it.'

'It'll be your day, too.'

'But you have made my dreams come true today.'

'I don't deserve you,' Edward said. 'But we can't hang about. I have to go to Bulgaria in three weeks.'

'I'll come with you.'

He kissed her again. 'Not this time, Gussie,' he said gently. 'There's already been fighting out there. It's no place for a woman. But I have to go. I seem to have sold a couple of boats to the King of Bulgaria.'

The Vicar and his wife *were* startled, but not disappointed. Augusta, they had considered, was going to be more difficult to marry off than the luscious Georgina who already had hordes of admirers.

'Isn't Gussie a bit young, though?' the Vicar asked.

'Father, I'm nineteen.'

'I always thought –' the Vicar's wife began, then she stopped and managed a nervous smile. The slender boy she had known was now a man, determined, self-possessed – even, she thought, just a touch piratical.

'Very well,' she said. 'We can arrange it for next spring.'

'Not next spring,' Edward said quietly. 'I don't know where I'll be by then.'

'Autumn then.'

'Too late.'

The Vicar's wife looked both startled and annoyed.

'We have to do it in three weeks' time.'

'Augusta, you aren't –?'

Augusta smiled. 'No, Mother, I'm not.'

'But three weeks. People will talk.'

'Let them,' Edward said.

'They'll think.'

'Let them.'

'It just can't be done,' the Vicar said. 'I would hope to have the Bishop perform the ceremony. He's an old friend and I'm sure he would wish to. I would assist, of course. And Alexander will have to be there to help –'

'If that bloody man comes within a mile of the church,' Edward said savagely, 'I'll . . .'

154

The Vicar went purple and his wife sagged faintly back on the settee.

'And what, pray, has Alexander done to make you take this outrageous view?' the Vicar asked.

'Never mind what he's done,' Edward said. 'But if we can't get married here without that toad being present, then we'll get married somewhere else.'

'Augusta,' the Vicar said, trying to keep his temper under control, 'what have you got to say?'

'I agree with Edward,' she said, in a small uncertain voice.

'He'll be most disappointed.'

'Good,' Edward said. 'But I don't think he'll raise any objections when you let him know.'

Suddenly Georgina was in the doorway. She was dressed in blue as usual and looked beautiful enough to melt ice. She had obviously heard everything as she took off her hat and gloves in the hall.

'Good old Gussie,' she said cheerfully. 'What a clever girl you are.'

'They're going to get married,' her mother wailed. 'In three weeks. Can't you do anything to dissuade them?'

'Knowing Ned, I doubt it. And I'm not going to try. I think they're very wise not to delay.' Georgina crossed to her sister and, putting her arms round her, hugged her. 'You clever girl,' Edward heard her whisper. 'Don't let him go. And don't take a bit of notice of Mother and Father.'

Augusta kissed her warmly for her honesty and Georgina crossed to Edward.

'Well done, Ned,' she said softly as she kissed him. 'You've got a much better bargain in Gussie, you know.'

The marriage service was performed by the Vicar three weeks later. There was no Bishop.

The reception was small and held at the Vicarage. Because of the hurry, there were few relatives and, apart from Egg, Aunt Edith and Maurice, not many people from the village. Alexander Owen-Smith was conspicuous by his absence.

They went to London for the honeymoon, arriving in the late afternoon and spending the evening at a show.

Afterwards Edward couldn't recall what it was because he spent the entire three acts deep in thought, tinglingly aware that he'd had a very narrow escape. Marriage to Georgina would have been a hell of continual worry and uncertainty.

Back at the hotel, the desk clerk handed Edward a telegram. It consisted of just four words. *'Congratulations, dearest Edward. Rafaela.'*

He wondered how she had got to know but then Orlandos had their agents everywhere. Someone must have seen the announcement in *The Times* and passed it on to her.

'Who's it from, Edward?'

'A friend in Italy,' he said. 'Her family took me in when the *George V. Cotterill* was wrecked. She and her mother were the only two in her family to survive the earthquake.'

'Were you in love with her, Teddy? Tell me, I shan't mind.'

'No,' he replied, though he wasn't sure he was telling the truth. 'The family were very kind to me and I did what I could to help. She's worth a great deal of money. Far too important to be interested in me.'

In their room, she studied him. 'Teddy,' she whispered. 'Do you regret what we've done?'

'Not for a minute, Gussie.'

He didn't need a drink but he was aware that formalities had to be observed and it was usual to allow the bride time to prepare. He felt curiously nervous, all thumbs and elbows. 'I'll just pop downstairs,' he said. 'I'll be back in a minute.'

Augusta gave him a little smile. 'I shall be waiting for you,' she said.

Heart beating, Edward sat in the reading room trying to absorb the newspaper. The trouble in the Balkans seemed to be increasing. The Greeks, Serbians, Montenegrins and Bulgarians seemed to be organising themselves very effectively. In Edward's mind it could only be for all-out war. It was time he headed back to the Mediterranean.

When he reached their room, Augusta was in bed and he crossed to the bathroom without really looking at her while she avoided his eyes by ostentatiously seeking a handkerchief from the bedside table. He noticed she was wearing a nightdress with a frill at the neck and that her hair was neatly brushed.

Cleaning his teeth at the washbasin, he stared at himself in the mirror, and found himself thinking of Rafaela again. It was as though time stood still and he was listening to her voice, seeing the line of her figure, and her face with its proud nose, the fierce dark eyes.

'Damn it,' he said out loud.

He was surprised to find the light was still on in the bedroom because he'd always understood that new wives liked to meet their husbands in bed for the first time in darkness.

Gussie looked as innocent as a child about to say her catechism.

She lifted her arms to him. 'Come along, Edward,' she whispered. 'I expect you know what to do.'

Gussie went with him to London to see him off on the boat train at Victoria. She had changed. Even in four days she had gained assurance and confidence, and she looked stunning in green with a feathered toque on her head.

They talked by the open door of the compartment as if they'd been married for years.

'I shall be back within a month,' Edward said.

'Will you take me to Bulgaria later when things have quietened down?'

'Of course I will.'

The guard came along the platform, making sure the carriage doors were all closed. Taking Gussie in his arms, Edward held her for a long time, then kissed her and turned away abruptly.

'I love you, Edward,' he heard her say.

23

The platform at Naples was crammed with people clutching suitcases. Even before the train had stopped, they began to scramble aboard, watched by a group of Italian police, caps tipped forward over their eyes, faces expressionless.

Edward found himself struggling against a dozen people trying to get in. In the second-class compartments, they were shouting and cursing, pushing children through windows and yelling at them to find places.

As he burst out of the door, he almost fell into Sam's arms.

'Welcome to Bedlam!' shouted Sam, his face covered in perspiration. 'Come on. I need a drink, even if you don't.'

'Well?' said Edward, when they had found a table in the first-class buffet.

But Sam refused to say anything until the waiter had served them. 'Guess what?' he said. 'I got married.'

'Teresa?'

'No, Rosina. She made most fuss about me going to Bulgaria. Teresa didn't seem bothered so I decided Rosina was the one who was interested. I'm enjoying it, Ted.'

Edward stared back at him, grinning. 'You might have waited until I got back,' he said.

'Rosie wanted to get on with it. The whole family was there. And after all it was me that was marrying her, not you. It was like a madhouse. About two million relatives, all crammed into the apartment. You couldn't move. There's another party tonight, now you're back.'

It was Edward's turn to look sheepish. 'Well, it doesn't matter, Sam. In fact, it's fair enough because I didn't wait either. I got married too.'

'Who?'

'Gussie.'

'This calls for another drink.' Sam signalled the waiter. 'I thought you were after the other one.'

'So did I.'

The two friends grasped hands warmly, then toasted each other with another glass of wine.

The toasts continued at the della Stradas. And the party seemed to include the whole street. Next morning, holding their heads, Sam and Edward tried to brief the family on what to do while they were away.

The *Maréchal MacMahon* arrived the following week. She had not run into any bad weather, but Edward and Sam insisted on examining the boats and crates. The French captain watched them with disgust written all over his face.

'You think I cannot look after my cargo?' he said.

To get at the hatches, the boats had to be lowered to the quayside and the crates containing tinplate and galvanised ware from Birmingham were hoisted out. Anxiously, they watched the boats hoisted back again two days later and lashed in place on the deck.

The ship stank of the mules she was carrying so they decided to eat ashore and join her at the last minute before she sailed.

They ate *cozze*, Taranto's celebrated large mussel, for dinner, and, aware they were heading into the unknown, drank rather too much wine. When they awoke next morning the ship was at sea.

After the sophisticated bustle at Athens, Smyrna was a warren of mud-brick houses, huddled lattice to lattice and roof upon roof amid winding precipitous lanes. Churches, mosques and houses were silhouetted against the sky in a higgledy-piggledy pattern.

Passing through the Dardanelles, they gazed at dilapidated farms, outhouses and rickety buildings, and in Gallipoli were treated to a vision of the biggest-breeched, longest-bearded, dirtiest, most stately old Turks in the Ottoman Empire, all smoking pipes as they sat on wooden platforms along the water's edge. The bazaars were full of men in shawl turbans, flowing fur-lined coats and bright sashes, in which were stuck silver-sheathed daggers and ornamented pistols. The women looked for all the world like bundles of washing set on top of yellow boots. Screw steamers, paddle vessels, barques and Mediterranean caiques bobbed in the filthy water of the harbour.

The *Maréchal MacMahon* anchored off Scutari. The town looked enchanting with a fairytale prospect of domes, minarets and pink-painted houses, their balconies covered with flowers and creepers. But when they went ashore they found the harbour choked with refuse that stank to high heaven. When the *Maréchal MacMahon's* boat ground on to a beach, gaunt dogs prowled about them, sniffing the debris along the waterline. The houses that had looked like pink sugar cake from the sea turned out to be windowless and filthy. The streets were rutted and rats, quite unconcerned, ran among stinking puddles of oily water. They were glad to get back to the ship.

Constantinople rose in spectacular terraces with a skyline of domes, snow-white minarets, golden cupolas, coloured walls, gable-ends and intricately carved roofs. But the streets were as narrow, fly-ridden and smelly as those in Scutari.

There was another long delay because once again the boats had to be hoisted to the quayside. Sam and Edward decided to take a horse-drawn taxi to a hotel in the European section of the city.

At dinner they found themselves sitting next to a beautiful blonde woman, who turned out to be Russian. She smoked cigarettes in a long amber holder, complained about the food and was clearly interested in Edward.

But their meal was rudely interrupted by a man in a fez and wide breeches.

'Are you the owners of the two boats on the quayside?' he demanded in English.

They could not deny it.

'Please accompany me.'

A carriage took them across the city to a large pink-painted building. It looked like a police station. Men with rifles balanced on their knees sat around the entrance hall.

Beyond the hall a colonnade enclosed a paved court like a cloister with a small square pond in the centre. The pillars were striped in twists of pink and yellow. Above the capitals the walls rose in arched ribs to a roof of carved and gilded wood. Pink jewel-like lamps glowed on the walls.

They passed through a maze of dimly-lit corridors until they reached a large room where a man smoking a hookah at an ornate desk rose to meet them. He spoke in French.

'You are –' he glanced at a paper in front of him '– Messieurs Bor– Bourdillon and Nan–' like everyone else he stumbled over the name '– Nankidno.'

They agreed they were.

'The owners of the boats on the quay. Bound for Batum.'

'Yes.'

'Are they naval boats?'

It was easy to see where the questions were leading. 'No,' Edward said.

'Are they designed to carry weapons?'

'They're pleasure boats.'

'Can weapons be carried on them?'

'That would make them top heavy.'

'Are they fast?'

'Very.' Edward was praying that the man behind the desk was no sailor and hadn't been serving in Arina at the time of the *Tahaf* and *Huda* incident.

'They could be put to naval use?'

'Every boat in the world could be put to naval use. Providing enough hard work and money were spent on them.'

'They are not men-of-war?'

'No.'

'Your customer?'

Edward and Maurice had thought of that one way back in England and fixed the advice note accordingly. 'Someone called Nabat. He may not, of course, buy the boats. We've come to demonstrate them.'

'His nationality?'

'Turkish, I believe.'

The two officials exchanged looks and it was clear what they were thinking. If the Turkish government found it necessary to have the boats, Nabat, as a good Turk, would be expected to hand them over.

The man behind the desk scribbled something on a piece of paper and handed it to Edward. 'Very well,' he said. 'You may go.'

'And the boats?'

'They may go, too.'

They were down at the docks early next morning on nervous look-out for Turkish officials or soldiers but no one came near them. When the *Maréchal MacMahon* left, the stink of the mules was worse than ever. Rain began to fall heavily and for four days the ship drove through a storm that kept them below decks. The bunks felt harder and more lumpy with every day and the stench grew so bad that they tasted mule with every meal they ate. Even on deck in the shrieking wind they breathed mule. They were surprised one evening to be invited to dinner by the Captain, who seemed to have mellowed in his attitude towards his English passengers. He was very free with the wine and the brandy, but nothing could blot out the smell.

'The mules are dying,' he said. 'And one of the muleteers who came with them has gone, too. Typhus.'

Batum stank of the waste from the oil refineries and the sky was choked with cloud. As soon as they arrived a launch appeared alongside the ship and the Captain was informed they were to be held in quarantine. There was malaria and cholera in the town.

They remained in Batum for two dreadful weeks. It poured with rain the whole time. There was nothing to read except Russian newspapers, and nothing to do.

Eventually, permission to continue was granted and, with the captain in a sulphurous temper, they headed north with a new cargo of drums of oil, citrus fruits and tea for the ports of Sebastopol and Odessa.

Their first sight of Russia was of the sheer cliffs of Balaclava.

A pilot was waiting to take them round Cape Khersonese into port by the naval base of Sebastopol. White houses gleamed in the sunshine and bells were ringing in the warm air.

'This is more like it,' said Sam.

As the deck cargo was lifted ashore, a fast, green-painted launch appeared alongside. It was long and low like the Bourdillons, but with a high cabin that ruined its lines. The man at the helm requested permission to come aboard.

'Pavel Ivanovitch, Count Khamlukin,' he introduced himself in excellent English. 'Russian Imperial Navy. My father is Admiral Count Khamlukin. I was admiring your boats. Would they carry torpedoes?'

'They've been used very satisfactorily,' Edward pointed out. 'One like these sank the Turkish *Huda* at Arina.'

Khamlukin nodded. 'Do they carry armour plate?'

'No.'

'Why not?'

'They're intended to be fast. The weight would slow them down.'

'How fast *are* they?'

'Thirty knots.'

'I presume such boats are for sale to anyone?'

'Of course.'

'Where will you put them in the water?'

'Varna.'

'I should like to see them perform.'

They removed the tarpaulins and allowed Khamlukin to climb into one of the boats.

'Bourdillon Mark III,' Sam said.

'Excellent,' Khamlukin said. 'But little comfort for the officers.'

'They're not built for comfort.'

Khamlukin smiled. 'For Russian officers, comfort is essential. Perhaps we ought to try your boat against mine.'

'With pleasure,' said Edward.

'As it happens, I am on the point of negotiating for a flotilla for the Imperial navy. If yours is faster, I could be persuaded to take them.'

Despite Khamlukin's smile and friendly manner, there was something about him that made Edward suspicious. But he was happy to accept the challenge if it meant another sale.

24

To the undisguised delight of the captain, the two boats were lowered into the water at Varna. The port itself was small, with a shipyard and workshops set at the end of a long bay.

Sam and Edward spent about fifteen minutes, checking that everything was in order, and were surprised to be hailed from a steam launch by someone with a strong Scots accent. The man wore what appeared to be a cross between Scottish and Bulgarian native dress. With baggy Balkan trousers and a red embroidered waistcoat, he sported a navy blue pin-stripe jacket. On his stomach was a watch chain strong enough to hold a bull and on his head was a Balmoral bonnet with a red bobble and tossing ribbons.

'The name's McClumpha,' he said cheerfully. 'Jock McClumpha.'

He said he was in business in Varna exporting lead and tin. He had a small fleet of coasters and owned a small shipyard at Burgas, south of Varna. He was also the British Consul, was married to a Bulgarian girl, and had two daughters. 'Fiona an' Rhadka. Fiona after ma mither. Rhadka after ma wife's. You must come home with me and meet them all.' Home was a low white building with red-tiled roofs and extensive grounds, called Khouton McClumpha.

His wife was a dark-eyed shapeless woman in native dress. Fiona and Rhadka, just growing into womanhood, were both doe-eyed and spoke English with a strong Scots accent. Sam gave Edward a huge wink. 'I think I'm going to like it here,' he said.

McClumpha insisted that they stay for as long as they wanted. He was blunt, warm-hearted and honest. He didn't like King Ferdinand. And he didn't care much for Khamlukin either.

Varna was quite a change from Naples. There were storks' nests in the trees, and eagles, kites and vultures wheeled in the sky over the thin green poplars that lined the dusty white roads.

The area was rich in vegetation. There were valleys of roses, with hazel, chestnut and walnut trees everywhere. The fields and woods were full of foxes, deer, wildcat, boar, squirrels, snakes and, so McClumpha said, even an occasional bear. Inland was a huge lake which echoed each night with the croaking of frogs which seemed to inhabit every garden and every scrap of waste ground.

The main street looked like a wide drain and its smell was reminiscent of the *Maréchal MacMahon*. But geraniums, begonias, roses, tall grass, butterflies and dragonflies offset the squalor, as did the fruit and hop gardens, the clinging vines and cherry trees.

The streets were cobbled, and in the square was a dilapidated fountain full of floating leaves where old men washed their feet and read the Koran. One street formed an Eastern bazaar and the domes of Turkish mosques rose decoratively above the houses. Most of the Bulgarians looked like bandits in sheepskin caps and suits of coarse yellow frieze, and at the lower end of the town, somewhat battered by Turkish shells, was a collection of huts occupied by gypsies, their hair glistening like black snakes. There was a town hall, a hospital, inns, a clock tower and Turkish and Bulgarian schools where *Oliveri Tvisti*, by Carolus Dickens, was popular reading.

It was like being transported back to an earlier century, with the bullock waggons, the women in yashmaks, the wandering goats and sheep, the pungent smell of garlic and straw.

But an attempt had been made to modernise the place. A station was situated outside the town, consisting of low red-tiled buildings and a platform on either side of a single track, for what was known as Shimen Difair, which Edward managed to translate back to its French origin, Chemin de Fer. Here one of the regular town entertainments took place as people assembled to see a train arrive, clapping as it halted and again as the passengers descended.

McClumpha found them a house and a couple of servants, as well as space in the small shipyard he ran, where they could work on their boats. They had a slip and a workshop and McClumpha arrived with his car full of tools and equipment. They hadn't got their own winch but McClumpha had a Burrel's steam traction engine that they used to haul things about.

There wasn't a peep out of King Ferdinand, and it took a while to acclimatise because they couldn't speak the language. But within a few days they could at least identify the beverages and the food on the menu at the little restaurant where they ate. At first, the men in the neighbouring workshops, moustached and heavy eyebrowed, were suspicious of them. The only friendly response came from a small black cat which liked to sit in the sunshine and watch them.

'Perhaps it understands English,' Sam wondered.

In the Balkan War, the Turks suffered a series of defeats with heavy casualties, and were obliged to sue for peace. But a change of government in Constantinople brought a change of heart and the peace conference broke up in confusion as fighting started again.

It was as sordid as all wars, but curious because of the fact that the reigning monarchs of the Balkan states were all in the field leading their troops.

Dislodging the Turks from the position they had taken up on the narrow isthmus west of Constantinople proved impossible and cholera quickly spread among the Bulgarian troops. The campaign in that area came to a complete stop once more.

Edward decided to check out the situation for himself, even though petrol was in short supply. It was a trip he wished he hadn't made. There were broken guns and carts everywhere and bundles of clothing that were dead men. Every house seemed to be full of cholera victims and, looking for a supply store, Edward stumbled into one which looked like hell. It was stacked with corpses and the living dead.

Only by volunteer ambulance groups, most of them raised in England or France, was any aid given, and the soldiers, exhausted, half-starved and sick, were largely being cared for by doctors and nurses from the other end of Europe.

Edward was beginning to wonder if he had not made a terrible mistake venturing into this backward country in search of custom. There was still no word from any representative of the King and Edward wondered if the setback to the Bulgarian Army in the south might have cancelled the deal.

Khamlukin, on the other hand, was as good as his word and, one hazy afternoon, turned up for a race that was a foregone conclusion. The Bourdillon raced ahead without them even advancing to full throttle. Returning to McClumpha's launch, they waited for the Russian to come alongside. He acknowledged defeat with a graceful smile.

'You win, Monsieur Bourdillon,' he said. 'You have an excellent boat there. May I try her?'

They allowed him to put the boat through its paces and he spent the rest of the day examining the plans and asking questions about spares. Eventually, Khamlukin threw down his pencil. 'I could persuade the Imperial navy to take a flotilla of these boats,' he said. 'Let's say six for a start, of which these are the first two. What are your terms?'

From the Russian government he would be able to accept the price in two stages, Edward said.

'There would be no need for that. The money would be paid at once. I receive it from the Treasury via the navy. I pass it on to you in the form of a bank draft. The boats to be handed over as soon as the draft is acknowledged.' Khamlukin paused for a moment. 'There is, of course, another question. It is normal to reward the agent for his services.'

'What had you in mind?'

'Fifteen per cent.'

'That's a bit steep.'

'Nonsense.' Khamlukin beamed. 'I know you business-men. You're like the Chinese. You ask a price that's high enough for you to come down and still leave a good profit margin. Neimhoff always gives fifteen per cent.'

The deal was agreed in principle, with no mention of the commission to be made in the contract.

The next day a message arrived via McClumpha that the officer in command of the naval base at Varna wished to see them.

He was a handsome young man with a moustache and a little too much flesh round his middle. His blue uniform was beautifully pressed and he wore white gloves, but the gold stripes on his sleeves looked a little frayed.

'Welcome, welcome, dearest sirs,' he said in careful English. 'I am the Lieutenant Roboshva. I have arranged to confront you. We have everything that is desired for you. The King's own basin and slip are prepared. I will inform Sofia that you are on tiptoe to receive the King.'

'Now what are we going to do, master?' Sam asked afterwards. 'You've already sold the bloody boats.'

'Not yet, Sam,' Edward said. 'Nothing's been signed. We haven't even shaken hands on it. Let's wait and see what happens.'

Two days later, Lieutenant Roboshva informed them that the King was due to arrive the following morning. With the Lieutenant was a small man called Drimic, the lawyer who acted for the King. He wore pince-nez, a tight frock coat, a shiny silk hat and immaculate spats.

'Monsieur Drimic is the man who acquired the King's seaside villa here,' Lieutenant Roboshva pointed out. 'He acts in the King's name. If the King decides to take your boats, it will be Drimic who will see that you receive a draft on the royal bank. It is a private transaction, of course. The King will arrive incognito as Monsieur Lazlo Ribovic.'

Whatever Ferdinand's views about anonymity, he arrived wearing a long brilliant yellow coat. He was about fifty, round-faced with greying hair, and he reeked of perfume. He had a moustache and pointed beard that made him look not unlike Edward VII, especially as his shape was roughly as rotund. But his nose looked like the fore-shortened trunk of an elephant.

'The bugger's wearing make-up,' Sam murmured, after they had been introduced.

Looking at the boats, the King gestured with a heavily ringed hand and began to pick his huge nose thoughtfully. 'How fast are they?' he asked in English.

'Very fast, sir,' Edward said.

'Show me.'

'You wish me to take the boat out, sir, and put it through its paces?'

'No. I wish you to take *me* out in the boat and allow *me* to put it through its paces.'

He waved aside the offer of an oilskin. 'It's a fine day,' Ferdinand said airily. 'And the sea's calm. And if the spray damages my suit, I do have another one.'

As the boat almost leapt out of the water, the King's curly-brimmed homburg blew off, leaving two wisps of greying hair fluttering in the breeze over his bald dome. But he was engrossed with the Bourdillon's performance.

Returning to the quayside, the engine popping and rumbling and surrounded by exhaust smoke and steam, they made fast and helped him ashore. For a while he stood contemplatively on the quayside, surrounded by soldiers, policemen and sycophantic officials.

'Could they be used as naval vessels?' he asked.

'The Italian Navy has a flotilla of them, sir.'

'Can they carry torpedoes?'

'They have done, sir.'

'I will have them,' he said without any further questioning.

'Both of them, sir?'

'Of course. There will also be others, no doubt. I will build my inshore fleet around them. But I will wish you to remain here for a few weeks to iron out any problems and familiarise my officers with them. That will be satisfactory?'

It wasn't satisfactory at all, Edward thought, and would be most *un*satisfactory to Augusta. But he had no option. Doing business with a King, even the King of a third-rate little kingdom, could do Bourdillons' reputation no harm at all.

As the King turned away, the little cat from the restaurant crossed his path. Ferdinand halted, and snapped a command to one of the officials who was scuttling along behind him. The cat stopped as the man approached, and, tail in the air, it made to rub itself against his pin-striped leg. Instead, the official raised his silver-topped cane and brought it down with a thwack on the animal's back. As it lay in the gutter, blood trickling from its nose, a policeman stepped forward and finished it off with a kick to the head. Picking the body up by the tail, the policeman tossed the cat into the sea.

'My officials will call on you tomorrow,' the King said. 'Contracts will be drawn up and, as soon as everything is in order, you will be paid. How do you wish your money? In one or two instalments?'

Edward swallowed. 'I have no instructions, sir,' he said. 'Except that in pre-contract letters I was informed I was to receive the money immediately the boats were made available.' He drew a deep breath. 'In full.'

Ferdinand scratched his nose. 'Oh ye of little faith,' he said gloomily. 'Very well. You shall have your money. In full. Drimic will attend to it.'

As the cars drove away, Sam said 'I suppose it doesn't bother you that you've now sold the bloody boats twice.'

25

However confident he might appear to Sam, Edward was worried about his double dealing, and resolved to see Khamlukin.

The Russian was staying in the only decent hotel in the town, and having dinner with a beautiful blonde woman. When he spotted them together, Edward slipped away to a nearby flower shop and bought an armful of roses.

'Monsieur Bourdillon. How nice to see you.' Khamlukin rose as he arrived at their table. 'This is my wife, Ilona Dimitrovna, the Countess Khamlukina.'

Edward laid on a little bow to go with the roses. But there was no mention that they had seen each other before in Constantinople.

'The flowers are lovely,' the Countess said. 'How kind.' And extended her hand. Edward managed to kiss it without falling over his feet.

Khamlukin asked him to join them at their table, where Edward trotted out some story about having to be in touch with England about the boats, and also having to go away for a day or two. Then he beat a hasty but polite retreat.

Sam was instructed to make sure that baskets of roses were sent daily to the Khamlukins' apartment, while Edward juggled with delivery dates and shipping movements. Then, to their surprise, Ferdinand's officials arrived to discuss payments and contracts and plans. Edward hadn't expected them so soon and had to think fast. In his capacity as British Consul, McClumpha was invited to oversee things and act as interpreter. Champagne and caviare were ordered, and a meeting was organised with Roboshva and several other shifty-looking men in a small private room set aside for them by the hotel manager.

There was a lot of arguing before signatures were put on paper, and after a while it dawned on Edward that, for all the detailed discussion, nobody was offering money. He took a new tack himself, and asked a question about the use to which the boats were to be put. Edward didn't think for a moment Ferdinand was the sort of man to enjoy tearing round the Bay of Varna simply for the fun of it. And Roboshva eventually conceded that the boats were to be taken to a place beyond Cape Igneada just inside Turkish territory which at that moment happened to be occupied by Bulgarian troops. Edward replied that the boats were not paid for and he had no intention of letting them go until they were. He was beginning to regret not letting Khamlukin have them.

'There is also,' he said 'a little more work to be done.'

'The boats were working perfectly the other day,' Drimic protested sharply.

'High-speed marine engines require the most scrupulous attention,' Edward insisted. 'The craft are highly tuned. We must be absolutely certain that nothing will go wrong when we go home.'

The meeting broke up without resolving delivery or payment.

'The buggers want to use them against Turkish shipping round the Bosporus,' Sam said. 'And before they've bloody paid for 'em.'

Apparently, peace negotiations had come to nothing, fighting had not halted, and Bulgaria was getting the worst of it. Edward had sent letters off to Augusta, as Sam had to Rosina, but there had been no replies. War was not good for any postal service. Even a wire to Egg produced no response. And what on earth were Ferdinand's intentions?

'Dinnae trust him lad. He'll welsh on ye,' said McClumpha, over a delicious glass or two of single malt.

'My advice,' the Consul said, 'is to move y'r boats further doon the coast. The King willnae give a damn. He'll have forgotten all aboot the bluidy things by now. Tell Drimic the sea is better there. Flatter. Calmer. Doesnae rust the boats so much.' McClumpha grinned. 'I reckon ye can think up somethin'.'

172

He fished out a grubby map. 'Burgas,' he said. 'That's the place. It's no' far north o' the Bosporus. I've got copper mining interests there, and a shipyard. I'll gi'e ye a letter o' introduction, and telegraph ma manager tae expect ye. Ye can moor at ma quay. The boats'll be safe there. The only problem is it's eighty miles away.'

'That's not a problem,' Edward said. 'We can follow one of your ships with drums of petrol aboard and top up when necessary.'

'There's plenty of little ports you can slip into if the weather shuts doon on the way. I'll supply the petrol an' oil and charts o' the coast, and I'll see ye have food an' a bottle o' this stuff. That should see ye through.'

'Where would I be without you?' said Edward.

'Up the creek, I reckon, laddie, without a paddle.'

When Edward next saw Khamlukin, he had heard all about Ferdinand.

'Has he changed his mind?' Khamlukin asked.

'Unhappily, no,' Edward admitted. 'On the other hand he doesn't seem prepared to pay. It looks as though the boats are yours.'

'Very good,' he said. 'I have been advised to hand you a bank draft as confirmation and down payment on the first two boats, with an option for four more.'

'And my cheque for the agent's fee will be in your hands immediately I receive the bank draft.'

Edward spent the rest of the evening with the Khamlukins, and drank rather more champagne than he intended. Several other Russians joined them, all accompanied by women friends and the evening got noisier and noisier, with many toasts and glasses smashed in the fireplace.

In a vain attempt to keep his head clear, he slipped away and drank three cups of black coffee. On his return, Ilona Khamlukina promptly filled his glass again, and made him drink Russian fashion with arms linked.

She also insisted on dancing. The orchestra consisted of half a dozen elderly men in rusty evening dress. The music was Viennese, and Ilona Khamlukina moved like an angel – an angel with the most seductive perfume and voluptuous body. It was hot and stuffy on the dance floor, particularly when they were dancing so close. The Countess whispered in Edward's ear that it might be cooler in the conservatory.

'Pavel Ivanovitch is a dull dog when he's been drinking,' she said as they sat down among the exotic potted plants. She placed her hand in Edward's and he felt something hard pressed against his palm. It was a key.

'My husband leaves tonight for Sofia,' she said softly. 'I have told him I don't wish to be alone at the apartment while he is away so I am staying at the hotel. The number of my room is on the key.'

She kissed Edward on the lips. 'You are a very attractive man, Edward Bourdillon,' she whispered. 'All Pavel Ivanovitch thinks about is money. His debts are enormous and his father refuses any longer to pay his bills.'

They saw Khamlukin off in a carriage.

'Goodbye, darling,' she murmured, as they waved him off. But her eyes were on Edward.

Trudging upstairs to bed, he realised that Ilona Khamlukina reminded him of Georgina. The thought of it suddenly made his collar feel tight. Gently blown on, he felt he might easily burst into flames.

Next morning Edward send a basket of red roses to Ilona Khamlukina's room, together with his card, her key, apologies and an excuse.

'There you are, you see, Sam. Everything open and above board.'

'She's a tart,' was Sam's only response.

'She's one of the hazards of doing business.'

But Sam was impressed by the size of the bank draft when it arrived. It was stamped all over with the seal of the Russian Ministry of Marine and signed by three different officials.

'Looks good,' he said cheerfully. 'Did Khamlukin get his commission?'

'Yes.'

'Did he want it in gold?'

Edward laughed. 'I sent a basket of flowers to his wife.'
Sam raised his eyebrows. 'The cheque was in a brand new wallet in the middle.'

'Time to go home,' said Sam.

'I hear you pulled it off, lad,' McClumpha said next morning. 'By the way, dinna pay your bank draft through a Bulgarian bank. Use a Swiss one, preferably in Sofia.'

Edward didn't argue. The next morning he took the bank draft to the Swiss Banking Corporation building and saw it safely deposited. The manager was impressed by its size and Edward's sense of urgency. In the expectation of further good business, he offered Edward a list of other branches in the country.

26

The whole McClumpha clan saw them off, Fiona and Rhadka in floods of tears. The sea was calm and the day full of sunshine as they headed south at half throttle, Edward leading, Sam just behind on the starboard quarter. They reached Denipopoulis during the afternoon. It was nothing more than a fishing village with a stone quay, and, when they moored alongside, the whole village came down to stare at them.

McClumpha's friend, Savoff, was waiting for them and, by the grace of God, he spoke Italian because he had once conducted trade between Montenegrin ports and Bari. He placed two of his men on the quay to protect the boats from enthusiastic spectators, then he took Sam and Edward to his home and fed them some Bulgarian dish they couldn't identify but which tasted delicious. He had some recreationary suggestions.

'Cotel,' he said. 'Fifty kilometres south. A fishing village. The following day you should reach Burgas.'

He gave them the names of men who could help and they set off the next morning with the whole of Denipopoulis watching. By the grace of God the weather remained good, the sea calm and the boats behaved perfectly.

'It'd be a good advert,' Sam said, 'if only somebody could see us.'

They made Burgas in the expected time. A friend of Savoff called Boris Enescu was expecting them and sent out a launch to guide them into McClumpha's little basin. It was just big enough for one small coaster, and the two boats were safely hidden by tall buildings of brick and corrugated iron. As soon as they stepped ashore they were handed a telegram from McClumpha.

'Oh, Christ,' Edward said.

176

Ferdinand's officials were looking for them and were on the point of paying up. It was important for them to return to Varna at once. Ferdinand had decided he needed the boats for his new war and was even prepared to pay for them from his own pocket.

McClumpha was at Varna station to meet them.

'Roboshva wants to know where you wish to receive the draft,' he said. 'They're suggestin' ye go tae Sofia. I'm suggestin' ye don't. No' in a million years. They'll probably wait for you and have it off ye before ye reach the station. Yon Drimic's as fishy as a barrowload of rotten herrings. Make him come here. You can have my people tae look after ye. When ye've got it, beat it. There's a Swiss bank in Burgas. Stick it in there. The Swiss won't let 'em get away wi' anythin'.'

He offered his office for the signing, and Russian champagne with small Russian pancakes called *blinochki* were laid on. Roboshva was the first to arrive, and didn't waste time confirming that the King's representatives were ready to pay.

Drimic turned up soon afterwards in a big green Fiat. 'I will arrange for the money to be paid into your bank in London at once,' he said.

'That wasn't the arrangement,' Edward said stubbornly. 'Payment was to be here. To me.'

Eventually smiles returned, everybody shook hands and Roboshva insisted on kissing Edward on both cheeks.

'And the boats?' he said.

'At Burgas,' Edward said. 'We had to move them because of the threat from Romania.'

It wasn't an unreasonable argument and the documents were handed over, together with a thick file of plans and instructions. The champagne was drunk and the *blinochki* eaten and Drimic passed over the bank draft. It was an elaborate document in scarlet, yellow and gold. Edward noticed it was drawn on the King's personal account.

They stood in silence as Drimic climbed back into his car, and set off up the hill into the town. Edward stared at the bank draft.

'Don't be presentin' it here, whatever ye do,' McClumpha insisted. 'Drimic has the banks in his pocket. Take it tae Burgas. Use the Swiss bank. An' I'll get y'r message tae Khamlukin but ye've no need tae worry about him. He willnae be back here in a hurry. He left a lot of debts and there are a few bum bailiffs lookin' for him. An', to cap things, his wife's run off wi' a Pole.'

As they burst out laughing, McClumpha continued. 'I'll go tae the station an' get y'r tickets. Ye'll also need cash. You stay here. Dinnae go oot an' keep the door lockit an' y'r heads doon.'

It was good advice. McClumpha shot off in his car while Sam and Edward collected their belongings. He was waiting in Reception as they left the hotel, and shoved a wad of notes into Edward's hand.

'We can never thank you enough,' Edward said.

'Pchah.' McClumpha shook him by the hand. 'It's ma job as consul, after all. Ye can pay me back when ye've time tae stop runnin'.'

Worried about Drimic, Edward had placed the bank draft in the inside pocket of his jacket and used a safety pin to make sure it couldn't fall out.

'If they want it back,' he said, 'they'll have to strip me.'

'They won't get that far,' Sam said, opening his briefcase. Inside was a revolver.

Edward grinned and lifted the lid of his despatch case. Inside there was a revolver of his own. 'Snap,' he said.

'Never mind guns,' McClumpha advised. 'Keep y'r eyes open. Ye need have no worries aboot the boats. If Drimic tries tae steal 'em for his own use, we'll move 'em. Intae Enescu's yard. They can be hidden there as well as in mine. I wouldnae trust yon Drimic not tae sell 'em again and pocket the money.'

Dark clouds were massing over the hills and heavy drops of rain began to fall as the train jerked into movement. Crowds gathered on the platform to applaud its departure, and Edward spotted Drimic and Roboshva. When he saw Edward leaning out of the window, he ran forward a few steps, pointing to someone in one of the coaches behind.

'Sam,' Edward said, 'I think we're being followed already. And if we are, it's because they're hoping to get this bank draft back. If Drimic has someone on this train they can only be looking for us. I suggest that at the first opportunity we drop off and catch the next train.'

'Here we go again,' grumbled Sam.

Provadiya was a small town tucked into the bottom of a range of mountains. It was packed with people who had left Sofia after the threat of invasion, and who were now trying to make their way to the sea. As the train stopped, Drimic's agents, both dressed in black with homburg hats, jumped down and mingled obtrusively with the peasant women squatting under the trees. Eventually, a red-capped guard bustled along the platform pushing people back on board. Whistles blew, flags waved and they saw the two men head back to the train.

'Right, Sam.'

Picking up their cases, they made for the door. Like all Continental railway carriages, the door had steps to ground level for the low station platforms.

The train was just gathering speed as they opened the door and jumped out. As they went sprawling, Edward saw one of Drimic's agents at a window.

Dusting themselves off, the two men picked up their belongings and headed for the station exit, surrounded by indignant railway officials.

'Come on, Sam,' Edward said. 'Those bastards'll be waiting at the next station. We'll have to think of something else.'

But outside, there was a livery stable which hired horses and traps.

'That's the answer,' Edward said. 'We'll follow the road. Can you ride? I can't remember.'

'No.'

'Oh, well,' said Edward. 'Too bad.'

'I'd manage better,' Sam groaned, 'if the wretched thing was fitted with a tiller.'

The road led into the hills, which climbed beyond them to a clear sky.

'We have around eighty miles to go,' Edward said. 'We should be able to reach Burgas in about three days.'

'What makes you think they won't be waiting for us at Burgas?' Sam asked. 'Why not cross the border into Greece?'

For three days, in increasing cold, they plodded along. There were few roads and, at every village, by signs and the few words they had learned, they were able to set themselves on the right route. The inns were few and far between but they found reasonable food and hard beds for the night. On the fourth day, they became aware they were being followed by two horsemen.

'Can you hit anything with that?' Edward asked, as Sam fished out his revolver.

'Shouldn't think so. How about you?'

Edward shook his head.

At the next village they took a loop road away from the main route south. They didn't stop to ask directions and wondered if they'd lost their pursuers. Towards evening, feeling more or less safe, they passed through a village called Picep, then turned back to the main road. Heading between rock-scattered hills in the last of the sunshine, they were wondering where to stay.

'We could sleep in the open,' Sam suggested. 'It wouldn't do us any harm for one night.'

A breeze had started which promised to make the night chilly.

'Hang on, Ted,' he said. 'We've got company.'

At a bend in the road by a rocky wall surrounding a field, two men waited. Two horses were tethered to a tree. Drimic's agents.

Edward's eyes flickered about them. There were dry-stone walls on either side of the road, and behind them a narrow hump-backed bridge which they had just crossed.

'What do you suggest we do now?' Edward asked.

'Rush 'em?'

'And get shot before we've gone a couple of yards? Let them come to us.'

It was a good guess. The two men walked over, while Edward and Sam sat waiting in the saddle.

'Paper,' said one of them in English. 'I want.'

Both men were holding revolvers.

'Very well,' said Edward, reaching inside his jacket.

But instead of the bank draft, he brought out the heavy revolver he had bought in Sofia and slammed it down hard on the man's head. As he did so, he saw the other man raise his gun and found himself looking down the hole in the barrel. There was a bang that echoed round the hills and set the horses dancing in fright. He saw Sam fall from his saddle, while the second Bulgar was flung sideways against the stone wall. He groaned once, then slid down against it to sprawl on the grass at its base, leaving a smear of red on the stones.

'Jesus,' Sam sat up. 'I hit him.'

Vaulting from the saddle, Edward bent to examine the two bodies.

'You not only hit him, Sam,' he said. 'You killed him.'

Turning to the other man lying crumpled in the road, he turned him over. Blood oozed from his nose and ears and his face looked like wax.

'In fact, I think we killed 'em both,' he said.

27

Stiff and saddlesore, they drew near the Greek frontier two days later. The place was bustling with soldiery. It had started raining and the dusty roads were already becoming quagmires. Along every pathway lay the debris of retreating armies. The sky was dark with buzzards and kites. And the wind from the mountains was bitterly cold. Every house they passed contained sick and wounded soldiers, with doctors struggling to help without drugs, bandages or lint.

Everywhere were broken carts and waggons and roofless and burned farm buildings. Dead horses and cattle made the place vile with their stench. Here and there they could see a huddle of grey clothing where a dead man lay. Moving about among the ruins were the shadowy figures of people who lived in the area, searching desperately for something that might sustain life, gaunt figures with hollow cheeks and burning eyes. Every scrap of wood had vanished and they were wrenching out the vines from the slopes to make fires. In some houses living and dead lay together, almost indistinguishable from each other. Starving dogs sniffed hopefully at doorways.

There were refugees everywhere. The suffering had brought a stillness over the countryside that was broken only by the cawing crows which hovered over the long caterpillar of human beings trudging northwards and eastwards.

As the rain persisted the mud grew worse. Near the village of Prosip they came across ambulance carts stuck in the mud, and, shortly afterwards, crossed the path of the battered and retreating Bulgarian army. The feet of the half-starved soldiers were wrapped in rags, their bodies swathed in old carpets and pieces of torn canvas. Nearby, they saw a group of hospital tents and a Red

Cross flag, a Ford car, ox carts and mule-drawn waggons. Wretched-looking soldiers swathed in bandages sat in groups, hunched against the cold.

As they approached, a woman emerged from one of the tents. She seemed little more than a girl, fair-haired with a long curl that fell over her nose, a neat figure and legs half-obscured by the long coat she wore over a nurse's uniform. She stopped in front of them and addressed a few words of Bulgarian Slav to them.

'Perhaps,' Edward said gently, 'it would be better if we spoke English.'

Her eyes lit up. 'You speak English?'

'We are English.'

'You are? What are you? Doctors?'

'I suppose you'd call us sailors.'

Gesturing towards the mountains, she said 'We don't see many ships round here. But it's good to see you. I'm with the British Women's Convoy Corps. We arrived when the fighting started last year. We're here with the assistance of Queen Eleanora of Bulgaria. Not that she's given much of that. We need help. We have to move the hospital. A pipe carries excreta past the building we're using to a cesspool that's only partly covered by rotting planks. Delightful. We've found another building that's usable but we can't manage on our own.'

'Madam,' Edward said uncomfortably, 'we'd love to be of assistance, but we have urgent business, which requires us to leave Bulgaria as quickly as possible.'

'I'm not a madam,' she replied. 'I'm a miss. Are you a spy?'

'Certainly not,' he said. 'I'm a businessman. Of sorts.'

'Then you can spare a day or two to help us, I'm sure. My name's Virginia Gogarty. There are seven of us, part of Mrs St John Halahan's group. She just dumped us here while she went off with the others to sort out supplies. One of the lorries has broken down, and it would help if we could understand the bloody language better. You don't speak it, by any chance?'

'Only a few words, I'm afraid.'

She was young and pretty and reminded Edward of Augusta. She had the same neat blonde hair drawn back

183

and tied with a ribbon. Even her voice sounded a little like Augusta's.

'The bloody people round here are perfectly prepared to carry the stretchers. But they haven't the foggiest idea what we want done when we get there. Every time we open the windows they shut them again. We have an outbreak of typhus and cholera, and no one to help. Please stay. If only for a while.'

'Have you got any transport?' Edward asked. 'I need to find a bank.'

'To deposit your loot?'

Ignoring her remark, Edward said, 'My friend, Sam Nankidno here, will stay with you until I return. As a hostage.' He smiled.

'Svilencic's not far away. They have a Swiss bank there.'

'Good. I'll go tomorrow. Now, what can we do?'

'You can go and tell those bloody Bulgarians to leave the windows open.'

'Why not smash the panes?'

'Why did I never think of that?' she said. 'Too well brought up, I suppose. You might also tell them not to throw scraps of food on the floor. It encourages mice and cockroaches, to say nothing of rats. This place is full of them.'

'I'll threaten to shoot anyone I see doing it,' Sam offered. 'I can hit anything at a distance of a yard.'

She turned to Edward. 'Have *you* got a gun too?'

'Yes.'

She grinned. 'That makes three of us then. Please call me Ginny.'

'Ginny,' said Edward.

'And you would tell me if you were a spy, wouldn't you?'

They worked until dark setting up the hospital and spent the night on the floor in the same room as the off-duty nurses. There were two British, Virginia Gogarty and a girl called Florence Mitchell, a Canadian and four Australians, all of whom had been recruited in England. They were all shattered and slept like logs.

'Here's a rum go,' Sam said as they shared the blankets round them. 'Never thought I'd share a bed with seven girls at once.'

★

184

At first light Edward set off for Svilencic with a Bulgarian driver-mechanic called Movisch. The ambulance had bone-juddering solid tyres and the road was rutted and very difficult. But they made it eventually to Svilencic where Edward insisted on Movisch staying in the ambulance with his revolver until he returned, in case anyone tried to steal it.

The clerk studied the signature on the bank draft and the name, Bulgarian National Bank, along the top, then insisted that Edward see the manager, a cold-eyed Italian-Swiss.

'This is on the King's personal account,' he said. 'May I ask how you came by it?'

Edward explained. 'You can check with the palace and with the firm of Bourdillons in England.'

'I'm not suggesting there's anything wrong, sir, but this is a large sum of money. I shall have to make some enquiries.'

'How long will that take?'

'I'm sure I can have an answer for you by this afternoon.'

In the event, confirmation came through quickly, and Edward was able to raise some much-needed cash. A biting wind made it difficult to light the ambulance's oil-filled lamps. And the only way to get the vehicle back on the road was to push-start it. The going was very slippery, and the lamps gave only a feeble glow and kept going out. They finished the journey with Movisch steering and Edward squatting on the running board, working the throttle by hand with the bonnet open.

It was in the early hours of the morning when they clattered back into Prosip. There was no sign of life, just a solitary light in the hospital building. Then the silence was broken by a shriek and suddenly they were surrounded by yelling young women.

'My God.' A lantern was held up right in front of Edward's face, making him blink. 'He came back,' cried Ginny Gogarty. 'Oh, thank you, Spy. I never thought you would. I'll never forget you. Anybody who can forget international secrets to help half a dozen lost women is a pearl beyond price.'

She stood on tiptoe to kiss him. Then the two men were hurried into a room at the end of the hospital, and someone found food and wine. It was only then that Edward realised how cold and wet and tired he was.

'We thought we'd lost you and our ambulance, too.' Ginny Gogarty said. 'I was beginning to wonder what the hell I was going to tell Mrs Halahan. "Sorry, Ma'am. I lent the ambulance to this spy." '

Edward smiled. 'I'm really not a spy, you know.'

'It doesn't matter to me if you are or not. The important thing is that you're here.'

28

The weather had been growing colder ever since they had left Varna and now violent storms howled round the mountain tops. Icy winds brought torrential rain, turning the ground to a quagmire. As Ferdinand's defeated army retreated the Turks took the opportunity to snatch back territory they had lost in the First Balkan War.

Typhus was rampant, and the bitter cold that drove the homeless to seek refuge and warmth in overcrowded quarters only helped the epidemic to spread.

Many of the men who found their way to the little hospital had frosbite which with neglect had turned to gangrene. Often the patients were two to a bed, but Ginny Gogarty and her staff fought to keep the dysentery, typhus and fever cases separate.

Patients and staff had all their hair cut short because that was where the lice laid their eggs, and the girls wore one-piece calico garments bound at the wrists, with Turk-ish-type trousers tucked into rubber boots or socks. Even the medical teams were at risk and one of the Australian girls had caught typhus and had had to be isolated.

As supplies dwindled, Ginny went to seek help from one of the Bulgarian hospitals in a town called Brzniko-vitsa. She took Edward with her as escort.

'One of the patients gave me an egg the other day,' said Ginny. 'We couldn't make out where he got it but it turned out he had the hen in the bed with him under the blanket.'

It was a wasted journey. The hospital was stinking and unventilated. There were few beds and what bedding there was, was swarming with vermin. Because of the cholera, the whole town was on the point of being quarantined. There were no trains, few rations, and no sugar, tobacco or milk.

They returned to find that the water supply at Prosip had vanished. Sam had already discovered that a conduit had broken and was struggling in the rain and sleet to repair it. But at least there was food. Movisch had once been a poacher and was a good shot. He brought back rabbits and wildfowl, once a roe deer, once a boar, sometimes stolen hens. One day he came back with his dark eyes blazing.

'Mister Edward,' he said, hardly able to stand still for excitement. 'I have found a baker. Two bakers, in fact. Unfortunately –' Movisch grinned '– they are Turks.'

'Where are they?'

'Only half a mile away, Mister Edward. I got lost and almost wandered into their camp. I was going to shoot them so the Turks would also have no bread. Then I thought, why not bring them here and let them make bread for us?'

That night, armed only with their revolvers, Edward and Sam followed Movisch out of camp. A dank mist cloaked their movements, and permitted them to get close to the Turkish camp without being spotted. The Turks looked in as poor a state as the Bulgarians, their camp a morass of glutinous mud. The cookhouse and bakery were behind a small red-tiled building with a hole in the roof.

'There's no sign of any sentries,' whispered Sam.

'Let's go get 'em, then,' said Edward.

They got back to the hospital just as the next day's watery sun came out. Florence Mitchell was trying to wash outside the girls' quarters and she shrieked in alarm as she saw the Turkish uniforms. The other girls came dashing out, Ginny brandishing her revolver.

'Who are your friends?' she asked.

'Bakers, Ma'am,' Sam grinned.

'With their own flour,' Edward added, motioning the

188

two fat and very weary Turks to put down the large sacks they were carrying.

Edward and Sam stayed with the Women's Convoy Corps far longer than they had intended. The onset of winter stopped all movement and they knew they were stuck until spring opened the roads.

Searching among the wrecked houses, they found a boiler and some tin baths, and rigged up a bath-house for the patients and orderlies and another for the girls. They threatened the death penalty to anyone who shut an opened window and gradually, with the fresh air, the typhus died. The Turkish bakers took their captivity philosophically, thankful not to have been murdered. Edward bullied them into actually washing their hands before they kneaded the dough. It took longer to impress the notion of cleanliness on the Bulgarian orderlies. They were in the main peasants, hardy, tough and smelling strongly of their scented tobacco, but in the end they fixed up a laundry and ran it because it pleased Ginny. They were all a little in love with her.

Three days before Christmas, Edward and Sam went to Svilencic in Movisch's ambulance, returning with the back of the ambulance crammed with knick-knacks.

They produced rolls of coloured paper and showed the patients and orderlies how to decorate the wards with paper chains. Sam dug up a small fir tree and, though the Bulgars didn't understand its significance, they watched open-mouthed as it was hung with paper decorations and lit with candles.

On Christmas morning, Ginny and Flo Mitchell led a procession of nurses into the ward with two bottles of slivovitz and a tray bearing gifts of tobacco and cigarettes. As the door opened, Edward nodded to Movisch who raised a hand and there was a great cry of, 'Sank you, Ladies, and Smelly Kissimass.'

The nurses stopped dead and on more than one face there were tears. 'Oh, Spy,' Ginny said, her voice choked. 'Oh, dear Spy. Dear Sam.'

'They've been at it all night,' Sam grinned. 'Rehearsing.'

★

189

January remained wet and cold and the roads were rivers of liquid mud, churned up by feet and the hooves of horses and oxen. When the redoubtable Mrs St John Halahan arrived, she turned out to be a small woman with bright red hair that was obviously dyed, wearing a floppy hat and a divided skirt. She eyed Edward and Sam coldly but had to praise the way the hospital and dispensary had been organised. When she left for Trnava to check on a series of recently set-up depots she insisted on shaking hands.

There was no way Edward or Sam could depart. Every route south was blocked by refugees, frightened, footsore and starving. Bullock waggons hauled pots, pans, babies, ancient wooden tools, bowls, benches, sacks, all crushed together in an inextricable mass, each cart guided by a man with baggy trousers or a woman, sometimes wearing a shawl, sometimes a Turkish yashmak. Old women struggled with goats, children wept with fatigue, mothers plodded with babies on their backs, their older children carrying what treasures they could from abandoned homes or driving a couple of donkeys or a flock of skinny goats.

According to Ginny, a very close watch was being kept on the frontier. 'You'd better stay here.'

So, not entirely unwillingly, they stayed.

One night, with the weather turned suddenly balmy. Sam turned up with several bottles of slivovitz. The two Turkish bakers baked cakes and produced instruments and began to play. Orderlies and those patients who were able linked arms and formed a ring. It started quietly, the feet hardly shifting, but then the steps became more pronounced. Movisch gestured at Edward to join and then to Ginny. One by one all the girls followed her into the circle.

A piano was brought up by lorry and somebody produced a mandolin, another a banjo and a triangular guitar like a Russian balalaika. As Sam played, Edward sang 'I'm a Flying Fish Sailor Home From Hong Kong'. Sam gave them 'Widdicombe Fair' and the girls sang 'If You Were The Only Girl In The World'. Finally they danced the foxtrot and the quickstep to 'Hitchy Koo' and 'Who Were

You With Last Night?' After the music stopped, Edward sat with Ginny Gogarty by the remains of the fire, feeling happier than he had for a long time.

A black and white cat wandered in and jumped on Ginny's lap. 'It wandered in out of the rain,' she said quietly. 'It had a broken leg, which mended very nicely, didn't it, baby.' The cat purred contentedly. 'I suppose,' she said. 'I suppose you won't be staying much longer.'

'I'm sorry,' he said.

She offered him one of the aromatic Balkan cigarettes everybody smoked. 'I never used to smoke,' she explained. 'But now we always carry them, to give to the patients. They need them so desperately and it started me off . . . I shall miss you terribly, Spy. Most of the time I'm scared stiff and wonder what on earth I'm doing here.'

He took her hand in his. For a moment, her fingers closed tightly round his, warm and strong, then she pushed his hand away.

'Don't,' she whispered. 'Don't, or I'll blub like a kid.'

Next morning, a big green Fiat drove past the hospital. Sitting in the back seat was Roboshva.

'They've found us, Sam,' Edward said.

'Is he the enemy?' He turned to see Ginny looking up at him.

'You might call him that,' he said.

He told her what had happened in the mountains to the north.

'What was the money for?' she asked. 'Arms?'

'Boats. But there's little doubt the King hoped to mount guns on them and use them against the Turks or the Romanians.'

She squeezed his hand. 'It'll be all right, Spy. We can get you away without you being seen. Leave it to us.'

The following afternoon, the car returned and parked outside the hospital. From a hiding place in the store Sam and Edward heard Roboshva asking in his precise English if they'd been seen. Ginny solemnly swore that she'd never seen any sign of anybody even remotely answering their description.

191

He hung around for some time, asking the other girls, but he got little change out of them. So he tried one of the patients. Flo Mitchell was quick to whisper something to Movisch who passed the word along.

'I shouldn't get too close,' Flo Mitchell said. 'That chap you're talking to is a raging maelstrom of typhus germs. It's very contagious.' On cue, the man groaned and coughed.

Roboshva moved on to the next bed.

'Cholera,' Flo Mitchell said.

Roboshva went pale and hurried away.

The next day, Movisch's ambulance set off south-west. It was driven by Ginny Gogarty, with Edward riding alongside her in the front seat, wearing a white jacket, Red Cross brassard and a false goathair moustache made by one of the Turkish bakers. Sam lay on one of the stretchers in the back with Movisch, covered in bandages.

'I hope to God Mrs Halahan doesn't find out,' Ginny said.

They reached the Greek frontier during the afternoon and Ginny kissed them both as they prepared to cover the last few hundred yards through the trees on foot.

'God bless you both,' she said. 'Mrs Halahan doesn't like anything demonstrative. She feels it indicates that women are frailer than men, but I feel very frail and very feminine. And very grateful.' She gave Edward a final extra kiss and squeezed his hand. 'Thank you Spy, dear. I'll never forget you.'

IV

1914 – 1918

29

They crossed into Thrace that evening. On the other side of the frontier, Sam took a deep breath.

'Feels safer already,' he said.

On the railway, there were delays and hold-ups all the way north, so they made their way on carts and waggons to Dedeagach and took a coaster from there to Salonika. From Salonika they both wired home before finding another coaster to Naples.

The della Stradas were on the docks to meet them, and cheered as the two men walked down the gangplank. Alessandro had grown enormously and it was obvious that Rosina was on the point of producing a baby. She clutched Sam and wept with joy.

It occurred to Edward that he might go on to Messina, until he heard that Rafaela had got married. To Count somebody-or-other. Apparently they had a sumptuous place in Rome, the Villa Rospodi, not far from the Borghese Palace.

Papa della Strada had news of a very different kind. An Austrian Archduke had been assassinated in Sarajevo. Archdukes, as Sam pointed out, were two a penny in that part of the world. So what was all the fuss about?

Edward did not delay his journey home, and at nine o'clock next morning he was at the railway station, with one battered suitcase, and a wicker basket stuffed with sausage, cheese, fruit, bread and two bottles of wine.

To Edward's surprise, the newspapers echoed Papa della Strada's concern over the assassination in Sarajevo, but they clearly thought the crisis would soon blow over. The sabre-rattling to the north was condemned as crude political manoeuvring.

As the train drew into the Rome station, on an impulse, Edward snatched his case from the rack and jumped out. Finding a cab, he directed it to the Villa Rospodi. It was a modern building, different from so much of the medieval architecture around it, and attractively situated in a park shaded with cypresses. The porter at the gate refused to let him in. However, he did make it clear that Rafaela wasn't there, anyway, and that Edward might find her at an apartment near the Orlandos' office in the Via Veneto.

The cab dropped Edward outside the door. It was an imposing building, constructed in the ornate style of the new Italian monarchy. A large note placed in the calloused hand of the concièrge produced the directions, and Edward made his way up a winding staircase to the second storey. The door was opened by a maid in pink with a white apron and cap. She was about to refuse him entry when a voice from inside the apartment called out, 'Who is it, Michaela?'

Edward brushed the maid aside and dropped his bag in the doorway. The apartment was enormous and lavishly furnished in yellow and gold. Obviously Rafaela was enjoying her wealth. She was standing by a table at the far side of the room with her back towards him. In a large, gilded mirror he caught a glimpse of an ivory face, hair black as a raven's wing, oblique eyebrows like brush strokes, large, slanting fearless eyes, and a firm full mouth like a streak of carmine.

She turned as he walked towards her. For a moment a look of pure astonishment was on her face, then she ran across the room and flung herself into his arms. For a while, gawped at by the astonished maid, they clung to each other, Rafaela's fingers stroking his hair, his cheeks, his neck.

The maid exited as discreetly as she could, and closed the double doors behind her.

Rafaela drew back, her breast heaving.

'You shouldn't have come,' she said.

'I had to.'

'It is all finished. I'm married now. As a matter of fact my husband is connected to the same family as you.'

'Is he here?'

196

'Thankfully not. He's in Messina on business.'

'I'm married, too, Rafaela. To a girl I've known since I was a small boy. I haven't seen her for months. I was on my way home. I didn't intend to . . .'

'So why did you?'

He didn't answer immediately.

'Why, Edward?'

He wanted to say, 'Because I love you.' But he couldn't. How beautiful she was, though. 'When the train pulled into the station, I could think of no one else but you.'

She said nothing for a moment then she drew a deep breath. 'You can't stay. I'm sorry. It's all too late.' Tears filled her lustrous eyes, but she didn't cry.

Suddenly formal, Rafaela motioned Edward to a chair and sat down opposite him. 'Tell me more about your wife. Do you have children?'

'I've hardly seen Gussie since we got married.' Edward said ruefully. 'And I've been stuck in Bulgaria for months because of that wretched war.'

'You have always had a knack for getting into trouble.' She smiled.

'I suppose you're right. I don't seem to be able to live a normal, straightforward life.'

For a while they simply sat there gazing at each other. It was not a painful silence, but so much remained unsaid.

'I shall be back in Naples,' Edward said eventually. 'I hope I can see you again then. And meet your husband.'

'Of course.' Her reply came automatically. But then she stood up and walked over to the fireplace. 'Oh, Edward. You shouldn't have come. I had begun to get used to another life, a life without you in it. I'm not sure if I can bear to see you again. Not now. Not under the circumstances.'

Edward got to his feet. 'Then I suppose I had better go.'

'Yes.'

'I'm sorry.'

'So am I. More than you know.'

Without saying another word, Edward took her hand and pressed it to his lips. Then he walked briskly out of the room.

★

The cross-Channel ferry seemed abysmally slow and Edward was fidgeting with impatience long before he reached Dover. The journey, even then, was far from over. He had to take the boat train to London, another train down to Portsmouth and from there a local train to Porthelt. It seemed to take aeons of time. But he did manage to send a telegram to Augusta, saying he was on his way, leaving her to work out what train he would catch.

It was late evening when he arrived. And there she was, waiting at the end of the platform.

Creek House was bulging at the seams with people, with Aunt Edith and the Vicar's wife weeping openly. Georgina came forward and kissed Edward on both cheeks.

'Clever Edward,' she said. 'I don't know how you manage it but you always manage to come home to a hero's welcome!'

Edward caught the sly smile on her face and looked round quickly for the curate. Maurice guessed his thoughts. 'He isn't here,' he said. 'He left the country. I heard he got a job somewhere abroad. Teaching theology. That sort of thing. Bit like you, Ned. Always knew how to fall on his feet.'

But, after a huge dinner accompanied by copious glasses of claret, having fielded a thousand questions, all Edward could do was fall asleep.

He didn't remember going to bed, but awoke some time in the night aware of Gussie next to him, warm and soft. Satisfied that he was home, Edward promptly fell asleep again.

The next thing he knew, the sun was streaming in butter-yellow beams through the windows and Augusta's lips were on his.

'Oh, Teddy,' she said. 'You can't believe how much I've longed for you.'

He drew her close, aware at the same time of a guilty feeling that he didn't entirely mean the endearments he murmured to her. He had known her too long, he felt suddenly. She was as familiar to him as his clothes, his own skin.

198

'Did you meet any other girls, Teddy? I promise I won't mind if you did. Well, not much, anyway. I'll just kill you.'

'I met a few,' Edward confessed. 'But the girls in Bulgaria look like bundles of washing tied up with string round the middle.'

She laughed. And he kissed her long and hard, and tried not to think of Rafaela.

They stayed in bed until hunger drove them out. Augusta seemed to be walking on air, and, smelling the old scents of the fields and the trees and the river, Edward found himself smiling with pleasure.

After lunch, Uncle Egg sat him down in the study and offered him a glass of port and a cigar.

'I've acquired a strip of land along the sea east of Southampton,' Egg said. 'We've already established a workshop there. It's got deep water and we can use it to build bigger vessels. And with all this bother on the Continent, we could be doing just that any minute.'

'Is it that serious, Uncle Egg?'

'I reckon. Still, let's forget that for a moment. We've been reorganising. I've got a youngster called Butler – Josh Butler – to help me in the design office. He's good. University background. Maths. Keen sailor. Knows what he's about.'

'Well done.'

'We paint all our boats yellow now, too, as you suggested. And people do call them the Yellow Perils as you said they would. But you can't miss 'em. It was a cracker of an idea. And we've not been coy about the name of Bourdillon. It's painted in huge letters across all the sheds. That was Maurice. He's pulled his socks up a bit these days and running the yard on his own. I've made him managing director. We shall need someone with more business and accountancy experience if we develop further, but Maurice will learn. What about you?'

They had obviously reached the crucial question. 'Me, Uncle Egg?'

'Well, your bonus will be tremendous. So will Sam's. I'm going to make you sales director. Would that suit you?'

Edward smiled. 'I'm not all that fussy what I'm called, Uncle Egg,' he said.

'Your salary's gone up, of course, Substantially.'

'Jolly good. I'm a married man now.'

'Gussie's a dear. She's missed you dreadfully.'

Edward took a pensive sip of his port.

'And Sam? How's he?'

'The best in the world. Saved my life. There's nothing he can't do.'

'Would he like to be called head of foreign sales? Something like that?'

Edward laughed. 'Something like that. And, of course, he's a married man, too.'

After three weeks of glorious sunshine, Edward began to wonder if he would ever want to leave England again. Augusta was in the seventh heaven to have him back with her. Life was perfect. Except that Edward could not get rid of the guilty feeling when he and Augusta made love that it was someone else he held in his arms.

To Edward's surprise, a letter arrived asking him to present himself at the Italian Embassy in London to be honoured once more for his feat at Arina, 'for the sinking of the Turkish ammunition ship, *Huda*, and the surrender of the gunboat, *Tahaf*'. By this time the incident had been magnified out of all recognition, either for propaganda purposes (because the Italians wanted to make sure of their British friends), or simply because the newspapers wanted to sell more copies.

Edward took Augusta with him. *The Times* he read on the train was full of speculation about the Balkan crisis. Austria was not satisfied with Serbia's reply to her ultimatum and had broken off relations. But according to the self-satisfied tones of the 'Thunderer', 'This is far from a real war. It is only a diplomatic manoeuvre, though a particularly violent one that must not be allowed to get out of hand.'

Augusta watched proudly as the Italian ambassador hung round Edward's neck the Order of the Crown of Italy. There were two other recipients – both Italians – and champagne was produced. Newspapermen, most of them representing Italian papers, were brought in, and their flashguns dazzled everybody and filled the room with smoke. Later Edward and Augusta dined quietly at the Café Royal before taking the train home.

Two days later, the press was wild with stories about Russian mobilisation. Reading between the lines it seemed everybody was engaged in a gigantic bluff. Considering the Russian move had put the Fatherland in danger, Germany was demanding that the Russians demobilise at once. This demand was refused.

August brought the news that Germany had declared war on Russia and, two days later on France, because of her alliance with Russia. The Germans were also insisting on free passage for their armies through Belgium. For the first time alarms were sounding in London. Britain had guaranteed Belgian sovereignty during the last century and could hardly back down now.

Maurice suggested Edward make an urgent trip to Paris.

'Firm who runs boats on the Seine,' he pointed out. 'Pleasure craft. Bateaux mouches, don't they call them? They have three orders with us. In view of the political situation they want to cancel. We need someone to go and tell 'em they bloody can't. How's your French?'

'Better than it was. Can I take Gussie?'

'Why not? I'd go myself – like a shot. Love a night or two in Paris – but I need to be here to stop Father overdoing things.'

Augusta, who had never been out of England, was thrilled at the prospect and bought a whole new outfit for the journey.

'We're only going for a couple of days,' Edward laughed.

She gave a little sniff. 'It isn't every girl's chance to go to Paris. It'll be wonderfully romantic.'

Dover and Calais were jam-packed with returning travellers, and the train to Paris was packed with Frenchmen, reservists to a man, who were off to join their regiments. At midnight, war was declared.

Flags had sprouted everywhere and the boulevards were packed with people, streetcars, cars and cabs moving past at a faster speed than normal. All seemed to be occupied by soldiers. Lorries roared by, crowded with men and kitbags. Patriotic slogans were shouted. Crying women and children kissed their menfolk goodbye.

It was impossible to get anything to eat in the hotel because chefs and waiters had been called up.

'Is it always like this abroad?' Augusta asked incredulously.

Edward went to the offices of the bateaux mouches people, where it turned out that the owner had himself been called up. His father, whom he had left in charge, had no authority either to write cheques or make decisions. There was nothing Edward could do.

Back in the hotel he found Augusta on the verge of tears.

'I want to go home,' she said. 'And I don't think I ever want to go abroad again.'

Nobody queried Edward's failure. The seriousness of the situation was clear to all, except perhaps Augusta, whose dream of a romantic Parisian interlude had been so rudely shattered.

At the yard, Egg was in a state of nervous agitation. 'It's war, Edward,' he said. 'I don't see how we can stay out of it. And war means business for us. Lots of it. The navy'll be crying out for our boats.'

'I don't know,' Edward said. 'The navy's like an exclusive yacht club for admirals. Most of them have never handled anything less than a battleship for years. They'll want to fight the war with big guns.'

'I'm not so sure,' Egg replied. 'I've had enquiries already. In any case if it goes on a long time, they'll need to push up production. Big ships need small boats to serve them. We'll need all the space we can get.'

Maurice was called in and they sat round the table arguing the thing out. 'Engines are going to be the problem,' Maurice said.

'So why don't we build more?' Edward said. 'We know how.'

'Money,' Maurice said bluntly. 'Expansion requires money. We've already gone almost to our limit acquiring the new premises.'

'If it's equipment for the navy, surely the government will pay.'

'Hrmph!' muttered Maurice. 'The government has some very funny ideas about money. They think that because a Rolls Royce chassis costs around a thousand pounds, the engine to go in it costs the same.' He gestured at the row of design drawings spread along the table, watched over by Egg's new assistant, Josh Butler, a blond young man who looked like a grown-up baby.

'We could sub-contract, Mr Bourdillon,' Butler said. 'There'll be plenty of small firms who'll lose civil trade with the war and will be glad to take on the work.'

'Who'll pay 'em?'

'Surely we'll get advances?'

It was decided finally to scout round smaller firms with a view to signing up a few for sub-contracting, but not to commit themselves in any way. It was also decided to make sure of supplies of timber, rope, paint, and all the other things they were likely to need.

'There's one other thing,' Egg said as the meeting closed. 'The Italians have increased their order to fifteen. But that, they say, will be the end because they're proposing to build their own at Motoscafo Armato SVAN. The boats for the Turks won't be allowed to go, of course, because they're expected to come in with the Germans. The ones you sold to Bulgaria are already there, but we'll not get permission to send any more. That's all right because the Admiralty will surely take any we have. The ones for Russia – well they *can't* go because we can't get them to their bases. We can't get them to the Black Sea because they have to go through the Bosporus which the Turks would never allow, and we can't get them to Kronstadt because the Germans control the entrance to the

203

Baltic. We could send them to Vladivostock but that's the other side of the world and they wouldn't do much good there. The Russians haven't any enemies in the Pacific.'

'However –' Egg smiled '– the Greeks have come up with a firm order, and we can get the boats to Switzerland through France. The navy's already started commandeering vessels being built for foreign nations. And the same rule will apply to us. Which raises a final point. At this moment there are four Bourdillons in Antwerp on their way to Finland. They represent a great deal of money. It was a private contract initiated by a man called Gerhardt Neimhoff. He's the agent for a Finnish shipping company in Turku and I believe he intends to use them as launches on his ships.'

'Name of the company?' Edward asked.

'North Baltic Shipping.'

'It's not Finnish,' Edward said. 'It's German and Gerhardt Neimhoff is neither a Finn nor an agent for a Finnish shipping company. He's a German arms buyer. You're selling to Germany.'

Egg sat bolt upright. 'Good God, boy, are you sure?'

'Quite sure.'

'Then we ought to stop them moving beyond Antwerp. Perhaps we can encourage the Belgians to buy them?'

'Why not the Royal navy?'

'Why not indeed? Someone ought to go across there and make arrangements.'

'Don't look at me,' Maurice said. 'Send Ned. He's the linguist. And a hero.'

'I'm not a bloody hero.'

'You've got a medal to prove it. Or is it two now?'

Egg looked at Edward quizzically. 'I have to agree with Maurice,' he said. 'There's one man for this job, and it's you.'

30

All naval ships had been ordered to coal and the great vessels began to leave Portsmouth for their stations, squadron after squadron of gigantic floating steel castles moving across a misty sea.

In London, pacifist speakers were mobbed and German traders, of whom there were plenty since Queen Victoria's marriage to a German prince, put up their shutters. Those wealthy people in the West End, of German descent, who had come to England with the Hanoverian kings, were busy hiding their ancestors' portraits in the cellars.

But mobilisation notices had not dropped through letter boxes in every street in the country as they had in France. Britain still relied on a volunteer army.

Then, suddenly, things changed overnight. From an obscure little town called Mons in Belgium came news of a terrible defeat. The papers were full of the names of men who had been killed. And the defeated British units, struggling across France, were the remnants of famous regiments people had come to believe were invincible.

Edward decided it was time he told Augusta about the Antwerp trip.

'But you've only just come home,' she stormed.

'I'm not going to war,' Edward insisted. 'I'm only going to Belgium to bring back our boats. We'll never get paid for them if they stay where they are.'

'Aren't the Germans going through Belgium?'

'Not that fast. I'm sorry, Gus. But I have to go.'

It required a street map of Antwerp to find out exactly where the boats were.

'Compagnie van der Essen,' Egg said, trying to avoid Augusta's frosty stare. 'The boats are lying at their wharf. Etiènne is an old associate of mine. He'll give you all the help you need. But you'd better hurry. Look.' He passed a newspaper to Edward.

The French were attacking in the Ardennes and Lorraine to win back the provinces lost in 1870. Arrows on the hurriedly drawn maps showed the Germans merely holding them while their right wing swung in a wide circle to the north to cut off Paris as they had in 1870. There was also a report of disaster off the Broad Fourteens. Three old armoured cruisers manned chiefly by over-age and over-weight reservists had been sunk in an hour by a single submarine.

'You don't want to believe everything you read in the papers.'

Edward looked up to see Sam, grinning from ear to ear.

'Thought I'd come and see what you were up to,' Sam shook his old friend warmly by the hand.

'What about Rosina?'

'She's here too. At my Ma's.'

'You're a sight for sore eyes, Sam. And you've turned up, as always, in the nick of time.'

Antwerp seemed to be on the point of collapse. A hastily assembled British naval brigade, mostly reservists or untrained recruits, badly armed and under-equipped, had been landed but had been surrounded. The city was in a panic expecting the Germans to march in at any moment.

The Scheldt was flat and greasy-looking as they swung into it and headed upstream. The great Hoboken oil refineries along the banks had disappeared in a great cloud of black smoke, burning oil running into the water so that there was a flaming current flowed in midstream. There were no steamers at their berths and the wharves were deserted. Beyond the buildings they could hear the thunder of heavy shells bursting along the outskirts.

But the lights of the city were still on, shining through a drifting drizzle on to the black water as they went ashore. Beyond the dark silhouetted buildings they could see rising columns of smoke and the air was full of floating scraps of charred paper and ash.

Almost the first thing they saw was a British van, with 'Typhoo Tea' plastered on the side, scarred by shell splinters. It had been used to move some of the equipment of the naval brigade to the front. On the driver's seat was an abandoned naval lieutenant's greatcoat, and Edward put it on against the rain.

The warehouses of the Compagnie van der Essen were silent and dark. Outside were four cradles but only three Bourdillons.

'What in God's name are we going to do with 'em?' Sam asked. 'The Germans will be here any day. And where the hell is the other one?'

Edward gazed at the wrecked houses and uprooted paving where shells had burst. Dead horses still lay in the shafts of smashed service waggons. There was no sign of life. A few of the houses still displayed a Belgian tricolour or even a paper Union Jack which had been put up to welcome the naval brigade.

Nearby was a barricade of felled trees and carts and next to that a church, where Sam and Edward decided to spend the night. Civilians slept in huddled groups round the walls on piles of straw. Old men kept watch, slumped on comfortless chairs, their veined hands folded patiently. A whining child was soothed by its mother, a girl who looked as young as Augusta. The priest informed them that the naval brigade had been cut off but many had got away.

It was impossible to sleep, although both men dozed off from time to time. At first light, they found a café and were able to obtain coffee and rolls. The owner's face was grey. As they left, a Belgian battery clattered past on the pewter-coloured cobbles. Above them a German monoplane seemed to hover, the sun shining through the varnished fabric of the curved wings.

Refugees appeared, moving northwards through the city, leading horses and carts, pushing wheelbarrows and perambulators packed with their belongings. The carts were full of old people and children, pale-faced and nodding with weariness. Behind them came some Belgian Army stragglers, bedraggled scarecrows, their narrow, hungry faces hollow-cheeked and blank with weariness.

Eventually, Edward spotted signs of life at van der Essen. The three boats they'd seen were still there and now the fourth had appeared in the water alongside a slip.

Etiènne van der Essen was a small bespectacled man who spoke English almost without an accent. But he could not conceal that he was desperately nervous.

'The Germans will be here within days,' he said. 'We can no longer hope to stop them.'

'Why is one of the boats in the water?'

Van der Essen sighed. 'I was going to use her. A kilo-metre away downriver there's a Dutch freighter, the *Mevrouw Koolhaven*, lying at the explosives wharf. She's full of ammunition for the Germans.'

'And what were you intending to do?'

'Blow her up.'

Edward reflected that you couldn't judge people by their looks.

'We considered filling the Bourdillon with explosives – I have plenty of stock in the warehouse. But the time setting for a fuse was too difficult. So I went to the library to find out and I read of a spar torpedo. We filled a steel cylinder with dynamite and packed it with mud from the river. All we had left to do was fit the detonators. I thought we might drive the boat at the ship's side and jump overboard. I think the French did something of the sort in the last century and sank a ship called the *Bayonnaise*.'

Edward remembered that ship, too.

But he was less concerned with doing damage to the Germans than with getting Egg's boats back to England. With extra drums of petrol stacked on board, it might have been possible to cover the distance, though from Antwerp the crossing could be treacherous.

Van der Essen promised the petrol, but, without crews and engineers experienced in sophisticated marine engines, Edward couldn't see how they could even get the boats downriver.

'Could we use one to tow the rest?' he asked. 'Or could we get them aboard a ship, perhaps?'

'Which?' van der Essen asked. 'We have two British vessels here – sister ships, *Liverpool Street* and *King's Cross*.'

Edward raised an eyebrow.

'The *Liverpool Street* is seaworthy but her bunkers are empty. The *King's Cross* has coal but her engines are out of action.'

'Great,' said Sam.

'Couldn't we coal the *Liverpool Street* and put two boats aboard her? Perhaps take the other one on a long tow?'

Van der Essen gave a sad smile. 'Are you aware of what a job coaling a ship is? She would have to go to the coaling wharf. And there are no tugs. They've all bolted for Ostend.'

'Has the *Liverpool Street* no steam at all?'

'Enough to work the winches, perhaps.'

'So why can't we work her up alongside the *King's Cross* and transfer her coal?'

'Do you realise how long it takes to coal a ship? We would need men. Many men.'

'What about all those refugees? Where are they going?'

'They are hoping to go to England.'

'Well, maybe they'd like to work their passage.'

The two old ships lay under a row of cranes just along the wharf. They stank of decaying hides and rotting potatoes mixed with the faint odour of tar and brine. They were old-fashioned with untidy clusters of derricks round their masts. The hulls had been painted black but the superstructures, which had once been ochre, looked as though they hadn't seen a paint brush for years. They were the archetypal tramp that plodded round the world carrying every kind of cargo under the sun.

By the grace of God they found a small tug called the *Boetje Otto* which had *not* vanished to Ostend and the skipper, a tough-looking Fleming, offered to help.

'Anyt'ing to stop de goddam Huns,' he said.

The master of the *Liverpool Street*, a man called Houghton, was sleeping off a colossal drunk in one of the nearby hotels. The master of the *King's Cross* had long since departed for England.

209

They hauled Houghton from his bed and dragged him to the café where they started filling him up with black coffee.

'We're commandeering your ship,' Edward said.

'You bloody young whippersnapper,' Houghton snarled. 'Who are you – navy?'

'Yes.' The lie came easily.

'Where's your uniform?'

'I had to ditch it. To pass through the German lines.'

Houghton pulled a face. 'Well, you're out of luck. My ship's out of coal.'

'We're going to bunker her. Know the *King's Cross*?'

''Course I do. Right astern of me. First time we've been in port together for twenty years. She's full of coal but the shaft bearing's gone and you can bet your last quid there won't be a spare in Antwerp.'

'What about your crew?'

'Bolted. Most of 'em, anyway.'

'Can you round the rest up?'

'Why?'

'We're taking your ship home. With her captain.'

Houghton was a stubborn man who had long given up hope of advancement. It took an hour of bullying and wheedling to get him to change his mind. But, as his hangover eased, he finally began to see what they were getting at. Seaman enough to know exactly what to do, he began to organise wires from the stern of his ship to pull her out past the bow of the *King's Cross* and lie alongside.

Somehow, they managed to round up the bedraggled remnants of his crew. There was an engineer officer and two or three of the black gang among them, and they knew their jobs backwards.

'You'll never do it,' Houghton said gloomily. 'You can't shift coal with half a dozen men.'

They ignored him. As the *Boetje Otto* nudged the *King's Cross* alongside her sister ship, receiving nothing more than a dent, a bent rail and a shattered derrick boom, the remnants of the naval brigade began to appear in the neighbouring streets looking for a means of reaching England. They were a mixture of Marines and sailors, unshaven, dirty and some wearing items of Belgian uniform because they had given their own clothing to the wounded.

One of the sergeants saluted and explained what had happened. He assumed, like Houghton, that Edward was a naval officer and instinctively looked for guidance. 'We landed on the sixth, sir,' he said. 'And went straight up the line. We never saw no Germans. Just Zeppelin and bloody Krupp shells lobbing over us into Antwerp. They sounded like the District Line on the London Underground going over. We were told to expect a Uhlan charge, sir. In the end we pulled out but we still didn't see no Germans. Is the war lost, sir?'

'Not on your life,' he said. 'How would you like to see home?'

'Not 'alf, sir. What you got?'

'I've got a ship with coal and no engines and a ship with engines but no coal. It needs a bit of elbow grease. Think you and your friends might like to lend a hand?'

31

While Houghton's men began to raise steam on the *King's Cross* to power her cargo winches, Sam occupied himself with getting the Bourdillon in the water on to a cradle and up the slip, and moving all four boats to the wharf where the ships lay. It didn't take long before one of the Belgian refugees approached, and, in halting English, asked if they could help in return for a passage to England.

By evening the quay was full of men, women and children. Sam found plenty of assistants, even women, willing to push the heavy cradles and work the crowbars. Winches started clattering and great canvas slings of best Welsh coal were dumped in clouds of black dust on the decks of the *Liverpool Street*, where it was pounced on by men with shovels and sacks.

With the derricks working, they needed more sacks and barrows, and Sam was dispatched to find them. He came back with his party, eyes gleaming.

'You know where we saw the 'Typhoo Tea' van,' he said. 'It's just like van der Essen said. There's nobody there. Only a watchman. He told me they all hopped it when the shells started dropping. He's off himself now. I can't tell you the amount of bang there is there. He showed us. We helped ourselves to their barrows and trolleys.'

They manhandled the equipment aboard the *Liverpool Street* and within minutes the decks were packed with sweating marines, floating coal dust and the rattle and clatter of winches, as coal swung from the *King's Cross* to the *Liverpool Street*.

'How long to raise steam for the main engines?' Edward asked the engineer.

'Four hours. We can do it in four hours.'

Edward was surprised to see a familiar figure appear on the gangplank. It was Alexander Owen-Smith, the curate from Porthelt. He carried a small suitcase and looked immaculate in a lightweight fawn suit and panama hat. As he stepped on deck, Edward stopped him.

Owen-Smith stared at the dust-blackened face. 'You,' he said, incredulously. 'What on earth are you doing here?'

'I'm taking this ship back to England.'

'In that case, I demand a passage. I'm a British citizen.'

'British citizens are working their passage.'

'You can't expect me to do that sort of work.'

'Then get off the bloody ship.'

Anger and petulance chased themselves across the curate's face. In the end he controlled himself and drew a deep breath. 'What must I do?'

'Take your jacket off for a start.'

The exchange was watched with interest by the coal-blackened Marines and refugees. Their fear seemed to have dispersed with having something to do and they were all more cheerful. Some of the women had gone into town to buy bread and doorstep sandwiches were thrust into the grimy hands of the hungry workers.

The coaling was finished by evening.

'Captain,' Edward said to Houghton. 'Why don't we tow the *King's Cross* home with us?'

Houghton guffawed. 'Don't talk daft, lad.'

'All we have to do is get her out of the river. The navy'll be out looking for lost British ships. They're bound to show up as soon as we're clear of German artillery. We could get two ships and twice as many people to safety.'

'Can't be done. We'd have to have the towing hook right on the stern. Anywhere else the tow would foul. That's why tugs have their towing hook in the middle of the ship. So they can turn back and forth and still keep the tow steady.'

'We've got the *Boetje Otto*.' Edward gestured at the Bourdillons. 'I came for those,' he said firmly. 'I'm going to get them home. For the navy.'

They found the skipper of the *Boetje Otto* was agreeable to attaching his ship to the *King's Cross'* stern and acting as a jury rudder to manoeuvre her downriver behind the *Liverpool Street*.

'So why don't you have a go?' Edward said to Houghton. 'And win yourself a medal. Think what your wife will say.'

Houghton laughed. 'She went off with the mate from the *Shulmar* two years ago while I was in 'amburg.' He glanced up at the towering structures of the dockside cranes. 'My cargo hoists have a maximum lift of three tons. We'll need one of them.'

'No problem,' said Edward. By his side stood a man in a blue suit and bowler hat. Behind him, a woman and two children were standing guard over their suitcases.

'Monsieur Schalcken,' he said. 'Dockyard manager. He'll work the crane in return for a passage to England.'

As Schalcken climbed to the cab of the crane, the boats were manoeuvred into position. Slings were fitted and one by one the boats were hoisted into the air and lowered, two to the *King's Cross*, two to the *Liverpool Street*. When they were lashed in place, the ships looked topheavy but Houghton wasn't worried.

'They'll be all right,' he said. 'So long as we don't have gale force winds.' He grinned at Edward. 'Christ, lad, pull this off and I'll have to hand it to you for sheer bloddy cheek.'

'We leave at first light,' Edward said. 'We'd better warn the naval brigade to bring in their outposts.'

There was no need. The outposts were already in.

'The German Navy's arrived,' an officer informed Edward briskly. 'Two armed trawlers with three-pounders on the bow and a machine-gun on the stern. The *Schwan* and the *Tolpel*. They're lying in a trot alongside a coaster name of *Mevrouw Koolhaven*.'

This was bad news. These boats would be lying across their path as they headed for the sea. 'We'd better check this out,' said Edward.

They found the trawlers without difficulty, moored alongside the little coaster at the explosives wharf. Men were moving from the warehouse to the ships. The old 'Typhoo Tea' van still stood under the trees.

'If we could put a match to that there warehouse,' Sam said, 'it'd go up a treat. The ship alongside would go up because it's full of explosives, too. And if *that* went up, so would them two trawlers.'

'How about a torpedo?'

'We haven't got one.'

'No, but van der Essen has.'

'They'd blow you out of the water.'

'I wasn't thinking of doing it from the water,' Edward said.

The 'Typhoo Tea' van's engine showed a marked reluctance to start, but Sam wasn't a fitter for nothing and, eventually, as he swung the starting handle, it roared into life. The sudden noise was drowned by the thud of shells to the east, and no-one showed the slightest interest from the quayside where the German trawlers were moored.

There was a crack as they removed a branch or two from the overhanging acacias as they turned, but then they were driving slowly down the shallow slope to van der Essen's warehouses and the quayside.

Van der Essen's foreman brought out the steel cylinder they'd been working on and gingerly located detonators against the top layer of explosive. Then he produced a cap made of wood. In it were three holes through which long metal spikes had been inserted.

'When they're pushed in,' van der Essen explained, 'they strike the detonators and set off the explosive. I hope it works.'

'You're not the only one,' Edward said. 'Get everybody aboard.'

Sam crossed himself. 'I'm not a Catholic yet,' he said, 'though Rosie insists on the kid being brought up properly. But a little prayer never does any harm, does it?'

As Houghton mounted the ladder to the bridge of the *King's Cross*, Edward climbed into the driving seat of the van. The 'torpedo' had been jammed into place over the mudguard so that it protruded a good two feet in front, and lashed securely into place. Remembering *Fairy*, Edward had seen that it was backed up with a baulk of timber to stop it from moving.

'I just hope I can get out in time,' he said with a grimace to Sam.

As the van climbed the slope to the main road, they both spotted the grubby fawn suit and panama of Owen-Smith.

Edward braked, and the two men jumped out. 'I bet the bastard's on his way to warn those bloody Germans what we're up to,' muttered Edward as they gave chase. Sam launched himself in a flying tackle which sent the curate crashing to the cobbles.

'What the hell are you up to?' Edward snapped, grabbing him by the collar.

'I don't wish to go with you.'

'You'll be interned.'

'Better than being killed.'

'You've changed your tune since yesterday. Tie the bugger up, Sam.'

His hands secured behind his back by his braces, Owen-Smith was bundled into the back of the van and they trundled slowly up to the road that ran behind the warehouses and parallel with the quayside.

'For God's sake,' Sam breathed as they manoeuvred with difficulty round a narrow corner, 'don't run into anything with that thing in front.'

At the top of the slope that led down to the explosives wharf, they parked the van and climbed out. Sam stuffed a handkerchief into Owen-Smith's mouth and tied it tight with his tie.

There was no movement near the explosives store but they could see a sentry near the door, silent and still in the shadows.

Sam pushed Owen-Smith against a wall out of the way of the blast, while Edward edged the van forward and slowly turned the corner. There was only an inch between the nose of the torpedo and a wall, and he was conscious of the dryness of his lips as the metal spikes leading to the detonators just brushed the bricks.

Then he lashed the steering wheel to the choke lever with a heaving line from the *King's Cross*. Shoving the throttle forward, he wriggled from the seat. As he did so, his jacket pocket caught the gear lever and wrenched it into neutral. With the hand throttle advanced, the engine began to scream. Edward wrenched at the jacket. It tore and he fell out of the door, the van's wheels only just missing his legs. As he picked himself up, Edward saw the sentry outside the store stare at the advancing vehicle and open his mouth to shout.

Engine screaming, the thick-spoked solid-tyred wheels rumbled faster and faster over the cobbles, but started to drift off course.

'Christ, Sam. It's going to miss.'

The van suddenly mounted the pavement. For a moment it looked as though it would fall on its side, and then it skidded into a brick building yards from the target.

Nothing happened. But then there was a roar and a tremendous blast that blew Edward on to his back.

The first explosion was followed by another that merged into a long sustained rumble. What seemed like a hot breath from hell took his breath away, searing his lungs as if from a blowtorch. Windows shattered. A wall collapsed and bricks and other debris flew through the air, including the driver's door from the van, which bounced and clattered before coming to a stop against a tree which had been stripped of all its leaves.

Desperately, Edward shielded his head with his arms and felt his hands beaten by bouncing objects. Slowly the noise subsided. Edward sat up. Sam was crouched, wild-eyed, against the wall.

There was nothing left of the explosives store. Just a great cloud of brown smoke lifting slowly into the air. As it began to clear, they saw that every scrap of the building was gone except for a broken wall no more than a few feet high and a pair of burning doors. The *Mevrouw Koolhaven* was nothing but a twisted iron hull. Beyond her, the two German trawlers leaned on one another as though exhausted, their bridgeworks shattered.

But of Owen-Smith there was no sign.

The *Liverpool Street*, with the *King's Cross* in tow, moved slowly down the river, with the *Boetje Otto* attached by a hawser to the stern of the *King's Cross*.

As they moved slowly past the half-submerged trawlers, they saw horsemen with lances and strange flat-topped headgear gallop down the slope. They were about fifty strong and were followed by a car carrying staff officers. Voices floated across the water and there were a few shots.

Bullets whacked into the yellow sides of the Bourdillons. As the firing grew heavier the people on the crowded decks crawled on hands and knees to the shelter of the deck houses and hatches. The shouting was renewed, but fortunately the Germans had nothing more powerful than rifles. The Marines on board returned fire, which discouraged the cavalry who were in an exposed position, and gradually, as the ships drew out of effective range, the firing petered out.

They cleared the city and were in the estuary by mid-day. By mid-afternoon they were in the Channel in a thinning mist, and eventually, a British cruiser carrying a commodore's pennant crossed their bows. An Aldis lamp began flashing.

'Do I reply, sir?' said one of the naval brigade to Edward.

'Got a lamp?'

'Yes, sir.'

'Tell him "*Liverpool Street*. Towing *King's Cross* and carrying refugees and four Bourdillons for the Royal navy." '

'How do you spell Bourdillon, sir?'

Edward repeated the message and grinned at Sam. 'It'll get into the newspapers, Sam. Wait and see. Nothing like a free puff for the old firm.'

32

The rescue of two unimportant merchant ships and four boats stood out like a small beacon in the darkness of defeat after Mons, the sinking of the three armoured cruisers, the fall of Antwerp and the loss of the bulk of the naval brigade. There was little to crow about so the propagandists seized on their small victory and it got full headline treatment. Egg was quick to explain to the newspapermen who turned up next day what 'Bourdillons' were, ending with the same comment Edward had made – these quick boats would undoubtedly be wanted by the navy.

By the time Edward and Sam stepped ashore at Harwich, the press was there in droves. The two men managed to extricate themselves from the crush, only for Edward to be escorted to one side by a grim-faced naval commander.

'I'd be obliged,' he said 'if you would shut up. A statement's being prepared. You'll get full credit for everything.'

'I don't want your bloody credit,' Edward snapped, short-tempered with tiredness. 'But Captain Houghton would doubtless appreciate a mention in your statement.'

The commander insisted on escorting Edward to see the admiral, a tall man with a hawk nose and bushy eyebrows.

'What the devil were you doing in Antwerp?' he demanded.

'Business.'

'I heard you were navy,' the commander pointed out. 'The captain of the *Liverpool Street* said you were.'

'I had to say something. To get him on his feet.'

The admiral and the commander exchanged glances. 'Pity you're *not* in the navy,' the admiral observed drily. 'We could do with a few like you. My chaps say you destroyed two German ships with a torpedo.'

'Three actually.'

'How in God's name did you manage that?'

Edward explained.

The admiral thought for a moment. 'So far most of *our* efforts with torpedoes have been a great deal less successful. The bloody things sink or go off-course.'

'This one was home-made.'

'How the devil did you deliver it?'

'In a 'Typhoo Tea' van.'

It took a bit of explaining but the admiral seemed satisfied in the end. 'And then,' he pointed out, 'they say you performed some miracle bunkering an empty ship, which you used to tow home a broken-down vessel. Both carrying refugees. How many?'

'I don't know. I didn't count them.'

'The navy did,' the commander said coldly. 'There were five hundred and forty-three. Perhaps Mr Bourdillon should have made a list.'

The admiral frowned. 'Bourdillon?' he said. 'Bourdillon? That name's familiar.'

'Arina,' the commander said. 'An Edward Bourdillon sank the Turkish ammunition ship, *Huda*.'

The admiral peered at Edward under his eyebrows. 'That wasn't you as well?'

'Yes, sir.'

'What exactly are you?'

'I'm foreign sales executive for Bourdillons, the boatbuilders.'

'You're in the wrong line of work!' The admiral turned to the commander. 'Give him a drink, James. He looks whacked. What's more, he's dropping coal dust all over my carpet.'

Edward would have been home earlier if he hadn't been required to supervise the loading of his boats on a ship bound for Portsmouth. But it was worth the wait. Egg pumped his hand – even Maurice looked pleased – and, behind her anger, Augusta's eyes glowed with pride and joy. Only Georgina hit the nail on the head.

'You're too lucky to be true, Ned,' she observed quietly.

'The navy are ready to sign on the dotted line,' said Egg. 'They've really got the wind up.'

In France, the Germans seemed to have been stopped. The fighting had settled down now to trench warfare, with the troops of both sides squatting in muddy holes in the ground in a system that stretched all the way from neutral Switzerland to the sea, neither side knowing quite how to get round the other.

At sea German raiders, despatched from German ports before the war, were lying across the shipping routes and sinking British vessels. One of them, the *Emden*, was caught by the Australian cruiser, *Sydney*, but another, the *Königsberg*, had sunk a merchant ship, the *City of Winchester*, on passage to Aden. Then, catching the old cruiser, *Pegasus*, in harbour at Zanzibar, she had blown her out of the water before disappearing again.

On the whole, however, England had been little affected by the fighting. Things continued very much as before, and the Vicar's sermons quickly slipped back to the tedious old platitudes. The War Minister, Lord Kitchener, predicted that the war would be a long one, but nobody believed him. It was confidently expected hostilities would end before the coming summer.

However, Egg's books were suddenly full of orders for picket boats, launches and lifeboats. The boatyard resounded to the sound of saws, drills and planes, the clang of hammers and the clatter of donkey engines. There was nothing much for Edward to do but see the sub-committee at the Admiralty, who were in charge of buying. Though Egg was still toying with the idea of his hydroplane, Edward could see little hope. On his desk was a letter which stated Admiralty policy quite plainly. 'There appears to be no necessity for the government to continue experiments in search of this kind of craft,' it said. 'The design of small quick boats for war would naturally have priority if it could be shown there was a need for them. But action at sea, as events have shown, indicates that most of the work will be done by the big guns of big ships.' It seemed a short-sighted attitude, considering how many submarines or fast launches could be built for the price of a battleship.

221

'I'm thinking of opening an office in London,' Egg announced one day. 'That's where the business is. If they won't come and see us, we must go and see them.'

'We're moving too fast, father,' Maurice said. 'We haven't got that sort of capital.'

Egg would have none of it. 'The office in London'll be only a sort of agency,' he explained. 'No big staff or anything like that. I've got Lord Northcliffe behind me.'

'With money?'

'Well, no. With stories in his newspapers. Publicity.'

Maurice didn't have much time for newspaper proprietors. 'He'll have some other scheme tomorrow,' he said.

'Bourdillons is fine,' Egg insisted. 'We're already under contract to other yards and, of course, we're sub-contracting ourselves for bulkheads and things like that. Don't worry. We have orders for four boats for different places in America and six for the Admiralty. We've also got four with smaller engines to go to South Africa. That chap, Leroux, you met in Switzerland, Edward. Because he runs a whaling fleet, he's been chosen by the South African government to find boats for harbour duties in Cape Town, Port Elizabeth and Durban, and he thought of us. It's a war order and I want you to take them.'

'When?'

Egg looked sheepish. 'Well –' he said '– now.'

'What's Gussie going to say?'

Gussie was plunged into gloom. 'You've only just come back. Why can't Maurice go?'

'Too fat,' Edward observed. 'And too unadventurous.'

As soon as he spoke, Edward knew he had said the wrong thing.

'That's the trouble,' she said sharply. '*You* aren't. You're itching to be off again, I know.'

She was dead right, of course. Returning to work, Edward had seen Sam absorbed smoothly into Bourdillons. But was tired already of sitting in long, dreary sessions of sub-committees at the Admiralty, of technical officers who knew too much and politicians who knew nothing at all.

'It's business, Gussie,' Edward said angrily when she challenged him about it yet again at dinner.

'You've only been home a few weeks.'

'Gussie, there *is* a war on. And the country depends on business to pay for it.'

'Father says it's up to everyone to carry on normally,' she insisted. 'He says wars can't be won by gadding about. He says we should leave it to the soldiers and sailors.' She was well into her stride now. 'Father says –'

'Bugger your father,' Maurice interjected.

'Maurice!' Aunt Edith cried.

'Well –' Maurice was furious '– what does he know about it? As Ned says, there's a war on and that means we don't go on living the same comfortable lives we did before. Everybody's working at the yard all hours God sends. Including me, which is something. And there's the Vicar prattling on and expecting people to take notice. It's a farce.'

Augusta tossed down her napkin and hurried from the room.

'Sorry, Ned, old boy,' Maurice mumbled. 'Unforgivable. Overtired, I suppose.'

Edward shrugged. 'It was bound to be said some time.'

He found Augusta sitting on the bed, her eyes full of tears. 'The trouble is,' she sobbed, 'men like you love wars. You can't wait to be off. But what about me?'

Edward put an arm round her shoulders but she shrugged it off. 'If anything happened to me and I died, you'd still go on with your work. The first person who came along and said, "There's a job for you in Timbuktu", you'd go. But if you knew you'd never go off anywhere again, you'd be devastated. Oh Teddy, how can you do this to me? What if you are killed? What would I be left with? The memory of two months. It's not much, is it?'

After the sinking of the three old armoured cruisers off the Broad Fourteens, there was a great concern about the threat of submarines, and the ship bound for South Africa went at full speed. It was an uncomfortable trip. The vessel shuddered so much under the vibration of the engines that even meals were difficult since the plates slid around the tables. Volunteer look-outs all

223

saw submarines. Porpoises and whales were regularly reported as enemy undersea craft, and there was an alarm almost every night.

But they reached Cape Town in record time, and Edward was pleased to find Leroux waiting there with his family at the Mount Nelson Hotel.

South Africa was keen to capture South-West Africa, a German colony just to the north of the Union on the west coast. However isolated it was, the Germans were noted fighters. No one expected it to be a walk-over. And before the colony could be captured, the Boer rebellion in the Transvaal and the Orange Free State had to be put down.

That wasn't all. There were too many small German enclaves in Africa, and fighting had broken out in Togoland and the Cameroons. In East Africa a campaign had started which looked set to range over vast territories, great lakes, mountains, jungles and swamps.

Mrs Leroux seemed pleased to see Edward. Krissie kissed him on both cheeks but seemed subdued. Leroux explained later that she had married a soldier who was now in the government forces at Vereeniging heading for Bloemfontein in search of the Boer general, De Wet.

Over at least two bottles of champagne, the two men discussed both the rebellion in the Transvaal and Leroux's ambitions to break some records in a souped-up Bourdillon. It came as a surprise when the manager of the hotel came over to say that Edward was wanted in Reception. Edward excused himself and was introduced to a couple of naval officers, Captain Covington and Lieutenant-Commander Higgins, who had insisted on a private room for their meeting.

Covington wasted no time in coming to the point.

'We want to take advantage of your advice and experience. Heard of the *Königsberg*? Light cruiser.'

'I know what the *Königsberg* is.'

There was a silence in which Covington shuffled a few papers. 'She sank the *City of Winchester*, then caught the cruiser, *Pegasus*, in harbour and blew her to bits. It set a few alarm bells ringing at the Admiralty, I can tell you. Jacky Fisher's idea of selling old ships from foreign stations to pay for his new dreadnoughts is coming home to roost.'

Higgins sniffed. 'Well, now the *Königsberg's* been found,' he said. 'In the Rufiji delta. Know where it is?'

'As it happens I do. I've been into Mombasa a few times. You'll have a hell of a job getting her out. It's like Hampton Court maze in there.'

'We've discovered a few things about her,' Higgins continued. 'A German survey ship charted the waterways of the delta. But so have we. There are four channels she could have used to get in there. We know she's acquired maps, fresh fruit, and coal from German East Africa. She's also rigged up a coast-watching service with field telephones and telegraph lines. What they haven't discovered though, is how to get out again without being seen, and we understand they have boiler problems.'

Covington spread out a chart on the table. 'She's here. Difficult to see because they've fastened trees and branches to the masts and funnels. Damaged machinery's been sent to Dar-es-Salaam and repaired. They've positioned machine-guns and heavy guns along the shore, and they have men in trees and in the mangrove swamps keeping an eye open. She'll try to escape. However –' Covington paused '– we've not been without success ourselves. We obtained the services of a seaplane, and a pilot with Mark I eyeballs. We're now covering three of the exits from the river, and we've sunk a blockship across the fourth. They're trapped.'

'So why don't you sink her?'

'That's where you come in,' Covington said.

'I guessed that would be the catch.'

'It's difficult to get close. Shallows. Sandbanks. That sort of thing. She's just beyond reach and she'll blow anything we send in out of the water. She can't get out but we can't keep three valuable naval vessels and supply ships sitting off the mouth of the Rufiji for ever.'

'Go on.'

Covington sighed. 'I suppose we could sink more blockships and leave it to the mosquitoes and the water to do for them. They've got malaria and typhoid on board. But we can't afford the time. We're expecting *Goliath*. She's old and no damn good for anything but she's carrying a fast launch. All our torpedo experts are in the Channel

225

and the North Sea waiting for the German High Seas Fleet to come out.'

'I'm not a naval officer.'

Covington smiled. 'I don't think that presents us with any problems,' he said.

Two days later Edward was kitted out in white tropical uniform with two gold bars on his shoulder, and his Italian decorations, plus a medal Edward didn't recognise.

'It's a new one,' said Higgins. 'For torpedoing those German trawlers in Antwerp.'

When Edward laughed, Higgins looked indignant.

'Well, you did, damn it,' he snapped. 'And brought home two ships and six hundred refugees.'

'But I'm not a naval officer.'

'You are now. And your commission's been backdated.' Higgins smiled. 'I've been in the navy twenty years and all I've got is a tidgy little thing they gave out for the Diamond Jubilee. You ought to be proud.'

Against his better judgement, Edward discovered that he was.

33

'*Dearest Gussie –*' as Edward wrote the sweat dripped off the end of his nose '– *I appear to be in the navy. I'm not sure how. I think I'm a pressed man, and it seems I won't be coming home as soon as I expected.*'

Even as he looked at what he had written, Edward knew Augusta would never believe he hadn't engineered it.

By this time there was a small fleet of ships off the mouth of the Rufiji, with attendant colliers, supply ships and a fleet of small boats scuttling about between them like water beetles.

Edward had settled down uneasily aboard the *Goliath*. She was a 17,000-ton ship, with four tall funnels and a colossally wide beam reminiscent of the brass and white paint ships of the previous century. She looked every day of her age, out of date, slow and useless. The ship's company could have been specially selected. They were overweight reservists, for the most part, none of them happy at being recalled to sea. Her officers, with very few exceptions, were of much the same vintage. Among them Edward was regarded as some strange sort of primeval creature who had actually seen war at close quarters. With the exception of an occasional bombardment, the navy had not been in battle since Nelson's day. Most of the men didn't have the first idea about what war entailed and didn't seem over-eager to find out.

The temperature had passed the 100-degree mark and, with no wind, it was like being in the mouth of an open oven. When a wind did blow, it was as if it came direct from hell. Everybody was suffering from prickly heat, tinea or some other form of skin complaint caused by excessive sweat. Writing letters was difficult even when you could raise the energy, because they were always smudged by the drops of sweat. It was necessary to place a towel or a blotter under the wrist to prevent the paper sticking to the skin. Swimming would have been pleasant but there were crocodiles and a fish like a pike that was liable to take a bite out of your legs.

All day the sun blazed down on them. It was almost impossible to stay in the cabins, and to risk exposure on deck was plain stupid. Awnings had been rigged up but they didn't reduce the sweltering heat. The air they breathed was sweltering. They could only console themselves that it must be a thousand times worse on the *Königsberg*, which was lying hard up against the river bank somewhere, its company a prey to mosquitoes and mangrove flies.

The hardships were made more irritating because the German ship had disappeared again. The first attempts to get near her had failed, with river mud choking condensers, pumps and evaporators. *Goliath*'s trudging launch, with its dropping gear for two 14-inch torpedoes, was, it turned out, Covington's idea of a fast motor boat. There had been a number of unrealistic suggestions for getting the torpedo to the *Königsberg*, including doing it with a skiff or even a dugout canoe, but none that looked like having the remotest chance of success.

The heat remained intense. The crew was so unhappy that the prospect of action was actually welcomed. *Goliath* moved close inshore, and set her steam launch and four motor boats in the water. They were all full of red-faced men, their clothes saturated with sweat, cursing under the load of weapons and equipment.

Edward studied them from the well of the launch. Nobody had asked his views – in fact, he hadn't got any – and the lieutenant in command of the launch, an older man called Crump, who had been in the navy for some time, could not hide his resentment about the way Edward had been instantly promoted to a rank it had taken him years to achieve.

They were dazzled by the glittering water as they left the cliff-like sides of *Goliath*. The object of the mission was to make an attack on the shore defences thrown up by the German commander. No-one was very keen because no-one fancied setting up camp in the mangroves.

At low tide the land was a maze of creeks and brown mud and the constant threat of malaria, blackwater fever, yellow fever, elephantiasis and other unmentionable diseases. In the searing heat of the day you could hear the silence. At night the delta came to life with the splash of jumping fish, the strange groaning sound from the trees and the sighing cough of crocodiles.

There was no talking as the little flotilla drew closer to the shore. The water was the colour of milk chocolate, and not far away a flock of grey pelicans bobbed up and down on the wavelets.

The sudden burst of firing made Edward jump and the pelicans vanished in a noisy clatter of wings. Edward saw splinters leaping from the gunwale of the steam launch within a few feet of his face. Tucking his head down, he peered across the water under the brim of his pith helmet, wondering exactly where the firing was coming from. Then he saw wisps of smoke among the trees and realised the Germans had lined the whole of the shore on both sides of the creek. A man yelped in pain and fell backwards into the bottom of the boat. There was blood on his face but, judging by the oaths he was using, he wasn't badly hurt. A line of bullet splashes in the water indicated they were under fire from machine-guns.

The boats began to turn away and several more men were hit. There was a sudden flash on the side of the steam launch and Edward saw the starboard torpedo chocks drop away and the missile they were supporting bellyflop into the water. The line of bubbles veered erratically through the fleet and he saw one boat after another take desperate evasive action.

From behind the trees a raft appeared. It consisted of two logs fitted with a small outboard motor. Between the logs was a torpedo.

'For God's sake,' Crump yelled. 'Talk about Fred Karno's navy. Starboard your helm!'

Fortunately the German torpedo was no more accurate than the British one. It swung round in a circle so that the Germans had to heave their raft to port as it whisked past them to run up on the mud and explode against a tree.

Both sides hooted with laughter. 'Ve exchange you,' one of the Germans yelled. 'Yours for ours. Zey are all as bad.'

It looked as though torpedo attacks were out of the question. To run the gauntlet of concealed defences through the maze of channels presented unacceptable risks to the boats' crews and the likelihood of getting close enough for a clear shot at the cruiser was remote. But the admiral in command, chivvied from Cape Town and London, refused to accept defeat. As they sweated uncomfortably through the following weeks, two Sopwith seaplanes arrived. Loaded, they couldn't get off the water and, stripped down almost to their spars, the pilots found themselves aloft without observers or bombs and with only an hour's supply of fuel. In that steaming corner of Africa the glue that helped hold the machines together started to run. The laminated propellers warped and the fabric of wings and fuselage shrank and became brittle.

Two weeks later, two strange-looking vessels appeared off the delta. They were around 300 feet long and 50 feet wide but they had only three feet of freeboard. Even fully laden they drew little more than six feet. Each had a single funnel and an 80-foot mast amidships.

'*Severn* and *Mersey*,' Crump said as he came back after a visit to the strange new ships. 'Built for the Brazilian Navy for use up the Amazon and taken over by us when the war started. Slow as snails and can't be long away from port, but they have two six-inchers and two four point sevens. They've seen some action off the Belgian coast and were going to be used at Gallipoli.'

More ancient aircraft arrived soon afterwards, but they were in bad shape. Edward's expertise with engines was called on. They experimented with fuel blends and adjusted the carburettors until the threads of the screws were worn. They trimmed and retrimmed the aircraft, and even removed the exhaust systems to build new ones. In the murderous heat tempers frayed quickly. On the other side of the world, ships were being lost on both sides from shells, torpedoes or mines, among them great

230

battleships and liners. But under the roasting sun of East Africa, hundreds of men were doing nothing but pursue one small German raider, struggling with out-dated equipment because everything else was being held in England for the expected clash in the North Sea with the German fleet.

Men began to go down with malaria and Edward was one of them. Taken to *Goliath*'s sick bay he eventually emerged weak and pale. But he continued to work on the engines, until they began to get something like a show from the aircraft.

'Let's go and have a look at this wretched tub,' said the pilot to Edward. 'And don't jerk around too much or we'll be crocodile meat.'

It was a great deal cooler at 1000 feet. The clatter of the engine made conversation impossible but Watkins soon pointed out the German cruiser that had defied their efforts for so long. It looked like a grey-green cigar covered here and there with foliage. Her sidescreens and awnings were spread, smoke was rising from her funnels and she looked surprisingly smart, considering how long she'd been there.

As they returned, the engine began to make clattering noises mixed with breathy sighs and choking coughs. Then it stopped altogether. The propeller came to a jerky halt. But the pilot knew his stuff, and they glided safely down to where a group of British whalers waited in case of trouble.

Returning to the mouth of the delta, Edward found shipwrights and seamen being drafted to the monitors to prepare them for battle. Their decks were being built up with sangbags. The compass and hand-steering wheel were protected with more sandbags and the bridge was screened with piled hammocks, while scores of men hung over their sides painting them the same green as the mangroves.

On Edward's birthday the monitors steamed down the coast, as close inshore as they could manage, to familiarise themselves with the landmarks and the route through the river maze. The following day there would be a high tide which would carry them over the mudbanks.

All unnecessary equipment had been removed. Galley fires had been extinguished. Every man was issued with four meat sandwiches, and baskets of oranges and buckets of oatmeal and water were placed about the ships.

At four in the morning, with the other warships in position to give support, the monitors began to creep forward, each towing a motor boat.

A mist shrouded the river and flotillas of pelicans clattered into the air with the first shot.

'Forty-seven millimetre,' someone said laconically. 'Over there. On the bank.'

As the firing started the motor boats drew back, ready to pick up survivors. Taking his boat to the sheltered side of the *Severn*, Edward waited as the three-pounders began to crack away to keep German heads down. Through lulls in the din, he could hear the high-pitched buzzing of the spotting aeroplane overhead. By 6.30, with the sun well up and the heat tremendous, the monitors slowed to a stop.

'Let go anchors.'

They were around 10,000 yards from the target and the first shots were short. The monitors were soon being straddled.

'They're firing four to every one of ours,' someone commented.

'It's a good job they're not hitting anything.'

A piercing yell came from one of the look-outs on the *Severn*.

'Torpedo!'

They could see the line of bubbles quite distinctly but couldn't work out from where the torpedo had been launched. Every gun in the area opened up and the torpedo leapt broken-backed from the water.

The din was terrific. Overhead Watkins was trying to drop bombs on the German ship. None of them scored a direct hit. But puffs of smoke rose from the water and the mangrove tops shook under the blasts.

The *Königsberg's* shells were falling on the river banks, hurling mud and bushes into the air. The *Mersey* had been struck twice and her forward 6-inch gun had been knocked out. The next shot hit her motor boat and

Edward saw it disappear in a shower of spray, planks, pieces of metal and human limbs.

Severn was also taking heavy punishment. The anchor was weighed and she began to move. The firing continued throughout the day. And, as the sun began to drop towards the horizon, the monitors headed back to the river mouth. As they came alongside *Goliath*, there were cheers from the men lining the rails as the exhausted boats' crews climbed back on board.

'Finish it tomorrow,' Crump said, knocking back a gin in the wardroom.

'It'll be nice to be in at the death,' Edward said drily.

'Not you, old boy,' Crump grinned. 'You're away.'

'Where to?'

'Some business on Lake Tanganyika, Number One says. They've got two motor boats. Real ones. That sounds more like your cup of tea.'

34

Edward climbed aboard the steamer, *Trent*, heading with sick and wounded for the field hospital on the Mbuni River. The monitors were preparing for another engagement, and as *Trent* reached the open sea, Edward heard the dull thudding of guns. A little while later, there was a tremendous explosion. A huge column of yellow smoke rose over the distant trees. At lunchtime the signals officer confirmed it was the *Königsberg*.

'Thank God for that,' Edward said. 'I hope the next job's a bit easier.'

When they landed under the shadow of Table Mountain, Edward was hurried to the base at Simonstown where the job was outlined by a pink-faced captain.

'Lake Tanganyika,' he was told. 'Thirteen thousand square miles of water and one of the longest lakes in the world. German East on one shore, Belgian Congo on the other, a bit of Northern Rhodesia in the south. The Germans have two gunboats on the lake based at Kigoma. We, as usual, have nothing. By attacking unarmed craft, the Germans control the lake. The tribes on the Belgian shore, having been treated like slaves by the stupid bloody Belgians, favour the enemy.'

Edward waited patiently for his role to be explained.

'We've discovered that a large motorboat can be carried from England to Cape Town and transported 1800 miles by rail to Elizabethville and Jadotville in the Belgian Congo. It can then be dragged by oxen and traction engines through the bush to Sankisia where it can again be loaded on a train to the Lualaba River on the Upper Congo. It can be floated down to Kabalo and from there go by rail again via Lukuga to Albertville on the shore of the lake.'

'Seems a hell of a long way round to fetch me all this way south and then send me back north again!'

The captain smiled bleakly. 'Unfortunately, we couldn't see any simple way of getting you across German East Africa to rendezvous with the boats.' We're not sending one boat, but two. They've assigned an officer to command the expedition, and qualified petty officers and technical ratings will accompany them. The boats are already on their way. We want you to catch them up. I presume you've been vaccinated and inoculated against smallpox and typhoid.'

The Lerouxs were still in Cape Town. They had just returned from Johannesburg where they had been attending the funeral at Vereeniging of their son-in-law. He had been an early casualty in the defeat of the rebel Boers.

Krissie insisted on picking Edward up in her father's car and taking him to Sea Point for dinner.

'I didn't love him,' she confessed. 'He was only interested in beer and cricket. Marrying him was Pa's idea. His family had money. They were in shipping. It all linked up with the business.'

'I'm sorry.' Edward couldn't think of anything else to say.

'Next time it'll be my choice.'

She put a hand on his thigh and Edward turned towards her. He was fully aware by this time that he had married Augusta on the rebound from her more worldly elder sister. Attractive and loving as she was, she didn't manage to ring bells. There could never be the deep-seated passion he had felt for Rafaela and – he had to admit it – continued to feel.

He kissed Krissie gently on the cheek. 'I think we'd better go,' he said.

Next morning Edward started the long journey north.

It wasn't full summer, but enough dust drifted through the slatted shutters of the railway coach to veil every surface. He caught up with the expedition at Elizabethville. Morale wasn't exactly high.

One of the officers, a slight but energetic man called Dudley, had seen service in the Boer War. He had qualified as a second mate in the merchant service and had ridden 200 miles on a bicycle along roads and native paths to join the expedition. He took to Edward at once.

'The commanding officer's a bloody lunatic,' he said bluntly. 'The last decent job he had was commanding the Downs Boarding Flotillas and he managed to have one of his gunboats torpedoed in broad daylight while he was ashore showing off to a bunch of women. Ended up in command of a desk at the Admiralty.'

Edward met Spicer-Simpson at dinner that evening. He was a large man with a beard, close-cropped hair and a twangy drawl. He wore a uniform he had designed himself for the expedition. It included a tunic like an army staff officer but with blue tabs in place of the usual red ones, a grey-blue flannel shirt, a navy blue tie, a naval cap badge and buttons, but army rank insignia. He studied Edward's medals with undisguised curiosity.

'I see you've had a bit of experience,' he said. 'But I don't recognise this one. What is it?'

'The Italian Order of the Crown, sir.'

'What did you get that for?'

'For sinking the *Huda* in Arina harbour in 1911, sir.'

Edward was aware of a few sidelong glances around him.

'I think you'd better show Bourdillon the boats,' Spicer-Simpson said to Dudley.

'Forty foot,' Edward said when he saw the Thorneycroft launches. 'Eight foot beam, three-eighths mahogany. Two hundred-horse Z6 engines, twin screws, nineteen knots.'

'Okay. I'm impressed,' Dudley confessed.

'Bourdillons built a few under contract.'

Called *Mimi* and *Toutou*, the boats were on cradles. With them, parked alongside the railway, were two huge trailers with solid rubber tyres.

'They'd better be good and strong,' Dudley said. 'We've got a long way to go.'

The trail had already been surveyed, and hundreds of Africans had cleared and levelled the track. Boulders had been removed, trees felled, and firewood stacked for the traction engines.

The two traction engines arrived soon afterwards, tall vehicles with huge steel-spoked driving wheels, high smokestacks, whirring flywheels and canopies to shelter the driver. They each came with a ten-ton trailer that had been constructed to carry the wood the machines would burn.

Two days later they set off. There were a 150 bridges in front of them, all old and rickety. It took twelve hours to cross the first stream they came to. The following day one of the traction engines, manoeuvring near a drainage ditch, was pitched sideways as the ditch crumbled. It took an age to get it upright. By the end of the month they found the specially constructed cradles for the boats were collapsing. Thirty miles from the place where they could join the railway again they foundered completely.

'We'll have to send back to the coast for help,' Spicer-Simpson said.

'Why not adapt the wood trailers?' Edward suggested.

'Do you know anything about it?' he was asked icily.

'Enough.'

'So what are we waiting for?'

It took several days to do the work, since not only had the trailer to be rebuilt but rudimentary A-frames rigged with block and tackle had to be constructed from local timber to lift the boats. Dudley was growing increasingly anxious. 'The rainy season's almost on us,' he said. 'If we don't get a move on we'll sink out of sight in the mud.'

But after the oxen arrived, the expedition managed to travel six miles during the day. Tsetse fly and disease-carrying ticks pursued them all the way to the Mitumba Mountains. The loads were hauled uphill by the traction engines, the oxen and by the sheer muscle power of hundreds of Africans. The descent was even more treacherous. The launches threatened constantly to run away and wreck everything. But thanks to the inventiveness of a grizzled petty officer, a series of blocks, tackles and ropes made it possible to lower the boats inch by inch to the valley below.

The constant worry was water, both for drinking and for the boilers of the traction engines. When search parties failed to produce enough, Edward and Dudley recruited a party of 150 African women from the local villages and, having found a tiny stream, led them back in a straggling column, each woman carrying a clay water pot filled to the brim on her head.

Sankisia, a wretched, fly-blown village, was the terminus for the narrow gauge railway to Bukama. The expedition was sweaty, dusty and exhausted, but there was a sense of mounting optimism. It took only two hours to cover the fifteen miles to Bukama on the banks of the River Lulaba. However, the steamer that was to carry them downriver was not there because the river hadn't been as low for six years.

'Why not float the boats down?' Edward suggested. 'We build 'em to float after all.'

'Too deep a draught,' Spicer-Simpson decided solemnly.

They went ahead nevertheless. Towed by barges rowed or poled by Africans, they set off downstream, with a fleet of dugout canoes following with supplies. The heat was appalling. The air was heavy with the dank, decaying smell of the river and the mud that was stirred up as the African labourers worked chest-deep in water, hoisting the launches shoulder high in the shallows to move them to deeper water.

A river steamer waited at Musanga. The launches were lifted aboard by dent of great effort and in constant peril of swinging out of control, and the steamer trudged off with traders, chickens, goats, elephant tusks, provisions, crates, boxes and bags, every spare inch of space stacked with wood for the steamer's fireboxes.

Reaching Kabalo, they transferred again to the railway which would take them via Lukuga to Albertville on Lake Tanganyika. The rains were still holding off. Nobody had succumbed to sunstroke or any of the abundant tropical diseases. And miraculously they reached the lakeside in working order.

'It was nothing,' Spicer-Simpson said, absorbing the praise like a sponge. 'Only required a little thought and effort.'

By this time, he was flying a vice-admiral's flag and, against the heat, had taken to wearing a skirt which was a cross between a sarong and a kilt. Edward was amazed to see his legs were covered in tattoos.

With the rains late, the tropical storms started. At first there was nothing more than a breath of wind that lifted little whorls of dust. This was followed by rumbles of thunder in the distance. Then the sky changed from grey to yellow to purple, and the storm burst in a hurricane of wind, thunder and slashing lightning. Enormous breakers rose on the placid lake, to crash ashore uprooting trees and demolishing native huts. They couldn't leave the boats unprotected and more long columns of Africans were engaged to haul tons of rock to the water's edge to construct a breakwater.

As they worked, the German gunboat, *Kingani*, steamed past on patrol. She looked like an out-of-date tug, but she did carry a six-pounder gun and tried a few speculative shots. But she was way out of range.

'Hadn't we better start arming our boats?' Edward asked.

'My thoughts entirely,' Spicer-Simpson said. 'Get the machine-guns out.'

'You'll not stop anything with machine-guns. Why not three-pounders?'

'The boats won't take three-pounders.'

'They did at Arina.'

Spicer-Simpson frowned but agreed.

During the first weeks of December the storms continued to lash the coast but *Toutou* was slipped into the water just before Christmas. The engines were tested and the first trial run was made.

Spicer-Simpson seemed to be permanently in a bad temper and an attempt to put up Christmas paper decorations was forbidden. But on Boxing Day, with boats now floating, everyone paraded for an inspection and church service in best naval style. Spicer-Simpson was reading aloud from the Prayer Book when a message arrived for him. Stuffing it in his pocket, he went on reading as if nothing had happened. Beyond him everyone could guess what it was about. The *Kingani*, on another circuit of the lake, was just rounding the point.

Spicer-Simpson didn't move until the service was over and the ship well past, then he ordered the chief petty officer to dismiss the parade and man the launches. It was a clear bright day with a rising wind, and thousands of Africans lined the shore of the lake to watch the coming battle.

As the two boats roared out of the recently built harbour Edward was ahead in a private Belgian motor boat called *La Belle Duchesse*, which they had borrowed, a slow vessel that was to be used as a decoy. She carried nothing but an old French Hotchkiss mounted on the bow and a crew of three. She flew the Belgian flag in the hope that such a defiant gesture would encourage the Germans to turn on her.

The *Kingani* moved slowly along the coast. She had passed that way often enough for her captain to be full of confidence. It came as quite a surprise to find *La Belle Duchesse* crossing his bows. The *Kingani* swung round and fired a shot that landed only 30 yards away.

'Steer towards the shot,' Edward yelled at the coxswain. 'They won't drop the next one in the same place.'

As the boat's bow turned towards the circle of disturbed water, a second shell landed in the spot she had just left.

'Follow the shot.' Edward looked about him for Spicer-Simpson. 'Come on, you clot,' he muttered. 'We're not just a bloody target.'

Another shell plunged into the water. Then they saw the two Thorneycrofts sliding into view to take up positions between the *Kingani* and her base. Spicer-Simpson in *Mimi* manoeuvred to starboard while *Toutou*, commanded by Dudley, swept round to port.

The German captain was still watching the *Belle Duchesse* through binoculars when he suddenly spotted the other two boats roaring towards him, white ensigns fluttering. He made no effort to change course, intent on finishing off the irritating Belgian challenge first.

The wind was making the lake choppy and all four vessels were rolling heavily. As the *Kingani* increased speed, a dark column of smoke billowed from her funnel. Another shot came dangerously close to the *Belle Duchesse* then, over the rattle of the engine, they heard the thump of the Thorneycroft's three-pounders, and the *Kingani*'s gun swung away to counter the new attack.

'About bloody time,' Edward said.

Blinded by the spray, he searched for their target. 'Where the hell is she?' he yelled.

'Starboard quarter, sir,' the engineer yelled back.

'Come on then. She can only fire forward. We might as well join the fun.'

Kingani was already in trouble. As she began to swing, trying to bring her gun to bear, the *Belle Duchesse* darted in, the Hotchkiss clacking away. A man on the deck fell, and, as the German vessel turned back again towards the slow Belgian launch like a deer harried by hunting dogs, the other two boats darted forward from opposite sides. A shell struck her near the 6-pounder and, as the *Kingani* swung away again, they saw her foredeck suddenly erupt in flames. A man on the stern began to wave what looked like a white tablecloth.

'Christ,' the engineer said. 'That was quick.'

The speedy end to the fight took them all by surprise and Spicer-Simpson, ever anxious to show off, took *Mimi* in with a flourish.

'Oh, Lor',' the petty officer coxswain said gleefully. 'He's rammed her, sir.'

The commanding officer and his crew were sent sprawling on the deck and, with her bow badly damaged, *Mimi* was backing off. As she ran for the shore to be beached before she sank, Spicer-Simpson was waving his arms frantically in an attempt to pass orders by semaphore. Neither Dudley nor Edward took any notice.

As *Toutou* removed the two survivors from the gunboat, it was Edward, as officer commanding the prize crew – one man from *La Belle Duchesse* and one from Dudley's boat – who hoisted the white ensign above the German colours.

35

By this time Augusta's letters were growing desperate. She had gone to London to work as a nurse but seemed unable to understand that Edward was now caught up in the war. She had seen him off to South Africa as a civilian and couldn't grasp that he was now part of the navy and no longer sole master of his fate.

Her letters had been chasing him round Africa as they had followed him round the Balkans, and he felt somehow that he had cheated her. He had not, he knew for certain, ever really been in love with her but he was convinced they could be happy together, if only because she was honest and kind. But he could not put out of his mind her complaint: 'I loved you and wanted you and you were never there.' He hadn't been much of a husband, but, remembering Krissie Leroux, he could at least feel that he had tried to be honest and faithful, and might hope that everything would come right when he was allowed to go home. Who would have thought that a war could last so long.

With the lake now under British control, the fear had ended of a native rising against the Belgians. Troops could move safely. The *Kingani* was hauled out of the water, patched up and refloated, with a 12-pounder mounted on the bow. It could only be fired forward because the recoil across the beam would have capsized the ship, but, with command of the area in Allied hands, other vessels the Belgians had not dared to launch before were put into commission and the fleet began to grow.

They had hardly finished their repairs when the second German gunboat was sighted looking for the vanished *Kingani*. She was twice the size of the *Kingani*, now renamed *Fifi*, and carried two 6-pounders and a Hotchkiss. When intercepted she was far too fast for *Fifi* and was beginning to draw away when *Mimi* roared ahead of her

242

and opened fire. Since the German ship's only usable gun in such a position was the Hotchkiss on her stern, she turned about to bring her six-pounders into action. *Fifi* drew inexorably closer. A well-aimed shot crashed into the Germans' engine room and water poured in. The German ship began to sink.

With the destruction of the German vessels Spicer-Simpson had removed the reason for his being there. It meant he was no longer a commander-in-chief but an ordinary naval officer again. He vanished homewards to the inglorious office job he had left only a short while ago.

His departure caused a realignment of men because the Allied armies in East Africa were in difficulties. The German commander was performing miracles with a scratch contingent of sailors from the destroyed *Königsberg* and German native soldiers who, contrary to expectations, remained loyal.

In France enormous numbers of men had been lost at Ypres, Verdun and the Somme. Every attempt to get at Germany by the back door – Gallipoli, Salonika and Mesopotamia – had suffered the same horrendous losses. The only strategy was simply to hold on. In East Africa, where the battles were minor affrays, the true enemies were disease, the climate, the swamps and the country itself. There wasn't a unit that hadn't been thinned by malaria, dysentery, blackwater, typhoid and enteric.

Men were in very short supply, and Edward was soon recalled to Simonstown where he was marched in to the captain in charge of appointments.

'I've got just the job for you,' he said cheerfully. 'Freetown, West Africa. Small boat pool. It's in a shocking mess. But you know about small boats. It'll be a doddle. You'll be able to sit on your backside ashore under the fan with a gin and let other people do the work.'

It didn't work out like that.

Freetown rose, white, brown and gaudy green from the Portugese Steps to Tower Hill, from Clyne Town to Kongo Town, from the Mohammedan quarter out beyond Kissy. Past the stained green statue of William Wilberforce, the Law Courts and the Cathedral. Past the seedy bars and cloth shops and up the slopes by the bungalows of the Creoles and the Whites, surrounded by the unpainted boxwood houses that abutted, dry and sundrenched, on the town centre, packed in by the mud and beaten-tin dwellings of the poor.

It was a place of riotous colour and noise. But Edward's office was comfortable enough with a fan and chief petty officer to run things. And the promised gin was available in the wardroom of an old liner moored in the harbour as a depot ship. Edward had been there only two days when Chief Petty Officer Jennings approached him with a problem.

'Sir,' he said. 'King Jim.'

'Who's King Jim?'

'It's not a him, sir. It's a village at the top end of the River Bunce.'

'What's it done? Sunk without trace?'

'No, sir. There's been a bit of trouble up there. The chief's a chap called Akeledi. Decent type. But he's flogged a white man.'

'And?'

'Well, we can't have these chaps doing things like that, can we?'

'What do you propose we do?'

'It's not what *I* propose, sir.'

'I imagine you have a general idea all the same, Chief.'

'Yes, sir. The feller he flogged is well known round here. Chap called Toby Golightly. He's an ex-officer from before the war and, begging your pardon, sir, he's a bloody nuisance. We're always having to bale him out.'

'What sort of a nuisance precisely?'

'Booze, sir. And women, sir. He won't leave 'em alone. He beats 'em up and, well – there's no other way to put it, sir – he rapes 'em, sir.'

'So why hasn't he been put away?'

'He has. They shove him in the lock-up for a bit to cool down, but then he starts demanding his rights as a white man and in the end they let him out again.'

'What's he done this time?'

'Chief's daughter, sir. Name of Florrie Akeledi. Picked the wrong girl this time. The old boy, Akeledi, tied him to a tree and flogged him.'

'Can't say I blame him.' Edward was unmoved. 'What am I supposed to do?'

'Missionary up there kicked up a fuss, sir. Said he couldn't treat a white man like that. Sub-Lieutenant Robertson thought he'd better nip up and see. He was running this place until you arrived, sir.'

'Chief, are you suggesting I go up there and sort it out?'

'Yes, sir, I am. It needs somebody with a bit of authority. I think Mr Roberston's going to walk into trouble. He's only young, sir, and I hear them tribesmen are out with spears and clubs.'

'Who was this bloody fool missionary who got him up there?'

'Chap called Owen-Smith, sir.'

'*What*?'

'Owen-Smith, sir,' he repeated. 'The Reverend Alexander Owen-Smith.'

'From Heidelberg, by God.'

'I don't know about that, sir. He's running the district for one of the mission societies. They're a bloody nuisance too, sir, begging your pardon.'

'Have we a boat?'

'Steam launch, sir. And a little motor boat for getting ashore.'

'Have 'em ready. With a party of men.'

'Big one, sir?'

'No. Little one. How long will it take?'

'Most of a day to get there, sir, then half a day through the bush. It's heavy stuff up there. I once went up after a deserter. He was glad when we caught him.'

As the boat plodded upriver with its load of men, they could see crocodiles basking on the mud. They weren't always easy to spot in the sunshine until one of them opened its mouth to reveal yellow gums and saw-edged teeth. Terns splashed like bombs into the river after fish, while pelicans took off and landed like the big ugly seaplanes with which they had hunted the *Königsberg*. A native fisherman, balancing upright in a pencil-slim dug-out, flung a circular net and a great Susu canoe sped past under a bellying sail towards the open sea. The helmsman held up a basket.

'Egg, boss?' he yelled. 'You want egg for cook?'

As they reached King Jim the launch glided to a stop and an anchor was thrown over the side. The smell of hot earth, sweat, river mud, decayed fish and excrement wafted from the land like the fumes from a heated dust-bin. Women left their corn-pounding and crowded round, black breasts rubbing against white arms.

The bush, with its high foliage and overhanging trees, was stifling. The trees seemed to hold down the heat so that all the men sweated endlessly in the hot breath of the land. They spent an exhausting night fighting off mosquitoes.

At midday they caught up with Robertson's party.

'Thank God you've come, sir,' Robertson said. 'I'm not sure I'm up to this job. But this Owen-Smith parson fellow insisted there was trouble and we should be here. We lugged the Lewis gun with us, too. Damn heavy in this heat.'

'Where is Owen-Smith now?'

'Well, he was with us when we set off but he seems to have disappeared.'

'Sounds fairly typical. Where does he hang out normally?'

'Here, sir. In King Jim.'

'Right. Where do I find the chief?'

'Over there, sir.'

About a hundred yards away from Robertson's party, a line of Africans had appeared. They carried spears and clubs and shields and wore feathers and monkey skins round their waists.

'The chief's the fat chap, sir. In the middle. Wearing the bowler hat.'

'Right. Stay here.'

'You're not going up to 'em are you, sir?'

'Have you got a better suggestion?'

'No, sir.'

'Right, then.'

Hitching up his shorts which were being dragged down by the heavy revolver at his hip, Edward began his lone walk across the parched earth.

The Chief also stepped forward, and there was a fidgety movement among his men.

'Greetings, Chief Akeledi.' Edward swallowed hard. 'We make palaver.'

'Greetings, Sah.'

'I do not come in enmity, Chief. I want white man, Toby.'

'He locked up, sah.'

'I know. I still want him.'

'White bosses always free Toby, sah.'

'Not this white boss, Chief. This one put Toby on ship. He go. For good. He not trouble Akeledi no more.'

It took a good half hour of discussion in pidgin before the Chief agreed to hand his prisoner over. After that, it was fairly straightforward. The natives gathered round Edward and one or two hands reached out to finger the insignia on his shoulders. With this curious escort, Edward walked towards the village. Robertson's men began to follow.

'Mr Robertson!' Edward roared. 'What the hell do you think this is? An Easter parade? Get your men formed up properly.' He turned to Jennings. 'See to 'em, Chief.'

With Jennings yelling a series of strident commands, Robertson's men shuffled into some sort of order to bring up the rear, Robertson pink in the face.

In the village, local beer was produced. Robertson stared at his with distaste. It was served in the bottom half of a beer bottle, which had been cut in two by part-filling it with oil and dipping a red-hot rod into it.

'Swallow it down, Robertson,' Edward snapped. 'The man's offering you hospitality.'

He managed it down without pulling too much of a face. The sailors didn't make the slightest protest and knocked back their drinks with relish.

Golightly was produced, an evil-looking man with a high-class accent and an even higher body odour. His clothes were filthy and he was unshaven.

'Bastard had me flogged,' he growled.

247

'Did it hurt?' Edward asked.

'I'll say it did.'

'Good. Tie his hands, Mr Jennings.'

Golightly exploded. 'What? Are you siding with these black bastards?'

'Did you rape the Chief's daughter?'

Golightly grinned.

'Right. Tie 'em tight, Chief,' said Edward. 'And place a guard over him. If the bugger lets him get away, I'll have his stripes.'

'You can't do this!' Golightly yelled. 'I'm a white man. You have to let me go.'

'Not this time.' Edward turned to the grinning Jennings. 'I think it's time we had a word with the Reverend Owen-Smith.'

The mission was surprisingly large and comfortable. They were met at the door by a black girl dressed in an elegant but decidedly old-fashioned dress. She was pretty and slim and wore green shoes that obviously had not been made in Africa. Her name was Ili Komorrah.

'Where is the boss man?' Edward said.

'The Reverend Owen-Smith has gone to Freetown,' she answered in excellent English. 'You will find him, I expect, at mission headquarters in Kissy Street.'

They set off as dusk was falling, with Robertson's boat bringing up the rear. Golightly was sitting on the deck of the steam launch with a sailor's foot planted firmly on him in case he tried to jump overboard. As they reached Freetown early next morning, Edward waved Robertson's boat alongside.

'Take the motor boat with you,' he said. 'I've got a job to do.'

He spent a long time checking the ships anchored in the bay, big ships, some of them with troops on board. They found one that was about to leave in convoy for England, and Edward climbed aboard and spoke to the captain and the officer commanding the troops.

After the ship had departed, Edward made a complete report to the Commodore commanding the station.

'You did *what?*'

'I shoved him on a troopship for home, sir. With instructions to the O/C Troops to see that the police pick him up and deliver him to the army. He's of military age and they've brought in conscription now.'

'Good God, you've got a nerve. Naval officers can't go around deporting people.'

'I just did, sir,' he said.

'Yes, by God, it seems you did. There'll be a devil of a row with the frock coats but I suppose I'll have to back you up. Now tell me more about this Owen-Smith fellow.'

'I've wondered about him for some time. But now I'm pretty sure. I think he works for the Germans.'

The Mission headquarters in Kissy Street was a shabby little place, crammed with black men with holier-than-thou faces and stacked with Bibles, prayer books and pamphlets.

'Alexander came here from the east,' the old clergyman in charge explained. 'He said he'd been caught in German territory by the outbreak of the war – in the Cameroons – and eventually arrived in Sierra Leone via Nigeria. We were glad to have him, of course. We'd just lost our man in King Jim to the navy as a chaplain.'

'Did he make many converts?'

The old man smiled. 'One can't ask too much in wartime. But he's been a great help with the troopships.'

'Doing what?'

'He goes on board and holds services. That sort of thing. The chaplains are always pleased to see him. After several weeks on a troopship, the men like a change of face. He's always happy to talk to them.'

'I'm sure he is.'

The following day, Edward headed back upriver to King Jim. Taking Jennings with him, he searched the Mission House with the black girl, Ili Komorrah, twittering after them like a frightened sparrow, trying to prevent them opening drawers and looking in cupboards. They found several of letters which appeared to have come quite recently from the Cameroons, which until late the previous year had still been German territory.

A fortnight later Edward went down with malaria.

36

The war seemed to have ground to a halt again. The Allies
were floundering in the slime of Passchendaele. The Italians had been routed at Caporetto, but there was one
small item of news that pleased Edward a lot. Italian
high-speed launches built by Motoscafo Armato SVAN
had torpedoed the Austrian light cruiser, *Wien*, in the
harbour at Trieste.

His own personal fortunes changed overnight.

'The Governor's heard about Golightly,' the Commodore informed him cheerfully. 'He's after your head for
usurping his job. I'd buzz off quick, if I were you.'

The malaria struck just as Edward's ship reached Suez.
His temperature peaked at 105 degrees at Cairo. But he
was oblivious. When he woke up in hospital, the first
person he saw was Ginny Gogarty.

'Spy,' she breathed, a wisp of fair hair drifting down
over her eyes.

She vanished at once and he could hear her outside the
door of the ward talking to someone on the telephone.
'You must come at once, Flo. Hurry.'

The nurse who appeared with her he recognised as
Florence Mitchell, one of those he'd met on the border
of Thrace.

'Oh, Spy,' Ginny said softly. 'Fancy finding you here.'

'I think I'm going to die,' Edward whispered.

'Don't you dare,' Ginny said.

Two weeks later, he was riding round Cairo with both
Ginny and Florence in a gharry, seeing the sights and
beginning to feel human again.

Ginny was a delightful companion and a joy to be near,
quite unaware of her own attractiveness. She behaved the

251

same with everybody whatever their rank, and was adored equally by the ordinary soldiers from the desert and by the senior medical officers.

She was a woman who could somehow shrug off the horrors she had experienced first hand. Edward and she dined together and danced at the affairs organised for officers and nurses. The evenings were warm, and Cairo, old, raddled, but exotic, could still work her charm.

To celebrate Edward's discharge back to duty, they took a carriage to the Pyramids. He was uncomfortably aware of her lustrous hair, her lovely figure, her wide grey eyes and soft, smiling mouth. She was absolutely enchanting.

Afterwards they went back to the flat she shared with Florence. It was on the top floor of a building whose bottom floor contained a garage and the office of a middle-aged YMCA worker. The moon was enormous, the night balmy and, riding home, aware of a growing warmth and trust between them, Edward kissed her.

'Aren't you supposed to be married, Spy?' she asked.

'Yes, I am.'

'Then should you be kissing me?'

'Probably not. But you're very special, Ginny.'

'Am I really, Spy?'

He kissed her again.

'You can't come back with me tonight,' she said. 'But tomorrow Flo's on duty and the flat'll be empty. She won't mind.'

He stared at her. 'Ginny, have you ever done this before?'

'No,' she said. 'You'll find me a bit of an amateur. But there's got to be a first time and I can't think of anyone more wonderful than you, Spy, dear.'

The following morning Edward was called to naval headquarters in Alexandria and given his orders.

'We have to protect the Suez Canal,' he was told. 'The only way we can do this is by advancing into the Sinai Desert and pushing up to Syria. But we're not ready for that yet and have to move extremely carefully after they

252

made such a mess of it at Kut. We're going to use boats. Small, fast boats which can move up and down the Canal at speed. You'll be in command. We can't waste your experience, Bourdillon. You'll be based at Ismailia half-way along the Canal. By the way, you've been upped a notch. As from today.'

It pleased Edward a great deal to meet Ginny that evening wearing the extra narrow stripes.

'Oh, Spy,' she said as she kissed him hello. 'I'm not the only one who's noticed how wonderful you are.'

They ate at Shepheards and took a leisurely gharry back to her flat. Inside, they stood looking at each other for a moment, both faintly embarrassed, then she moved into his arms. Her cheeks were cool from the night air.

'I love you, Spy,' she said. 'I didn't realise it at first. But I do.'

'I love you too, Ginny.'

'No, you don't. Perhaps, even, *I* don't love *you*. But war's a funny time to make your mind up about things like that.'

'Maybe,' he said.

'Everybody's living artificial lives, and when it's all over you'll go back to your wife and live happily ever after. Is she pretty?'

'She looks a bit like you.'

'How nice for you. You can consider me her under-study.'

'What about you? Don't you have a boyfriend?'

'Dozens. But it doesn't mean anything, really. It's just having a pretty face and a cheerful disposition. They hang around in the corridors just to say good morning to me.'

'Nobody special?'

She put her arms round his neck. 'Oh, Spy,' she said. 'It's a bloody complicated business, isn't it?'

'You're awake.'

'Yes, I'm awake.'

'Thinking of England, home and beauty?'

'Yes.'

'Does it hurt, Spy?'

'Sadly, Ginny, no, it doesn't. Something's gone. Perhaps if I'd stayed at home and there'd been children, it wouldn't have. But it has. We never had time to put down roots, I suppose. I try very hard to tell myself everything will be all right, but I have an uneasy feeling it won't.'

'Your poor wife.'

'Yes. I feel that, too. Because she's everything she ought to be. But . . .'

Ginny sighed. 'I've been in love once or twice, Spy. Unfortunately, there was always something missing. The man was good-looking, clever, adoring. But what I wanted wasn't there. Until now.'

He turned to look at her.

She smiled. 'I mean, you're what I've been looking for,' she said. 'I don't make a habit of this kind of thing. All we can do is simply enjoy it while we can because it *is* wonderful when you're with someone you love. Flo's boy friend works with the Foreign Office and he has a luxury flat. She's self-indulgent enough to enjoy being in it so we can come here whenever it suits us.'

'No, Ginny,' Edward said slowly. 'I'm afraid we can't. I'm leaving Cairo tomorrow.'

'Oh, no. Not already. Where are you going?'

'Ismailia. I've been made Admiral of the Canal Fleet. That's what the extra stripes are for.'

Their meetings were not so frequent but they still managed to see each other. Edward's job was not an arduous one; most of the time it consisted of sailing up and down the canal, stopping at one of the canal harbours to check on his command. He had four boats available to him. Edward thought at first they were Egg's hydroplanes but they turned out to be Thorneycrofts. Egg had not moved fast enough.

The Thorneycrofts had stepped hulls, and had been designed as torpedo boats from an idea developed by three young officers of the Harwich destroyer force. They were shallow enough to go over North Sea minefields to attack German ships at their base. They were slender little craft and the crews had to clamber about them because they had no real deck. The foredeck was rounded to give the boats a cigar shape and right aft was a counter a yard long built to hold the torpedo.

A dry-voiced torpedo artificer described the method of launching.

'From the stern, sir,' he said. 'Then the boat turns away. The discharge velocity's the speed of the boat less the velocity of the impulse that launches the torpedo backwards. Very successful, sir, with eighteen-inch torpedoes. The depth-taking's very good.'

The torpedo rested on its side on rails in the trough on the stern. 'Discharged by firing a charge of a thousand grains of cordite into an explosion vessel,' the torpedo artificer explained. 'The gas forces a bell-shaped ram against the head of the torpedo and shoves it down the trough and over the stern.'

It was obvious they wouldn't be putting the canal at risk by torpedoing anything there, so the torpedoes and the platforms that supported them were removed to improve the boats' speed. They were now able to reach the astonishing speed of over forty knots, which was brought down to around thirty-five when guns were mounted.

It was soon obvious there was little to fear any longer from a serious attack from the desert because the Turks were being driven back. There was one desperate attempt by a boatful of fanatics with dynamite to destroy the canal, but they were spotted by an aeroplane. The message sent Edward and one of his skippers, an aggressive Scots boy called MacNab, roaring up the canal, creating confusion and alarm among the ships passing through. Cries of fury were hurled by the Arabs doing their ablutions and the women doing their dhobying on the banks, who were almost swept away by the wash. But they arrived before the Turks had set their charges. It was all over in a matter of minutes, leaving one man wounded and a row of dead Turks still clutching their explosives.

As the Allied troops crossed into Sinai, there was less and less for Edward to do. And he slipped away with increasing regularity. The train journey only took an hour or two, and there was Ginny waiting, dewy-eyed and desperate for love.

'I'm beginning to feel like an old married woman with her husband away on business,' she admitted. 'Do you think we should be doing this, Spy?'

It was a question he couldn't answer.

The odd letter from Augusta began to catch up with him. She was still in London and reported that she wasn't the only one to pray for the war to end. The only hope was that now the Americans had joined the Allies, it surely couldn't take much longer. Otherwise, she had been worked off her feet at the hospital, with some new strain of influenza, which was laying low both young and old.

Meanwhile, the Revolution in Russia toppled the Tsar and it was obvious that the Germans, free now to fight on a single front, would make a great effort before the full power of the United States could be brought to bear. The blow fell on the British Army near St Quentin in France. And, with the Germans rushing once more for the Channel ports, the old outcry came for a second front. The Mesopotamia and Gallipoli sideshows had come to nothing, but there was still Salonika in Greece.

There had been nearly half a million men there ever since the beginning of the war to keep an eye on the armies of Foxy Ferdinand of Bulgaria, who, Edward guessed, had never had any intention of getting himself too involved with his German allies. All he wanted was a large slice of Macedonia. But now, with the old plan revived to hit at Germany's back door by going through Bulgaria, Ferdinand was due for his comeuppance.

When Edward received orders to report to Alexandria, he decided it was a marvellous excuse to take Ginny on a short holiday.

They celebrated their arrival by making love in their hotel bedroom. While Ginny slept, Edward got dressed. He was already late for an appointment with Admiral Covington.

'Ah, Bourdillon,' said the Admiral. 'Met you before, haven't I?'

'Yes, sir. Cape Town. You whipped me into the navy when I wasn't looking.'

Covington laughed. 'Of course, of course. Just been looking at your file. Quite a career. North Africa with the Italians. That *Huda-Tahaf* business. Antwerp. Rufiji. Tanganyika. You spent some time in Bulgaria, didn't you?'

'Yes, sir. Selling boats, sir.'

'To King Ferdinand, I believe. Ever meet him?'

'Yes, sir.'

'What did you think of him?'

'Not much, sir.'

There was a pause. 'Do you know the South-east of Bulgaria?' Covington said eventually. 'From Svilencic up to Varna?'

'Very well.'

'Then you're the man I need. We have to draw off troops from the Western Front so we're going to push north and east from Salonika. As you know, the men and guns have been there for most of the war. Bulgaria's sick to death of the whole wretched business. One good shove will finish her off.'

'And me, sir?' Edward said faintly.

'We need someone to handle the shipping when we get there. You'll take your flotillas. They're no longer needed on the canal. You'll have your officers to run the boats. You'll be in command but, since you know Bulgaria and no one else has much of a clue, you'll be attached to the staff for intelligence purposes. Full commander this time, of course. That suit you?'

Edward left in a daze. He had no wish to be a full commander nor to go to Salonika or Bulgaria.

He didn't dare tell Ginny at once. Throughout dinner, she chattered brightly, although she could see there was something on his mind. He was poor company.

And it wasn't long before she said, 'You're going away again, aren't you?'

Edward nodded.

Tears filled her eyes, but she didn't cry. 'Where to this time?'

'Back to bloody Bulgaria. I'm sorry, Ginny.'

She wiped her eyes and smiled. 'Then we had better make the most of the little time we have left together,' she said.

37

Salonika was a bedlam of men, guns and ships ready for the move northwards. Edward's boats were ready for instant action but he couldn't imagine them ever being used. They had brought all their gear, the launching platforms and the torpedo troughs, the fittings for depth charges, the 3-pounders and machine-guns, the tools, the mechanics, the torpedomen and marine fitters.

The sea in the Gulf of Salonika was an exotic green, and the town had a distinct Eastern style, with its minarets and mosques, relics of Turkish rule. The front line was forty miles to the north round Lake Doiran.

Built of lath and plaster, the town had been destroyed by fire the previous year and everywhere were the blackened scabs of its passage. The streets were still covered in sooty ash, and when the Vardar blew from the west the air was full of it, too.

Within a day or two, Ginny's letters began to arrive. Though she seemed to have accepted that he would go home to England and his wife when the war finished, there was no hiding her feelings because they shone through every line on the paper.

Augusta's letters, however, had stopped. Edward could only assume that they were being addressed to Egypt. One came from Egg, however, months out of date. Apparently the firm was enjoying an unparalleled run of prosperity. There was also one from Aunt Edith and, surprisingly, one from Maurice who didn't see eye to eye with Egg about the future.

'Nobody will want to buy boats when the war is over,' he said. 'You'll be able to pick them up for two a penny.'

Augusta's letters finally arrived. They had been addressed to the hospital in Cairo and forwarded, he suspected, by

Ginny. They gave him the news but not much else and it wasn't hard to detect irritation with him.

The general in command of the Allies was a Frenchman called Franchet d'Esperey, and Edward constantly found himself dragged in to endless staff meetings where a naval captain called Bois d'Effre asked questions on the general's behalf.

'Will Ferdinand resist?' he asked.

'From what I know of him,' Edward said, 'he'll be concerned only with preserving what he has – chiefly what he personally possesses.'

'I think he will be luckier than he deserves if he keeps his throne,' Bois d'Effre smiled.

'Would you be prepared,' he interpreted for d'Esprey, 'to meet the King and explain our position, the numbers we have, the fact that he doesn't stand a chance in hell?'

'With great pleasure, sir.' Edward smiled.

'You realise,' Bois d'Effre said later, 'that you will be going into Bulgaria in civilian clothes. You could be shot as a spy.'

It wasn't difficult to slip across the frontier. Edward had been supplied with plenty of money and was able to acquire an old Peugeot for the trip north. The car was pretty clapped-out and petrol was very scarce. Edward drove only as far as Burgas, where he contacted Enescu at the boatyard where they had delivered the two Bour-dillons. To his surprise, they were still there, completely forgotten in the confusion of the war. But Enescu's fitters had taken good care of them.

Enescu also found him a place on one of the coastal steamers going to Varna. McClumpha was delighted to see him. There were tears in his eyes and squeals of delight from his daughters.

'I want a meeting with the King,' Edward explained. 'If not the King, then one of his ministers.'

McClumpha thought for a moment. 'Ah reckon ye're in luck, laddie. Drimic was brought intae the government. I think he fiddled it tae get a grip on all the money that was being spent. He still has a house here. I could contact him. He'll contact the King. In the meantime, ye stay here.'

The first meeting was with Roboshva. His smile was as fixed as ever, and made no mention of having searched the border area in 1914 for Edward. He promised to contact Drimic, and a week later Drimic himself appeared in McClumpha's office.

'I speak for the King,' he said.

'I prefer to speak to the King personally,' Edward said.

Drimic eyed him warily. 'I'm afraid I don't think that will be possible,' he said.

'I think,' said Edward, 'that it would be to the King's advantage to spare me a little time.'

He kicked his heels in Varna for a week, and then a message arrived. A meeting had been arranged at Krivodol near Plevna. It was a picturesque village in a sheltered valley, surrounded by a number of curious mounds that were said to be the tombs of Greek settlers from the Byzantine period. After taking the train to Plevna, Edward was met by a car and driven in warm sunshine to a low white house with red roofs set among eucalyptus trees and apple orchards. Armed police were on guard but Edward wasn't even frisked to see if he might be carrying a gun. Drimic came to meet him, and gestured to a room on his right. As they sat down, a girl in native dress appeared with coffee and slivovitz.

'You have come as an emissary,' Drimic said. 'You have arrived carrying a white flag.'

'I have come,' Edward said, 'to advise *you* to produce a white flag.'

Drimic choked on his strong sweet coffee, and Ferdinand suddenly appeared. He had obviously been listening outside the door.

'Majesty,' Drimic said as they rose.

The King was in uniform but he sported no badges of rank. He looked older and greyer and more lined. His eyes seemed to have shrunk while his nose had increased in size. 'Please sit down, gentlemen,' he said wearily. 'Now, Mr Bourdillon, you have come to tell us it's time we ended our part in the war. Is that not so?'

'It is, sir.'

'I never received my boats,' the King said. 'I paid for them and they were never delivered.'

'They are waiting for you even as I speak,' Edward said. 'At Burgas, where they have been since 1914. Minister Drimic knows their location.'

The King looked hard at Drimic who went pink.

'And I no longer want them,' said Ferdinand, 'since I shall have no use for them. Will you buy them back?'

'I didn't come here to do business, sir,' Edward said. 'At least not that kind of business.'

Ferdinand shuffled in his seat and ran a finger round his collar. 'Of course not. Well, I will *give* you your boats back. They are yours.' He glanced at Drimic. 'If Minister Drimic doesn't have any other plans for them, that is. I expect the war got in the way. Now, what exactly do you wish to discuss?'

'I have no power to grant or promise anything,' Edward explained. 'But I am instructed to inform you that you will not be pursued or accused if you instruct your army to lay down their arms.'

'But I would be advised to leave Bulgaria?'

'That's up to you, sir. We want the war over as quickly as possible. Germany can't hope to carry on if her allies leave her side. Austria is already negotiating. And Turkey.'

Ferdinand sat in silence for a while. 'I was a flea in Europe's ear,' he said slowly. 'I caused trouble. I know that. But I made Bulgaria a country to be reckoned with. I changed the capital from a dreary Balkan village to a city and I brought the railway to Sofia and the coast. And my reward is this.'

'There must be no demolitions. Railways and port installations must be left exactly as they are. Troops are to withdraw from strategic points.'

'Which are?'

'It isn't my job, sir, to tell you that. You know them better than I. If you agree, Allied plenipoteniaries will arrive for any meeting we can agree to.'

Ferdinand managed a wry smile. 'They have thrown you in at the deep end, young man, haven't they! If I wished I could have you shot. You arrive in civilian clothes when you are an Allied officer and we are at war.

And you have no documents to prove you are who you say you are. Am I right?'

'Quite right, sir.'

'And suppose I did have you shot?'

'I shouldn't like it very much. And I don't think that it would be in your best interests.'

Absent-mindedly, Ferdinand picked his nose. 'Perhaps Vienna might be bearable,' he said. He swallowed his slivovitz in one gulp. 'It doesn't look as though I have much choice. I have just been defeated by your armies at Dobropole and I fear we are beyond any hope of recovery. You can inform your superiors that they can send their plenipotentiaries, soldiers, ministers of state and prison warders. I give up.'

At the end of the month Ferdinand asked for an armistice, withdrew from the war and headed for Vienna. Southern Europe was suddenly wide open and the Allies could advance directly to the Danube. Then came the news that German agents, in defiance of Ferdinand's agreement, were destroying port installations. Clearly they were going to have to hurry.

By the time they reached Thrace, it was obvious that the congested roads, which were always unmetalled and invariably in a terrible state, were holding up the vast convoys of lorries, carts, guns and supplies. Bois d'Effre suggested a fast-moving column of half a dozen armoured cars, with lorries to supply them, to head swiftly for the coast.

The cars were Crossleys, Daimlers and Rolls Royces which had been used in the desert in the surge northwards to Damascus. The crews were British but the lorries were full of Frenchmen who, following Napoleon's precept, saw nothing wrong with living off the land. As soon as they reached Burgas, Edward headed for Enescu's yard. MacNab was due to bring round his boats by sea, because Turkey was expected to sign an armistice within days.

The two Bourdillons were still there and, to make sure the French didn't take over the yard, Edward hung out a

Union Jack, left a guard under a petty officer and stuck up a black-lettered notice, *British Naval Yard. No Entrance.*

He did the same thing at McClumpha's in Varna, since there was also a considerable danger from looters.

38

With the war in Eastern Europe over, shipping began to move again in the Black Sea. But they were harassed by Bolshevik Russian ships from Sebastopol and Odessa who kept stopping vessels. They insisted on examining papers and conducted vigorous searches for Russian refugees.

In November, with the army on the Danube, the Russians stopped the *Yokub*, one of McClumpha's ships. McClumpha happened to be aboard travelling to Constanza. When Edward visited him at his home he found him in bed, with a black eye, a cracked rib and bruises all over his body.

'I've been operatin' up and doon this coast for over thirty years an' never had trouble. Your Russians are gettin' too big for their boots. Ye should tak' oot one o' y'r boats an' sink a few o' them.'

Guarded, as often as not, by two fast motor launches that cruised up and down alongside them, the Russian squadron consisted of an old battleship called the *Sverdlov*, a cruiser that had once been the *Priz Pavel* and had been renamed *Lenin*, a destroyer, a supply ship, and a gunboat which was the one that usually caused the trouble. She was old with a high superstructure and looked not unlike the *Tahaf* at Arina.

MacNab arrived with two of the four boats from Egypt before the end of the week. There was another boarding by the Russians the following week and more beatings. Bois d'Effre sent a protest to the Russian base at Odessa. The officer who delivered it was treated with contempt, and shortly thereafter another of McClumpha's ships was stopped. Bois d'Effre decided to deliver an ultimatum and dispatched Edward, dressed to kill with a borrowed sword, and MacNab, complete with aiguillettes, as his aide.

As his climbed aboard the *Sverdlov* Edward could not help noticing how dirty the ship was. The crew looked surly and he saw one of them relieving himself against a gun turret. The Russians were sloppily dressed with hardly a uniform in sight. Nevertheless, a bosun's pipe twittered and the sailors pressed forward, clearly impressed by the gold on his cap and sleeves. An older man who looked like a petty officer pushed through the crowd, accompanied by a man in a leather coat and what looked like a railway porter's cap. The petty officer could speak French and they exchanged greetings in that language.

'I'm running the ship,' the petty officer said. 'And this is the political commissar. He's here to see we behave ourselves. One of these days I'm going to chuck him overboard.'

Edward offered a cigarette which the petty officer snatched with great enthusiasm. 'I'm here to deliver an ultimatum,' he said. 'We object to you stopping our ships.'

The petty officer shrugged and pushed the commissar forward. He spoke no English nor French but, with a rough translation by the petty officer, Edward managed to make himself clear.

'Our ships are proceeding about their lawful business,' he explained. 'If Russian ships interfere any more we shall be obliged to take action.'

The petty officer translated and the commissar laughed, snapped his fingers contemptuously and launched into what appeared to be a political diatribe. The petty officer obliged once more.

'He says the glorious revolution has freed the people from the bondage of rules. The Russian people will do as they think fit.'

The argument continued in this vein for half an hour then the petty officer drew Edward to one side.

'I can guess what you're intending, sir,' he said. 'Just try to avoid involving me, please.'

He showed Edward round the ship. Breech mechanisms, sighting instruments and rangefinders looked rusty and dirty and Edward suspected that the magazines and shell rooms were probably half empty. There were bullet holes in the panelling of the wardroom where the officers had been murdered.

The petty officer produced some vodka, which Edward knocked back without animosity. He was then escorted back to the deck. He noticed that several of the sailors had donned caps, as though faintly ashamed of their grubby appearance.

At the ladder, he turned and saluted. While not exactly returning the salute, the petty officer raised his hand in a farewell gesture.

As he settled himself back in his boat, Edward looked up to see dozens of heads hanging over the rails watching him. The leather-coated commissar took the cigarette from his mouth and flicked it contemptuously into the boat. The glowing stub fell at Edward's feet.

'Right, you bastard,' Edward thought. 'I'll see you again.'

Within three days, scorning of Edward's ultimatum, the Russians shelled the ferry from Constanza to Burgas, killing several people. As soon as they received the news Edward set off with the two launches, followed by two of McClumpha's tugs. The launches arrived just as the ferry slipped beneath the water.

There were dozens of people floundering in the sea and the launches moved quickly to pick them up. On his return, Edward faced Bois d'Effre, red in the face with outrage.

'I have heard from the general,' the Frenchman said. 'He has agreed that it's time we hit back.'

They got the Thorneycrofts tuned up in a matter of hours, and treated the Russian squadron to a view of them moving along their line at a distance of half a mile.

The Thorneycrofts were not fitted with guns, torpedoes or depth charges. A gun banged once from the *Sverdlov*, but it wasn't clear whether this was meant as a warning or not. The straight runs changed to manoeuvres, the two boats working together, driving along the side of the

Russian squadron, then opening out in two great arcs to meet again in the same spot.

The remaining two boats from Egypt failed to arrive as expected, which left Edward with only one boat armed for depth charges and one for torpedoes. The Russian ships and their accompanying launches were still doing their slow, untidy patrol north and south, always just inside Bulgarian waters. It was worked out that during the early hours of the morning they would be about three miles off Varna.

'We'll do the job with what we've got,' Edward decided.

Summoning the two crews to his office, he explained what he intended, outlining the time of slipping, speed on passage and in action, and the cruising positions. Torpedo depth setting was not discussed because there was only one torpedo – on Edward's boat.

Setting off in the dark, they drove to in the shelter of the bay. Not far away, Edward could see MacNab's boat. Somewhere ahead the Russian squadron was trailing past in a long untidy line. Mist drifting over the sea made visibility poor and as he swept the horizon with binoculars it seemed to be bare. Then he spotted a faint hump, then another and another.

'There they are.'

The Russian ships were nearer than expected and the crash start was enough to wake the dead. Within minutes they were on top of them, the Russian vessels growing rapidly in size as they approached.

Waving to MacNab, Edward watched him swing away round the stern of the squadron, then they were roaring towards the *Lenin*. At the last moment the Russians came to life. They were within 500 yards when a gun fired and a column of water lifted just ahead.

'Splendid,' Edward said. 'According to international law that allows us to fire back.'

At a range of not more than 150 yards he yelled to the torpedoman and heard the thump of the ram and the splash as the torpedo shot out astern. Looking back as they swung away, he saw the torpedo leap out of the water like a porpoise and thought for a moment that the attack had failed. But then there was a flash abreast the cruiser's after–funnel and a column of black smoke rolled up into the sky.

'Enemy to starboard, sir.'

As the torpedoman sang out the warning, Edward saw the two Russian launches hurtling out of the mist. Swinging the helm, he roared at speed between them and had the satisfaction of seeing their shots hitting each other.

As the launches fell away astern, one giving off clouds of steam, he put the helm over again and swung in a wide circle towards Burgas. Shutting down, he looked around for MacNab who was making his approach from the other side of the Russians. An enormous column of water rose at the stern of the gunboat and MacNab emerged towards them through the shell splashes.

Daylight dawned as the two boats stopped alongside each other. In the distance the Russian ships were still moving slowly in the direction of Sebastopol, but the gunboat had stopped and the *Lenin* lay in the water with a distinct list to starboard.

'I shoved my depth charges right under the stern,' Mac-Nab grinned. 'I was so close the starboard strake actually rubbed against the side of the ship.'

It was a very satisfying moment. MacNab had disabled the gunboat and at the very last minute Edward had finally lived up to his reputation. He had torpedoed a proper ship with a proper torpedo launched from a proper torpedo boat.

V

1918–1922

39

Two days later hostilities in Europe ceased. The weather was grey and drizzly and a cold wind blew from the east. For a while, it didn't seem possible that men would no longer die because some stranger on the horizon had squeezed a trigger or pulled a lanyard.

It left them feeling dazed, but with the certainty that the future would be very different from the past. The only satisfaction was that they had survived.

The war had left Europe shattered. Thousands upon thousands of homeless people wandered about its roads, stateless, sick, penniless and desperate. Then the 'flu epidemic arrived in Greece, Bulgaria and Eastern Europe with the power of a bomb.

Some doctors thought it was yellow fever or bronchial pneumonia, but then they heard it had started in Spain and it began to be known as the Plague of the Spanish Lady.

Men began to go sick in dozens, and outside the hospitals there lay rows of corpses as if there had been a great battle. The ambulances were on constant alert in Varna and a curfew was put on the town to keep military personnel away from where the infection was busiest.

In places like Germany, where the naval blockade had left the people starving, they were dying in thousands and the germs were travelling at tremendous speed across frontiers, striking in the United States, South America and Australia.

In Buda-Pesth the churches were closed down. In Italy the shaking of hands had been forbidden in case it was a means of carrying the virus. Yet, remarkably little was being reported in the papers. It was the ending of the war

271

plus the fourteen points for peace presented by the United States that grabbed the headlines.

There were still no letters from Augusta, and Edward could not help wondering if she had fallen ill. A letter from Maurice arrived, however. Maurice's letters always managed to find him, correctly addressed and without delay. He couldn't understand why Augusta's didn't.

'Over here,' wrote Maurice, 'it's all "Hang the Kaiser". The election seems to have been a bit of a fraud and the people who've been elected all seem to have done very nicely thank you out of the war.'

The second paragraph contained a shock. 'Father died in October. It was the 'flu. I'm running the show now but I expect we can find a corner for you to shove your oar in when you return.'

It was only on the second page that he got to the point. 'Well,' he wrote, 'here we come to it. I've put it off until now because I didn't know how to say it. But, dear old boy, prepare yourself for a blow. Augusta has left you. I think she grew tired of waiting. I know it wasn't your fault but I think she always felt it was. She's gone off with some American. They plan to live in New York. He seems a nice enough chap, though, I have to say. Of course, all hell broke loose. The Vicar retired to pray. Mrs Vicar had hysterics. I'm sure they won't change Gussy's attitude. She says you can go ahead and get a divorce; she won't contest it. Her new boyfriend's a lawyer and she expects him home for dinner every night. I suppose it's just one of those wartime disasters. There are a lot of them about. I've got one myself. I married Georgina and I don't think for a minute it'll last.'

Cairo looked the same' as ever but there was no Ginny. Her flat was empty and her friend, Flo Mitchell, had no idea where she was.

'You know what she's like,' she said. 'There are all those people in Poland starving and dying of influenza, typhoid and cholera. I'll bet she's there somewhere. She just upped and went as soon as the war ended.'

Edward took himself to headquarters and said he hadn't

been home for four years and it was about time his case was given some priority. He went via Naples. The della Stradas had survived but had been profoundly shocked by the terrible casualties of the war. Italy had been hard-hit by the influenza pandemic. In Rome people had died at the rate of 400 a week. Because displays of grief had been forbidden, no bells tolled, and funeral processions, wreaths and black-edged notices were banned. Apparently the carpenter-boatbuilder Sam had hired became something of a local celebrity when he had succumbed to the disease.

'He came round as the coffin lid was screwed down,' Pappa della Strada said. 'When he sat up the mourners took to their heels.'

Alessandro had served in the navy as a fitter on SVAN motor torpedo boats, but saw no future in his own country. His mind was set, as it always had been, on emigrating to the United States. The whole family was considering following him as soon as he was settled. They had heard little from Rosina, stranded in England, but they knew Sam had gone into uniform.

Patriotic demonstrations were insisting on Trieste and Fiume becoming part of Italy. They were being heavily supported by Benito Mussolini, the journalist who had made his mark with his revolutionary paper, *Avanti*. The streets were full of men who were little better than gangsters. They called themselves Fascisti.

Edward had chosen a circuitous route that took him via Antwerp and he was delighted to find Etienne van der Essen still running his company and in good spirits. On the last night before crossing the Channel he was invited for dinner, and while they were drinking brandy van der Essen produced a small file. It included letters, stamped documents and a passport.

'Your friend, Alexander Clifton Owen-Smith,' he said. 'When the war ended, a commission was set up to investigate Belgians who had collaborated with the Germans. I was part of it. We found these documents at the Villa de Hootje, which was their headquarters. Your friend worked for the Germans for over two years before he disappeared. I believe he went to Africa.'

273

'He did,' Edward said. 'I ran across him.'

'I hear he's turned up now in Hamburg, with one of the anti-Communist groups. There's a German passport here. It's in the name of Aleksander von Rauche.'

Under the winter frost England looked shabby and pinched. Edward didn't stop long in London, considering his service with the navy terminated.

His reception at Creek House was muted. Aunt Edith had not recovered from the shock of losing her husband. And Georgina was in London.

'Where she spends most of her time,' Maurice said ruefully.

He was making a good job of running the firm, and for the first time in their lives the two men sat together feeling companionable over a drink and a smoke.

'They're talking in the House of Commons of "Back to normal",' Maurice said. 'But things can't be like they were. Everybody sank more money than they should have into their businesses because of the war. Nobody now seems able to accept that the old days of easy prosperity have gone.'

'What about Bourdillons?' Edward asked.

Maurice shrugged. 'Father made some bad mistakes – like not getting his hydroplane out before our rivals. The customers we had in Germany aren't in the market any more. We'll have to lay people off and production's going to drop to a minimum. There'll be bankruptcies. We also had to bring in semi-skilled men and women to take the place of men in the forces, and the unions are beginning to shout the odds. British industry's dying on its feet.'

Maurice took a long drag on his cigarette, and watched the smoke he exhaled rise up towards the ceiling.

'For a time I had "By appointment to King Ferdinand of Bulgaria" on the letterheads, but that didn't last long, did it? Oh, and there was one interesting sale. We sold six high-speed launches to a chap in Chicago. Nobody's allowed to buy booze there and our boats are to be used to deliver illegal liquor. They even carried out experi-

274

ments to increase the speed and were kind enough to pass the results on to us.'

Maurice paused. 'I'm sorry about Augusta, old lad,' he said. 'If it's any consolation, she's making it easy. I don't expect the same from Georgina when my turn comes.'

40

The future looked gloomy and Edward took little interest in the boatyard. Going to the library in Portsmouth, he acquired a medical directory and looked up Ginny's father, Sir Patrick George Gogarty.

Taking the train back to Porthelt, as he walked from the station, his route took him by the Nankidnos' cottage. As he passed, the front door flew open.

'Not so fast, Ted. Where do you think you're going?'

The two men shook hands, and embraced warmly.

'Somehow, I didn't think you'd be here. I'm sorry, Sam. How are things? My goodness, it's good to see you.'

Inside the house, Rosina greeted him with a shriek of delight, and old Mrs Nankidno brought out a bottle and then another.

'So what are we going to do now, Sam? Are you due for demob?'

'They've asked me to stay on. Only for a few months. It'll mean a bigger demob grant. It'll pay for Rosina to visit her folks in Naples. It's the Russians. They've been getting very stroppy indeed.'

'I had a run-in with them – in the Black Sea.'

Sam smiled. 'There's a plan to have a go at the buggers in the Baltic.' Sam looked faintly sheepish. 'So it's Riga first stop. I feel I owe the navy something. They made a gentleman of me, Ted. They gave me a commission. I'm not just a bloody fitter any more.'

'You never were just a bloody fitter, Sam.'

The following day Edward took the train to Waterloo. In the hope of impressing Ginny's parents, he wore his uniform. Sir Robert and Lady Gogarty were exactly as Ginny had described them, both good-looking, grey-haired, stately and rather formal. But they received him graciously and he was asked to stay for lunch. They had no idea where their daughter was, however, and were as concerned as he was about her.

'She was always independent-minded,' Sir Robert said. 'If you find her,' he continued, 'for God's sake ask her to get in touch with us. I could even arrange to send her supplies. She must need help.' He paused. 'That is, of course, if she's still doing the same job. Or –' he paused again '– if, and I suppose we have to face up to this, if she's still alive. The last we heard she was in the Balkans.'

There was one hope. The headquarters of Mrs St John Halahan's Women's War Convoy was in Jermyn Street in a small down-at-heel building where they occupied the top floor. It appeared that Mrs St John Halahan herself had left the organisation and was now in Ireland, espousing the cause of Irish freedom.

'They say she wears a revolver,' the woman behind the desk told Edward. 'Like Annie Oakley.'

'What about Virginia Gogarty?'

She shrugged. 'We've heard nothing of her since 1918 when she was in a hospital in Cairo. We think she's in Latvia. We heard she took a ship from Hamburg to Riga.'

41

The politicians of Western Europe were determined to bring the Bolshevik Russians down. They had been putting agents into Petrograd for months, and supported White Russian Armies in the Ukraine, Vladivostok and the far north round Archangel. The fiction was that it was to help the Russian people decide their own future. In fact it was simply to stop Communism spreading west.

British, American, Czech, French and Japanese soldiers were fighting in Russia in struggles they didn't understand. In the Baltic, the worry was that the Russians would take over the new small states of Lithuania, Latvia and Estonia. Ironically, British and German soldiers found themselves marching side by side to preserve German estates in East Prussia.

The navy had no objection to Edward joining the party for Russia. They were only too glad to have someone who had already proved he knew how to use torpedo boats.

There was a flotilla of destroyers, a group of inshore minesweepers, oilers, store ships, and fleet auxiliaries, a squadron of RAF planes and a small seaplane base on the foreshore of the beach, which was also used by the locals for a daily dip. Both sexes swam in the nude, much to the delight of the sailors.

Making enquiries at once for the Women's Hospital Convoy, Edward found no one had ever heard of it. There was no chance to search, because a raid had been planned on Kronstadt, the Russian naval base. The object was to destroy the Russian warships. After that the winter ice would complete the business of sealing the harbour until the following spring.

Kronstadt was guarded by forts built with shallow-water approaches, so the job could only be done by coastal motor boats. A cruiser converted to an aircraft carrier arrived to act as parent ship. Aboard were engine room artificers, torpedomen, ordnance artificers and wireless mechanics and operators. The men who were to operate the boats were all experienced and the senior officer, who was to lead the raid, had won the Victoria Cross earlier in the year for torpedoing a Russian battleship. Because of his rank, Edward was hauled in to help with the flood of signals, letters and reports on stores, weather, discipline and repairs.

Mail arrived irregularly but there was a packet from Maurice whose letter informed Edward that Augusta was arranging to have an American divorce. 'It's obviously still no good waiting for you,' he added.

There was another letter which had been sent from Bulgaria. Tearing it open in the hope that it was from Ginny, Edward found it was from old McClumpha offering him a job. He was touched by the gesture and was on the point of writing to explain the position when everything came to a halt as a date was fixed for the attack on Kronstadt. It was to be disguised as an air raid to keep the Russians' eyes away from the sea and it required careful timing because the boats (45- and 55-footers) would have to run under the forts guarding the entrance.

Four of the boats carried two torpedoes and the rest one each, but their speed had been reduced by the mounting of machine-guns and depth charges. The bigger boats, with two engines and two screws, were easier to manoeuvre but the task would not be simple because the crafts were still not built to go astern.

The chief problem was the possibility of collision, with fast boats moving about in the darkness in a restricted space. It was decided, therefore, that the first three boats would enter the basin well ahead of the others because they had to fire their torpedoes at high speed. At lower speeds, the missile was likely to dive to the bottom and blow up the boat which had launched it. This wave, Edward's, though it would be the first to face the music, had a sporting chance of escaping in the confusion, before the second wave arrived.

The fine Baltic weather broke, and the summer calm gave way to days of westerly gales which caused the water to pile up in the Gulf of Finland where Kronstadt lay. It meant a rise of two or three feet in depth and greater safety in slipping past the forts which guarded the base.

The boats carried a crew of three – skipper, torpedoman and engineer. Edward had hoped to have Sam with him, but it was decided that Sam's experience was of more use at the base. He was to remain behind as base engineering officer, and Edward was allocated a new torpedoman.

Edward went to check him out. The fellow was in the mess, singing softly to himself – ' "There was Brown, upside down, mopping up the whisky off de floor –" ' He turned as Edward tapped him on the shoulder, and his face split into a huge grin.

'Francis Xavier McWilliams, by all that's holy. What are you doing here?'

'Same as you, Oi reckon. Oi was naval reserve, y'see – only for the money, o' course – but when de war started Oi was in, like it or not. 'Sno too bad. Oi had to swim a bit at Jutland but Oi'm over that now.'

'Did you actually volunteer for this?'

McWilliams grinned. 'Officers volunteer, other ranks get drafted. I read about yez in the papers. 'Twas you, wasn't it? 'Tis a good boat ye've got. 'Tis desperate fast she is.'

'Did you ever get married, Paddy?'

'Ach, sure. Two little 'uns. Me wife's from Portsmouth. She keeps me on the straight and narrow. Oi haven't been in throuble for two years. The poor cratur was widowed by Jutland. The little 'uns aren't mine.'

'I'm needing a torpedoman.'

'Well, strictly, Oi'm a torpedo artificer and work ashore, but, sure, Oi'd like that. Oi took the shore job because Oi didn't want to make me wife a widdy woman again. But just this one time, Oi reckon. It'll be like old times.'

The night before the raid there was a party. Beneath the reckless gaiety, however, there lurked the certain knowledge that not everyone present would return from the mission.

As they waited for dusk next day, fitters crouched over engines, checking, testing and rechecking, with Sam looking over their shoulders. Torpedomen went over their launching gear again and again until they were absolutely confident everything was in working order.

In the late afternoon, the crews appeared clad in jerseys, seaboots and oilskins. McWilliams grinned. ''Tis a quare old business, this,' he said. 'With me afther sinkin' what Oi believe in.'

The boat behind Edward's sent out tremendous flashes from the exhausts as an engine kept backfiring. They soon lost sight of the other boats though their wakes remained visible. The badly tuned boat was still making a tremendous din and spitting out flames from its exhaust.

It was cold and there was a layer of mist like a grey blanket over the sea. They moved cautiously, all of them trying to keep an eye on the boat in front, the sound of the engines at low revs barely audible over the swish and rush of the water. It was a tense journey because Russian destroyers could be out searching, and for the most part it was carried out without a word being spoken. Paddy McWilliams was fiddling with his switches and controls and the fair-haired engineer, a mere shape in the darkness, began to whistle nervously.

'Stow it,' Edward said quietly.

Eventually they could make out lights ahead, most of them small, and there was a glow in the sky in the east that obviously came from the streets of Petrograd. Manoeuvring at low speed because the wakes could easily be seen, the boats were slipping now between the forts that guarded the entrance to the Kronstadt Channel. At first there was no reaction then the forts opened fire. But the searchlights were not switched on and the firing died away.

Swinging in a wide circle, it seemed their spray and the whiteness of their wash must be like beacons in the darkness. But there was no boom across the entrance and as they sped past the RAF was already above them, dropping bombs and machine-gunning the batteries. Attention diverted, the Russians were firing into the air and the flashes lit up the sea. As Edward entered the harbour, the guardship anchored outside spotted them and for the first time they came under fire. The aim was high, however, and did no damage.

Ahead they saw a tremendous flash and knew that one of the leader's torpedoes had found its mark. More explosions followed ashore.

As they ran in, the impulse charge that drove the torpedo out of its trough misfired. McWilliams swung at it savagely with a mallet, according to misfire drill. The torpedo leapt out with a whoosh.

'There she goes, the darlin' thing,' McWilliams yelled as they swung away.

The delay had caused the torpedo to run slightly off-course and it exploded against the side of a large store ship. Swinging round in a narrow arc, they skidded out of the harbour, as another torpedo went off. Burning ammunition was flung high into the air. The boat behind them was still throwing out huge flashes from its exhausts and the Russian guns swung on to it. Caught by the firing, it burst into flames. Edward saw it break in two, then disappear abruptly beneath the black water. Two searchlights probed the water, blinding Edward as they pinpointed his boat. And then they were hit. Not by the enemy, but by a boat from the second wave.

Edward was flung over the wheel with a force that knocked all the breath from his body. McWilliams disappeared beneath his feet and the fair-haired engineer vanished overboard.

The two boats remained locked together for a while, then the other one managed to draw away. But its bow, crushed by the collision, went down and it disappeared in seconds. By a miracle, Edward's boat remained afloat, and was even able to move ahead. He searched the water for the missing engineer and anybody else from the other boat who might have survived, but the steering was gone and it was impossible to manoeuvre.

McWilliams gave a shout and Edward saw a figure struggling in the water. They dragged the man aboard but it wasn't his fair-haired engineer. With the engines idling, they stared across the dark water calling his name.

As machine-gun bullets began to peck viciously at the water, Edward decided there was little hope of picking anyone else up and began to move away. McWilliams bent over the man they had rescued.

'Sure, Oi think he's dead,' he said.

Somehow they managed to pass the forts but were heading south in a wide arc. The boat seemed to go better at speed, but suddenly there was a colossal crash that knocked Edward on his back.

McWilliams lay sprawled across the bows, and Edward could see blood on his face. The boat was clearly sinking. Before he knew what was happening he was swimming for his life.

McWilliams floated nearby, buoyed up by the air in his oilskin. Edward tried to support him. He held on until the icy water numbed his fingers. McWilliams slipped away and vanished.

'Oh, Christ, Paddy,' Edward moaned. 'No.'

He swam round in a circle, shouting. But there was no one to help. Edward realised that, if he were to remain alive himself, he had to direct his energies to reaching the shore. His heavy leather coat threatened to drag him down. It was a struggle to get it off, but Edward succeeded without swallowing too much water.

How long he swam, he didn't know. But he made it to the shore. Dragging himself from the water, he heaved himself upright. He was frozen to the bone, exhausted, and still in Russian territory.

Scrambling from the beach, Edward headed inland through a huddle of tall firs. After a while he came to a road and set off along it, boots squelching. As daylight came he spotted a barn-like structure ahead of him.

Inside there were a few crude farm implements, a plough with a wooden blade, a primitive rake on wheels. The barn had a straw-filled loft. There was no ladder but he managed to climb up and flung himself down in the straw.

When Edward awoke, he guessed by the position of the watery sun that it must be late afternoon. He judged himself to be 60 or so miles from the Estonian border and guessed that he should reach it in four days. The chief problem was food.

A scraping noise below him, made Edward start. Scratching the hay from the floorboards of the loft, he peered down. A woman, round as a barrel, was staring upwards, alerted by the trickle of chaff through the cracks in the floor of the loft.

'*Dobroye utro,*' he tried.

'*Bozhe moi.*' The woman opened her mouth to scream. Edward put his finger to his lips and shook his head.

'*Zdravstvuite.*'

Edward was unlikely to get very far, he realised, with nothing more than 'Good morning' and 'hello'. He took a chance and jumped down. She watched him nervously, but it was clear she was more curious than alarmed. He pointed to his mouth and, fishing in his pocket, produced what money he had. It was damp and stuck together and he had difficulty in peeling it apart.

'*Amerikanski?*'

'*Nyet. Anglichanin.*'

Pointing down the road, she mimed holding a rifle to her shoulder. He got the impression she was trying to tell him there were British soldiers not far away. Again he pointed to his mouth and offered the money. She looked at it with interest but shook her head.

'*Kasha,*' she said and pointed down the road again, beckoning him to follow her.

They set off together and in the distance he noticed a low sod-roofed building with a wisp of smoke rising from the chimney. As they walked he tried to find out more about her with the few sentences of Slav he had picked up. He grasped the fact that she owned the farm but that her husband had been shot by the Communists.

'Klavdia Kusobev,' she said, tapping her chest.

'Edward Bourdillon.'

She nodded. 'Ed-vard Boo-dillon. *Khorosho.*'

'Kasha' turned out to be a crude porridge in which the kernels of the oats crunched under his teeth. But the woman also provided bread and tea, unsweetened and without milk in Russian fashion. As he ate, she sat opposite him, watching with apparent fascination.

'*Khorosho?*'

He nodded – '*Khorosho.* Good'

He rose to his feet and indicated he should be on his way. She shook her head.

'*Bronevik,*' she said. '*Bronevik.*' She made a noise like a car. Edward couldn't work out what she meant. But there was another barn behind the farmhouse and she indicated it was there he should rest.

He spent the day lying in the straw, dozing. But his senses were alerted, later in the afternoon, by the sound of an engine. Peering out, Edward saw the woman trudge slowly along the road. Beyond her was a crude armour-ed car, steel plates bolted to a motor car body and a machine-gun mounted in the back.

Convinced she had betrayed him, he sneaked out of the barn and took cover behind a group of trees to watch the armoured car, which he now realised was the '*bronevik*' she had been warning him about. Two men in leather coats carrying rifles climbed out. He waited for the woman to denounce him but she shook her head and pointed to the east. The men stood talking and smoking, then climbed back into the car and set off in the direction from which they had come.

Edward emerged from his hiding place.

'*Chinovniks,*' she said, when she spotted him. '*Duraki.*'

She prepared a sort of bacon stew and they ate it with black bread, just the two of them sitting alone in the shabby, smoke-filled farm room. Afterwards she produced a bottle.

'Vodka,' she said and, fetching two thick glasses, almost opaque from long use, she poured out tots for them. The spirit clawed at his inside. She poured two more larger measures and they sat back, grinning at each other.

By this time it was dusk and she indicated the road, then pointed at his uniform jacket and shook her head. Producing a sheepskin jacket and fur cap, she indicated he should put them on.

'*Khorosho,*' she said. '*Polushubok. Papakha.* Good.'

She took away his jacket and handed him a cloth in which she had wrapped dry porridge, a lump of dark bread and a chunk of fatty bacon, then pushed him to the door. Edward didn't know how to thank her. Then he re-membered a phrase McClumpha's daughters had taught him. He hoped it meant the same to a Russian.

'*Tsaritsa moyevo serdsta*,' he said. 'Queen of my heart, *Spasibo*. Thank you.' And he bent forward to kiss her on the cheek.

Her ugly face went pink with pleasure and she struggled to find a reply. Then she stood up straight. '*Bozhe king khrani*,' she said. 'God save King.'

42

It took him five days in bitter cold to reach the frontier. He walked between dusk and dawn and hid in the fields during the day.

The frontier consisted of nothing but a line of trees and he walked across it without difficulty. The first people he saw were German soldiers who were helping the Estonians set up their buffer republic against the Russians. The British consul in Narva provided him with a train ticket to Riga where he said there was a British Army headquarters. He also provided money for a meal, an old civilian jacket of his own and a clean shirt.

The train was crowded with refugees, and the smell of unwashed bodies and old clothes was overpowering. Because Riga had been unexpectedly occupied by Bolshevik sailors, the train took a circular southerly detour to Yelgava. At the station, Edward found an RAF flight sergeant with a Crossley tender who was awaiting officers from a ship from England, and he directed Edward to British Army headquarters, where he was received with some surprise. 'We heard you were dead,' he was told. 'Your family's been notified, I'm afraid.'

The officer tried to explain the general situation. 'As far as I can make out,' he said, 'everybody's fighting everybody else. We've got White Russians towards the Chinese border and round the Crimea. And they're taking quite a beating. Naturally. Their officers are afraid of being shot in the back by their own men. And the British-led troops are German territorials. It's a funny old business. And Poles. It's a terrible mess, if you ask me.'

Edward was none the wiser.

No-one had heard of a women's voluntary ambulance corps in the area and Edward decided to try the hospital.

The hospital had once been government offices but had been taken over for British sick. It was still in a chaotic state, constantly besieged by civilians begging for treatment that couldn't be given. What was needed, simply, was food. But nobody had any to give and the RAF men, who were living on barges on a nearby canal, handed out every day thick slices of bread and jam to starving children. The fields had been denuded by hungry people who had been surviving on dried fish and bread made of rye straw for nearly two years. The hospital knew of no women's ambulance corps.

Eventually Edward made his way by train to the port of Libau. It had been evacuated during the war by the Russians who had destroyed the port facilities and burned stores. The entrance had been closed by blockships and it seemed to consist solely of shattered buildings and half-submerged vessels.

The train drew in a day or two after a mutiny by White Russian troops and, as Edward stepped into the forecourt, his arm was caught by a British military policeman.

'Hang on, sir,' he said. 'I should keep out of the way if I were you.'

The condemned ringleaders had just been brought into the station forecourt. They were blessed by ringleted priests, sprinkled with holy water, and kissed before being lined up against a brick wall. And then, without further ado, they were shot.

There were no ships heading westwards but finally it was decided to send a guarded train via Berlin. Travelling with diplomats and the control commission's agents were a few wounded men and Edward. He was supplied with a civilian suit and overcoat and a passport. 'They won't stop civilians,' he was told. 'But they don't like Allied soldiers one bit.'

It was a dreary journey through the empty plains of Poland. Every time the train stopped for more carriages to be hooked on it was surrounded by starving families. The blockade which had forced Germany into surrender had still not been properly lifted, and everywhere there were soup kitchens. The peace conference at Versailles was still debating the political issues that had arisen from

288

the war, but seemed to have no time to address the most critical issue – the starving people of Europe.

Germany was a battlefield. The returned soldiers detested the politicians who had let them down. On every street corner there were armed men who had refused to be demobilised, still wearing steel helmets and manning machine-gun emplacements. More than once, Edward heard small-arms fire, and saw scattered groups of fugitives, some in sailors' uniforms, pursued by grey-clad army men.

At Berlin the train was switched south to Dresden because of trouble in Brunswick. At Dresden they were told it was going no further because fighting was halting all traffic.

There seemed to be no alternative but to try to find a hotel for the night. In the growing dusk, Edward went into a nearby bar.

The place was thick with smoke. Gaunt civilians were warily watching a group of soldiers, their coal-scuttle helmets on the seats alongside them. There was only one place, alongside a woman who was sipping a cup of coffee she held in both hands as though to warm them.

Edward gestured at the empty seat and she lowered the cup and smiled. She was wearing a leather coat and a fur hat. Beside her lay a soft leather bag that looked big enough to carry a machine-gun. He ordered a coffee and a weinbrandt. The coffee was terrible but the spirit sent a warm glow through his body.

'You are English, I think,' said the woman.

'Yes.'

'The English are not very popular here. Especially with those gentlemen over there.' She nodded towards the soldiers.

He smiled. 'You speak very good English.'

'I was three years at school in England. I am Leni Haeft.'

'Edward Bourdillon.'

The soldiers on the next table were listening to the conversation.

'They would like to know who you are.'

'I'm not important.'

'They think you might be a left-wing politician. A Spartacist. A Marxist. An American or British sympathiser.'

'I'm just someone who needs a hotel for the night.'

The woman finished her coffee, then said, 'I think you'd better come with me.'

As he rose to follow her, Edward noticed that the soldiers had disappeared. But he wasn't surprised to see them again as they stepped into the alley at the back of the bar.

'Quick,' said the woman.

As they ran, they could hear the thud of boots behind them. And rounding the corner, they came face to face with a soldier. He had a pistol in his hand. Without thinking, Edward swung the heavy carpet bag he was carrying. It caught the peak of the steel helmet, and the strap round the soldier's chin jerked his head back. There was a clunk as the helmet hit the wall, and the soldier sagged to the ground.

As they raced across the street, there was a burst of firing. Edward realised it was coming from a group of men in naval uniform in the archway of the building alongside the station. A Mercedes lorry with a swastika painted on the side was their target. The lorry screeched to a standstill and a group of uniformed men leapt out, and returned fire.

Edward and the woman made a dash for the station, and sheltered, panting, behind a pillar, as a hail of bullets chipped at the stonework.

'Nothing like a nice quiet evening stroll,' said Edward.

The station was deserted. Using what cover they could, since stray bullets were ricocheting all over the place, they crossed to the other side and comparative safety.

Edward offered to carry the woman's bag. It weighed a ton. She snatched it back. 'It is all right,' she said. 'I am used to it.'

'What's in it?'

'This and that.'

Eventually they reached a block of flats and the girl produced a key. 'Here we are at last. The Haeftenstahls, I'm glad to say, are rather more hospitable than those people back there.'

'Is that your name?'

'My real name is Elena von Haeftenstahl. My family have estates in East Prussia.'

'Are you a Communist?'

'Let's say I believe in people. My parents never did. That's why they're in East Prussia and I'm in Dresden. I'm a socialist.'

'Like Lenin.'

'Lenin is a Communist. There is a difference.'

Her apartment was well furnished, with soft chairs, good pictures and attractively shaded lights.

'Plenty of people have stayed here before,' she said. 'People on the run from the Freikorps. There is a spare room. The Freikorps would also like to talk to me.' She produced a bottle and two glasses. 'The trains won't run for days now. But you're welcome to stay until they do.'

She made them both a sandwich. 'It isn't much but it will have to do.'

'Tell me,' said Edward, enjoying the coarse bread and sausage. 'Why do you carry a gun?'

'They shot Rosa Luxembourg. They're not going to shoot me.'

'Couldn't you prove you're not a Spartacist?'

'You don't think they hold trials, do you?'

'Perhaps I could get you out.'

'And then what?'

'You'd be safe in England.'

'Doing what?' Her look was one of contempt. 'A job as a German governess? No. If Germany is in agony then I'll suffer with her.'

43

Leni Haeft had a long classic face that reminded him of Burne-Jones' portraits. But there was a harsh resolve that occasionally made her features set like iron, and the delicate beauty vanished.

When he awoke next morning, Edward heard a man's voice in the salon and decided that perhaps Leni had a live-in lover. But he changed his mind when he met him. The man was young, with a thin neck, unkempt hair and thick spectacles on a large nose.

'Rudi Goltz,' she introduced. 'Our propaganda expert.'

Goltz gave Edward a surprisingly sweet smile. 'I'm a reporter on the *Zeitung*. I do what I can for the party in my spare time.'

He listened in silence to Edward's story of his Baltic experiences but could not hold back when he heard about the attack on Kronstadt.

'The Russians are as bad as the Freikorps,' he said hotly. 'They're both trying to squeeze human heads until they're the right shape and the right colour. Ludendorff's a madman. So's Goering. Lenin's not much better. And the National Socialists grow more powerful every day. They'll go the same way as the Fascists in Italy. They're a political party now. Are you political? You should be. It's the duty of all intelligent men.'

Later in the day he came back to the flat with a single-sheet newspaper, badly printed, with it's title, *Rote Fahne*, in red. 'Circulation's gone up,' he shouted. 'From three hundred to three hundred and one. The tide is turning!'

Edward was unable to read the spidery German script but he knew the title meant *Red Flag*. Then he saw the name 'Leni Haeft', followed by his own name, or something resembling his own name – Edward Danny-Boy Dillon.

'What's this?' he demanded furiously.

Leni laughed. 'I fear Rudi doesn't always get it right.'
She crossed to him and kissed him on the cheek.

Edward's anger quickly subsided. 'Aren't you being a
little rash to allow your name to be in the paper?'

'I suspect Rudi's trying to build me into another Rosa.'

The trains were still not running. There were reports of
fighting in Berlin and elsewhere between Spartacists,
Communists and the soldiers of the Freikorps.

Leni sat down beside Edward on the sofa. He could feel
the warmth of her body and caught her sweet perfume.

'Will you please put your arm round me?'

Edward did so and she lifted her face to be kissed. He
obliged, wondering what he was getting into this time . . .

Leni couldn't stand being cooped up for long. Her favourite place was called the Rattsherrnkeller, whose main
room was surrounded by wooden statues of city council-
lors dating from the Middle Ages. There was always a
small orchestra on a dais, classical musicians playing
dance music for a pittance because they were reduced to
penury by inflation. It gave the beer cellar an air of unreal
gaiety.

They ate and drank there on a number of evenings, but
Leni sometimes couldn't help being gloomy. 'I used to
come here often in the old days, when I was a student at
the University. I got engaged in this very room, you know.
He was a doctor of philosophy.'

'So what went wrong?'

'He was killed on the Somme. Such a waste.'

One morning a friend of Leni's, Walther Busch-Schatter,
turned up. He was lean-faced, with lank, dark hair which
almost hid his eyes.

'They're after you,' he said to Edward, fishing a newspaper from his pocket. It was called *Die Stelz*. There you
are – Edward Danny-Boy Dillon. It says you're a Red

activist and that you're wanted for the murder of a Freikorps soldier at the Grosse Ziege Bar on the fourteenth.'

'I didn't kill anyone.'

'They say you did. And that's good enough for them. You've been identified by a chap called Von Rauche. Aleksander von Rauche. The Jew-Catcher.'

There was a tap on the door and Rudi Goltz appeared. He laid a revolver on the table.

'That all you have?' Busch-Schatter asked.

Soon afterwards two other men arrived. They looked like students and appeared to be carrying fishing rod cases. But when they opened them, they contained army rifles.

'They're here to protect me,' Leni said.

'From what?' Edward stared at her, shocked. Suddenly she looked small and frail and older than her years. Her face seemed grey and drawn and the shadows under her eyes had become hollows so that in the poor light her face looked like a skull.

'I'll stay, too,' Edward said.

'Don't be damned stupid,' Busch-Schatter said sharply. 'That's just what they want. To find foreigners involved in what they consider a German problem. You'll have to go south. They're watching all trains west, and that's where they'll expect you to go.'

Two more young men arrived, also armed with revolvers.

'I can get you on a train at Pirna,' Busch-Schatter said. 'It goes to Munich. Don't get off en route. From Munich I'd head for Vienna, but of course it's up to you.'

'Wouldn't it be a damn sight easier if I just went to the British Consul?'

'The consulate is surrounded by the Freikorps.'

Edward didn't hesitate any longer. His few possessions were stashed away in a small bag, which he collected from the spare room.

'Try to do something for us,' said Leni, and gave him a brief goodbye kiss.

The door slammed behind them, as they clattered down the stone steps to the hall. Busch-Schatter then turned towards the concierge's rooms at the back. A door was held open and Edward found himself in a tiny yard, with the cold night air on his face.

Passing through a series of alleys, none of them smelling very fresh, they finally emerged on to a street. Down the middle ran a set of rails.

'We wait for the tram,' Busch-Schatter said.

There was little traffic about, a car or two, a lorry, a horse-drawn cart, an old man pushing a heavily-laden pram. In the distance the lights of a yellow tram with its linked trailer headed towards them.

Edward and Busch-Schatter found themselves crammed in with a sweating throng.

Just as the tram was about to start, a burst of firing broke out and they both heard the shattering of glass. Busch-Schatter held his head in his hands.

'Poor Leni,' he muttered.

The firing continued in sporadic bursts, then stopped. Down the street they could see the front of Leni's apartment block. Men were coming out, laughing and carrying weapons. Then some others emerged carrying blood-stained shapes.

'Don't say or do anything,' Busch-Schatter whispered. 'Tomorrow they'll announce they were being taken in for questioning, and shot as they tried to escape.'

'What the hell is going on here?'

'Nothing good.'

Edward crossed the border into Austria without difficulty. Salzburg looked even colder than Dresden. He was still horrified at what had happened and sat in stunned silence every bit of the way, sick at the fatalistic way Leni Haeft and her friends had gone to their martyrdom. How Owen-Smith must have hated him – for throwing him out of the Vicarage, for forcing him to work as a coalheaver in Antwerp, for breaking up his unimportant little spy cell in West Africa.

On the way south he came to a decision. He could have headed for one of the Channel ports or thrown himself on the mercy of the della Stradas in Naples. Or he could head for Sofia and telephone old McClumpha. There was no point in going home. There was nothing to go home for. The episode in Dresden had crushed him. He needed light, sunshine and optimism.

Sofia hadn't changed much. It was a little shabbier than it had been and, like Vienna, it was suffering from the dismal after-effects of the war.

The telephone system had never been very efficient but Edward spent the last of his money on a decent hotel, who succeeded against the odds in making the connection.

'Och, laddie,' McClumpha said. 'We'll be gey glad to see ye. Stay where you are. I'll arrange wi' the hotel to supply ye wi' money. They ken me well. I'll pay the bill and they'll advance you the train fare against ma name. Now, tell me, will ye be takin' the job I offered ye?'

'Yes.'

It was a change to hear someone laugh.

44

McClumpha, widowed now, provided Edward with a small house overlooking the sea on a promontory above Varna. He had an elderly cook and a maid to look after him and an old Darracq with solid tyres to drive. His arrival was celebrated with a raucous party from which he had hardly recovered before he was obliged to stand alongside Fiona's groom, a painfully shy young man from Burgas, who turned out to be related to Enescu. A very small world, Edward reflected.

The wedding took place in a small Byzantine church. Bride and groom were decked out in a mixture of furs and traditional costume. They walked to the ceremony and there seemed to be roses, real and paper, everywhere, along with ribbons and the traditional bowers of olive leaves.

There was a small choir, much kissing of holy images and the wedding party had its wreaths and bouquets consecrated. At the door, everyone embraced everyone else.

Music was provided by a band consisting of miniature bagpipes, flutes, accordions and heart-shaped fiddles. The girls wore headdresses and aprons, and eventually all of them – from old babushkas down to grandchildren – joined hands and started dancing in a long line. Then the bride mounted a chair to smear honey on the ceiling to indicate her promise of everlasting sweetness to her husband. And McClumpha had to be put to bed by Edward.

Bulgaria had suffered less than Germany, and Varna had none of the gloom of Berlin and Dresden. The wedding had been an overwhelmingly gay interlude that momentarily locked away the miseries of the war. As life returned to normal, Edward made arrangements through the Swiss bank for Paddy McWilliams' 'widdy' to be traced through the naval welfare organisation and sent her a large cheque from his account. He wished he could have done more.

McClumpha made arrangements for his ships to be in Russian ports as the horde of refugees arrived from the north. For some time now, he had been using his ships to ferry Tsarist refugees from Odessa, Yalta and Novorossiysk to Prinkipo, Constantinople, Batum, Burgas and other places round the Black Sea. The whole area was awash with refugees, and McClumpha, for all his good heart, remained very aware that business was business.

For two weeks, Edward ferried backward and forward in one of the old man's coasters, the *Hamtun*, between Yalta and Constantinople. He had heard there were British nurses in Russia with the Whites, and he never gave up his search for Ginny Gogarty. She could have been in any of the ports he visited. They were already crammed with people trying to escape the advancing Reds, and McClumpha's ships crossed and recrossed the Black Sea, picking their way through dubiously charted minefields laid during the war by the Turks, Russians, Bulgarians and Romanians.

As the army advanced, the railway lines were jammed with refugee trains, one following the other head to tail, engine to guard's van all the way to the coast.

Odessa had fallen, and the Reds were murdering everyone who did not show a belief in their cause.

Every vessel McClumpha possessed was despatched across the Black Sea, McClumpha himself taking the *Yokub* to Odessa, while his son-in-law headed for Yalta. It fell to Edward to go to Novorossiysk, which turned out to be an absolute hell-hole. It was full of penniless refugees, filthy beggars and every kind of criminal under the sun. There were even a few of the old aristocracy whose arrogant belief in their own immunity had encouraged them not to hurry for safety. Many were now living in squalid cellars stinking of the creosote with which they tried to discourage the lice that crawled everywhere. The place had become a vast camp of wretched people, and, as the ropes of McClumpha's old ship were thrown ashore, Edward found himself wondering when the horrors were going to cease.

Fat merchants offered suitcases full of useless White roubles for a passage. Young girls desperately tried to get themselves married to British servicemen. Women of high birth were prostituting themselves with barge captains and the owners of small vessels for a passage.

As the demand increased, the fares rose. But McClumpha demanded fares only from those who seemed to have plenty – and there were still many of them, clad in fur coats, their pockets full of jewels, some even demanding that their cars be taken on board too.

Eventually most of the large steamers and passenger-carrying ships vanished with their human cargoes and only the smaller ones remained. Soldiers of the British Mission to the White army were pushing field guns and ammunition into the dark water of the harbour, and tanks were being used to smash aeroplanes and then also being driven into the water. By this time the Reds were shelling the harbour and the refugees panicked. They swarmed along the waterside in thousands, the exhausted and elderly squatting hopelessly round bonfires of rubbish. One or two youngsters tried to swim out in the freezing water to a ship but were lifted out, dried and put back ashore. One of them made a second desperate journey to the *Hamtun* and was lifted out, thawed back to life in the engine room and pushed into Edward's cabin to recover.

As the *Hamtun* cast off, scattered rifle fire sounded against heavier artillery fire. In the town, murder, rape and every kind of bestiality was the daily norm. The place was rocked with explosions as petrol tanks were set on fire, wafting a pall of smoke across the bay. All sorts of rubbish floated in the water – trunks, clothes, furniture, the corpses of human being and animals. The sick and the dead lay where they had collapsed.

45

As they returned, exhausted, to Varna, spring began to conceal some of the horror with greenery and flowers.

Edward enjoyed working with McClumpha. It was simple for anyone with experience, and he found himself travelling by car, train and ship between Varna, Burgas, Constanza in Romania and Vilkova at the mouth of the Danube. On one occasion he travelled up the Danube with McClumpha and Rhadka, who had dropped her boy-friend since Edward's arrival, from a delta so wide it was hard to tell where the Black Sea ended and Romania began. Business also took him south to Batum, Alexandroupolis, Salonika and Piraeus. Occasionally, well-disguised and with a false passport, he found himself in Odessa.

There was more to do in his leisure hours than he had expected, with concerts and amateur theatricals, even racing, though the horses varied in size from cavalry mounts to shaggy ponies, and the jockeys from blue-jowled thin-faced men to stalwart farmers and overweight rose growers.

There was game in the deep valleys, and the lakes behind the town were the home of countless snipe, wood-cock, geese and duck which rose in honking hordes into the blood-red sunsets.

The Bulgarians loved football, and even played a form of cricket which they'd learned originally from the British soldiers who had been stationed in the area during the early stages of the Crimean War. The football was played on a stony sloping pitch with lopsided goalposts and no crossbar, so when the ball was booted high the question of whether a goal had been scored or not was resolved by a noisy argument that involved both teams, the referee and most of the spectators. Cricket was played in much the same spirit. In the evening, the local families congregated to sing and dance. Every other person seemed to be a fortune teller and they all believed in ghosts, vampires and werewolves.

Occasionally, Edward found himself in Smyrna or Constantinople, where it was impossible to be unaware of the tension that was ever-present in the Middle East. The legacy of the war was hatred, distrust and muddle. Under the Versailles agreement, Turkey had to surrender large tracts of territory inland to the Greeks in return for their support of the Allies.

'One o' these days,' said McClumpha, 'yon Turks are goin' tae turn roond an' bite you Greek buggers in the bum, you see.'

Realising that Edward's interests lay elsewhere, Rhadka confronted him.

'You do not like me,' she said, pouting.

'Of course I do, Rhadka.'

'Then why do you avoid me so much?'

'I'm not avoiding you.'

'But you do not love me. You love some other body.'

'Yes, Rhadka, I do.'

'Does she not return your love?' Rhadka sounded as though she had grown up on the Bulgarian equivalent of *Peg's Paper*.

'I think so, Rhadka.'

'Then why do you not ask her to marry you?'

He laughed. 'Because, Rhadka, I don't know where she is. I keep hoping I'll find her.'

'I'll help you. I'll find her and explain that you have rejected me because you're in love with her.'

For a month or two Rhadka wrote to acquaintances and school friends in other parts of the country, searching for a British voluntary nursing corps. She had some success, but none of them knew of Ginny. But her enthusiasm cooled as she became interested in a young lawyer she had met at the post office during her regular visits, and before long she announced her intention of marrying him.

301

It was the usual noisy affair of dancing, singing and eating, and as Edward watched the two youngsters disappear in a borrowed car for their honeymoon in Romania, he felt desperately lonely.

The uneasy state of affairs round the Bosporus seemed to be growing worse by the day. It was common knowledge by now that the Turkish Army, like the German Freikorps, were refusing to accept the defeat of 1918, and just waiting for the opportunity to make trouble. But, after enduring generations of Turkish occupation, the Greeks were only too keen to get their own back. Atrocity stories fanned the hatred as Greek slew Turk and vice versa in a vicious tit-for-tat.

Everywhere he went, Edward asked questions about Ginny. And one day, he felt at last he might be on the right track, when he heard rumours that a British nursing unit had been at Kilkis, north of Salonika. But, this story proved to be without foundation. Letters flew backwards and forwards between him and Ginny's parents but they too had heard nothing.

Reluctantly, Edward was forced to consider that she must be dead, perhaps a victim of the great 'flu pandemic. At the end of two years, at the beginning of 1922, he announced that he intended to return to England.

McClumpha sighed. 'I'm sorry, laddie,' he said. 'Ye've been like a son tae me but I cannae stop ye. What'll ye do wi' yon boats at Burgas?'

It hadn't occurred to Edward to do anything at all with them. He had sold them to King Ferdinand, and, as far as he was concerned, they were no longer his.

'Take 'em wi' ye, lad,' McClumpha advised. 'They're only takin' up room an' me an' Enescu want to open up the basin there for repairs.'

'They're not mine.'

'They're nobody else's, laddie. You sold 'em tae King Ferdinand and Ferdinand has gone. Take 'em away. They'd make a nice bit o' cash for ye when ye reach home.'

It was an idea, and McClumpha was prepared to offer practical help. 'I've got the *Hamtun* goin' south,' he said.

'Callin' at Constantinople, Smyrna, Salonika and Naples. I'll carry 'em there for ye for nothin'. A sort o' partin' bonus, ye might say.'

'I don't know what to say,' said Edward.

'I want tae get Smyrna sortit oot,' McClumpha went on. 'I dinna trust yon Turks, y'see. They've been mutterin' ever since the glaikit people at Versailles offered the place to the Greeks. I think I'd be wise to leave. I dinnae want tae have tae *fight* ma way oot. I hold tin concessions and I want tae clear 'em up.'

At Burgas, on the way to Constantinople, Edward and McClumpha had the first intimations of trouble. The Greek soldiers who were supposed to be watching the Turkish Army in the Turkish hinterland were in difficulties. Greece was bankrupt, the winter had been severe, clothing and food were short. Equipment had been delayed and the leadership was demoralised. And still the Turks waited, their passions at fever pitch, until finally the Greeks had nervously decided to retreat.

By the time the *Hamtun* reached Constantinople, the vengeful Turkish Army was hard on the heels of the Greeks. The retreat rapidly became a rout, with the soldiers dragging in their wake thousands of Greek civilians and setting fire to villages all the way to the coast.

Smyrna itself was a cosmopolitan place with every language in the world gabbled along the waterfront. It was well developed, with a golf course, a race course and an opera house. The bars were open and selling what they called 'American Skoch Misky', and the Greek and Armenian beauties who giggled and waved from the windows of the rooms above the busy streets were said to double up as agents for the Bolsheviks. There was the constant throb of zithers, mandolins and guitars, but behind them a murmur of fear. Everyone knew the Turks were coming.

The harbour was a perfect crescent at the end of a long bay, and, when the *Hamtun* arrived, it was crowded with ships. There were two British battleships, three cruisers and six destroyers at anchor, three American destroyers and numerous French and Italian ships. The water was littered with anything that would float. There were Levantine caiques, and massive freighters from every nation in the world except Greece. Their last ship had already nervously slipped away, carrying with it the Greek Army headquarters and all the officers of the Greek administration.

There had been no rain since May and a cloud of yellow dust hung over the carts, cars, carriages and people. McClumpha didn't waste any time in removing the cargoes that belonged to him and closing down his interests. The shipping agent wailed his protest, but McClumpha was adamant that the Greeks were failing to provide protection.

The first of the Greek wounded began to arrive. The trains rattled in, heading for Chesme. Then came the fleeing soldiers in ox-carts, trucks and handcarts, on camels, horses and mules, all dusty, hungry and begging for food. Behind them was an enormous cloud of civilians, dragging exhausted, crying children. Institutions like the YMCA offered to take them in, but mobs of terror-stricken women had begun to besiege the entrances to the consulates.

The first of the Turkish cavalry arrived soon afterwards, swords and bayonets rusty with dried blood, their high black fezzes emblazoned with the red crescent and star.

The Turkish quarter of the city was already decked out with red cloth, from windows, gas lamps and shop fronts, but the railways had ceased to operate as the Greek and Armenian employees bolted for the safety of the ships. Suddenly dozens of small vessels and fishing boats sprouted the Stars and Stripes because the Turks loathed Britain for backing the Greeks.

Disciplined Turkish infantry followed the cavalry, and there was nothing to stop them. The Greek Army had no leadership. For a short while, it seemed as if the occupation would remain under disciplined control, but then, returning from the British consulate, Edward saw Greek and Armenian shops being looted.

'Time to be off,' he thought, as he heard distant shooting.

46

McClumpha's manager had crammed his office with terrified refugees, who all started yelling as McClumpha and Edward arrived. Then there was a heavy knocking on the door. Peering out of the upstairs window, Edward saw a group of grinning Turkish soldiers outside.

'Man the machine-guns!' he roared.

There was no gun, but the Turks bolted.

Within hours the Armenian quarter of the city had become a charnel house, with mattresses and furniture scattered about the streets, and broken glass. Bodies lay in the gutter, and from back rooms they could hear the screams of girls being raped.

No-one tried to stop the havoc. The Allies, so determined to work together to crush the Turks three years before, now refused to work in unison and had no intention of working alone. The following day, the fires started. Fanned by the wind, the flames spread rapidly, until the sky turned a fearful orange silhouetting Greek churches and eastern mosques alike. A Greek freighter not far from the sea wall was also blazing fiercely, while three crammed lifeboats struggled to get clear.

The orgy of looting and rape continued unabated. People were whipped, stabbed, shot and flung into the sea. Yet in the bay lighters were still loading tobacco and figs for New York.

Watching from the *Hamtun*, Edward could see people fourteen deep along the sea wall, the parcels in their arms already ablaze. It was like the last days of Pompeii.

Desperate men began to launch small boats and even build makeshift rafts to float out to the ships. Only the French were handing out boarding passes. The British and American ships, not allowed by their governments to interfere, viewed the spectacle with grim indiffe-

rence. In wardrooms, gramophones were turned up for
'Smile Awhile' and Caruso singing 'Pagliacci' and naval
bands gave concerts to drown the hideous din on the
waterfront.

In the end, with McClumpha's revolver in his belt,
Edward ordered the two Bourdillons to be lowered and,
cramming them with people, used them to tow boats and
rafts out to the ships.

Hauling a string of boats alongside an Italian liner,
Edward shouted to the men on deck. 'Do you have any
refugees aboard?'

The answer was blunt and unequivocal. 'I have no
orders.'

Prodded by the people behind him, Edward offered
money and within five minutes, the refugees were allowed
on board. As he helped them up the ladder, they kissed
his hands, even his feet.

The Turks gave an ultimatum to the Greeks and Arme-
nians to depart and, in an attempt to avert a holocaust,
ships finally began to arrive from Mediterranean ports.

The *Hamtun* could do no more. She was crammed to
the gunnels with people. By this time the town was a
wreck stinking of charred flesh. Telegraph wires were
looped above pavements strewn with broken glass, stones,
torn paper and blowing chaff. Here and there a burned-
out car smoked. As he made one last quick search from
the quay, Edward ran into a group of wailing Greek girls,
some barefooted, in nightdresses or underclothes. They
had been rounded up by Turkish soldiers and were being
driven like sheep to an empty hotel.

When Edward protested, a Turkish soldier presented
the point of his bayonet to Edward's throat. He had no
choice but to stand and watch the wretched girls being
herded inside. At the last moment, one of them wrenched
herself free. She was wearing only a slip and, as a soldier
grabbed at her, the slip tore away in his hand and she
managed to break free, quite naked, as the hotel door
slammed shut and the screaming began inside.

Offering the distraught girl his jacket, Edward was shep-
herding her towards the quay, when a family struggling

with a group of cavalrymen swept across their path. The Turks, wielding clubs, had hammered the solitary man in the group to his knees.

'Wait here,' said Edward. Possessed by an overwhelming rage he flung two of the Turks aside. A club hit him hard on the side of the head. As he staggered from the blow, he was hit across the forehead. Unable to see properly, Edward dragged McClumpha's revolver out of his belt and fired it blindly. He heard a man yell then, abruptly, the fighting was over, and he was being lifted gently to his feet.

'Hurry,' he croaked. 'Get to the boats.'

Through a blur of blood he saw he was being supported by the girl who wore his jacket.

As he fell into the boat, he was made aware that he had rescued a Greek family of a father, mother and two daughters. The father was injured, too, and the two of them sat together in the *Hamtun*'s saloon while McClumpha and the woman tried to staunch the bleeding.

The *Hamtun* was almost sinking under her load. The Greeks on deck stared bleakly towards the dying city, in the full knowledge of the fate that lay in store for the men and women who remained.

Many of the refugees were being dumped by unscrupulous captains on barren islands, and left to fend for themselves. But McClumpha was determined to see his cargo safely to where a government could take proper responsibility.

As the ship drew alongside in Salonika, the Greek Edward had rescued went ashore, his head still heavily bandaged. Within half an hour a large black limousine drove him back to the quayside, and the man, dressed now in a dark suit, climbed back on board.

'I have not rewarded you,' he said to Edward.

'I don't need rewarding.'

The Greek's eyebrows rose. 'You saved my life and the lives of my wife and daughters. I must do something in return. But if you refuse to accept a reward, perhaps there is an alternative. I am Aristotle Maniopolis. I handle the shipping here in Salonika. I lost one of my ships and several launches to the Turkish arsonists. I need to replace them. Suppose I buy your boats from you. That way, you will simply be doing business.'

He named a price that made Edward's hair stand on end, and he could almost hear Sam's indignant bleat, 'That makes the third time you've sold those bloody boats!'

As the boats were taken ashore, Maniopolis offered Edward hospitality in his home for as long as he wished to stay. Edward had not been unaware that his older daughter was very attractive and that she had been eyeing him sideways ever since they had left Smyrna. On reflection, Edward thought, he had better decline.

Having arranged for his money to be transferred to the account he still held in the bank in Lucerne, Edward took his farewell of McClumpha over a five-course meal in the best hotel they could find.

As his old friend headed back to the ship, Edward contemplated the shipping office across the square. He had already bought a ticket to Naples, which he took out of his pocket and tore into four pieces. Turning on his heel he went in search of a livery stable.

Before dark, on a skinny old horse – all he could buy – he was heading eastwards against a tide of exhausted, sick people that stretched for miles.

As the dawn came, Edward came across the shattered Greek Army, blank-faced, unshaven and hungry, with groups of civilians among them. The railway couldn't cope with the numbers, and the people, mostly peasants, were driving what cattle, donkeys, mules they had left. It was pouring with rain. Under a tree he saw a man spread a blanket over a woman in labour, while a small girl watched with wide, horrified eyes.

The rain continued to fall as Edward rode eastward through Thrace. He had travelled the same road in 1913 in his escape from Bulgaria, and again as they had advanced from Salonika in 1918. He was passing small hospitals set up by the Red Cross and other groups, as well as a few American organisations who seemed to be the only people in the world who cared about the appalling mess the statesmen at Versailles had allowed to develop. On the fourth day, he saw a long low building with a red-tiled roof and a group of vehicles outside that looked like ambulances.

The place was full of groaning people, some in beds, most lying on the floor. A nurse barred his way at the door. She looked shattered but unbelievably clean.

'Are you a patient?' she asked in English.

'No.'

'Relation?'

'No.'

'Then you can't come in here.'

'I think I can,' Edward said, pushing gently past her.

A small figure half-way down the ward held an enamel kidney dish containing instruments. She was issuing instructions in a mixture of Greek, Bulgarian and Russian. She was a lot better at it than when he had first met her.

'Ginny,' he said.

Handing the kidney dish to one of the other nurses, she stood for a moment, just looking at him. Then she blew a wisp of hair off her nose.

'Spy,' she cried. 'Spy.'

He caught her in his arms. She seemed featherlight. Her fingers touched his face and her eyes were wet.

'I read that you had been killed in Russia.'

'I'm not that easy to kill. And I certainly wouldn't have gone without saying goodbye to you.'

VI

1922–1923

47

Ginny was desperately pale, thin and overworked, but this lent her delicate features a beauty that was even more intense than before.

'It's wonderful to see you again, Spy. I thought I'd lost you for ever. But now that you are here, please tell me if you're going to stay.'

'I came to find you, Ginny. I'm not planning on going anywhere.'

He told her briefly about how Augusta had decided she couldn't hang around any longer, and how he could hardly blame her.

'It's God's judgement on me,' Ginny said. 'For being bad. I harboured such wicked thoughts about you. God punished me for them. Now He's rubbing it in. You shouldn't have had them, He's saying. And now He's sent you back so I'll feel even more guilty. He's a lot cleverer than people think.'

'We can get married as soon as we get back to England,' Edward said.

'Why can't we just live together? It's quite fashionable since the war, I believe.' Her response was matter-of-fact, but her eyes glowed.

As governments began to help, the hospital gradually emptied of patients, and bigger organisations took over. But it took all of five months before Edward and Ginny took a ship home.

Maurice met them at Southampton, and was obviously quite bowled over by Ginny.

'You must move into Creek House,' he said. 'When Father died and I married Georgina we split it in two. Now Mother's decided to go and live with her sister in

313

Winchester and Georgina abandoned ship some time ago.' He paused. 'As it happens, though, I do plan to get married again myself. Do you remember Alice Appleby, Ted? She lost her husband on the Somme. She's got a nipper, so I'll have a ready-made family.'

'Father left everything to me,' Maurice continued. 'But he left precise instructions to look after you. I wish things were better. I've thought about selling out. It would make me quite comfortably off. I'd split the proceeds, of course. But I do have to take my ex-wife into account. She is a definite drain on resources. Do you know, I hear she's back with Owen-Smith.'

Edward could hardly believe his ears.

'Oh, yes. He's a candidate in a parliamentary by-election. For Hamworthy and Ulston. He's standing as a Conservative, and it's solid Tory round here. He can't fail.'

Edward stubbed out his cigar. He was remembering Smyrna and the words of Walther Busch-Schatter, who had helped him escape from Dresden. 'If you get a chance to shoot a politician, do so. You'll be doing the world a service.' Well, he couldn't shoot Owen-Smith, but he could destroy him just as effectively.

'No,' he said. 'I don't think he will get in.'

Maurice looked startled. 'You going to put up against him? If you are, you're too late. Closing date for nominations is long past. Polling day's next Thursday. I didn't think you were interested in politics.'

'I'm not,' Edward said. 'But I'm going to make damned sure that bastard doesn't get in.'

The Labour Party's local committee almost fell on Edward's neck, but he swore them to secrecy. 'We have to move with extreme care on this. This fellow is as devious as a rattlesnake.'

He went to see Sam, who had just left the navy. Edward showed him the documents van der Essen had given him, told him what he had learned in Sierra Leone and Germany and explained what he intended to do.

'It had to be tomorrow night,' he said. 'It's the last chance before the by-election, so we've got to hurry.'

'Why don't you just go to the police?' Sam asked.

'I will. Afterwards.'

Sam studied Edward's grim face. 'I don't like it,' he said.

'Nobody's asking you to,' Edward snapped.

Sam was silent for a moment then he shrugged. 'It'll be as well to have a bit of support,' he said. 'As soon as you start flourishing those papers they'll try to shut you up. Still, I know a few people who'll help. Ex navy-types who've got a few grudges themselves.'

'Are you sure they'll come?'

'You bet your life they will.'

The Town Hall, decked out with blue muslin, was packed, and Owen-Smith was on the platform when Edward arrived. He looked fatter than when he had last seen him. His hair was smoothed down so that he looked like a sleek snake. Georgina was also on the platform, sitting at the back. Her parents were on the platform, too, to give their former curate support.

Looking as innocent as an angel, Ginny sat near Edward, Maurice and Alice, surrounded by a phalanx of ex-navy men.

The chairman was Colonel Scholes-Dever from the Manor House at Porthelt. He introduced Owen-Smith. The ex-curate was an able speaker, with a dramatic delivery and a ringing actor's voice. The audience listened attentively. There were only a few interruptions and no catcalls.

'Any questions?' Scholes-Dever was on his feet again. 'I'm sure our candidate will be delighted to answer them.'

'What did he do in the war?' Sam shouted.

Hamworthy and Ulston was near enough to Portsmouth to be almost a naval constituency, and the war was still close enough to be a subject of considerable interest.

'The candidate was in West Africa,' Scholes-Dever said. 'He was doing a splendid job for the government in an area not known for its salubrity.'

'What about in 1914?' The questions were deliberate.

'In 1914,' Scholes-Dever said, 'he had hardly had time to become involved.'

Edward was pleased to see Owen-Smith frown. And in her back-row seat on the platform, Georgina started to fidget.

'The candidate *was* involved in 1914,' Edward stood up to speak, so there could be no mistake about what he said. 'And there are several men here who can tell you what he was doing.'

'And what *was* that?'

'He was in Antwerp when the Germans arrived.'

There were a few loyal shouts from Owen-Smith's supporters for Edward to be silent, but he persisted. He explained what he had been doing in Antwerp and pointed out that in the audience there were several members of the naval brigade whom he had met there.'

Owen-Smith rose quickly. 'This man is a fraud,' he said.

Edward took no notice. 'I'd like to ask what the candidate was doing in German-held Togoland in 1915.'

'The candidate was never in German-held Togoland,' Scholes-Dever snapped.

'Ask him. Ask him also how he came to be in the German-held Cameroons and what was he doing in Sierra Leone after that?'

'What exactly are you getting at, sir?'

'I have here a set of papers. The name on them is Clifton Alexander von Rauche Owen-Smith.'

'Get rid of that man!' Owen-Smith shouted.

For a minute or two the meeting was in an uproar. Edward remained standing, holding up the papers. There were furious yells from Owen-Smith's supporters but they grew noticeably fewer, and when Scholes-Dever hurriedly tried to close the meeting there were cries of, 'Let him speak!'

Two or three stewards moved down the aisle to remove Edward. They were met by a solid group of ex-naval men.

'This is monstrous!' Scholes-Dever shouted.

'Let him speak! Go on, mate, give it to 'em!'

This time the shouting died quickly. Everybody was hanging on to Edward's words. The whole story came out – Antwerp and Togoland and the Cameroons and Sierra Leone. Edward described where he had obtained the documents that proved his case. Owen-Smith sat motionless in his chair, white as death. A woman wearing a blue rosette rose. 'It's a filthy lie!' she screamed.

'No, Madam,' Edward said. 'And after the war your candidate was still in Germany, betraying people to the Freikorps. Many were murdered. Ask him. I was there. Mine was one of the names on the death list.'

There was a shocked silence. Then a roar went up from the Labour Party contingent, along with shouts of, 'Hang the bugger from a lamp post!'

By this time all semblance of a serious political meeting had vanished. Half the audience began to creep out. The rest were on their feet, yelling. The Vicar and his wife hurried for the exit and when Edward looked up again, Owen-Smith had vanished, too. He was all for going after him, but Sam grabbed his arm.

'Leave it be, Ted,' he said. 'You've finished him. The police'll do the rest.'

The newspapers next morning gave the story front-page treatment.

'My God, Ned,' Maurice hooted. 'You're worth a guinea a box.'

A string of visitors turned up, including the police, who wanted to know a lot more about Owen-Smith. Edward tried to be a bit more lenient this time. 'I suspect that when he found himself trapped in Antwerp,' he said, 'his first concern was to avoid the discomfort of internment and no more. But he allowed himself to be enrolled by the Germans. Have you caught him yet?'

The inspector shook his head. 'We went round to his hotel but he seems to have disappeared. It won't be easy to find him now. He has money and a big family behind him. There was a lady there, however, who seemed fairly angry.'

'At him?'

The inspector smiled. 'Not exactly, sir,' he said. 'At you.'

48

Not surprisingly, Edward found himself cold-shouldered by the local members of the Conservative Party. In the main street at Porthelt, they crossed the road rather than speak to him, and when he had a meal with Ginny at the Royal George, the silence that fell as they entered the dining room could have been cut with a knife.

'They don't seem to like you very much, Spy darling,' Ginny said.

'Can't say I'm too fond of them either,' replied Edward with a large smile. But, while Edward was kept busy at the boatyard, he was more than aware that Ginny also was being ostracised by the local women. She was fortunate to have Alice in the house and Rosina nearby.

'Perhaps I should set up on my own somewhere else,' he suggested.

'I shouldn't,' Maurice advised. 'People are going bust all over the shop.'

'We'll emigrate then. Australia, Canada . . . New Zealand.'

It wasn't easy to adjust to life after the war. The old order had been overturned, and in its place a bitter and confused system struggled to make sense of things. But Maurice was undeterred by the prevailing gloom. He had dug out Egg's plans for the hydroplane and was studying them with interest. 'Might be something in this still,' he said. 'With the right engines, she could go at one hell of a lick. Feller called Gar Wood's just shoved the world speed record up to over eighty miles an hour. That's some going. Perhaps it's time to look at a new design ourselves . . .'

A letter arrived from Augusta, full of apologies and explanations. Edward wrote back at length. It was the war, he said, as much as anything, that had destroyed their marriage. But he admitted, too, that he had not been the ideal husband. Two days later he married Ginny at the register office at Hamworthy.

A letter came one day from Fricky Leroux, the South African from Saldanha. Edward had almost forgotten him. The last time they had met was in 1916 as he passed through Cape Town on his way to Lake Tanganyika.

'I've got a boat,' he wrote. 'And I'm going to break some records. I'm at Luino on Lake Maggiore and I need help. I want you and that little skellum who worked with you. I'll pay you both well, plus any expenses. Can you come?'

Sam was dubious about Leroux's chances. 'Still,' he said, 'it would be a holiday and Rosina will jump at the opportunity to go back home for a bit.'

'I don't think Fricky knows enough about high-speed boats to go in for records,' said Edward. 'But perhaps we can stop him breaking his neck.'

'Go for it,' Maurice advised. 'You might sell him something.'

Ginny agreed, and was secretly relieved that Edward had invited her to join him. She was determined to finish decorating their living room and main bedroom, and arranged to follow with Rosina in two or three days.

For Italy, the war had ended in a rash of Communist-inspired strikes and an industrial recession made it impossible for a government to be formed. The new Fascist party, led by the journalist, Mussolini, was playing up the dangers of Bolshevism, and gathering enthusiastic support both from the middle classes and nervous industrialists. They had marched en masse on Rome, and the coup ended with Mussolini as prime minister.

It was impossible to ignore the groups of black-shirted men, when Leroux met them with a car at Luino.

Leroux's daughter, Krissie, was waiting on the verandah of the hotel. She had grown plumper and pronounced frown lines were an indication that two failed marriages had left their mark. She shook hands warmly with Sam and greeted Edward with a kiss that warned him to be on his guard. Behind her stood a tall good-looking man with a wild shock of hair. His pockets bulged with papers.

'This is Leonid,' Leroux said. 'Leonid Sazyko.'

Sazyko greeted them in English but with a heavy accent.

'He's a White Russian,' Krissie explained. 'He was in the Russian air force and had to flee when the revolution came. He found his way to Cape Town. He's a genius.'

Sazyko grinned broadly.

Sam scowled.

As they ate that evening, Leroux produced the plans for the boat he'd built. It was not large, but was long and low with a high stern where the engines were housed, from which a battery of enormous exhausts protruded like gun barrels.

The bow was just above the waterline with a deep chine and what looked like the wings of a giant ray sprouting from the quarters to touch the water on either side.

'We fitted them as stabilisers,' Leroux explained. 'She lifts her nose at speed and planes with only the tail touching the surface of the water. It reduces resistance, but she was wobbling a bit and the wings hold her steady. They were Leo's idea. Gar Wood can't do any better than us with *Miss America II*.'

'I thought Gar Wood reached 77.79,' said Sam, unconvinced by Leroux's optimism. 'He's since pushed it up to 80.57.'

'We can reach that easily,' Leroux said.

Sam examined the plans. 'What kind of engine has she got?'

'Two six-cylinder seven-fifty-horse Rolls Royces. Navy surplus, from an airship. We fitted a heavy flywheel in place of the airscrew, a starting handle and a modified water pump. She has a straight drive and no gearbox.' Leroux grinned.

'Gar Wood had *four* aero engines driving four propellers,' Sam pointed out. 'Modified Liberys producing sixteen hundred horsepower.'

'My boat will do over a hundred miles an hour. When we break the record every navy in the world will be after her. Bourdillons can build 'em for me.'

'What speed have you made so far?' Edward asked.

'Eighty-five.'

'How does she handle?' Edward asked.

'There's a tendency to swerve a bit at speed. But we fitted the wings and a steel plate to the underwater body of the boat.'

'What's the lake like for the job?'

'Not perfect. The water's not always smooth and you get unexpected gusts of wind that make it a bit tricky for ultra-light craft. We'll have to wait for a good day because –'

'Because what?'

Leroux shrugged. 'Nothing. It's going to be great.'

49

The night was warm and there was a huge silver moon hanging over the lake. Krissie insisted on joining Edward in his room for a nightcap, and clearly expected to stay. A few years ago, Edward might have succumbed. But in the nicest possible way he suggested that she should leave.

By the time they met again next morning for breakfast, it was clear that Sazyko was the beneficiary of her attentions, and he was happy to comply.

Leroux took them all off to the lake in a big Fiat. The *Lightening* lay at a wooden jetty which had once been used for pleasure steamers. Leroux had hired it with the nearby slip and wooden workshops. There was a team of Italian mechanics and one South African who seemed entirely out of his depth. 'Just keep an eye on the speed,' he said. 'We don't want to overdo it yet.'

Alongside the jetty the hatches were removed. Sam and the mechanics did a last-minute check on the engines, while Leroux joined Krissie on the jetty.

Sam and Edward strapped themselves in and pulled on the flying helmets and goggles that had been provided. As Edward took the wheel, Sazyko started the starboard engine, and then slipped into the tender.

Swinging the wheel to face the boat up the lake, Edward opened the throttle. Despite the stabilising fins, the boat immediately showed a tendency to veer to starboard and, as the bow lifted, the view decreased and the spray grew worse. A heavy bumping started at a speed considerably below full potential and Sam made urgent signs to slow down.

They turned in a large circle, then, swinging to face down the lake, Edward accelerated again. The bumping and bucking returned and, as speed increased, rapidly became so uncontrollable that Edward slammed the throttles closed. The boat dipped its nose and lifted its stern as it came to a stop in a cloud of steam and spray.

'She's got the power all right,' said Sam, 'but I'm not sure it's attached to the right boat!'

As they were towed alongside the jetty to the clicking cameras and the applause of spectators, Leroux greeted them with a slightly nervous smile.

'What do you think of her?'

Edward climbed ashore and attached the painter to the ring on the jetty.

'I think you've got a long way to go, Fricky.'

Leroux could not hide his disappointment.

'You've got a hell of a power plant. I think it would drive a much bigger boat at the speed you want to achieve. But I think those wings you added are dangerous. They're lifting her too high out of the water. At a hundred miles an hour, she'd be so high the hull would be causing wind resistance. You've got to keep her down so she goes into it like an arrow, not like a brick wall.'

'I think you're talking bloody rubbish, man.' Leroux flushed. 'The next good day we have, I'm going for the record.'

Against their better judgement, Sam and Edward worked hard on the engines.

'This boat,' Sam said, 'is a bloody fraud. With those wings they fitted it almost flies. Your friend, Leroux, wouldn't know a good engine from a bit of clockwork. And this Sazyko fellow's just chucked a few ideas together that he got from a book and Leroux's swallowed them hook, line and sinker. But if he wants to commit suicide, I suppose that's his business.'

When Ginny arrived with Rosina, the two couples celebrated with dinner at a lakeside restaurant. But it was a muted affair. Neither Sam nor Edward could conceal the fact that they feared for Fricky Leroux's safety. The weather, which had remained overcast and blustery for sometime, began to improve. And after two days of sunshine, Leroux decided to make his attempt. The press were informed and cars and busloads of people lined the water's edge. A squad of black-shirted men were helping the police to keep order.

'I want you in the other seat,' Leroux said.

Edward shook his head. 'Not me, Fricky. Sazyko should be there. It's his boat.'

'You're just yellow,' Krissie snapped as they met later in the hotel bar.

'Think what you like,' said Edward. 'I've told your father what I think about his boat. If he chooses not to listen, that's his affair.'

The jetty bustled with engineers, technicians and press, while Leroux, Krissie and Sazyko were talking with the Italian mechanics. The boats containing the timekeepers had taken up their positions on the lake, but even now nobody was certain that the water was right. By the middle of the afternoon, however, the slight breeze had died down and the water was like glass.

'Can't you stop him, Spy?' Ginny asked.

'Nothing in the world's going to stop him now,' Edward said.

Leroux was grim-faced, and Sazyko obviously nervous, as they climbed aboard the boat. The spectators hushed.

The starboard engine started with a bang, followed by the port, and the boat moved slowly forward. When the boat was no more than a speck in the distance, close to the officials' tender, Edward saw the sun glint on the polished hull as it turned to face them.

The rumble of the engines became a full-throttle roar, as the boat raced towards them in a cloud of white spray.

'By God, he's fast,' Sam said, in genuine admiration.

The word went round that Leroux had reached 90 miles an hour.

'I wouldn't have believed it,' Sam said. 'He's only got to do it the other way and the record's his.'

There was a long pause before the throttles opened once more. And the crowd yelled with excitement. The boat was screaming towards them now, bow up, only the stern in the water. Through the binoculars Edward watched tensely. Sazyko was flapping his hands, but Leroux's head was down as he struggled with the wheel. As the boat approached them for the beginning of the measured mile, the nose began to lift. The engines sounded powerful, but the bow looked too high and seemed to be lifting higher and higher.

'Shut down!' Sam shouted, although he could not be heard.

'Pa!' Krissie wailed. 'Oh, Pa!'

Suddenly the engines screamed and there was a gasp from the crowd.

The boat bounced twice, shot into the air, turned a somersault, then dived in a backwards loop into the lake. The sun made rainbows of the drifting spray.

The officials' tender accelerated down the lake, but by the time they arrived at the spot where the *Lightning* had vanished, the only trace of boat and crew was a floating leather cushion and a smear of oil.

50

After the funeral ceremony, Sam and Rosina decided to head for Naples to see Rosina's family. Edward and Ginny elected to stay on for a few more days, but it seemed that it was not Edward's destiny to lead a quiet, calm and uninterrupted existence.

'A telegram for you, Signor Commandante.' The manager himself brought it to their breakfast table.

'HAVE BEEN SEARCHING EVERYWHERE FOR YOU. IMPERATIVE YOU CONTACT ME.' Signed, Zoparella.

The telephone line sounded as though cats were fighting in the junction boxes, but it was just possible to make out what was being said.

'You must come to Messina, Signor. As soon as possible.'

'Is the Signora in trouble?'

There was a pause before Zoparella's voice came again. 'No, Signor,' he said slowly. 'There are no problems now. This is business. You are needed here. A great deal of money is involved. I have been instructed to ask you to bring an engineer with you. The name of Ingenièro Nanchino has been suggested. All his expenses will be paid, of course.'

'Let's not worry about that, Carlo. I think I can persuade Signor Nankidno to come. But I'd be glad if you could give me some idea what it's all about.'

But Zoparella would not be drawn.

'I've been asked to go to Messina,' he told Ginny.

'Your old flame?'

'That was over a long time ago.'

She smiled.

'And if you are worried, Sam will be coming along as my chaperone.'

327

They were met at Reggio di Calabria by Zoparella. 'We will go to my office,' he announced.

He seemed unusually solemn.

'Can you tell me now what this is all about, Carlo?' Edward asked.

Zoparella held up this hand. 'I beg you to wait, until –'

'Until the Signora arrives?'

'No, Signor Edward. Not the Signora. Just me and Evrone and Avvocato Montesi. I have booked rooms for you at the hotel. But I have to ask Ingenièro Nanchino if he would mind waiting there until the first part of our business is concluded.'

Sam wasn't bothered, and they dropped him off with the luggage at the hotel. Edward couldn't make head or tail of it.

'Why aren't we going to the Casa Orlando? Why isn't Rafaela here?'

Zoparella hesitated for a moment before he answered. 'The Signora,' he said, 'is dead.'

It hit Edward like a blow in the face.

'I'm afraid it's true, Signor Edward. It was the 'flu that started it. My father died of it. So did many friends. The Signora caught it. She recovered but it left her weak. Two months ago, she insisted on visiting the docks at Genoa where we have interests. It was cold. She caught a chill. It turned to pneumonia.'

The car drew up at Zoparella's office, and Edward climbed out in a daze.

Seated at a table, Edward pulled himself together and studied the three men. Zoparella had lost a lot of hair. Evrone had grown fat. Montesi seemed thinner and graver than ever.

From a drawer in his desk Zoparella produced photographs which depicted a funeral in all the barbarous majesty of Sicily, with draped horses wearing tall black-dyed plumes, and black curtains edged with silver on the hearse. A crowd of mourners walked behind among whom Edward recognised the three men facing him, and their wives, all heavily veiled.

Evrone shook his head. 'A tragedy,' he said.

Zoparella took a deep breath. 'Signora Rafaela,' he said,

'made sure she put her affairs in order before she . . . before she died. Avvocato Montesi will explain in more detail but, briefly, she left shares in the organisation to me, to Carlo and to the avvocato. It makes us extremely wealthy men.'

'What about her husband? Wasn't he included?'

'Her husband was killed last year. An automobile accident in America.'

'Poor Rafaela.'

'She also left documents for you,' Zoparella confirmed. 'And a lot of money.'

'Why me?'

'You are a director and shareholder of Orlandos. You have been ever since 1909.'

Edward could hardly believe his ears. Rafaela had talked about giving him a directorship once upon a time, but he had never given it a second's thought.

'The Commandante, as you may know, was an engineer. He produced an engine, a fine marine engine. It was the Signora's wish that you should examine it and give an opinion on it.'

'Where is it?'

'At the Casa Orlando.'

'So that's why you wanted Sam along.'

There was a long pause.

'She loved you, Signor Edward. She always did.'

51

Casa Orlando was empty and heartbreaking in its silence. As they climbed from the car, Zoparella pointed towards a grave. It was very simple with a small headstone. Not for Rafaela the huge mausoleums wealthy Italians adored. Discreetly Zoparella and Sam left Edward alone.

He stood for a while, and felt tears roll down his cheeks. Then he knelt and tried to say a prayer. He had never been a religious man.

A new workshop had been built at the back of the house, near the spot where Edward and Rafaela had buried the looter after the earthquake. In the centre of the room stood a bulky object covered with a white sheet. Zoparella switched on an overhead light, and removed the cloth.

In front of them stood a huge engine on a steel stand, its various parts in different colours among the gaudy leads and pipes and copper exhausts.

'This is the Uschetti marine engine,' Zoparella said. 'Petrol driven. The Commandante felt it was years ahead of its time. It has been tested in a boat over fifteen metres long, and it gave a speed of forty knots. On board was a weight equivalent to two heavy machine-guns and two torpedoes. This is without doubt the marine engine of the future. What do you think?'

'We can hardly judge something like this in five minutes,' Edward said. 'But a day or two ought to do it. Is there somewhere we can run it?'

'There is a boat in the Orlando basin at this very moment equipped with the twin of this engine.'

The boat was of wooden construction with thin double-diagonal planking on light timbers backed by stringers and more rigid frames. Zoparella introduced them to a small, swarthy man in overalls.

'Tomaso Spoli,' Zoparella said. 'He can hold his tongue.'

'How long have we got?' Sam asked.

'As long as you like. But, of course, we'd prefer an answer sooner rather than later.'

Guided by Spoli, Sam and Edward checked the controls.

'Beautiful boat,' said Sam. 'A real beauty.'

The engines started with a bang and a rumble. Casting off, they moved slowly into the bay with Spoli at the wheel.

'Take her well out,' Edward instructed. 'Away from prying eyes.'

'She feels good, Ted,' said Sam.

As Spoli opened the throttle, the bow rose but the spray was flung out sideways, and the boat held steady in the water with none of the dangerous lift that had killed Leroux.

They took her well out to sea and put her through her paces – tight turns, sudden stops and crash starts. She performed immaculately.

'Shove in one of those electric petrol pumps,' Sam said later. 'And a supercharger and – oh, God, Ted, you've got a bloody miracle. This is a fifty-footer, Ted with one engine. Imagine a sixty-footer with two. It would carry everything any navy could want and still be fast.'

'It would eat petrol.'

'Why not fit two smaller auxiliary engines as well? Each eight or ten horsepower for cruising at low speeds. You could clutch the engines somehow over to the Uschettis when you wanted extra power.'

'It's superb,' Edward told Zoparella later. 'Both the power plant and the boat. I wish they were mine.'

'They are,' Zoparella said.

'Are you prepared to emigrate, Sam?'

The two men had been left to discuss Rafaela's proposition in an outer office. The idea was for a joint partnership to develop the engine, and finally to take it to America.

'Sounds all right to me,' said Sam, incredulous at this unexpected good fortune. 'Rosina won't mind. Alessandro's there already. Florida will suit Rosie fine. She'd have the whole damn family there in a couple of years.'

'So is it a deal?' said Edward.

'It's a deal,' said Sam, with the widest grin Edward had ever seen.

They shook hands.

'Then shall we go back and inform the three wise men of our decision?'

'After you,' replied Sam, inclining his head as he opened the door.

'There is one final condition, you see,' Montesi told Edward. 'We could not disclose it until you had agreed about the engine. If you had refused – and I have to confess no one thought you would – I was to handle it as best I could. But, now you have accepted responsibility, I will explain the main reason why it was left to you. Everything depends on your answer.'

Montesi paused and took a deep breath. 'The Signora left a child,' he said. 'She hoped, and prayed, that you would take her and care for her.'

Edward didn't see himself as a father to someone else's child, but he felt confident that Ginny would not raise any violent objections.

'I'm sure that will be possible,' he said at length. 'Where is the child?'

'At my home,' Zoparella said.

'The child isn't Uschetti's?' he asked cautiously.

'No, Signor Edward,' said Zoparella. 'The child is yours.'

52

'Why did she never tell me?'

'She had her reasons, Signor Edward. I think she felt you could not be saddled with the responsibility.'

'I'd never have turned her down. How old is the child now?'

'Thirteen.'

Edward's thoughts were in a turmoil. He wondered what on earth Ginny would say and suddenly panicked that she might not be as understanding and supportive as he had imagined at first.

'What is her name?'

'Nicoletta,' said Zoparella.

The child was achingly like Rafaela. She even had the same confident manner. The sight of her left Edward with a sense of aching regret and guilt, combined with an overwhelming tenderness that he had never experienced in his life.

'You're my father,' Nicoletta said. It was a statement, not a question.

'Yes.'

'Where have you been?'

'I've been at war.'

'The war's been over for over four years.'

He knelt and held her. She put her arms round his neck. 'Mamma told me all about you,' she said. 'She said you were very brave.'

'Perhaps not as brave as your Mamma made out.'

'Oh, yes. She showed me newspapers with your name in them.'

The child gravely studied his face. 'You're not Italian.'

'No.'

'Why not?'

'Does it matter?'

'No. But you speak Italian.'

'My mother – your grandmother – was Italian. She belonged to the same family as your stepfather.'

'Why am I to go with you?' she asked.

'Because I loved your mother, and she asked me to take care of you. We'll be going to America. Will you like that?'

'Is it like Italy?'

'Parts of it.'

'Can I come back when I want?'

'The Casa Orlando has been left to you, Signor Edward,' Montesi pointed out. 'Until Nicoletta comes of age.'

'Your mother seems to have thought of everything,' said Edward. 'But I do wish she had told me earlier about you.' And he bent his head and kissed her.

While he waited at Reggio di Calakna station for the train back to Lake Maggiore, Edward took Rafaela's letter from his pocket. He had already read it a dozen times.

'Dearest Edward,' she had written. 'You will have made your decision, and I know it will have been the right one. I am leaving you the Commandante's engine and boat because I want them out of Italy. Since 1918 our country has changed out of all recognition. I don't trust Mussolini and I fear that Europe will find itself at war again in twenty years' time.

'I hope you will learn to love our child. God and the Blessed Lady listened to my prayers. I have told Nicoletta everything. She is under no illusions. I have made it possible for her to admire you. I wanted once to tell you about her, but you couldn't stay, and, for one reason or another, I never did. But I prayed,' the letter continued, 'and I have brought her up to go to church and listen to the priest. I owed you so much. You made Orlandos when I would have let it go and sold everything. It was your confidence in me that made me decide to take it on. So I leave you our daughter because she is the best thing I can give you in memory of my love. Because I did love

334

you, dearest Edward. But it is now too late. We shall meet again in Heaven.'

Sitting on a bench in the railway station, Edward wept.

He sat down on a block of stone, which was part of the remains of the old station destroyed in the earthquake of 1908. His legs wouldn't support him and he hadn't realised he was crying. How could anyone love someone else so unswervingly and so unselfishly as Rafaela had loved him for so many years? She had not only loved him, she had thought constantly of him, and of the day that he could claim their child.

Ginny was there to meet him at the station. Taking a cab, they drove to the Via Vittorio Emmanuelo and sat together in the sunshine.

'I'm probably not going to explain this very well,' Edward said. 'But what I want you to know is that I love you, more than anything else in the world. I've led a far from perfect life, and, in many ways, I've paid for that. And now I discover, after all these years, that I have a child – Rafaela's . . . It's a terrible thing to ask of you, but I do ask it. Will you help me? Will you help me bring up this child as if she were ours?'

Ginny didn't reply immediately.

'We were very young,' Edward said. 'I feel now that I betrayed her, as I betrayed Augusta. But in my heart, as I know it now, there has only been you.'

'And you, Spy,' said Ginny, 'are the only man I've ever loved. If we can't work this out, what hope is there for us?'

He held her close and kissed her.

'You're a wonderful woman, Ginny,' he said. 'I don't deserve you.'

'But we deserve each other,' said Ginny with a smile. 'And that's what counts.'

THE END